PRAISE FOR
WHEN THE STARS FADE

"A tremendously ambitious first novel, a galaxy-spanning tale of 'hard science fiction' that tackles interplanetary diplomacy, [and] the realities of combat in the vacuum of space."

–Scott Tipton
New York Times *bestselling author, from his foreword*

"*When the Stars Fade* captures the human dimension of warfare. Invasions, insurgency, devastation, and an incongruous war game hold a mirror up to our Republic's experience over the last decade. It calls to mind Tom Clancy's *The Hunt for Red October* and is a sound addition to any professional development library."

–Lt. Col. Mark Johnston, US Army Reserve

"Korenman is adept at engaging the reader in action across the continuum of future war from the fleet actions of maneuvering battle groups and fighter formations to the small unit tactics of planetside soldiers. But where *Stars* truly comes into its own is with boots on the ground, where Korenman, with each lavishly detailed, well-crafted scene, reminds us again and again that now and in the far future, victories are won by individual men and women taking the fight to the enemy. The characters here are crisp and no-nonsense, and ex-military readers will smile at the authentic radio banter they trade on the tactical net–apparently in Korenman's future, some things never change."

–Cmdr. Paul Wynns, US Navy Reserve (retired)
Pilot, S-3B Viking

"Adam Korenman is a compelling new voice in military science fiction. His prose puts you right in the cockpit, on the bridge, and behind a rifle on the ground with such authenticity you can almost taste the salt in the jargon."

–Chris Herschel
Owner and Game Designer, Trial By Fire Games

"*When the Stars Fade* is an immense tale of epic proportions that hits upon many of the most beloved aspects of great sci-fi."

–Jodi Scaife
Fanboy Comics

ABOUT THE AUTHOR

ADAM KORENMAN, a captain in the United States Army, has been writing fiction most of his life. It started with notes from his "parents" to his teachers. Later, it exploded into short stories and now a full-length novel.

He's a contributor to several online periodicals and absorbs as much science as his mortal body can take.

He lives with his wife in Los Angeles, where he plans to keep writing until his fingers fall off.

This is his first book.

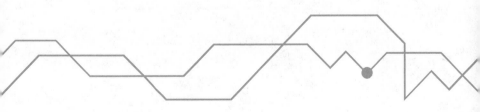

WHEN THE STARS FADE

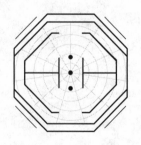

A CALIFORNIA COLDBLOOD BOOK
RARE BIRD BOOKS
LOS ANGELES, CALIF.

WHEN THE STARS FADE

THE GRAY WARS: VOLUME ONE

ADAM KORENMAN

A California Coldblood Book | Rare Bird Books
453 South Spring Street, Suite 302
Los Angeles, CA 90013
rarebirdbooks.com
californiacoldblood.com

Set in Goudy Old Style

Lt. Col. Mark Johnston's quote for this book reflects his opinion alone
and does not reflect the official policy or position of the US Army,
Department of Defense, or the US Government.

Cover art credits: Algol Vector Art and Illustration; Enrico Agostoni;
Galyna Andrushko; Iurii Kovalenko; Mehmet Reha Tugcu

Cover design by Leonard Philbrick

Printed in the United States
Distributed by Publishers Group West

10 9 8 7 6 5 4 3 2 1

Publisher's Cataloging-in-Publication data

Korenman, Adam.
When The Stars Fade / Adam Korenman.
pages cm.

Series : The Gray Wars.

ISBN 978-1-942600-09-1

1. Space warfare—Fiction. 2. Outer space—Fiction. 3. Science fiction. 4.
Action and adventure—Fiction. I. Series. II. Title.

PS3611 .O735 W54 2015

813.6—dc

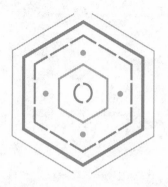

To my parents, who inspire me to do better.
To my brother and sister, who drive me to try harder.
To my friends from high school, who gave me the characters.
To my friends in California, who held me to a higher standard.
And to Scott Tipton, who told me that writers finish.

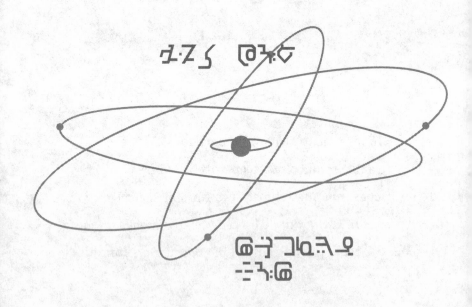

ACKNOWLEDGMENTS

It feels strange to be back here so soon. When I finished *When the Stars Fade* a few years back, I told myself it was ready for print. I moved on. And yet, some part of me never quit dreaming of how it could be changed and molded into an even better product.

Shortly after I proposed to Corinne, I met with a dear friend, Robert Peterson. Bob had written about a million books at that point and was something of a mentor/business partner to me. He impressed upon me that there was a chance to take *When the Stars Fade* to a new level, starting with a real, live publishing deal. The catch? I had to revisit the recently completed novel and break it up into two books.

At first I was terrified. I thought then that I had already bled everything onto the pages. I was sure there could be no more gold spun from straw (and yes, I know how egotistical it sounds to compare my writing to gold, but this is my foreword, so there). After a while, however, I realized that this new opportunity would afford me the chance to correct what so many fans had commented on: the science.

Then I remembered that this was science fiction, so I decided to focus on characters instead.

This is my definitive edition. This is *The Gray Wars* as it is meant to be. From an epic, if flawed, trilogy to a (hopefully) driving and emotional hexology. Everything I could squeeze out of my veins went into this, and all I can do now is hope it is enough.

So, without further ado, here is some stuff I wrote.

-ADAM KORENMAN

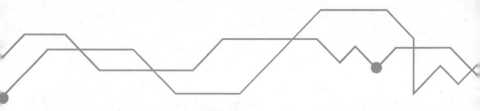

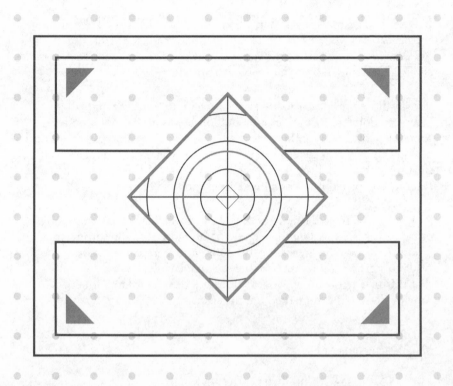
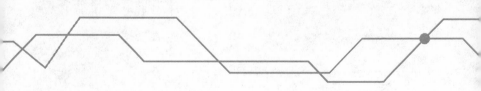

FOREWORD

BY SCOTT TIPTON

When you start to see a little success as a writer, a curious thing happens. Suddenly everyone you know is also a writer, even if they've never published a thing in their entire lives. Sometimes they've never even finished writing a thing in their entire lives. And now they want you to read what they're working on, as if you've somehow cracked the code and can just swing open the door to a life of book tours and movie deals, canapés and caviar.

We all know it doesn't really work like that.

Sometimes, you can politely beg off, explaining that you can't read their knockout, can't-fail idea for a *Star Trek/Land of the Lost* crossover series, because you're working on *Star Trek* already and don't want to risk being accidentally influenced by their work. Sometimes you agree to look at something and have to find a way to be polite about the work, because you know your friend doesn't really want to hear the truth. Sometimes they insist, and sometimes you lose a friend.

And sometimes, if you're really lucky, someone will hand you a book and you realize you've already been friends with an incredibly gifted writer; it's just that nobody knows it yet.

That's what happened to me when Adam Korenman handed me a copy of *When The Stars Fade*.

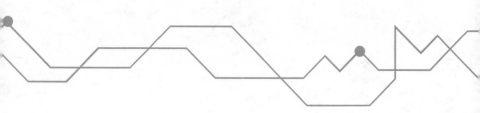

What Korenman has done in the pages that follow is take a lifetime of influences in science fiction, film, video games, comic books—all the things he loves—and masterfully fused it all with the kind of real-world insight, fears, and experience that only come from being at the controls of a three-million-dollar M1A1 Abrams battle tank (Mr. Korenman's day job, believe it or not). The result is a tremendously ambitious first novel, a galaxy-spanning tale of "hard science fiction" that tackles interplanetary diplomacy, the realities of combat in the vacuum of space, and most of the other tropes you see in countless "war in outer space" stories, only here it all feels so much more...*tangible*. It's approachable, even identifiable, thanks to Korenman's keen ear for dialogue and dead-on instincts about character.

Sure, it's a big outer-space war epic. But it's about people. And it's got heart.

One of the best compliments a writer can get from another writer is a simple "Damn, I wish I'd written that." As much I'd like to be able to say that, I know I'd never have been able to write *When the Stars Fade*. But I'm delighted to have it here to enjoy.

And Korenman will get the book tours and caviar all on his own, no doubt.

NOVEMBER 2015

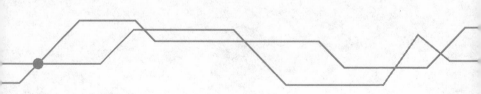

WHEN THE STARS FADE

PROLOGUE

THE KING'S

FLEET

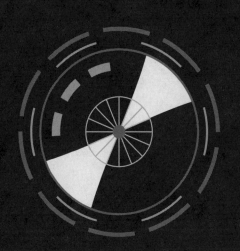

THE KING GAZED OUT at the stars of creation and rejoiced. In his galaxy, one hundred billion twinkling lights hinted at the possibility of a trillion unknown worlds. Somewhere in the endless spiral were creatures rising from the dirt and seeking out the truth. All He needed to do was to find them and bring them into the fold.

At His command, the Armada left the safety of the Home System and began the journey outward. Watching the massive ships tear free from the planet's grasp and ascend into the black night, the King stirred with emotion. He would see the end of this crusade, and the banner of his kingdom would rise over countless worlds in triumph and glory, but this galaxy would be his grave. He imagined what could exist in the Far Keeps, the blossoms of white and blue and yellow that floated just out of reach. In the end, He accepted that even Gods must have their limits.

In the sky overhead, the Elder Star churned and tumbled. It had long ago collapsed into darkness, well before the Horde took a single step on dry land. The King gave his thanks to the True Father and asked for a blessing of protection for his brood. There were untold dangers lying ahead, and so He prayed for His children's survival. Then, settling down on a throne of bone and rock and skin, the King waited for news of victory.

It didn't take long.

———

PART
ONE

LUNA

"We didn't find gods in the stars. Only darkness."
-Tractate of the Guiding Light

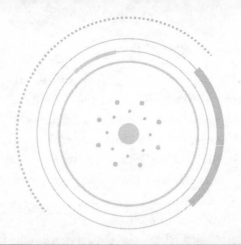

October 12, 2236
New Armstrong Station
Luna

E ARTHRISE ALWAYS TOOK HIS breath away. Standing on the bustling train platform, the old man breathed in recycled air and yawned. His first coffee stirred restlessly in his stomach while a second warmed his hand. The freshly pressed fabric of his uniform hugged his shoulders and waist. He didn't stand out, even with all the medals and ribbons on his coat. This was Luna Station, and there were plenty of veterans around.

"Come on," a voice said. "We're going to miss the train."

Commodore Hiro Osaka turned to face his escort, a handsome young soldier whose name was already forgotten. The sixty-year-old officer took a sip of bitter liquid and grimaced. He couldn't wait to get back to his boat. *Midway* always had fresh Paradiso brewing in the galley. Hiro gestured for the soldier to lead the way to the tram. Fort Yonkers waited at the end of the line, along with briefings and paperwork and, just maybe, a little sleep.

Hiro stole one last glance through the triple-paned window. Through the cloud and heavy satellite cover, he could just make out the island of Japan. His father's home stood out as a vibrant green crescent against a deep blue canvas. His heart swelled at the sight. Hiro paused. He'd seen the homeworld from Luna—the moon—many times before. Why this feeling now?

"Sir? We really need to go."

He nodded. "Lead the way." Hiro matched the soldier's brisk gate and followed toward the sound of an arriving train. He let the odd sensation drift to the back of his mind for later inspection. Right now, he had a more pressing concern. *Midway* needed to get off Luna.

Earth Orbit

ON THE OPPOSITE SIDE of the moon, in the absence of the sun's light, space began to bubble. A small weather satellite drifted too far off course, its fuel reserves depleted long ago and never refilled. As it meandered into the depths, it suddenly sparked and shuddered. Blue light engulfed the satellite in its final moments, before the truck-sized capsule vanished into the ether.

Beside this new vortex, a dozen motes of light winked into existence and began to grow.

Terran Space Initiative (TSI) Observatory Andretti Crater, Luna

THE WAIL OF AN alarm shocked Raymond Lee awake. He rubbed his eyes and looked at the computer screen. Glowing text popped onto the monitor, creating an endlessly scrolling list of notices. Raymond thought first that the machine had glitched, but then he saw each alert came from a unique ISP. Of the three hundred satellites controlled by the observatory, nearly all were calling for help.

Raymond hadn't been with the Terran Space Initiative long; he'd only just been promoted to full time. TSI paid well for the graveyard shift, and the long hours left him with enough time to study for school. During his orientation, he'd been taught what to do in case the AI controller broke down, or if there was a fire in the lab, or if the CO_2 filters malfunctioned. No one ever brought up an invasion.

A number of satellites reported anomalies consistent with a spatial disruption; something was leaving interdimensional space and arriving near Earth. Raymond double-checked the coordinates, relieved to see they were nowhere near the Earth gates. An invasion force would have to arrive as close as possible to the station, otherwise they'd never survive more than a few minutes. This strange signal seemed more and more like a transport ship using an old traffic code.

It had taken Olivia—his boss—a full six hours to explain, but Raymond figured he understood enough about the science of space travel to be absolutely terrified. Given the advances in quantum mechanics, quantum physics, and something called AeroSpatial Disturbance Theory, there were now three ways to cross distances in space: Standard, Stride, and Blue.

The first was simple and had been around for hundreds of years. Normal engines and rockets could propel any vessel at what was known as Standard speed. This was good for travel between stations, in orbit, or from a planet to a moon. Ships used their rockets and zipped about, agile as figure skaters.

For longer journeys, intrasystem travel required Strider drives. At Stride speed, the time it took to cross the Solar System dropped from decades to days. Precise calculations were required to avoid slamming into an asteroid at Stride speed, but given the network of relays in the system, it was a fairly painless process. Not every ship had the Slush Erbium Drives—or sleds—built in, so smaller craft often had to hitch a ride.

The final form of travel, and infinitely more dangerous, was Blue. Discovered only a century before, and more regulated than any other form of travel in history, Blue Space allowed interstellar travel and became the backbone of the colonization movement. The first probe sent into Blue Space transmitted a report back via FTL one week later—from over one hundred lightyears away. Using nodes—building-sized relay stations around the colonies—ships could pinpoint their destination within a few kilometers and arrive hundreds and billions of kilometers away in a manner of days, if not hours. The only requirement for "safe" travel was a linked terminal at both ends of the journey. Otherwise a ship could exit Blue Space anywhere in the universe. *Anywhere.*

But what made a Blue jump *really* terrifying was the fact that, aside from the evidence that it worked, no one in any field of science understood *how.* Ships ripped into the fabric of space, emerged unscathed, and all of it happened without solid proof that it made any logical sense. TSI devoted one quarter of its budget every year to plumbing the depths of Blue Space in search of answers, but so far had come up empty. That thought alone convinced Raymond that he would never, in a million years, travel through the "Blue Tunnel." Especially with the stories one heard about civilian ships that never exited and simply floated in another dimension for eternity.

Curiosity kept Raymond's mind racing. He found himself at the telescope controls, not entirely sure why he was there. The powerful lenses responded to his commands, rotating until they faced the indicated coordinates. The entire room spun on a disk, bringing the table-sized glass plates to bear. Raymond tapped out sequences on the keyboard, bringing up a view of a brilliant expanse of nothing at the edge of the planetary plane.

The massive monitor displayed the star-filled sky, but little more. Raymond saw comets streak by in the distance, the strobe lights from two weather stations on far orbit, and the red and yellow pulse of a relay station. Nothing. And then, something.

No, Raymond thought. *What is that?* He leaned forward and tapped a button on the keyboard to increase the focal length. A small point of light came into view, barely the size of pinprick. As Ray watched, the dot expanded rapidly, becoming as wide as a hangar and pouring blue rays across Lunar space. A dozen more pinpricks flared into existence, peppering the space around the enormous Blue exit. A cold fist gripped Raymond's chest.

Jesus, it's a goddamn invasion. Raymond grabbed his headset and dialed the link for the SP Operation Center. He rubbed his shaking hands together furiously as he waited for the operator to pick up. Raymond watched the Blue funnels spew out twisted black shapes. He switched to a higher-powered lens, and the objects grew in size. Hulking battleships and frigates hurtled through space, spewing blood-red energy in their wakes. As the Blue Space exits began to close, he had counted twenty total ships.

"Sector Patrol Luna, this is Operations." The woman's voice on the other end was crisp and clear. "What is the purpose of your call?"

"This is Raymond Lee, TSI station Andretti. I have a major situation here."

"Andretti, if this is a civil incident, you need to contact TSI Control. Do you need their information?"

"No. What? Listen to me, I have unauthorized Blue Space exits in..." He threw files off his desk until he found the map of the space above Luna. "Quadrant forty-five, sector twenty-one."

The operator paused, typing on her computer. "I don't have any reports from Terra. Andretti, I need you to authenticate this channel."

Shit. Raymond squeezed his eyes shut, trying to remember the code for his station. He nearly panicked until he saw the note posted above his computer. "Uh, seven-four, er, nine-one-oscar-zulu-zulu?"

A longer pause. "Andretti, this is Operations. We authenticate, seven-four-niner-one-oscar-zulu-zulu. Send coordinates when ready."

Raymond read off the coordinates from the telescope. The armada of ships had slowed down and seemed to be forming up into a battle group. The largest of the vessels, what looked like a giant beehive, was surrounded by the smaller craft.

"Andretti, we confirm contacts in Lunar space. SP will take over from here. Continue to monitor the situation, but if contacts come within fifty kilometers, seek out shelter immediately."

The line closed. Helpless, Raymond watched the hypnotizing shuffle of ships move into a battle group and creep toward Earth.

Dr. Markov Ivanovich sat on a wooden bench near heavy double doors, waiting for his turn to speak. The impressive hallway of NYU's new Silver Center stretched endlessly in each direction, curving around in a massive circle. The seven-story structure overlooked the Hudson River, one of the few unobstructed views in the ever-growing city. Skyscrapers reached toward the stars in every direction, connected by a web of Sky Rails.

Markov placed a hand on his knee but failed to stop his restless leg. It bounced constantly, relentlessly. He swallowed, then swallowed again. His chest felt too tight. He checked his buttons to make sure they were in the correct order, then checked his padded binder. Indeed, all of his documents were in order, just as they had been ten minutes prior, and the half hour before that.

"You need to relax," a heavy voice said opposite Markov. Sasha Otravlyatovich regarded his liberator. Sasha had been rotting in a gulag on Phobos when the infamous Dr. Markov recruited him. Despite having spent thirteen years chained to a wall, Sasha was reluctant to leave the comforts of a UEC dungeon, even one on a planetoid as unforgiving as Phobos.

But when Markov told him the old government had been disbanded as part of a treaty with Mars, Sasha agreed to leave. As their transport lifted off from the small moon, Sasha found himself one step closer to the culmination of his life's cause and goal:

A free and unified Mars.

But now Sasha didn't know *what* he stood for.

"If you spook the Joint Chiefs, this project dies tonight."

31

WHEN THE STARS FADE

"I can't relax," Markov said, eyes lingering on Sasha's scar, which stood out on his face in the fluorescent light.

"This is too important for relaxing. Everything we've worked for..."

"I did nothing," Sasha replied. "You're the mad scientist."

"Fine. Everything I've worked for depends on getting this grant."

The heavyset man leaned back on his bench opposite Markov. His black leather coat still dripped on the floor from the rains outside. His skin was monstrously pale—a souvenir from a long stay in prison. "Tell me again why we can't use the Cove?"

"The Fade uses the Cove," Markov said, referring to the Fleet Analysis of Intelligence Division, known in the armed services as FAID, or colloquially as *the Fade*. The mystery of what went on in the myriad of onyx buildings they maintained around the galaxy led to many conspiracy theories and cheesy thrillers on the Net. "I won't have their greasy fingers getting into all my projects."

He was about to say more when the double doors opened. Both men turned to face a pretty young redhead. She smiled and gestured toward the chambers.

"Dr. Ivanovich, the Joint Chiefs are waiting."

Sasha picked up a soggy newspaper from a nearby table and starting reading. Markov swallowed a final time, stood, and walked into the room.

There were seven men waiting inside the chamber, all dressed in their respective uniforms. Admiral Walker, the commander of Fleet, sat front and center on a dais. On his left were members of the military, all four-star generals or their naval equivalent. On his right were the Joint Chiefs, dressed in civilian suits. Markov nearly gasped when he saw another familiar face leaning against the wall, barely concealed in shadow. Chief of Staff Jerry Ahmad needed no introduction; he was the face of the new government, as famous a man as High Chancellor Burton himself.

"Doctor," Admiral Walker began. "Thank you for making the trip. How is Titan this time of year?"

Markov's mouth tasted like sandpaper. "Cold. I really appreciate this opportunity. I know that the last conference wasn't my best showing, and I agree with you saying I needed time to develop my ideas and sift through the chaff to find—"

"Markov," Walker said, cutting the young man off. "We've listened to almost sixty presentations today. Let's cut to the chase."

The doctor sniffed. "Right. Okay." He opened his binder and pulled out his tablet. The thin sheet of polymer was clear as glass, but lit up at his touch. He swiped on the screen, sending the information to a massive projector on the wall to his right. "The guidance you gave for this task was pretty simple: provide a new method of dealing with terrorist operations in the Systems. You said to make it man-portable and as safe for the soldiers as possible."

General Sanders yawned. "We know the rules, Doctor. We made them. Get to the point, please."

"Of course, General." He advanced his slide show rapidly. "What you're looking at is my proposal for the new and improved CROWN Mark V."

There it was. Markov had said it, and the room fell insantly silent. Sasha braced for the backlash.

Markov had been a genius since childhood, excelling in math and science at an early age. He'd been discovered by the headmaster of a prestigious school for gifted youth and graduated early to join the United Earth Council's Department of Science and Research. Markov quickly earned his stripes as the UEC's top mind. When Mars revolted, he was chosen to find a swift solution.

His idea had been the Carbon-Reinforced OverWear Network armored suit, or CROWN. Using simple neural networking, a single soldier controlled a twelve-foot-tall, armored battle suit. The intent had been to create a weapon any soldier could learn to use.

Too bad it was a disaster.

And everyone in the room knew it.

Markov pressed on, "Using a proprietary method, we can enhance a soldier's survivability by a factor of—"

Walker cut him off again. "Are you fucking serious? CROWN? Is this a joke?"

Markov's mouth opened and closed without sound.

Sanders seethed. "I still have nightmares about your *last* round of tests. One of my men had a seizure when your contraption went into a forced reboot. We found him at the bottom of a lake, sealed into a CROWN suit like it was a goddamn tomb."

"Please, I know the name isn't popular, but this is a completely new system." He flipped through his presentation until he found a series of action shots. "Look, you can see the results clear as day. These suits enable a soldier to run faster, jump higher, and fight longer than any other human in existence. This is the evolution of power armor, and it doesn't require a license to operate. You could slip one on right now and go fight."

Markov continued, "And that's just the beginning. We're experimenting with new protein-based dermal enhancements to make the human body more capable and adaptable. All I need is a team, a lab, and willing candidates, and I can have a working operations unit in under a year. Send seven of my soldiers into a Red Hammer den and you'll never worry about them ever again."

"You're still using SQUID," Walker said. "Doctor, let me be blunt. I don't like this. I don't like that you're using century-old tech. I don't like that you've stubbornly refused to try ANGEL networking. And I especially don't like you wasting this committee's time when you have zero governmental support." The admiral rubbed his temples with both hands. "The budget is tighter than ever this year, and you've given us no reason to trust you with a single cent. You do understand the reason behind this project, don't you?"

Markov nodded quickly. "The Martian rebels?"

Walker dropped his head into his hands. "Jesus, Doc. Mars is pacified. That generation has all but died out. Why would we want to prepare for a war we already won?"

"The prompt for this project referenced the Guardian initiative. I just thought—"

"That we were fighting Red Hammer with armored knights? They're just a grubby militia living out of cheap motels." Walker sat back and exhaled through his teeth. "Markov, until you get a Councilor on board or the goddamn sky starts to fall, this committee will not pay any more attention to your mad science. You need to go."

Markov's head sank. He switched off the projector and collected his things. "I understand, Admiral. I'm sorry for wasting your time."

Walker stood along with the other members of the committee. "I don't think it's just our time that was wasted here." The men marched from the room in a single file, disappearing into an annex behind the dais.

The doctor was so busy moping that he barely registered movement by his shoulder bag. He nearly shouted when he saw Chief of Staff Ahmad leafing through his notes.

"Sir, I'm so sorry," Markov said. "You startled me." He took a moment to catch his breath. "I didn't know the Federate government was watching this project so closely."

The chief of staff nodded but didn't look up. "The office of the high chancellor has no interest in wasting money on defense projects, especially when our greatest threat is a psychopath from Mars." He glanced at the trembling scientist. "Relax, doctor. I'm on your side. I think CROWN never really got a fair shot. Then again, I didn't watch three men's brains melt when they tried to wear it. How much field testing have you done?"

"Tons," he offered quickly. "My team is small right now, just six of us, but we've been making some incredible advances with the tools available." He fidgeted. "Titan is a great place to build ships, but the facilities there are lacking in the proper equipment for my needs. Please, give me a small space on New Eden. I guarantee the results will astound you."

The chief of staff shook his head. "Out of the question. As far as the Joint Chiefs are concerned, this is the last time this project will ever see the light of day. Understand?"

Markov felt ill. "I do."

"Good. Now go back to your hotel and clean up. I want you ready to present this to the Centurial Council in a few days."

"What?"

"We're voting on funding to new Special Projects. If you can make a better case, this might just pass muster. And for god's sake, change the fucking name. Everyone in the four systems knows about CROWN."

Markov bobbed his head up and down. "I'm actually headed to Kronos after this. I want to catch the end of the Crucible. Perhaps I'll find some new test candidates for CROW—for my power armor. I'll write a new report tonight on the flight over."

Chief of Staff Ahmad held up a hand. "No rush. Just get me something good to present to the high chancellor. He could use the win." He walked toward the door where his assistant, the young redheaded staffer, waited. "And I'm serious about keeping this quiet. As soon as people hear about new defense projects, they act like the sky is falling." He paused at the door. "And enjoy your trip to Kronos. I hear it's lovely this time of year."

Kronos
Third Moon of New Eden
Eros System

KRONOS WAS HELL.

From orbit, the medium-sized moon was a uniform brown, broken only with canyons and mountains. What little water existed on the planetoid was buried deep in the ground, accessible from the many wells built on the surface. It was a place where no human would ever dream of living.

Naturally, it was the Army's favorite training center.

While the citizens of nearby New Eden went about their days, the soldiers of the 185th Combined Arms Battalion endured the Crucible. For five months straight, the mixed units trained in high intensity combat. Wearing advanced simulation gear, they fought for every inch of defendable dirt in a hundred-square-kilometer arena. Aside from bragging rights, the top performers could hope to join the ranks of the infamous Black Adders, or maybe earn a coveted slot for Team Hercules.

The slow rotation of the moon meant thirty-hour days, most of which was spent under the blistering heat of nearby Eros. The soldiers had been cut off from the outside world for half a year and were eager to get home. While generals and politicians and weapons manufacturers watched on, the men and women on Kronos prepared for the end.

LYING IN A SMALL outcropping of rock, Joshua Rantz of Charlie Company tried to still his breathing. His tan uniform and gray ceramic armor blended well with the bleak terrain, but a moving target still stood out like a sore thumb. Closing his eyes, Josh measured each breath in a slow four-count. In the dim light he became just another boulder on the canyon wall. The sun had just set, cooling the training area to a blissful ninety-eight degrees. Josh raised the shade film on his visor and gazed at the beautiful horizon. The blue star made an impressive show every evening, turning the sky into a watercolor with every shade of purple, red, and orange.

"You're dead." The deep baritone was felt as much as heard.

Josh opened his eyes and looked up at a mountain. Dax Goodman, his fellow Charlie Company soldier, was nearly three hundred pounds of sharp muscle. He looked every bit the sports celebrity, with his bright white smile and dimpled chin. Dax tried hard to maintain a serious expression but lost it after a few seconds. He offered a beefy hand to Josh and hoisted his friend to his feet.

"Alexa's in position?" Josh asked.

"Just getting set up, Sarge."

"Stop that."

"You got it, Sarge."

"I'm not kidding." Josh shot Dax a mean look. They walked side-by-side toward base camp through a wide canyon. There probably wasn't an enemy for miles, but they still paused every few dozen yards to scan their surroundings. Months of living in a combat zone—even a make-believe one— had imprinted new instincts. Corners were now dead zones. Shadows were possible threats. And every sound could be the last they ever heard. "In a month, I'll be a corporal again and all will be right with the world. I'm not earning the pay, so what's the point in pretending I'm a sergeant?"

"All right," Dax said, holding up both hands. "You got me." The darkness swallowed the huge soldier, his brown skin blending into the surroundings. "Rank looks good on you, though."

Josh glanced down at the chevrons on his uniform. They were borrowed off of Sergeant Luker, who had taken a sniper round a few months back. That had earned Josh his battlefield promotion, as well as control of the squad. There were dried red droplets on the rank, leftover dye from the sim-round that "killed" Luker.

"Bravo's done," Dax said suddenly. "Alexa got the word from the XO. First Platoon took them out at first light. Picture-perfect ambush."

They arrived at their improvised patrol base, buried in the canyons. Accessible from only two directions, it was a perfect spot for a tactical pause. The squad was invisible unless the enemy stumbled right in. A sentry held them at gunpoint and waited for the password, then waved them through and resumed his guard.

Dax set down his DaVinci Heavy Machine—a massive three-barrel monster—and sucked down mouthfuls of water. "Just Delta..."

"And Alpha," a voice said. Alexa Haines jogged over. She had stripped down most of her armor, with the exception of the simulator vest. If she removed that, she'd be automatically killed for breaking the rules of the Crucible. Still, it was cooler than wearing all fifty pounds of her scout gear. She sweat from every pore, but still looked cheerful as ever. "XO says we need to stand by. Something's happening at the FOB."

We've been standing by for three days. Josh paced irritably. "Delta still has more boots on the ground. If we don't pick a few more off, we're coming in third place. That means no extra leave."

Alexa punched Josh's arm. "Had a big weekend lined up? Hot date?"

Josh dodged a second punch and blushed. "No. I mean, that's not what I'm saying. We shouldn't settle for anything less than a total win."

"I'm pretty sure Alpha's already locked that up," Dax said.

Alpha Company had sailed through the first few months of the Crucible with endless momentum, conducting blistering assaults against their opponents. Now, with a little more than a month left, they were relaxing in an easily defendable position at the North side of the training area. If they made it to the end without suffering more losses, they would win the event without lifting another finger.

Josh turned to Alexa. "Have you...been working on it?"

Her face brightened. "I thought you'd never ask." She led them to the center of camp where a map rested on a large boulder. Her red hair had grown long during the half-year exercise, and she wore it in a tight ponytail. The armor across her right shoulder bore a long crack—earned during a tense struggle with a Delta sniper. "They definitely don't have this hill covered. I've counted their patrols three times, and no one watches it." She tapped the map. "I mean, it's suicide to attack from here, but still."

Josh rubbed his chin. "I'll work that part out. Just keep a tab on their movements."

"What is all this?" Dax asked.

"I asked Alexa to take her scouts and find out about Delta's FOB. We've got a little more than five weeks before this all shuts down." Josh tapped the map where a cluster of red dots had been drawn. "We can take Delta out before then. I just need to convince the XO. If he gives me two platoons, I can get Charlie into second place in a single night."

Near Earth Orbit

THE FIRST INVADER SLIPPED free of the swirling Blue portal and shot out into the Sol System. Forward rockets fired, slowing the heavy craft until it was nearly stationary. Its iridescent silver hull shimmered in the light of Sol, the system's small yellow star. The engines cooled, venting puffs of green and white gas into space.

Seconds later, three more vessels joined the larger ship, popping into existence with flashes of blue light. Their numbers grew steadily as a variety of large and small craft entered human space. Finally, the Blue Space funnels shrank and faded, leaving behind an armada of silver and blue. The alien craft looked cobbled together in haste, with different colored panels and sloppily repaired hulls. They ranged from small saucers to enormous, cigar-shaped cruisers. Engines ignited, and the strange collection of ships advanced toward the human homeworld.

With all eyes watching the interlopers, few even noticed the second series of Blue exits opening just a hundred kilometers away.

October 13, 2236
Lunar Sector Patrol Center (SPC)
Luna

CAMERON DAVIS AND GEORGE Locklear sat at a table in the quiet mess hall, nursing steaming cups of coffee. A few other pilots ate their meals in silence, ignoring the overpowering smell of whiskey and beer wafting from the two men's table. George sat with his head on the table, groaning. Cameron seemed unfazed by a night of poor decision-making, and barely suppressed his smirk every time his friend winced. Their flight uniforms were clean, if not fresh. They'd changed out of their dress blues a half hour before.

Like most members of Sector Patrol, their uniforms were recycled from Fleet. The tiger-stripe pattern in gray and blue had long ago changed to a hexagonal charcoal for the Active component. There was no malice in the decision; it made no fiscal sense to spend the money on brand new uniforms for the weekend warriors. Still, to members of SP, it felt like just another in a long list of slights by big brother Fleet.

Folks called the military the "fourth pillar" of the government. It broke down into five functional areas. There was the Army, designed to defend planets and moons. Marines were trained in similar tactics, but they only served aboard ships or stations, a fact that disturbed anyone with even a passing knowledge of the branch's history. The Navy had long before been rebranded as

Fleet. It covered everything from pilots to commanders.

Finally there was SP, the reserve forces that acted as jacks of all trades. That included Cameron and George.

Cameron leaned his long frame back in the plastic chair. He fit the uniform just right, creating a striking figure. His wingman George, on the other hand, seemed extra frumpish in his too-large jumpsuit. A few coffee stains on the sleeves didn't improve the look.

"I told you that last shot was a mistake," Cameron said.

George looked up with red eyes. "No, you said the *second*-to-last shot was a mistake. You didn't see the one after." He hiccuped, choking back a sudden surge of bile. "Or the two after that."

"Are you okay to fly?"

He grinned, tapping a subdued black badge on his chest. "I'm an ace, son. A hangover is just part of the job." His stomach gurgled, and George fought to hold down his meager breakfast. "Anything on the board today?"

Cameron turned toward the massive briefing screen, looking for the flight list. Strangely, the board was empty. Not even the runs from the previous night. Normally, the names and routes for dozens of wings would be laid out for the day. He was about to say as much to George when the panel suddenly flashed white.

An alert bell rang out in a sudden shotgun blast of white noise. They clapped hands over their ears in defense. Red strobes activated, washing over the room. The entire hall leapt to attention, accompanied by a cacophony of shouting voices. They glanced around, completely disoriented by the ready alarm. Then, one by one, they registered the meaning of the noise. Cameron nearly knocked over the table as he bolted toward a comm terminal and activated the line to

OpCenter. George joined him quickly, massaging his temples as he walked up. He'd brought his coffee over and sipped from the steaming mug.

"What the hell? We're off this weekend. It's supposed to be a holiday."

"That's next weekend. It's Thursday." Cameron raised an eyebrow. "What holiday happens on October thirteenth?"

"Leave George The Hell Alone Day." He yawned, limbs splayed out like a cat. "What do you think?"

Cameron shrugged. "Could be another passenger liner lost thrusters." It was the most likely possibility. Ever since the recession hit, interstellar cruisers were going longer and longer between repairs and refits. They'd handle a call like that once a week at least. SP advertised as the reserve component of Fleet, but it was more like being a space cop.

The crowd around the station grew, and Cameron felt dozens of eyes on him as he waited for the operation center to connect. Someone finally silenced the alarm, but the startled pilots still huddled and shivered like wet dogs.

When the monitor lit up, they found themselves staring at General Burnside, the elderly post commander. Cameron immediately went to attention, while George merely stepped out of the camera's view. After a moment, they both realized it was a recorded message.

"What the hell?" Cameron stammered. "This is new." He looked over his shoulder at the remaining crowd, shrugging.

Burnside was old but tough. A former infantry officer, the three-star general ruled the base with a firm hand. SP personnel often found their passes revoked for minor infractions. It didn't stop the civilians from acting like imbeciles, but anyone in uniform behaved as professionally as a West Point graduate. George had nearly exploded the first week. Cameron found the transition smoother.

Burnside spoke, his voice tired and full of gravel. "Attention. This is General Lawrence Burnside, commander of Federate Reserve Post Yonkers. Earth and her moon are facing an imminent threat. All pilots report to your hangars and you will receive full briefings. Godspeed." The feed cut out.

George looked at Cameron, bewildered. "Imminent what?"

Cameron took off out of the mess hall and down the corridor, with George struggling to keep up.

Fort Yonkers
Luna

FORT YONKERS HADN'T BEEN built for Fleet. That much Commodore Hiro Osaka knew. Grown from the skeleton of the first lunar colony, the sprawling base lacked the facilities and equipment to properly care for anything larger than a six-man Griffin. The complexities of a Terran carrier seemed to baffle the gaggle of civilian engineers that pored over the flagship like ants on a picnic. Two weeks into the refit and they were already a month behind schedule. The fifty-year-old officer had walked the halls of his ship only hours before and had been horrified by the disastrous mess left behind. Cables hung down from the overhead panels and entire sections of the walls were missing, exposing the innards of the vessel.

As the commander of Carrier Battle Group Sol, Hiro oversaw a flotilla of the most advanced ships in the Terran Fleet. But even without the support craft, Hiro had the Alpha vessel.

Midway, the Terran flagship, was unlike any carrier before it.

Designed during the final days of the Emigration War, she replaced the fallen TFC *Shiloh*. Three times as large, and holding eighty more fighting craft than her predecessor, *Midway* had become the unquestioned symbol of the Federate's supremacy in the dark skies. It wasn't hard to see why; unless someone saw her in person, they never believed the stories of her size.

In recent years, even as newer ships of the line flew out from the various yards over Titan and Phobos, *Midway* had remained a sentinel in Terran space. Her crew could populate a small town or conquer a small moon. Though armed only with standard weaponry, the carrier was a match for any fighting vessel in the known universe. Hiro's weapons officer lamented that they never installed some of the latest and greatest tools of destruction, but a forty-inch gun still packed a hell of a punch. Which made it all the more frustrating to have it under repair, collecting moon dust.

Alarms sounded throughout the base, muted now that the initial alert had gone out. The commodore seethed at the idea of sitting idly by while Mars launched an attack. Hiro looked out the small glass window next to him, imagining he could see the red planet. It was such an unimaginable distance away—but unbearably close for a military man. He took a final look at his prone and gutted berth before heading back down the hall. The civilians and soldiers he passed stared at him as he walked by. With his closely cut gray hair and piercing blue eyes, Hiro was as recognizable a face on a military post as the high chancellor himself.

He pinched the bridge of his nose, his other hand holding a small clear phone to his ear. He didn't like the new model— the synthetic material wore too quickly and felt tacky against his cheek. His jaw clenched and relaxed, and he tried to slow his racing pulse.

"I don't care about the old plates," he said. His voice was calm, but he felt acid rise in his stomach. "I can't fly until you replace the port hangar's armor shielding." Hiro paced back and forth in the hall, his eyes locked on a distant point of the Earth's surface. "You have until I reach the OpCenter to give me a better answer. When the fighting starts, I'd better be up there." He hung up, lingering in place to soak in the spectacle. For a moment he considered calling his daughter, maybe asking to speak to his grandson, but it was already late. With a sigh, he put his phone away.

The commodore turned to walk toward the operation center and nearly collided with two young men running down the corridor. They stopped cold when they saw the golden star on Hiro's collar, the scarlet "S" designator at the top point. Each snapped off a crisp salute, which the commander took a moment to reflect on before returning. The ranking officer walked around the two pilots, glaring as only a superior can. His perfectly polished shoes clacked on the tile with a satisfying echo.

"What unit are you with?" Hiro asked.

The taller of the two turned to speak. His flight uniform was clean and pressed, with creases along the sleeves. Silver pilot wings crested his lapels with a large "A" in the background. "Sector Patrol, Wolf Squadron, sir." His friend, a head shorter with dark and unruly hair, grinned in agreement. "We're responding to the alert."

"Names?"

"Lieutenants Davis and Locklear."

Hiro stared at the growing number of winking Blue portals in the distance. "You had better get moving, boys."

He saluted, signaling for them to run off. The shorter one immediately began speed walking away, but the other remained a moment.

"Is that your ship, Commodore?" The young man pointed out the nearby window. From almost any area inside the post, the supercarrier could be seen. It blocked most of the view, not that there was all that much to miss. Just a sea of gray stretching to the horizon.

Hiro smiled. "*Midway* has been my home for seven years now, but I can never claim her as my own. She belongs to the crew and the pilots, to the engineers who brought her to life. Though she does do what I ask. Most of the time." He took a moment to take in the younger officer. The dirty blonde hair was a bit long for regulation, but he couldn't deny the man possessed a powerful bearing. Hiro liked him right away. "What is your name again, pilot?"

"Davis, sir. Cameron Davis." He scratched his head. "We sort of met before, sir, at my commissioning ceremony. You talked about the battle at Phobos, said it made you wish you'd been a pilot again."

"Did we speak then?"

"No. I was laid up in a chair in the back. My Dodo bricked out fifty yards from the deck. I was lucky; only sprained my neck. They had me on so many meds, I slept through my pinning."

"But you remembered my speech?" Hiro asked.

"Some things stick with you."

Hiro looked at Cameron's shoulders, noticing the silver bar on either side. He almost called him a Junior Grade, but he recalled that SP worked off the Army ranking system. "May I ask you a question, Lieutenant?"

"Of course, sir."

Hiro stared out the window, fingers brushing against the cold glass. His breath fogged the view when he pressed his face closer. "Why SP? Why not Fleet?"

"I failed the health test."

"Really? You look perfectly fine."

Cameron tapped his chest. "Hypertrophic cardiomyopathy. Fancy way of saying I have a genetic disposition towards a bad heart. Fleet wouldn't accept my packet without a letter from a doctor saying I would live forever."

Hiro nodded. He'd seen so many good soldiers turned away from service because of geneticism. "What does the disease do?"

"For now? Nothing. But, if the wrong things happen, my heart gets thicker and I can't pump blood as well. Makes it hard to be a pilot." He waved off the look the commodore was wearing. "It doesn't bother me, sir. Sector took me, and they let me fly whatever I want. Besides, I'd never fit in with the active side. Too rigid."

Hiro turned his eyes on him. "Is that right?"

"Sorry, sir. No offense meant."

The commodore let the moment dilate. Then he smiled. Cameron felt like he'd just received a stay of execution.

"Well, Lieutenant Davis, I'll see you in the air. Good hunting."

Cameron grinned. "Thank you, sir." He became serious, extending his hand to his superior. "It's an honor to meet you, Commodore."

The commodore took his hand. "It was very nice to meet you, Lieutenant Davis."

The pilot saluted and ran off toward his friend.

Hiro watched him go, then continued on to the operations center.

ADAM KORENMAN

THE LONG STRETCH OF connected pods stank of stale air and rust. SP had been relegated to the older section of post, in the units left over from some of the first attempts at a lunar colony.

Cameron normally enjoyed a leisurely stroll through ancient history, but now they raced past it all until they arrived at the shuttle to the hangars on the opposite end of the base. When the door opened, they boarded the automated craft and waited for it to launch.

"What the hell is this, Cam?"

The taller pilot looked out the window, admiring a series of sparkling dots clustered in the distance. It was impossible to make out shapes this far away, but the patterns of their movement were mesmerizing. "Looks like an invasion." He and George stared in awe at the spectacle. "Are those rebels?"

"Mars ships are always red," George said. "It's like they have to color coordinate with the dirt. Lonz used to say it was a branding thing. You remember Lonz?" The shuttle bobbed and weaved past different hangars. They watched a wing of Sparrows—small fighters with thin, fixed wings—launch from magnetic rails and race to join the SP battle group growing in the sky. "It's all hands on deck. They're even deploying Junos Squadron."

Cameron followed George's finger to where six Griffin bombers were lifting up from their pads. The long-necked craft handled like barges, but their heavy-duty ordnance could turn the tide of a battle. Their wings were in the VTOL position, bent midway so the rockets could fire straight down; they were much too heavy for MagRails. Even in the lower gravity, it took a minute for the immense craft to push off the dirt. Clouds of moon dust billowed and swirled around, coating every surface.

"Approaching hangar W, stand by for landing." The automated voice was followed by a chime, and Cameron and George braced for the usual rough stop. Another relic, the shuttle was older than either of its occupants. It hit the landing surface with a screech, lurching to a sudden halt. The doors hissed as they pressurized to the airlock before opening.

INSIDE THE HANGAR WAS a frenzy of activity as ground crews raced to launch their fighters. Wolfpack comprised only FS 115 Phoenix II superiority fighters, a single-winged craft that dominated the sky—at least until the Phoenix III had launched 15 years back and rendered "the Deuce" obsolete. Now the craft was a hand-me-down from big brother Fleet. The cool gray metal glistened in the harsh lighting, and the fighters on the rails shimmered as they grew near the purple barrier that separated the building from the elements outside. Cameron and George quickly spotted Captain Newman, the SP commander for Yorktown Air. Standing a head taller than anyone around him, Newman barked orders into radios and urged crews to work faster. An aide stood nearby, shouting into a phone. Even with the roaring engines of launching fighters, it was the loudest corner of the room.

"Captain," the aide said. "*Normandy* has two squadrons aboard, but *Stalingrad* went up without an escort. They were shadowing while the new commander got his sea legs. They have plenty of anti-air, but they're not adding much to the fight."

"Where does Gilroy want us?"

The aide searched around a nearby table until he found his dusty tablet. He tapped the screen, bringing up a holographic map of lunar space. "Sector is in a scouting position here and here, near the Alpha contacts. I'm still being told to wait for our flight order."

Newman nodded, taking the information cooly. Fleet problems were now his problems, and his peaceful drill weekend was long gone. Newman noticed George and Cameron standing a few paces away and waved them over. He returned their confused salutes and put them at ease. Rubbing his bloodshot eyes, Newman silently prayed for a cup of coffee. Like everyone else, he'd been asleep an hour before.

"Lieutenant, you two are the last in the hole. Wolfpack is at half strength today, so you're taking over the Squadron as Wolf One."

"Sir?" Cameron asked. "What happened to Lieutenant Rico?"

"Down with a bad bug. And another six are in the drunk tank with the MPs. I can't fly them, even with this shitstorm. You'll do."

"Roger, sir."

George looked around, taking in the reality of the situation. On the table, a trio of screens showed zoom-ins of the two unknown armadas. George studied the ships' strange designs, trying to place their origin, but he'd never seen anything like them. His palms felt suddenly cold. "Captain, have they said what we're up against?"

The field officer shook his head. "It's not Mars, or at least that's what they're saying. Could be that splinter group out of Colorum. Be prepared for a fight. People don't show up unannounced just to shoot the breeze. Once you're out there, rendezvous with the rest of SP and stand by."

Cameron took in the information, his mind flipping through scenarios. Even with the colonists of the red planet pacified, the Federate had no shortage of enemies in the outer sectors. "Those don't look like converted mining vessels, sir. Have they been converting old derelicts or something?"

Newman sighed, clenching his jaw and counting to ten. "Lieutenant, I know about as much as you right now. What I do know is that these ships are in violation of the Vienna Pact and Sector is part of the mission. So shut up, get in your ship, and get up there."

George interrupted, placing his palm on Cameron's chest. "What's the rally point?"

"*Savanna*," Newman said.

George immediately took off and ran over to his fighter. The hangar crew already had the ladder out for him, and they handed his flight bag up after he sat down in the cockpit. Cameron realized he hadn't moved yet and followed suit, climbing into his ship. The newer Phoenix had cushioned interiors and poly-crystallic screens with a refined holographic overlay. Cam's fighter was pieced together from eight different versions of the Deuce, and looked it. One computer flickered green while another beamed images in sickening orange. It had taken him months to be able to process the kaleidoscope.

In the cockpit, Cameron flipped on the master power and waited two seconds for the computer self-test to complete. He reached behind his head and pulled out his helmet from the stowage rack. The water line was still connected, and he bit down to test if it was full. A sweet mixture of water and electrolytes filled his mouth. He squeezed the baggy and shook, hearing the slosh of a half-empty bladder. *Won't be out more than an hour. It'll be fine.* Cameron pulled his helmet

WHEN THE STARS FADE

on and plugged into the communication box. Immediately he heard traffic from Wolfpack. It was the usual buzz: what people thought of the mission; if anyone knew something new; did so-and-so get lucky last night.

Switching to a local line, Cameron spoke. "George, you read me?"

"Lima Charlie, Cam. This shit is crazy." George leaned back as a flight crew chief—an attractive woman with bright green eyes—tugged his harness tight and checked for frays in the straps. As she pulled away, George held up a hand. "No kiss for good luck?" The chief smacked his helmet hard enough to make him wince, but she still blushed. George laughed and pulled his canopy shut, waiting for the magnets to connect and seal. He listened until the locks clicked twice before giving the crew a nod. The Heads-Up Display, or HUD, read green, meaning the cockpit was now pressurized and ready for launch.

Cameron felt, rather than saw, the crane grab his fighter and begin moving it toward the rails. It wasn't as efficient as launching from the airfield, as only two fighters could take off at once, but the magnetic launcher allowed crews to immediately enter the battlefield rather than waiting to taxi out into the vacuum. Cameron connected his flight suit to the hoses inside the craft. Zero-G combat was a fairly different animal than planetary dogfighting, but the human body was the same. The flight suit would help keep him conscious during even the most intense fights. Air and water flowed in hoses around his legs and torso, contracting and relaxing as the system came online. When needed, this would keep blood in the right places.

"This is Wolf Two—shit, Wolf One—show me attached on rail two."

"Wolf One, this is Yankee One-Two." Captain Newman's voice came through calm as a schoolteacher over the line. "You are cleared to launch in minus sixty seconds. Good hunting."

"One-Two, this is Wolf Six," George said. "I'm on the rail, show me outbound." He toggled his power amp. The engines whined in response.

The Phoenix began to vibrate around Cameron as the magnets picked up their spin. Once the green light came, the hangar crew would switch his arresting magnet forward and propel him to launch speed in under two seconds. He remembered the first time he'd launched off a rail. George had been telling jokes into the radio from the ground, and Cameron had turned to make a face at him. Three weeks in a neck brace had cemented that lesson: *face forward on launch.*

"George, test control jets." Cameron watched as the twenty vertical and horizontal nozzles on George's fighter spit out white flames in sequence. Once in the vacuum, those jets provided precise control of the craft. Had the fight been planetside, the Phoenix had standard flaps and ailerons for gravitational warfare. "You're green, spot me." He activated the jet self-test and watched the numbers count up. A yellow light came on for number fifteen. "Damn it. I thought they fixed that last month."

"Yeah, still sputtering. That's fifteen, right?"

Cameron banged his helmet against his headrest. "Same shit, different day. Like I *really* needed to turn right anyhow."

"Hey, the day everything works right the first time, call in sick. The universe is clearly trying to kill you."

An alarm chimed in their cockpits. "T-minus ten... nine...eight..."

Cameron pulled his restraints tight. His left hand rested on his engine control and missile guidance stick while his right gripped the yoke. He pressed his head back against the rest and waited for the sudden acceleration. George howled over the intercom, laughing maniacally as he always did before launch. The engines spun faster and faster, the whine deafening. Cameron only heard the mad thunder of his heart.

One moment all was still, and then the stars rushed forward at three hundred kph. Cameron sank into the molded seat, his vision blurring, his stomach somersaulting into his back. Then they were clear, rocketing out of the lunar atmosphere with the dusty ground falling farther and farther behind.

Mobilization and Training Equipment Site (MATES)
Fort Yonkers
Luna

"I DON'T CARE WHAT your status is, goddammit. I want *Midway* cleared to launch in fifteen minutes."

Hiro rarely swore, but the engineers on this post infuriated him. He glanced at a nearby radar screen, watching red dots populate the black monitor. The newcomers had yet to fire a single shot, but Hiro wasn't about to wait for an olive branch; they had dropped an armada directly into Terran space. That called for a firm answer from *Midway*.

Unfortunately Hiro was grounded, thanks to the chief engineer, a civilian.

"Commodore, we have personnel on board completing the refit," he said, looking sleepy. "Half your plumbing is still ripped out, and most of the lights are on emergency power. I've got doors chocked open and entire sections of hull removed so we can access the wiring. A week ago you asked for my estimate, and I said one month. That still stands."

Hiro's head throbbed, but he forced his voice to steady. "I don't need my men in the latrine, chief. And the crew is trained to operate in pitch black if necessary." He leaned in close, smelling mustard on the man's breath. "Listen carefully. I'm ordering my team aboard, and any man you have left is going to be conscripted onto the crew for the duration of this incident. And if you don't have those docking clamps deactivated by the time our engines fire, I will personally guarantee you end up in front of a firing squad."

Hiro left him whimpering in place and stormed away. Outside the OpCenter, Hiro took out his phone and dialed his executive officer, Captain Earl MacReady. The two longtime friends had served with each other for twenty-five years, back when Hiro was a fighter pilot and Earl a radar operator. The commodore knew he could trust the XO to get things ready while he contacted Fleet and developed the situation from the ground.

Earl picked up on the second ring. "Hiro? Jesus, it's four in the morning. What's going on?" Hiro filled him in on the invasion. "Christ. I'll have the master chief get the crews up to speed. Most are going to be racked out. When do you want to ship out?"

Hiro thought for a moment. "Thirty minutes."

"We'll be at battle stations in half that."

"Thank you."

"Shit, I can't even try to go back to sleep now. Have I ever mentioned you're a prick of a boss?"

Hiro chuckled. "I'll see you aboard." He disconnected and immediately placed a call to Admiral Gilroy at Fleet Command. He waited while the line was redirected through the relays down to Earth. Despite the incredible distance between them, the field-grade officer sounded as though he were only a few feet away.

"Admiral Gilroy speaking."

"This is Commodore Osaka, sir. We have a situation developing over Luna."

"That's putting it fucking mildly."

Hiro could hear the two-star admiral shuffling around at his desk. He tried to remember the time difference and figured it was around noon in Vienna. There were other voices in the background. Aides more than likely, from the condescending tone the admiral used with them. Gilroy was a career soldier, battle-hardened and brutish. He never could grasp the political side of the military, which was why he was still searching for his vice admiral slot.

"Commodore, I'm looking at some disturbing readings from a TSI observatory and a panicked transmission from a Sky Guard captain. What can you tell me?"

"A few minutes ago, a battle group jumped into quadrant four-five-two-one. They aren't responding to any method of contact, though thus far they haven't shown hostile intent. I have SP completely mobilized, and I'm working to get *Midway* in the fight."

"Whoever this is, they made an illegal jump into Earth territory with a group of warships. I want the welcome party to get them the hell off the front porch. Are they Martian? Raiders?"

Hiro pondered the idea. "I don't believe so, sir. Mars doesn't have the tech to pull a maneuver like this. Can't be raiders, either. These are...different, sir." *Not of this world? Not human?*

Gilroy shouted something to an aide. "All right, Hiro. Get your group in the skies and form a block. Fleet is mobilizing as we speak, and I'll have *Valley Forge* out to join you in two hours."

"What about *Sidney?*" Hiro asked.

"I'm bringing her in personally. TFC *Normandy* and *Stalingrad* are already in sector with CBG Solus, but they're at half strength," Gilroy said, referring to a Carrier Battle Group. "We're gonna outnumber them by a hair." He dropped off the line as one of his aides shouted something in the background. Hiro waited patiently. "Commodore, what were those coordinates again?"

"Right on top of us. Q-four-five-two-one, off the Luna map."

Admiral Gilroy didn't speak for a minute. "Describe the craft you're seeing."

Hiro pulled out his crystal tablet and scanned through the images. "Silver vessels, varied shapes. Looks to be cruisers, destroyers, and fighters. Green or blue lights coming from their engines, we think."

"Then who the hell are the black and red ships coming from the other side of the goddamn moon?"

Hiro took off toward *Midway*, his heart pounding in his ears.

Toronto, Canada

THE SOLDIER SAT IN a darkened den, smoking and watching. His throne was a worn leather couch, his fiefdom a chilly speakeasy in Toronto. A ribbon of smoke coiled from his cigarette. Piercing blue eyes stared at a television screen. A news anchor reported on the situation over Earth.

"Terra Node has initiated the Clear Skies Protocol, so we are urging all viewers to set down immediately and seek out shelter. No word on if this is in fact a Martian invasion, but speculation is high."

"Giving me credit already?" the man said. He drew the words out with a faint southern drawl. "Appreciated, but this ain't my style." A young woman approached from the back, offering a bottle of beer. The man took it with a grin, handing the pretty girl a folded credit note. She tucked the bill into her bra, winked, and went to serve more drinks. "Hell of a Reformation Day." The man turned to share his little joke, but no one paid him any attention.

Around the room, groups of men busied themselves with various tasks, mindful to keep their noise down while their leader watched the TV. Some cleaned rifles, others played cards. Mostly, they sat and thought about the week to come. The mission had taken almost four years of planning, months of preparation, and now could crumble with the smallest slip. Not that they worried. They were never to concern themselves with failure, or the possibility thereof. Only the mission.

The soldier smiled. If a younger version of himself walked in the room, he wouldn't even recognize what he'd become. There wasn't a proper word for him. Rebel? Terrorist? Monster? Hell, he was fine with "disillusioned soldier," but the media loved to portray him as some kind of anti-establishment nutjob. No matter. The hour of judgment was approaching so rapidly that he rarely slept anymore, lest he miss it.

From inside one of his many hideaways, the soldier known as Jonah Blightman waited for his moment of triumph. Soldiers of the Red Hammer had waited too long for vengeance, but now that time was at hand. He looked down at the sprawled notebooks on the coffee table and began to go over his plan, beat by beat. It was complex, but not overly so. Contingencies were in place should anything go awry. And, in Jonah's experience, plans like this had a tendency to stray off the intended path.

If they succeeded, they would undo the damage of the past ten years in a single hour. An entire galaxy of people would know the extent of the lies told by the Federate. Jonah knew that the odds might fall against him, and that this would be his last trip out, but the time for doubt had long passed. So instead, in that Toronto speakeasy, he prepared for his hour of glory. Looking over the plans for the attack, he felt a familiar numbness growing.

While Jonah looked at the reports from his various cells, one of his veterans approached. The old man smiled with a scarred face and placed a small tablet in front of his leader.

"Everything is set, and the delivery boys are in place."

"Good," Jonah said. "Now let's talk about Buenos Aires. The casualty estimates still feel too low."

The Front
Lunar Space

CRAFT FROM EACH SIDE filled the wide gap between Earth and Luna. The Terran Fleet continued to pour out of hangars on the moon and in nearby stations, staging off-center from the two unknown groups. On either side, thousands of strange ships flew into formation. The silver saucers and cigars of one group shimmered on the black canvas. The others were harder to see but appeared more menacing, with thorny black and red hulls.

No signal sent to the alien armadas had elicited a response. The two strike groups drifted toward each other, each well within range of long guns and missiles, yet no one dared to take the first shot. In the Terran Fleet, fingers twitched over controls and triggers, anxious for anything to happen.

CAMERON AND GEORGE RACED toward the front. Their engines kicked in automatically as soon as the craft were far enough from the hangar. With the twin slush-hydrogen jets spewing out a steady stream of white and blue fire, the Phoenixes cruised out of Luna's gravity on their way to meet up with the rest of the air wing.

The skies were clear, which was oddly terrifying. A normal day between Earth and Luna would see hundreds of thousands of ships coming and going to the various stations, outposts, and colonies. Having an empty canvas of black night in every direction felt wrong. Cameron's view was only blocked by the massive Terra Node. The monolithic diamond-shaped station hovered between the homeworld and her satellite. Most of the time, Terra served as a travel hub into and out of Sol space. Today it was a fortress, bristling with armaments.

"Sector Patrol Luna, this is Wolf One. Sight me inbound on approach vector four-two."

"Wolf One, this is *Valley Forge*. Approach on flight path Whiskey Seven, on your HUD."

Cameron looked out over his port wing at George. "Shit, wrong channel." They shared a look of uncertainty before Cameron went back to the radio. "*Valley Forge*, Wolfpack is Sierra Papa. Please advice which net to switch to."

"Wolf, this is *Valley Forge* actual."

Cameron straightened up. Commander DeHart's smoke-charred voice was unmistakable. Head officer of the supercruiser *Valley Forge*, he was second-in-command to Terra Node, which essentially made him second-in-command of the Sol System. That the station had committed its own security detachment meant the threat level had jumped dramatically. "You will rendezvous with elements of Earth's SP and form on CBG Terra's flank. Fleet has operational control of this task force. *Valley Forge* out."

George laughed nervously. "Well, now I'm sure this isn't just a drill."

"Wolf, this is One." Cameron let out a breath he'd been holding. "We're escort for *Savanna*. Tight cluster, nexus formation."

"Roger," came the expected response.

"Cam," George said. "You almost sound like a leader."

"Not my first wing."

"Did I ever apologize for that? Though, to be fair, you're the one who let me bring the Maneton inside the armory."

Cameron was about to respond when a shadow blotted out the light around him. He looked up, his mouth dropping open. Engulfing all space above his puny fighter, the enormous girth of the TFC *Midway* emerged overhead. The ship was a half mile long, with hangar bays that spanned its length. An escort wing of Phoenix III fighters flew in graceful figure eights around the hull, quad-rockets leaving parallel streaks behind them. As the carrier passed, driven by sixteen fusion-cell engines, Cameron made out crews inside the hangars prepping the bomber squadrons for launch. The almond-shaped Seed craft sat on rapid-deployment rails along with dozens more strikers. Soon they disappeared from view as the flagship joined its group outside the standoff between the two mysterious formations. Medium-sized frigates and much larger destroyers took position around the supercarrier while a heavily armed battleship arrived from the rear.

"Fuck," George blurted.

A curt female voice came on: "Please keep the line clear unless issuing an official report."

"Open net, man," Cameron hissed.

George quickly switched to a secure channel between him and his wing. "Sorry, guys." The young pilot gawked at the front line. "But seriously. Fuck."

The two armadas were a study in contrast. The one on the left was a hellish swarm. A gigantic black hive-carrier spewed forth squadrons of tiny ships whose glossy hulls glistened with red markings like bloody runes. The fighters flew in swirling clouds of three dozen, perfectly matching speed and direction changes. Four acorn-shaped cruisers flanked the flagship, cannons peeking out the front of their pointed hulls. Ten destroyers—long, scooped craft with turrets covering their skin like spines—edged slowly toward the other side of the battlefield. Finally, mixed in with the other vessels, spherical missile frigates drifted like space debris.

Opposite the hellish swarm, the silver flotilla was all elegance. Their supercarrier, a crescent of platinum and gold, glided on glowing engines toward the fray, surrounded by a gleaming array of cylindrical cruisers and destroyers. The fighters and bombers were all-too familiar in their shape.

"What do those look like to you?" George asked.

"Oh, I dunno. Disks, maybe? Or dinner plates?"

"They're saucers, Cam. *Flying* saucers. It's an alien invasion."

"That's stupid. There's no such thing." But Cameron's voice wavered.

Cameron and George finally arrived at the edge of Fleet's blockade. Wolfpack, made up of seven Phoenix II fighters, floated alongside the missile frigate TMF *Savanna*, a.k.a. "the bulldog," a nickname it earned from its silhouette, which looked like an English bulldog poised to pounce. The 130,000-ton vessel carried a payload of 600 Trebuchet missiles, 1,400 Ram dummy rockets, 40 Brimstone warheads, and 10 nuclear munitions—colloquially called the "Ten Plagues" by the crew.

"*Savanna*, this is Wolf One. I'm on your starboard side." The green lights of the craft's right dorsal fin bathed Cameron's fighter. He looked up and saw a gunner flash his target strobe; a friendly taunt from the under-gunned ship. Crews of missile frigates knew that without an escort they were slag-in-waiting. Cameron lifted his wing and opened the munition doors, showing off his own assortment of toys. That earned another flash from the frigate. "Wolfpack, this is our rally point. Leash is thirty klicks."

"I'm on your six, leader." Ensign McLane's battered fighter appeared in Cameron's rear camera.

"I see you," Cameron said. "Scan your sectors."

George glided up alongside his wingman. "If I need to puke, can you cover me?"

"That's it. You're done with bourbon."

"But I'm a good ol' Kentucky boy. It's in my blood to drink the brown water."

Cameron laughed. "Nothing you just said was true."

George was about to retort when the sky in front of them exploded. "Holy shit—what the hell is that?"

From the darker armada, a maelstrom of red energy— plasma bolts and missiles from the various ships—launched at the silvery craft. The dam burst, and the two formations exploded into attack. Silver craft roared at their enemies, firing salvos of green energy that blew holes clear through the dark armor. The carriers and cruisers deployed countermeasures to disrupt the incoming fire, but the heavier slugs passed right through and shattered hulls. From the surface of Earth, the light show was visible even in the daytime sky.

"Shields up, teeth out! It's starting!"

Kronos

Josh knew something was wrong the moment he made the call. He and his platoon were holed up so he could call the FOB, or Forward Operating Base, to check in with the rest of Charlie. Normally, such a call would be answered by the RTO—radio telephone operator.

"Calico Six, this is One-Two," Josh said. "Radio check?"

More static. Then a burst, what sounded like gunfire, and another moment of silence.

An angry voice finally spoke: "Who the hell is it?"

"This is One-Two," Josh said. "Who is this?"

"Lieutenant Sandford. I've taken command at the FOB. Are you secure?"

Josh exchanged confused glances with Dax and Alexa. Sanford was pretty far down the rungs; that she'd taken command meant Charlie was getting clobbered. "Yes, ma'am. What's the situation at the FOB?"

Over the radio, the unmistakable sound of a DaVinci's barking echoed again and again. "Pretty well fucked, One-Two. Alpha's got us pinned on all sides."

"We can be there in twenty." Josh gestured for Dax and Alexa to round up the troops. "We're only twelve, but we're fully armed up."

"Negative, One-Two." Sandford paused to return fire with her pistol. "We're blown. I'm in the Alamo." She took a deep breath. "Initiate Plan C."

Holy shit! "Ma'am, I promise, we can get to you in time. The Alamo is damned secure. I should know. I helped set it up."

"You're a good man, Sergeant. I appreciate the offer, but I've already primed the charges. I'll see you at Camp Noble, sooner or later." The line ended as Sanford pulled the zero switch, burning the radio frequencies on her end. It would prevent anyone from using the equipment.

Josh dropped the radio and stumbled away. He shuffled aimlessly for a minute before ending up just outside the patrol base, on a low rise that faced the sunset. Eros had long ago dropped below the horizon, but New Eden's many moons reflected the star's light down onto Kronos.

"What now, Sarge?" Dax stayed back a few yards, but not to give his friend space. Someone his size was simply too easy a target on high ground.

Alexa went right over to Josh. She was almost two inches taller, but she made sure she remained eye level. "What did they say?"

Josh swallowed. "Plan C is in effect. We're to zero out radios, burn the strip maps, and go to ground. If any Charlie elements make it through the next twenty-four, we'll rendezvous with them in F-forty-one."

A pillar of smoke rose four miles away, punctuated a moment later by a tremendous explosion. The ground shook. Josh pulled his helmet off and let it drop into the dirt. "The Alamo has fallen."

"So what? We're supposed to hide here for another day, then crawl to the rally point?" Alexa squeezed his arm. "We still have your plan."

"It won't work," Josh said. "We need at least a platoon. We're only twelve people."

Alexa leaned in. "It's still a plan."

Dax lumbered closer. "We can do it. Take out Delta. At least get Charlie to second place."

"No," Josh said a little too forcefully. "We don't have the manpower, we don't have the firepower, and we don't have any way to get into that base." He slumped down on a large rock, dropping his head into his hands. "It's not good enough. I'm not good enough."

"Bullshit," Alexa said.

Dax squirmed. "Language."

Josh shook his head. "It won't work." He faced them, crestfallen. "I know I missed something. A small detail that won't be obvious until we make some huge mistake. If the XO were here..."

"He's not," Alexa said. "He's dead. Well, fake dead, but dead enough to us. We've got each other, we've got ammo enough for a big push, and we've got you."

Dax joined his friends, placing a heavy hand on Josh's shoulder. "Coach always said it's better to make an okay move *now* than wait for a great move to come to you later."

"Yeah, listen to Coach. That man won three rings for New Freeman." Alexa seemed unfazed by the smoking ruin of her Company in the distance.

Josh pushed past his friends. "We're not talking about the Grudge, where you're evenly matched. This is us against two of the best Companies in the Battalion. Alpha and Delta always dominate the Crucible."

"Sure," Alexa said. "But this is the first time *we've* been through one. I think Charlie Company's day is due." She lost her smile when she saw Josh's face. "But if you're ready to throw it in, then fine. I'll get my fire team to start digging trenches if we're gonna be here long." She stormed off down into the camp, bumping Josh's shoulder as hard as she could.

Dax and Josh watched the dust settle at the Alamo. The charges were mostly powder and reactive salt. No one was hurt, but symbolically, that pillar meant the end of the safety net.

"If I messed up before, we always had the Company to bail us out." Josh sighed. "Now it's just us. We're all alone."

"Did I ever tell you about my first goal?" Dax pulled his large helmet off and slung it under his arm.

Josh smiled. "Yes. A dozen times."

"Fine. But you're missing out on a great story."

"That I've heard before."

"I've heard the gospel before. Doesn't mean I don't feel it every time."

Josh had to give him that. "So, what does the good book say about this?"

Dax thought for a moment. "'Glory in our sufferings, for suffering produces perseverance; perseverance, character. And character'?" He grinned at Josh. "'Hope.'"

The Front
Lunar Space

"All stations this net, this is *Midway*. Hold fire, I say again, hold fire."

Cameron looked down at his hands, surprised to find them shaking. He turned to his wingman but for once George was silent, staring open-mouthed at the spectacle. Cameron looked back at the surreal beauty of the battle. Silver craft exploded in a dazzling rainbow of colors, and black Y-shaped fighters spiraled and erupted, leaving glowing red nebulas in their wake.

"Can you track them? I can't get an acquisition lock." The voice came from another pilot in the SP line. Cameron realized he couldn't get a lock on signal from his passive radar. The system was designed to pick up on space debris, but seemed dumfounded by the new ships.

"What do you think, George?"

The pilot pulled his attention reluctantly from the battle. "Laser lock should work. We could try getting closer, but I'd rather not."

"Afraid of a little action?" Cameron teased.

"Nah," George said. "Just feeling particularly lazy at the moment. Let someone else draw suicide detail."

Cameron felt around his belt and located his good-luck charm. Regulations prohibited jewelry, but the small silver cross had more than religious value for the pilot and he loathed to be without it. Still, rather than risk strangulation, he had found a better place to stow it than around his neck.

"Wolf One, *Valley Forge*."

Cameron took a quick sip from the line before answering. "This is Wolf One, go ahead."

The operator on the other end of the line spoke softly, almost anxiously. "FRAGO to follow. Standby for *Valley Forge* actual." Cameron's pulse quickened. Seconds passed while the radio transferred to DeHart. Fragmentation orders were usually passed out by communication officers, not commanders.

"Wolfpack, *Valley Forge* actual. You are ordered to close with unknown vessels in quadrant forty-one-thirty-two and scan using active radar. Once a proper signal is acquired, you are to check for radio, laser, and beam traffic in order to identify what net these ships are using for communication. You are to hold fire unless fired upon. Do you understand?"

Cameron couldn't answer for a moment. "Sir, you want us to paint unknown targets?"

"That is correct. Ensure all safeties are engaged before moving out."

"Captain," Cameron stammered. "Couldn't that trigger them to attack?"

DeHart mumbled something away from the mic. Cameron could swear he heard the phrase "dumb shit Sector flyboys." "They haven't so much as sniffed in our direction yet. No reason to suspect they will now."

"Unless we start bouncing target signals off their hulls. Sir."

Valley Forge continued: "Your orders are clear. Brief your pilots and move. *Valley Forge* out."

Cameron stared out his cockpit at the distant cruiser, absolutely dumbfounded. That Fleet could so casually dispatch SP into a violent collision of unknown warships infuriated him. A Sparrow, piloted by a Fleet scout team, could get in and out without risking fire from the enemy. The Phoenix packed a punch, but the older second-series models were far less maneuverable than the new fighters. And given the acrobatics the unknown vessels seemed capable of, Cameron had every right to feel uneasy.

"Wolf Squadron, this is Wolf One." Cameron cleared his throat, unhappy with the orders he was about to give. "We're going to move in on the unidentified ships in quadrant forty-one. ROE hasn't changed, but we're going to paint them with active radar to determine if we're able to achieve target lock. Once you have acquisition, maintain line of sight and try to get some data for the ghosts in the Fade. We're dividing into

Flights, so break into your fighting pairs. Wolf Nine, you're the odd man out, so you're with George and me."

George snickered. "Who the heck is Wolf Nine?"

"Cut it out, Locklear." Ensign McLane pulled his fighter up alongside George's. "It's a dumb joke, and I'm getting really sick of it. I'm gonna tattoo my ID number on your chest when we're done here."

"I'll hold him down for you," Cameron said.

"Devil's threesome?" George chuckled. "I'm in, but my safe word is 'doily.'"

TSC Valley Forge
Lunar Space

ABOARD THE SUPERCRUISER VALLEY Forge, Commander Sam DeHart paced the bridge. The size of a bedroom, the operation center of the half mile-long ship sat dead center and twenty feet below the top hull. When the first battle cruiser sailed from the International Orbital Ship Yard back in 2101, the bridge sat atop the vessel and gave the officers on the deck a magnificent view of the stars and any action that occurred on their plane of the battlefield. That design choice lasted until the first pebble smashed through the diamond windows, killing the command-and-control structure for the entire ship.

Subsequent models placed the bridge in a safe position, and numerous cameras fed live images to a wall of monitors all around the room. It made for a more impressive view—and a more dynamic one. At any moment, a direction could be called up and viewed with incredible detail, allowing for full 360-degree situational awareness. And, most important, the chain of command would be maintained unless an attack achieved a catastrophic kill.

Captain Fuller, the executive officer, stood near the battlefield projector marking positions on his personal tablet. Though DeHart had a mind for ship-on-ship warfare, Fuller's specialty remained the big picture. It wouldn't be long before he commanded a ship of his own—in fact he could have had any vessel of Destroyer class or under already. Yet the allure and prestige of the Cruiser, the last true warship the Fleet possessed, called to him. DeHart would, in short order, be promoted to commodore, and he could either take a carrier or a desk. Not that he felt there was much of a difference.

"It's a dogfight so far," Fuller said. He watched the graphical display more than the monitors around him. The computer used images from the various cameras to create a three-dimensional model of the battlefield. But without proper tracking signatures, the smaller craft jumped around erratically whenever they moved beyond the cameras' line of sight. Fuller had placed a whiteboard next to the display and was taking notes on each ship type by hand. "These two frigates," he pointed to two floating spheres, "seem to be air-denial. They're building a wall of shrapnel around that carrier."

DeHart, from his chair above the main tier of the bridge, watched the action on the monitors. "Both sides have cruisers. Why aren't they engaging?" No one answered. DeHart often posed his thoughts aloud as a part of his mental process. It took some getting used to. A lot of new crewmen would try to answer his questions, but one withering stare from the commander was enough to teach them when to respond and when to stay quiet. "It could be our presence is putting them in a defensive posture. They don't know which side we'll come in on."

"And if a round from a cruiser misses its target and hits us, or one of the civilian stations..." Fuller let the thought die in the air. "It's not a bad theory, Commander. It could be this is a new form of martial etiquette."

The CO stared blankly at his second-in-command. "Are you saying this is a British line formation brought into space?"

Fuller shrugged. "If I'm the only person thinking it, then lock me up. We don't have ships that use weapons anywhere near this design. I'm not familiar with all of the Cove's dirty little secrets, but I think I'd remember catching a glimpse of one of *these* being built at Colorum." He pointed to the two unknown battle groups. "These aren't humans, Sam. They don't have to think like we do, nor do they have to behave like we'd want them to."

DeHart bit his thumb. He didn't want it said aloud. There wasn't any proof either way, but the evidence stood on its own legs at the moment. No ships like these existed anywhere in Terran space; or, if they did, they were the best-kept secret in human history. But to take that leap, to say the word "alien," it was too much.

"Commander, I recommend we pull SP back. If we get in the middle of their intergalactic barroom brawl, we're dragging ourselves into uncharted waters. And it looks pretty deep from here on the shore."

DeHart nodded. "Pass it out to SP. Recall to former position and hold."

"Intel is going to be upset you didn't get a scan."

The commander sighed. "Right now I'd rather deal with a ghost than a little green goblin."

Wolfpack
Lunar Space

CAMERON, GEORGE, AND ENSIGN McLane flew in a tight formation just to the rear of the unknown black fleet. Wolfpack had spread out across a line of a thousand kilometers so as to appear less aggressive to the alien ships. *Alien*—the word sounded wrong the first time Cameron had said it, but he was hard-pressed to find a better description. He'd never visited the colonies before; that trip was out of his budget. Once, while serving as a skycap pilot over Europa, he'd seen strange lights that seemed to chase his Sparrow around the small research station. But those were just vapor wraiths. This was something far more...otherworldly.

"McLane," Cameron said. "Did you ever hear back from the Fade?"

"Nah. Assholes don't see SP as enough experience."

George snickered. "You applied for an intel position? You do realize you have to be smart to do that, right?"

"Shut up, Locklear."

"Make me, buttercup."

"All right, all right. Cut the chatter," Cameron said. "We're almost in range."

The dark fighters appeared to have been built with the sole purpose of looking as scary as possible. A three-wing design gave the hull a distinct Y-shape, and the red splotches across the glossy black metal resembled animal markings or war paint. Radar and sensor array spikes popped out at odd angles across the body. Two gray barrels hung under the smaller wings—the main cannons—and fired rapid bursts of red energy at the far-off silver craft. Sound didn't carry in the vacuum, but the resonation from each salvo echoed inside

Cam's cockpit. The engines leaked thermal energy in a red stream behind the vessel as it flew.

Up close the missile frigates no longer resembled perfect spheres. Made of six layers of rotating disks, the warships spewed out a steady barrage of heat-seekers that locked onto targets and gave chase. The cruisers revealed a secret up close as well: a gargantuan barrel that protruded from the nose and seemed to run the length of the ship. Every few minutes the main gun would fire, rocking the entire ship as a breach dropped out the rear of the vessel to expel gasses. The engines had to rev to max power just to keep the ship from rocketing backward with each shot. Flying this close to the giant vessels played havoc with Cameron's nerves, but he focused on the mission.

Ensign McLane volunteered to be the one to scan the ship. His fighter was relatively old, but had recently received a new port engine. If the active radar caused the aliens to grow hostile, Cameron and George could hold the line while the younger pilot escaped. As the ensign's Phoenix closed with a solitary Y-fighter, George pulled off to his flank to watch for other ships. They hadn't said a word in twenty minutes, save guidance on flight patterns. When they neared a slow group of alien craft, the silence finally broke.

"This is maybe the second dumbest thing you've ever gotten me into," George said. He was sweating. His arms were stiff from holding the yoke so tight.

"Second?" Cameron looked off at a distant explosion. A silver fighter broke into thousands of pieces as a missile connected. He was lost in the image for a moment. There wasn't much debris left after the fireball, and no evidence of a pilot trying to punch out. "This is way worse than Angela Hershbach."

"Angela would have ruined my life. *You're* only trying to kill me."

"First of all," Cameron began. "Angela was a catch. She had a robust figure, a smile that most members of the species would not find alarming, and she could whittle with her feet. Plus you always wanted to grow a mustache, and she was clearly the best teacher."

George jerked his ship to the side to avoid a fiery chunk of debris. "All good points, but she also smelled exactly like hydraulic fluid. Woman never spent a day in her life around heavy machinery, but every inch of that apartment reeked. I spent a full day digging through her stuff looking for an empty bottle of H-twelve."

Ensign McLane couldn't resist getting in. "You spent a day rooting around in some lady's apartment while she was out?"

"No, McLane." Cameron suppressed a laugh. "That would have only been sad. George looked through her stuff while she slept on the bed."

"Hibernated," George shouted. "It's how her kind recovers after a session of passionate mating." All three pilots laughed.

Cameron's collision alert sounded. He looked around for a moment but couldn't see any source of danger in his flight path. He adjusted his height, dropping down two meters. Better to trust the sensors than to run into some unseen debris. His kinetic shielding would protect him from smaller fragments, not chunks of wrecked fighters. "I invited you to a party at a friend's apartment. You're the one who got blasted on coolers and ended up neck-deep in mistakes."

The alien fighters had drawn far away from the main battle, performing some elaborate banking maneuver that seemed excessively slow and deliberate. It took a full thirty seconds before they were pointed in the right direction again. Cameron and his wingmen fell in behind, ready to complete their mission.

An alarm sounded across their comms. McLane panicked, jerking his fighter laterally for a moment. He regained control, but tripped the toggle on his stick and activated his laser lock. The Phoenix's active radar projected out and found the nearest object and began creating a firing solution. Laser locks were used when the target had no readable signature, such as an asteroid or chunk of debris or an alien spacecraft that refused contact. The L-DAR, even more so than active radar, worked like a tracer round. It almost guaranteed a targeting solution, but drew a gigantic line back to the fighter for the enemy to follow with their own weaponry.

"McLane, you all right?" Cameron's heart pounded in his chest, but he recognized the alarm as a distance warning, not a threat detection. They had crossed beyond the range of their supporting vessels and the fighters warned that they should turn back. "We're working without a net. Stay sharp."

The radio squawked and a female voice came over the net. "This is *Valley Forge*. All SP fighters are recalled to position. All SP fighters are to return to Fleet position, time now."

"Seriously?" Cameron stared at his radio, dumbfounded. "Why the hell did you send us out here then?"

George whistled. "Common sense wins out. That's ten bucks, McLane."

"We didn't have a bet going," the ensign said.

George pulled alongside the ensign's fighter and shrugged. "I don't think that's how it works, but I can understand your confusion. Tell you what, I'm a fair guy. I'll settle for a beer."

At once, all three fighters' collision alarms sounded. Cameron looked across their formation, noticing both pilots react as well. Something pulled at his mind, a sudden thought racing through. He looked up and noticed they were flying alone. The alien ships had vanished.

"Contact rear! Disperse!" Cameron jerked his yoke to the right. Jets on the port side of the fighter fired off, propelling the craft away. One nozzle sputtered without effect, slowing the turn. A bolt of red energy grazed Cam's wing, digging a divot along the underside. A warbling note informed the pilot that his compressor valve was gone. Another two inches and it would have been the whole wing.

George and McLane dodged left and down, avoiding incoming fire as they separated from their wingman. Cameron looked over his shoulder and saw a trio of Y-fighters bearing down from their six o'clock position. His stomach lurched. They were all on him. "*Valley Forge*, this is Wolf one. Under fire, I say again, under fire from enemy fleet."

Presidential Tower
Vienna, Incorporated States of Europe

THEY SAT IN A half circle around a polished wooden table, all eyes watching the twelve glowing screens on the far wall. Each monitor showed the attack from a different angle, with a statuesque reporter spouting guesses about the situation. Chief of Staff Jerry Ahmad, along with his aide, stood off to one side and whispered to one another. When the older man was satisfied, he walked over to the large, well-dressed man in the seat of honor.

Alexander Burton, high chancellor of the Terran Federate, barely looked up as his closest advisor approached. He sat hunched forward in his leather chair, hands cupped over his mouth, brow furrowed. His normally crisp suit grew deep wrinkles from the awkward position. The dim light made his brown skin look even darker, but hid the stubble he'd forgotten to shave away. Finally, he managed to pry himself away to look at his friend.

"What is it, Jerry?"

The chief of staff sighed. "Admiral Walker finally made it to Terra Node. The station is secure, and all civilians have been moved to the emergency areas. Sol and Terra Battle Groups are moving in on the enemy as we speak."

Alexander nodded and swallowed a lump in his throat. "Do we have confirmation? Is it Mars or not?"

"The Unions were never good at keeping secrets, Alec. These vessels didn't come from any human shipyards."

"Jesus."

"We need to draft a speech." All eyes turned to Jerry's aide and goddaughter, Adeline Quinn.

She leaned closer to the high chancellor. "Sir, this is first contact with an alien race. Doesn't matter how this fight turns out—we need to have the first word about it in the morning."

Alexander scratched his chin scruff. "Why not now? Won't that make more sense?"

The aide shook her head. "With respect, no one wants to hear from you right now. They're glued to their televisions, and that won't change until the cleanup gets underway. Unless one of those ships crashes on your front lawn, you're not getting in front of a camera until tomorrow morning."

Alexander made a face. He wasn't fond of people treating him like a child. Still, the woman made a valid point. "What's your name, miss?"

"Adeline, sir. Been working for Jerry—sorry, Chief Ahmad—for about a year now."

"Well, Adeline, why don't you get with my speechwriter and work up a first draft?"

Her face lit up. "It would be my pleasure, sir." She walked swiftly from the room, barely hiding her excitement. When Alexander turned back, Jerry had taken the nearby seat.

"Did you read the proposal?" Jerry asked.

"Are you serious? You want to talk about it now?"

"Alec," Jerry urged.

Alexander's face darkened. "I don't like Dr. Ivanovich. We've been over this before."

"He gets results. CROWN may have been a PR nightmare, but it provided enough raw data for the Cove for ten years. And don't forget Team Hercules. They're wearing most of his designs."

"I've got sixteen weapons manufacturers with bids to replace all of it," Alexander said. "Ivanovich is a nutcase, and I'm not going to offer him more guinea pigs to torture."

Jerry glowered at his boss, his shoulders tense. "Alec, do you remember when you told me you were the wrong man for this job?"

"I remember."

"Do you remember what I said?"

Alexander nodded slowly. "You told me, 'Someone is going to be high chancellor. Someone is going to sit on the high throne and decide humanity's fate. Shouldn't that be someone who will at least try to do some good?'"

"We had other contenders, Alec. Men and women with plenty of experience. Some were even from the right side of that war. I fought for you because you'd demonstrated the most important aspect of being a leader—you made difficult and unpopular decisions in order to keep people alive." Jerry tapped the folder on the table. "We're here to do right by our species. We lose sight of that, and we're no better than every dictator in history. Markov may not be a popular choice, but his work could give us the tools we need to survive. He's a necessary evil. A *really* necessary one. We need to get him on board before a less scrupulous person snatches him away."

"Stop," Alexander said. "Shut up and let me think." He rubbed his temples. "We're not having this conversation. Not right now. Get Walker on the phone and get an update on Fleet's positions out there."

Jerry almost shot back but thought better of it. He rose, reaching for his palm-sized phone from the table. "It won't be Walker," he said as he placed the call. "Gilroy was already mobile when this started. He's running the battle."

Alexander's eyes bugged out. "Gilroy." He clenched his fist and bit his knuckle. "As if my day weren't already perfect."

Hostile Front
Lunar Space

"Lock on target."

"Get him off me!"

"Stay still! I've got you." Cameron blinked a droplet of sweat away from his eye. In zero gravity, moisture built up and hung around until it had enough density to move out on its own. At fighting speed, however, it ran like a river from the pilot's nose to the back of his head.

"Shit!" McLane's fighter listed, spewing smoke and sparks. "Port side wing is hit."

Cameron let his speed drop, sliding his Phoenix behind the Y-fighter trailing his wingman. When the laser lock found the target, he loosed a single missile, a medium-range ship-to-ship Harpy. It tore through space and pierced the alien craft beneath the engine. The Y-fighter burst into three flaming chunks, spewing a nebula of red fuel. Cameron drove through the debris, pinwheeling to knock loose bits of slag. "At least they go down easy."

"Like a Luna girl." George opened on the fighters with his twin Kraken gauss cannons. Compressed tungsten ripped into a fleeing vessel, rupturing the ammunition beneath the cockpit. Its back blew out and the ship drifted away, gutted and dead. The enemy destroyed, Cameron and George led their crippled wingman toward their own front. McLane's Phoenix was chewed up but still flying. Every few seconds a pinch of fuel would hit the burning wing and flash out, rocking the entire body. George dropped back to watch for more aliens, but they seemed to have turned attention on the larger frigates and destroyers.

"How you holding up?" George asked.

McLane checked his instruments. "It'll keep, I hope. I lost port jets completely, so no right turns until we get back." He chuckled. "Chief's gonna take this one out of my ass."

George scoffed. "How many birds have you lost?"

"Lost? None. I've broken three."

"Pittance," George said. "Lieutenant Davis over there, war hero that he is, has totaled seven of Sector's decaying fleet."

McLane seemed shocked. Cameron was flying alongside and could see the expression register on the young man's face. "What the hell are you doing to them?"

"Riding 'em hard, and putting 'em away wet." Cameron grinned. It was something his dad always said, though he only had a vague idea what it meant. He struggled to catch his breath and calm his racing heart. He hoped his wingmen didn't hear the staccato in his voice. "I'm just stress-testing the girl." He bit down on his water line so hard his jaw hurt.

George cracked up and drifted off course. He caught himself and corrected, but he was still red-faced and teary-eyed. He realized, after a moment, that the tears weren't stopping on their own. He wiped at his face with a gloved palm. "The last time, Chief Webb said he was going to make Cameron build his new ship out of the old ones." Something winked on his computer, grabbing his attention.

Cameron started to retort when a bright flash blinded his left side. The Phoenix bucked violently starboard. His head smacked against the canopy. A sharp ringing in his ears drowned out the world. He saw stars. Alarms warbled. The ship twirled, riding the concussion wave for a moment before Cameron regained his senses enough to wrestle back control.

George's voice was muffled. "You motherfuckers!"

Everything slowed to a crawl and then, suddenly, sped right back up.

Cameron saw he was facing directly toward the heart of the battle. Thousands of warships swarmed the larger vessels, lighting up the darkness of space with an endless rain of fire. A bolt of red streaked past the cockpit and blinded Cameron. When he looked up again, he saw George racing after two Y-fighters with guns blazing. Outside the cockpit, fiery debris drifted through space. A piece of matte-black metal floated by, trailing glowing embers.

Along the side it read "W-9."

Ensign McLane was gone.

Ice water ran through Cameron's veins. He pressed his right foot down hard, activating the afterburner. Pure hydrogen flooded the engine, rocketing the fighter forward. Missiles rained out from the wings, tracking targets down with discrimination and removing them from the field. His right hand gripped the yoke tight, finger pressed hard against the trigger. His Krakens barked and rattled, tracer rounds chasing each target.

"George," Cameron said. "I'm coming up on your five. Break left." The Phoenix carved a path through the sudden sea of broken ships, hull denting slightly with each impact. "We need to rejoin the Fleet." His heart caught in his throat and Cameron realized he'd never been more terrified in his life. He started his combat breaths, willing his body to stop shaking and focusing on simple tasks. *Flip the target switch. Activate lock. Fire four and six. Die, you sonofabitch.*

George loosed a Harpy and pulled back on the throttle. The missile connected and blew the alien craft into pieces. "Cam, Fleet's already here."

The war raged all around them. They were no longer on the outskirts of the battle; they were at its very core. Fleet fighter squadrons battled with the nimble Y-shaped craft, aided in small part by the silver saucers. The sleek, silver saucers weaved in and out of debris fields and line formations, searching for the opportune shot.

Heavy destroyers launched huge Hull Reduction warheads at the opposing side. The thirty-foot missiles bore deep into the center of the alien frigates, trailing an explosive cloud. When they detonated, the HRs ripped the hull apart like a can opener. The TFC *Stalingrad* held at the rear of the formation, a smoldering hole punched straight through her main engine compartment while her escort slugged it out nearby. *Valley Forge* had arrived at the center of the fray, firing main guns at the battleships while building a cloud of flak to disrupt the enemy craft. Every few minutes, her monster 50s would loose two huge slugs toward the nearest capital ship, punching building-sized holes into their black frames.

Midway, looming over the battlefield, fired surgical shots from her five-meter-long guns into the enemy carrier. The hive-shaped warship shuddered with each ten-ton round, explosions racking the deteriorating body. A missile frigate placed itself between the flagship and *Midway*, only to disintegrate when the projectile rammed straight through its hull.

"Cam, a little help here."

Cameron snapped back into the fight. He dropped his throttle, letting George and his tail come into view. The Y-fighter banked hard left, trying to evade Cameron's fire. Before he could lock on, the ship slammed into what remained of an alien destroyer, smearing itself along the battered metal surface.

"What the hell?" The alien craft hadn't tried to swerve or change direction at all. Cameron shook his head clear and turned back to the fight at hand. They'd found a sweet spot in the battlefield, away from the main effort. Cameron sucked on his water line, taking mouthfuls of the solution down with each sip. He tasted copper. "George, I need a minute."

"Take your time," he replied. "War's not going anywhere."

Cam's hands moved in a blur, snapping switches and flipping toggles. His computer ran an immediate diagnostic and battle update, gauging fuel and ammunition consumption in a few seconds. Satisfied with the feedback, Cameron reset the system and took watch while his wingman did the same. He silently willed George to move faster. Every second they stood still, the chance of an attack increased.

After what seemed like ages, George's collision lights flashed, and he moved out.

"Cam?"

"Yeah?" He could hear the strain in his friend's voice.

"What are we gonna do about McLane?"

Cameron touched his face and his fingers felt syrupy blood. "Focus on the fight. I'll write the letter."

"He had a sister."

"I know."

George was silent for a minute. "We met his dad at the family event last year."

"I know," Cameron said softly. But nothing inside him felt calm. Guilt rolled his stomach like a snowball, growing bigger and faster with each moment. *You fucking idiot. You just let him die.* The *what-if*'s came faster than expected, spinning his brain in circles. And then, as suddenly as the fear arrived, it was gone. There was still work to do, and he was in charge. "Get on my six and keep me covered. Fangs out."

Together with George, he raced toward *Savanna* to rejoin with the rest of SP. The frigate loosed the rest of its payload of warheads at the stream of incoming ships. Having pushed too far forward of the main battle line, *Savanna* sat unprotected and vulnerable and the enemy made all haste to capitalize. Squadrons of alien bombers, hideous crab-shaped machines, unloaded a relentless bombardment onto the stranded and crippled battleship.

"Come on, George," Cameron said, hitting his afterburner. "She won't take much more of this." He activated a signal beacon to all friendly fighters. "Wolfpack, on my position. It's hunting season."

JONAH BLIGHTMAN STARED AT the monitor, watching the incredible events unfold. A news orbiter struggled to keep up with the action. Ships from every side burst and crumbled on screen, spilling debris onto the battlefield. Every time a human vessel took a hit, the news anchor would immediately speculate about the loss of life.

"What you're seeing now is the *Savanna*, one of our frigates. The warship normally carries a crew of six hundred. We have Andrea Lautner, wife of Lieutenant Edward Lautner, who is currently fighting for his life in the skies over Earth."

Jonah turned the sound down and focused his attention on a warm lager to his right. He hadn't felt this good in years. "Brooks," he shouted.

The bartender waddled over. He was by and large the fattest person Jonah had ever seen, but he was jovial and, most importantly, a sympathizer.

"Whaddaya need, Jonah?"

"A round for the bar. On me." He slapped down a wad of bills and raised his beer. "To our brave soldiers in the sky. May the gods watch over them." The crowded bar cheered and raised their own drinks. Jonah drained his glass and gestured for a refill. He felt a hand on his shoulder and spun around.

Victor, his second-in-command, stood at attention. He carried a large tablet and a barely concealed pistol under his overcoat. Numerous craters on his face made him a hard man to miss. "Sir, the operation just passed phase three."

Jonah pumped his fists. "Yes. I loved phase three. That was a personal favorite of mine. Sorry to see it go, but glad it's done."

"You're drunk," Victor muttered.

"Yes, just a hair. I don't know if you've been paying attention, but there's some pretty exciting news on TV. For once."

"I don't see how this affects us."

Jonah lost his buoyant personality. Everything about him darkened at once. He grabbed Victor's shoulder with surprising strength and drew him close. "Everything that affects humanity affects us, you imbecile. There's no point in trying to start a revolution if you don't have the means to defend the population once you're done." He pointed at the screen. "Whoever those fuckers are, they just became a big variable in our little scheme."

Victor regarded his superior coldly, but made no move to break the hold. "So?"

"So? We need to rethink phase four. And especially phase five. I need you to send out the word that everyone moves up the due date by a month."

That got Victor's attention. "That's impossible, Jonah. We've planned this out to the detail. There's no room for change."

"Any plan without flexibility will break at the first sign of resistance." Jonah smirked. "The first Blightman said that."

"I know," Victor said. He pushed away from his boss. "I was with you when he said it. What I meant is that we've planned out the timeline very carefully. Certain things have to happen at the right time. If we move this up, we're bound to lose more than a few foot soldiers."

"Sacrifices must be made in a time of war. Right now, the Federate is learning that first hand. We need to use this opportunity. In one month, we teach them their second lesson."

THE HIGH CHANCELLOR SAT at the table, a glass of bourbon within arm's reach. Jerry paced the room with the other staffers, yelling at someone on the other end of the phone. Alexander was reaching for his glass when his aide, Arthur Roden, took a seat in front of him. Arthur was his usual immaculate self, spit-shined and perfectly tailored. Alexander wondered if he'd been up all night grooming himself for his entrance. Probably.

"*Midway* is taking a beating. We don't want to lose that ship."

Alexander nodded. "Who's commanding her?"

Authur leafed through his notes. "Hiro Osaka. He's a vet, well decorated. Says here he turned down three promotions to admiral so he could stay with the ship."

The high chancellor smiled. "I should have done that."

"Sir?"

"Times like this, I really hate wearing this suit." He tugged at his shirt and tie. "I used to feel in control, when I wore the other uniform. Now, I'm grasping at smoke."

Authur choked back his first comment and waited to formulate a thought. "Sir, there's no one in the universe who could have seen this coming. We can't kick ourselves for not realizing an intergalactic war was on the rise. All we can do is find the opportunities and exploit them while the timing is right."

Alexander shrugged.

Jerry stormed over, throwing his phone down on the table. "We're losing ships, but so are they. And, a small spot of good news, it seems we have friends up there. The silver armada either understood our broadcast or just doesn't see us as a threat."

"Broadcast?" Arthur asked.

"We put it out in every language, and a binary print that some scientists thought to use. Basically it said, 'Stay out of the way.'"

Admiral Gilroy, watching from a large display, coughed loudly. His large, bald head dominated the screen, close enough that the staffers could see the vein bulging in his temple. "High Chancellor, with all respect, I need you to reconsider my request."

Alexander glared at the screen. "You're out of your mind if you think I'll even consider it. Ronin protocol is completely unnecessary."

Gilroy snorted. "Chancellor, this is only the tip of the spear. Just because you're scared of a little political fallout doesn't mean we should risk the whole goddamn planet."

Alexander rose to his full height. Fire burned in his eyes. "I won't hear another word about this, admiral. I will see stars fall off your shoulders if I hear it again. Am I understood?"

The officer looked ready to explode, but buried his anger and ended the call with a curt nod. Arthur and Jerry exchanged worried glances.

After a long pause, Jerry said, "He's not wrong."

"Are we seriously talking about this?" Alexander looked at a second set of monitors. Images from the battle over Luna flashed on screen. "What the hell is going on today?"

Jerry leaned in close to his boss. "The last I checked, sir, there were fifty thousand members of the special-forces units in Sol and about a million men wearing any uniforms. The military is still rebuilding. You need boots on the ground. *Now*." He sat down at the table, resting his head in his hands. "Perhaps we should revisit the draft."

Alexander stared coldly. "This is a nightmare, Jerry. Let's not make it worse."

"All wars go to ground eventually, Alec. I'm just being pragmatic. It won't be popular..."

"That's an understatement," Arthur said. "It's political suicide. We'd all be out of the job at the next election, and that's assuming one of the Pillars doesn't try to impeach."

The chief of staff tapped his lower lip, his eyes locked on the various monitors. "We need something to show the public. A new project that can demonstrate a decisive step toward combating these new threats."

"We don't even know what these new threats are," Alexander said.

"Nonetheless, we need something." Jerry pushed the CROWN file closer to the high chancellor. He locked eyes with his old friend. "It doesn't have to fix the problem, just buy us time to find a better solution."

Alexander put his head in his hands. He couldn't bring himself to look up. "Fine."

Arthur's phone rang and he stepped out of the room. He could be heard in the hall shouting for a moment. Before anyone could speak, he popped his head back in. "Sir, New Eden has one hundred thousand soldiers stationed on the surrounding moons that can be deployable in the next forty-eight hours. The Black Adders have a battalion that's just finishing their deployment to Kronos."

The high chancellor blinked to clear his eyes. He felt the room still spinning. Burton had been raised to believe in the system—that doing the right thing would lead to the right end. He sneered at the thought. That ideology hadn't prevented his father's murder. He downed the rest of his drink.

"Tell them to activate every unit in the system. When those soldiers are finished training, I want them ready to deploy."

Arthur frowned. "Shouldn't we pull them all in now, sir? Why the delay?"

"Because they're green," Jerry said. "Most of them haven't seen a day of real combat. Pulling them out of training now will only shake them up more. Better to let them finish."

Alexander nodded. "Jerry, get me another drink. I have a feeling it'll come in handy." He looked around for his chief of staff, but Jerry was already gone.

Hilton Hotel, Vienna
Earth

MARKOV READ OVER HIS proposal for the umpteenth time. He'd worded it perfectly, using layman's terms so that it would be understood. How had they not seen what he was building? This wasn't just about winning some silly fight with rebels. This was about the next fight. This was about the very future of humanity.

How shortsighted these politicians can be.

He sipped from his glass of ice water. The liquid tasted grainy; expected, given the amount of additives he'd thrown in. Markov couldn't stand clear water. It felt wasteful. He hoped to one day cure the need for water altogether, but he hadn't found the time to devote to that side project.

CROWN. It always came back to that one failed experiment. Successes are quickly forgotten, but one public failure will follow you for the rest of your life.

His phone rang, and he planned to ignore it. But on the second ring there he was, standing next to the half desk with the small, clear rectangle in his hand. The image on screen was just a silhouette, so the call was from a secure line. That piqued Markov's curiosity.

"Hello?"

"Dr. Ivanovich."

Markov recognized the chief of staff's voice immediately. "Mr. Ahmad. This is unexpected." He glanced at the television on the far wall. Like everyone on the planet, he was glued to the events overhead. "What can I do for you, sir?"

"Have you left for Kronos yet?"

Markov's pulse accelerated. "No. Why do you ask?"

"I want you to leave as soon as the sky is clear. Let me know where you're departing from and I'll arrange the travel."

"I'll need two tickets. I have a partner—an advisor really. He'll need to come as well."

"That's fine. Bring whomever you need."

"And you might be interested to know that I requested a place from where to view the Crucible and was refused."

"That's been taken care of. I've reserved you a place. It takes about a day to reach Kronos this time of year. You can watch the highlight reel until you get there."

Now Markov's heart really raced. He already had most of his clothing packed away. He held the phone between his ear and shoulder and excitedly gathered the rest of belongings. "I'll need twenty candidates."

"No."

The scientist stopped and frowned. "Sir, if this program is to work, there needs to be a plan for attrition. I only expect to lose fifty percent, but I still need to have a margin of error."

"You can take seven. Make sure they're able to meet your standards first."

"There's no way to know."

Jerry ignored him and continued on. "And you're not taking the top ten percent either. In fact, it would be best if you went for runts. Otherwise I don't think I can sell Casey on this."

General Casey came to mind all too easily. He had shot down more than a dozen of Markov's projects in the past. "Fine. I'll make it work. But when I get these soldiers, they are mine. No taking them back until the project has run its course. That's the only way I can get you any kind of results."

"You've got a deal, Doctor." Another voice called for the chief of staff, but was too far away to be audible. "Oh, and one more thing. I'm keeping this under a pretty tight lid. There are only seven people in the universe who read your report. Let's keep it that way."

"Why?"

Jerry sighed. "Let me be frank. Your proposal is ghoulish, Doctor. Mad science at its most insane. It's fucking bonkers."

"I see."

"I don't think you do. On page fifteen, you talk about something called 'organ restructuring.' I don't even want to know what that means."

"I think you've made your point."

"Markov, you have a list of 'defects' that need to be removed in order to make the perfect soldier. One of them is *empathy.*"

The doctor pinched the bridge of his nose. "Are you done?"

"Not even close. You mention 'removing sex organs' in order to limit fraternization?"

"That's enough! You're taking portions from the abstract out of context. Has the world gone so completely stupid that no one can read a simple scientific thesis?" He stopped when he heard Jerry cackling on the other end of the line. "Oh... you're making fun of me, aren't you?"

"Doctor, I've always thought you were ahead of your time. But I'm the sole member of your fan club. The generals hate you, and no one from the Council would ever risk associating with you. I know the end results are for the benefit of humanity, but I can't let this get back to the high chancellor. So let's keep this on the black list. As far as the rest of the universe is concerned, Project CROWN does not exist."

TFC Sidney
Earth Orbit

ADMIRAL LAWRENCE GILROY STOOD on the bridge of the young carrier, *Sidney*. The sleek, new ship came with all the bells and whistles befitting an admiral's command, but it was by no means the largest vessel in orbit. It was a sore spot for the veteran commander, but one he pushed aside for the moment. On the ground, when there was no war to fight, Lawrence never felt sure of anything. Up here, with the smell of blood in the water, he was in his element.

"*Midway*, I need you to drop three hundred meters on the plane and let *Valley Forge* take the key spot. *Moscow*, you're too far forward. Pull back to phase line Green and wait for your escort. *Henderson*, I need an update on your ammo to the G-four in the next sixty seconds. And for fuck's sake, where does *Savanna* think the war is headed?"

He stood in front of the battle projector, a massive three-dimensional display of the field. Glowing icons represented the unknown enemy armada in relation to Fleet ships, the moon, and Earth. By moving the pieces around with his hands, orders were sent to the navigation officers of each ship automatically. It was a massively complex game of chess.

Lawrence blinked away droplets of sweat, every ounce of him focused on the task at hand. "*Valley Forge*, where's my heavy fire?"

Captain DeHart's voice rang out from speakers in the room. "Tubes were hot, sir. We're sending it now."

In the display, tiny yellow dots appeared near the icon for *Valley Forge*. They flew straight toward an almond-shaped ship, impacting with a small, flashing marker. A hit.

"Direct hit on target bravo-foxtrot-three-one."

Lawrence smiled. "Keep it up, Sam. I'm sending in a few frigates to up the pressure."

"Admiral," Commodore Osaka spoke up on the Net. "Only the bravo ships are hostile. We can redirect the Terra Group to the Lunar side."

Lawrence glanced at a second set of monitors, which showed a live feed from the battle. Sure enough, the silver ships were focused solely on the other unknowns, while the black-hulled vessels targeted everything in sight. "All groups, this is *Sidney*. Execute Lunar tide and focus all effort on bravo targets."

Holy shit, he thought. *We're winning.*

Hostile Front
Lunar Space

AN EXPLOSION ROCKED CAMERON'S Phoenix, throwing him into a tumble. Without his port control jets, he was unable to break the spin. George came up fast on his side and rapped his wing against Cam's, halting his momentum. They flew in perfect sync, the adrenaline rush from the initial attack mellowing to a dull tingle. In the back of his mind, Cameron knew McLane was dead. But there wasn't anything to be done except take down every threat available. With George covering his weak side, Cameron tore into the enemy with a vengeance. His Gauss cannons spat out bursts of metal at anything trailing red.

The Wolfpack never arrived, save the two fighters still in the air. Three pilots had taken missiles to their engines before firing a shot, and the rest were aboard *Midway* with "critical hull damage"—they were shot to hell. Instead, Cameron and George fell in with Helios flight group, harassing the alien bombers and protecting *Savanna*'s evacuation. Fleet craft dove in and out of the cloud of shrapnel, chasing after the swarming enemy ships.

Savanna listed hard to port, her starboard side a mangled mess of shredded armor and burning fuel. Her hundred-meter frame belched fire and smoke and shuddered with every decompression. Ten-person ExoPods launched in constant succession from the battered frigate, racing for the rear. As Cameron flew past the flaming hull of the missile boat, an escape craft caught a bolt of red energy and exploded into slag and shrapnel. Bits of steaming metal hit Cam's kinetic barrier with flashes of white and blue.

"I count two pods left," George said. Outside his canopy, a black cloud billowed from the open launch tubes. The aft section of *Savanna* collapsed in on itself, the hull losing integrity faster and faster. He saw what looked like a sea of wiry debris floating away from the frigate. As he drew closer, the debris became a stream of bodies—crewmen sucked clear of the vessel. George turned away and winced. "Jesus. This is bad."

"I know. We have to do what we can for whoever's left."

Midway's executive officer came over the net. "Helios squadron, open a flight path along quadrant forty-four to forty-three via sector eighteen. Clear a line for these pods."

"Wolfpack, you copy that transmission?" Helios leader Lieutenant Young pulled his fighter alongside Cameron. The Phoenix III resembled her older sibling in form, but had larger engines and a sharper wing design. Three silver bars painted on the hull designated the ship as squadron leader.

Cameron looked over. Lt. Young wore the new booster suit, an armored version of Cam's own flight uniform. The polarized visor and added bulk made Young look like a mad robot. The SP pilot was instantly jealous. "I'm on board. Wolfpack will take nearside security." He dropped throttle, using his thruster jets to guide his fighter in closer to *Savanna*. His left side dragged more than usual; the hit from before was getting worse. "George, shadow me. My port side is trash."

"Roger, closing in." He spun the Phoenix to get a better look at his buddy's hull. "Well, number fifteen won't be a problem anymore. It looks like someone chewed on the wing."

"Great," Cameron said. "Let's see how long she lasts. I'm not going home until the field is clear."

The Phoenix shuddered in response to Cameron's acceleration. The fighters ran under the belly of the frigate. Debris bounced off the glass sounding like a heavy rain. As Cameron started his turn around the port side, the second-to-last ExoPod launched, narrowly avoiding his fighter. The escaping shuttle joined Lt. Young's ship and rocketed toward *Midway*.

ADAM KORENMAN

DELTA HAD BUILT THEIR patrol base in the perfect location. Hidden from view on three sides and nearly inaccessible from the fourth, the small plateau allowed observers to spot incoming enemies from kilometers away, and made an easy attack impossible. The rear spanned a sheer cliff face, and only one guard post had been set up to watch the ground below. All the other entrances were manned by heavy machine gun teams that rotated throughout the day to ensure the crews were awake and ready.

Alpha's ambush on Charlie hadn't gone unnoticed, and Delta's captain had brought the camp up to fifty percent strength. For every soldier who slept, ate, or went to the latrine, another had to be up in position with their rifle ready. Every infantryman moved with a purpose, the tension building with each passing hour. It was a little frustrating to lose to Alpha again. Still, second place would earn promotion points for the officers and earn the enlisted men some much-needed time off to spend with families. They'd had zero contact outside the moon for months.

SITTING IN HIS POST, watching the light fade, Corporal Juan Hernandez struggled to stay awake. Months of intense combat, combined with a constant lack of sleep, had drained him of any motivation. After mouthing off to one of the lieutenants, he'd earned a permanent post watching the cliffs. It wasn't the worst thing that could have happened. Private Murphy was still in the stockades after he'd been caught toying with some of the POWs. Still, staring out at vast nothingness for twelve hours a day didn't make the time pass any faster. He told himself to tough it out, to let the rest of the Crucible run by so he could go back to the barracks and shower off the months of suck.

At the base of the sixty-foot cliff, something glinted in the rocks. He barely noticed. The sun burnt so many of the stones into glass that spotting a reflection wasn't unusual. The other moons of New Eden often reflected light onto Kronos for hours after sunset. Besides, intel still had Alpha holed up in their fort while Charlie attempted to nip at their heels. The game was almost in the bag. He daydreamed about his girlfriend back in Buenos Aires, how she would be waiting for him in their bed when he took his leave.

Something shifted in the sands below. Juan leaned over the railing of the tower, peering through his scope. He couldn't make out any shapes. All he saw was the orange sand below. From the middle of a small outcropping of rocks came a flash of yellow. Before he could react, the round smacked his visor just over his right eye. Immediately, electrical charges activated in his suit and brought him down without a sound. The echo from the shot died out quickly, unheard in the camp. As a mild sedative made its way into Hernandez's body, he smiled. For him, at least, the games were over.

"Great shot."

At the base of the plateau, Josh patted Alexa on the back. He'd watched the round fly and saw the soldier go down. They'd observed the position for almost two hours to make sure no other guards appeared. If he'd guessed right, Josh figured they wouldn't change shifts until midnight. It made for a perfect window of attack. It would take them that long to scale the cliffs and get into position.

The rock wall wasn't exactly vertical. In places, erosion had created natural handholds and steps. While it was far from easy going, the squad could make the plateau in less than an hour. They were outnumbered two to one, but surprise of this magnitude paid dividends.

Dax's eyes walked up the rock face, growing wider every second. "Are you sure about this?"

"Hope so."

Josh took lead, climbing hand over hand up the wall. Wind pulled at his arms and legs, threatening to dash his body against the sharp rocks below. He pressed his face against the hot stone, taking each inch with utmost caution. After a few minutes, the dark was so pervasive he had to search for each handhold by feel. He slipped more than once, his foot catching a weak mound of rocks, and ended up hanging by his fingertips. His arms ached all the way to his shoulder blades, and sweat stung his eyes. Every few vertical feet he would stop and sip from his CamelBak. Dax appeared alongside him, out of breath.

"How is this a good idea?"

Josh paused to suck in a bellyful of air before responding. "I figured you needed to lose the weight. I just didn't want to say anything in front of the squad."

Dax grinned and kept climbing. Despite his size, he moved nimbly up the rock wall, reaching the landing before the rest of the squad. Josh struggled to keep pace. His hands were beyond cramped. Each time he pried his fingers from one rock they refused to work for several seconds. The twin moons Castor and Pollux rose on the horizon as the soldiers made their way higher and higher toward the enemy base. Dax reached down and pulled his friend the rest of the way to the summit. Josh rolled onto his back and carefully slid toward the camp.

Sandbags had been placed to protect the watchtower from fire below, and they provided excellent cover as the squad assembled. In a few minutes, the twelve survivors of Charlie Company owned the blind spot in Delta's base.

"My fire team will take the two guard towers." Alexa pointed to the vague silhouettes on either side of the camp. "We can make a three-point kill zone and take this whole place down." She had to concentrate to keep her voice low. "We're gonna make it to second place!"

Josh shook his head. Lights from the camp—Delta had never been great about working in the dark—illuminated the young sergeant's face. He looked brighter, more focused than he had been only hours before.

"We're not here to take second. Delta still has mortars and enough ammunition to make a good stand. We're here to refit."

"For what?" Dax asked.

Josh smiled. "We're going after Alpha."

Alpha Company
Kronos

STAFF SERGEANT ZEV PEREZ stood outside the commander's quarters and brooded. The sun had been up for only an hour, and the temperature already topped 116. Sweat poured down from the band in his helmet and dripped into his eyes. It felt like a burning weight rested on his back. His fingers blistered when they gripped the hard plastic of his rifle. This wasn't his first tour on Kronos, but the heat never got any easier. His mouth tasted of sand and foul combat rations. Every time he moved, clouds of red dust billowed off his muscled frame. But now he stood still as stone.

With a month left in the exercise, the captain of Alpha Company had decided to call it quits. No more offensives, no more raids. With Charlie Company down to a handful of soldiers and Delta content to hide, there was no real reason to risk a single life—simulated or not—in any more missions. The soldier in Zev screamed at the idiocy of it all. Hiding in a fort was no way to finish a training exercise.

Every day since the order came down, Zev had met with the commander and screamed until his throat was raw. The raid on Charlie had been executed to perfection, and he saw no reason to not use the same tactics on Delta. If their intel was right, they could easily take out what remained of the company. Even if they lost a few soldiers in the attack, it was worth it to ensure Delta was wiped out of the game. Beyond that, it was the right call tactically. Had this been a no-bullshit ground war, leaving an enemy to regroup and rearm was the worst call to make.

The first sergeant agreed but was too spineless to stand up for one of his soldiers. Zev stood a head taller than anyone in the unit and didn't mind using his size as a tool for negotiation.

As he stood there, Zev's gaze wandered around the base at the rest of his unit. Soldiers ambled from building to building or loitered in the courtyard. Some sat at tables playing cards while others rested in the shade. Their weapons hung on their backs, out of easy reach, or were left in their bunks. They looked like men on leave, not ones in active combat.

The door opened, and the commander stepped into the sun. He wore combat boots and trousers, with only a royal purple undershirt under his combat vest. The officer shielded his eyes with one hand and stifled a yawn with the other. Zev wanted to spit. How was this the same man who had guided them through the last few months? Still, respect for rank had to be maintained.

Zev came to attention but did not salute. "Sir, Staff Sergeant Perez reporting." He waited for the commander to put him at ease.

Captain Redmond stretched with a grimace. His muscles were tired, but the expression was actually meant for the troublesome NCO. They'd done this dance almost every day for the last few weeks, and he didn't see why he had to keep up the charade. He was in command, and Zev was supposed to follow. It should've been as simple as that. But Zev, the veteran E-6, didn't know when to let off.

"Sergeant," the captain said. "Nice to see you this early."

Zev remained ramrod straight. "It's actually near eight, sir."

Redmond checked his watch. "So it is. What can I do for you on this fine scorcher of a day?"

"I thought we could revisit our conversation. Sir."

The CO started walking away. Zev shook his head and fell into step, allowing the commander to be just slightly forward and to the right. As they passed other soldiers, young privates and sergeants openly saluted the captain. He cheerfully returned the gesture. It turned the sergeant's stomach. No field discipline. And they'd done so well the first month.

"Sir, I really think it's time we sent the scouts out to try and locate Delta's position."

Redmond shook his head. "Not this again. Zev, we're not in combat. This isn't the war. Why risk losing points unnecessarily when all we need to do to win is stay put and enjoy the end of the hot season?"

"Because it teaches bad habits to the soldiers."

"Zev, I'm tired. We've been through this. You're a good soldier, but this conversation is over. Now head back to your bunk before I lose what's left of my patience."

Zev was about to say something less than respectful, but caught himself just in time. He saluted—another no-no in the field—and spun on his heel. He passed gaggles of soldiers, who greeted him with a "Hey, Sarge" and a big smile. He ignored them, not stopping until he was back inside his barracks. He had a platoon of well-trained infantrymen under his command, and they would obey his orders without a second thought. Any one would be a golden candidate for the Black Adders, he was sure. As soon as he stepped into the room, every man and woman rose to their feet. They wore their armor even inside, though their helmets were grounded on the cots. Each carried their rifle in a combat sling, not flung over their shoulder like a sack of laundry. Zev allowed himself a moment of pride.

"Sir, we're ready to move out on your order."

Zev gritted his teeth. "At ease, men. We're not going out. CO is locking down the fort."

A collective groan echoed in the tent.

"I know," Zev said. "But it doesn't mean we aren't going to train. I want everyone in full battle-rattle in ten minutes. We're going to the slopes to practice assaults on the empty buildings. Then we'll hit combatives for a few hours. There's still a month to go before we ratchet down, and I don't plan to spend a minute of that playing grab ass here."

"*Hooah!*" came the shouted reply.

Zev watched his platoon scramble to armor up and move out. He wiped a sheet of sweat from his forehead and strapped his helmet down. There was still an enemy to fight, and he was going to be ready for them when they came.

COMMODORE HIRO OSAKA SPAT out his orders, sending wave after wave of bombers to continue their assault on the alien fleet. What had seemed daunting at first had since become a tragically easy battle. The black armada, for all its impressive design and aggression, simply could not match a well-trained and coordinated strike-force. Reacting to the attack in a by-the-book fashion had led to three-quarters of the warships destroyed in six hours, with almost every fighter and bomber in the air smashed by overwhelming superiority. The silver craft had all but pulled away from the sortie.

Hiro made his rounds from one side of the bridge to the other. He didn't worry about the senior enlisted men. They were used to the shock and horrors of war, in such a way that they became inured even to the unexpected. It was the younger enlisted, the seamen, and even the newer officers who worried him. Hiro made sure to spend a few minutes with each person, not so much asking questions as allowing them to see a picture of calm acceptance. It was a technique he'd learned from his father, an ever-wise martial-arts instructor.

Calm waters can bear any weight.

Hiro's executive officer, Earl MacReady, stood by the board, taking the tally of the ship's injured. He smiled as Hiro drew near. "A lot of scrapes and bruises, and hangar A's crew chief suffered pretty severe burns pulling a pilot from a wreck. We're all pretty banged up, but that's it. Not a single death."

"Very good," Hiro said curtly.

The executive officer frowned. "What? Hiro, this is unbelievable. I've never heard of a battle this one-sided in history."

"But that's not what will be remembered about this day." The old commander sighed, his face etched in lines. He beheld the carnage. Smaller carriers burned as they were towed back to repair stations. Fighters continued the mop-up operation even as rescue efforts began. "We're not alone in the universe. We should be celebrating, not washing blood off bulkheads."

"Sir?"

"I've been waiting for this day my entire life, Earl." A quivering eyelid was the only crack in Hiro's mask. "Do you remember Chief Karanam? From back at the academy? She used to tell the most amazing stories about her time flying with the Fifth Corsairs."

Earl nodded. "The Frozen Fifth."

"So you did pay attention in class." Hiro watched a medic attend to the ballistics officer, setting a broken wrist. "Adrift in a void of black ice, burdened with the knowledge they might never be saved. They were pioneers, the Fifth. Sent on a mission to find life in our arm of the galaxy. Karanam was the flight leader on that trip."

"Really? I don't remember her saying anything about that."

"I asked her after class," Hiro said. "I would stay behind every day to beg more from her. She told me about the Orion cruise, jumping from star to star looking for habitable worlds and friendly neighbors. They found so much, but not at all what we expected." He beamed. "Have you seen a picture of a leviathan up close? They're remarkably beautiful creatures, unlike anything found on any world."

Earl nodded. "Space whales. I've seen my share from afar."

"Miraculous." Hiro watched a Seed bomber group, escorted by Sector pilots, conduct an aggressive run against the enemy. "That's what I hoped to find one day. But not just some creature that happened to live in space. I wanted to meet an equal. I needed to know for sure."

"Know what?"

Tears brimmed in Hiro's eyes. "Are we alone in all this wonder?" He faced the monitors, watching the battle come to a brutal end. "We are not, it seems. And that this knowledge was bought with death is a curse I cannot bear."

As they watched the screens, the final alien carrier fired a slug into the dying *Savanna*. It sucked up the return volley without any signs of damage. "What would you like me to do, sir?"

"Concentrate on support and repairs," Hiro said. "But no one lowers the alert. Not until every last bastard is dead."

The Front
Lunar Space

CAMERON AND GEORGE FINISHED towing the overstuffed ExoPod to *Midway* and released their lines, allowing a recovery ship to grab the shuttle and carry it the rest of the way. They turned back into the fight to see *Savanna*'s engines suddenly ignite, pushing the heavy frigate toward a huge enemy carrier. Whittled down by overwhelming fire, every cruiser, frigate, and destroyer from the black fleet burned in a floating sea of melted metal and shattered hulls. As *Savanna* approached, the last remaining fighters launched a desperate counterattack.

"And the Lord God looked down upon the Egyptians, and he saw what they had done to His people." The voice echoed over the open Net. It came from *Savanna*, from the bridge. "And he struck them with his outstretched arm and a strong hand."

Cameron stood on the breaks. Jets fired from the front of his fighter, halting all forward momentum. George had to swing around to rejoin.

"What is it?" George asked.

The voice on the radio continued. "Blood, Frogs, Lice, Pestilence..." An electronic chime punctuated each word as something came online.

Cameron didn't answer at first. His face was white as a sheet. "God, no. He's armed them."

"Who's armed what?"

Alien fighters swarmed the frigate. The bolts and bombs tore into the damaged hull, but momentum carried *Savanna* past the field of broken ships. With a stomach-wrenching crunch, the missile frigate drove deep into the belly of the carrier, fire spewing from the collision. The impact fused the two crafts, sending them on a wild spin. Debris spiraled around the derelicts as they tumbled together.

"All ships," Cameron cried out. "Clear the area. I say again, *Savanna* armed her nukes."

From every direction, enemy ships converged on the human warship. In every direction, the humans fled.

SAVANNA ERUPTED INTO A blue star, engulfing the ships around it. Floating wreckages dissolved under the intense heatwave and the incoming fighters disintegrated. A trio of alien bombers ran straight into the inferno, disappearing in smaller puffs of orange and white. The ball of light and fire expanded rapidly, stopping only a few kilometers from the Terran front lines. A massive concussion wave rippled through space, knocking hundreds of satellites out of orbit and causing a rolling blackout across Luna. Dust kicked up from the blast swirled into a thick cloud that moved slowly across the moon's face.

Cameron and George rode the turbulence back toward *Midway*. There was nothing they could do but hope their worn, old ships could take the punishment. Alarms sounded louder and louder, but all were drowned out by the terrifying creaks and pops from the hull.

Without any oxygen, the fire put itself out. As quickly as it started, the violence ended. Squadrons of Terran fighters searched the area to confirm that the battle had been won.

It had. Partially.

All of the alien ships from the dark armada were destroyed, but the second alien navy-the fleet of silver ships-remained.

Huge undulating balls of slag floated in space, drawn slowly but inexorably back toward Earth, along with the derelicts and debris. Lieutenant Young and the rest of Helios squadron began escorting rescue shuttles to pick up escape pods or ejected pilots. Lumbering Dodos and nimble Valkyries wove through the cluttered field in search of life. The remaining Fleet forces, including newcomers from CBG Sol and Venus SP, took up a blocking position between Earth and the silver navy. There hadn't been a single shot exchanged between the humans and the other aliens, but blood was in the water.

Valley Forge rotated toward the largest vessel, opening up every weapon port as it fired a salvo of flares into no man's land. It was a posturing move, meant to intimidate. If that didn't work, the twenty battle-scarred destroyers and frigates alongside the cruiser did the trick. As the carrier groups arrived toward the rear, pilots began taking bets about which side would strike first. No one wanted to be right.

Aboard *Midway*, Hiro sat in his chair and waited. He had survived the first part of the battle. Perhaps he could make it through the next.

At the center of the room, at a large computer station, Ensign Nari Suffra received an alert. As the communications officer for *Midway*, she handled all incoming and outgoing signal traffic. What caught her eye wasn't the message. The source stopped her heart mid-beat.

"Commodore," she began, her voice wavering.

Hiro's smile dissolved. He recognized the tone of the young officer's words and his own pulse quickened. "What is it?"

Nari pointed to her screen, ashamed at how badly her hand shook. "It's a message. No encoding." She swiped away images so only the words remained.

Hiro walked over and leaned down, staring dumbfounded at the message. His mouth dried up. Fighting to swallow, he typed a rapid reply and sent it out. Standing back up, Hiro moved quickly to the wall and grabbed the communication handset. His free hand tapped an agitated beat against his thigh.

Sam DeHart's voice came over the line: "*Valley Forge* actual."

"Sam," Hiro said. "Tell the fleet to hold fire. No matter what they see, no one shoots at the silver ships."

"What are you doing, Commodore? We should push them out of the system before they decide to bomb a city or blow up a goddamn planet."

"They haven't so much as grazed one of our scouts. If they wanted to attack, there was plenty of opportunity before. This is an order, Commander."

ADAM KORENMAN

Sam was silent for a long time. Then, simply, "Understood."

Hiro cleared the line and activated the PA. "Attention, *Midway*. This is Commodore Osaka. All soldiers stationed on this ship are to report to Alpha hangar immediately. I repeat, all soldiers are to report to combat stations in Alpha hangar."

Ensign Suffra turned in her chair as Hiro ran toward the door. "Sir?"

Hiro turned, his hand on the frame of the door. He looked at his second in command. "Earl, you have the bridge. They're on their way here."

Kronos

JOSH GRIPPED HIS RADIO, set his jaw, and keyed twice. For five seconds the silence persisted, and then the world erupted. Fire from both towers tore into the tents in the center of the camp. Josh saw two men standing in the center of the base cut down in a single burst. Shelters exploded as the sim rounds ripped through them. Soldiers would have been sleeping, completely oblivious to the frenzy around them. He almost felt bad for Delta. A group of soldiers shouted to attack the towers, and they charged back toward his position. As the riflemen approached, Josh and his team picked them off one by one.

Josh let the machine guns work through the camp, saturating the area with fire. There was no reason to hold back. Either they won the fight and secured ammunition from Delta's stock, or they would run out and be killed. He watched the massacre unfold, firing sporadically at soldiers trying to escape. Even if a few managed to run east out of the camp, they would either wander until the ending siren a few days later, get picked up by the safeties, or get killed by one of Alpha's sniper teams.

When Dax's tower went silent, Josh knew the fight was over. He called over the radio. "Cease fire, cease fire." The northern post quieted. "Hold positions, we're moving in." He called his small team of shooters together and they formed a line. Weapons at the ready, they marched forward to clear the area.

Two soldiers popped up from behind an overturned storage bin. At first they didn't recognize Josh and his group, then they went for their rifles. The team dropped them quickly and moved on. In the center of the base they found Captain Thornton and Delta's First Sergeant. Throughout the exercise, Josh had found the simulated "death" that the soldiers endured slightly unnerving. The sedatives produced a pleasant dream state that lasted two to three hours, in which time the safeties on the course came in to retrieve the soldiers and move them to the staging areas until the exercise ended. The corpses looked peaceful which, combined with a lack of blood, made the scene surreal.

Josh knelt down by the enemy CO and pulled his dog tags out. He pulled his radio from his shoulder, surveying the damage his squad had caused. "Dax, Alexa. Bring it in. Leave the gunners in position and tell them to watch for anyone coming back our way."

A few minutes later, he had his team leaders with him in the battered command tent while the team policed the bodies. Delta soldiers were laid out under a tent near the front for easier access by the safeties. The rest of the squad went through the camp and retrieved weapons and ammunition.

"Man, that was awesome," Dax said, slapping Josh on the back. He unstrapped his DaVinci and set it on the ground, its barrels still red and smoking. "The captain would've loved to see this."

Josh beamed. "It was all you guys. Delta never even saw you coming." He tugged at his collar to release some heat and gagged at his own stench. "Jesus, I need a shower, bad."

"No need to swear."

Josh rolled his eyes. "Yes, mom." He took another breath, feeling better than he had in weeks.

Alexa took off her helmet and wiped her sweaty forehead. "Quick says the armory is stocked. Mortars, mines, grenades, transpo—you name it, it's ours."

Josh nodded, making a mental checklist. "We can't sleep here, but we can't leave the ammo. Put together a detail and start distributing everything we can carry. We're moving out as soon as we're full up. We'll find a place to set down."

Dax's jaw dropped. "Why can't we stay here? Everyone's dead."

"We just made a hell of a lot of noise. Even if Alpha doesn't know where this place is, they know something went down in this direction. It's not worth waiting around for them to find us just to grab an extra hour's rack."

"He's right," Alexa said. "If I were a scout out there, I'd be talking this one up all night. At the very least, they'll send a team to watch this canyon in the morning." She took a drink from her pack. "We'd be spotted when we left."

The big gunner sat down on the ground with a grunt. "So we find a better place to crash, and then what?"

Josh pulled out a map and laid it on the ground. He took a pencil from a pocket on his forearm and drew a circle over a small, black, square symbol in the top right of the grid. As his team leaders watched on, Josh placed a series of symbols around the black square, designating entryways and egress routes.

"What's that?" Dax asked.

"That," Josh said, "is Alpha's fort. Delta had been monitoring their activity in order to stay out of the way. They never planned to attack, but wanted to know how to take over if Alpha ever left."

Alexa leaned in closer, her excitement growing. "Last I checked, Alpha's almost at full strength. And we're just twelve guns."

"When the safeties get here, they'll release a casualty report." Dax scratched his head. "By seventeen hundred, Alpha's gonna know we're the last ones standing."

Josh held up a finger. "Can't be helped. It's more than a day's hike to Alpha's base, and not on easy terrain. But that's exactly where we're headed." He pointed to the stores of combat rations near the armory. "I want every last meal packed away. If we need to make a cart to carry it all, so be it. We're taking it all."

"Why? We only need one per day." Alexa scratched her sweaty head.

Josh pulled off his helmet. "Alpha's going to expect us soon. They know how important it is to maintain momentum. So we're gonna wait. Head back to our patrol base, shore up defenses, and go to ground for the next two weeks."

"Two weeks?" Dax laughed. "We'll be crawling up the walls by then."

"Longer if we need to," Josh said. "I want them complacent when we show up. I want them to doubt whether or not we even have the balls to take them on. Then, when they're at their most cocky, we're coming in hard."

Dax smirked. "So you've got a plan?"

Josh pointed toward the ammunition shed, or rather, just behind the structure. Underneath a faded brown tarp, two open-air trucks collected dust. "They parked them right at the start of the games. I'll bet they still have a decent charge, and we can throw a few panels up at sunrise."

"Trucks are noisy," Alexa said. "And they're going to kick up a lot of dust. Alpha will know we're coming." Josh stifled a grin, and Alexa made a face. "What?"

Josh held up a stack of reflective patches. One side was all hooks and fasteners—the Army's oddball name for Velcro—while the other was covered in reactive tape. Even in the dim light, the soldiers could easily make out the large "A" in the center of the badge.

A...for Alpha company.

"We're headed to Alpha's base, and they're going to roll out the red carpet when we arrive."

TFC Midway

CAMERON AND GEORGE SHARED a deadpan stare. Between them, gliding on a flat stream of blue energy, a silver vessel unlike any they'd ever seen followed a human escort toward *Midway*. Aside from a shimmering green bar across the front of the craft, Cameron couldn't find a seam in the iridescent hull. Along with a full squadron of Phoenix fighters, silver saucers wove in and out of the formation. Their acrobatics came across as playful, but also demonstrated unbelievable maneuverability. A membrane of blue force field coated the ship, shimmering into view every time a bit of dust or debris flew into the shuttle's path.

The hangar floor was bare, save enough space for the craft to land and a good fifty soldiers on all three levels. Cameron and George looped around, docking on the top tier while the silver vessel hovered in place at the bottom. The dull thrum of the engines reverberated through the entire section of the ship, vibrating deep within the soldiers' chests. As three spindly legs descended from the bottom of the shuttle, it seemed like the only sound in the world was that churning and grinding bass note.

Hiro jogged down the steps, an attachment of security guards and aides rushing to keep pace. For an older man, he was surprisingly spry. He jumped the last step, landing in front of the humming spacecraft. Easing between the growing crowd, the officer inched his way to the front.

There was no way to describe the ship without calling it alien. No metal known to man reflected light the same way, nor did there exist an engineer with such incredible skill. It was seamless, and the curves and angles were too perfect to be something off an assembly line. Around the room, a single thought passed through the minds of all present.

Who, or what, was about to emerge?

A line of light bisected the pristine hull, soon joined by other beams that crisscrossed the ethereal metal until a doorway formed. Steps emerged from the inside, dropping down until they touched the floor. Thirty seconds passed without a single sound, save the hiss of steam and the ebbing whir of the engine. From within the unknown vessel, footsteps approached.

It wore a simple suit of black and silver. The pattern on the fabric swirled as though made of gas. The lithe gray creature wore no breathing apparatus; either their species used oxygen or simply didn't require air. Its small, dark eyes darted back and forth, and its long slender hands gripped a bulbous silver weapon tight. A distant observer might mistake it for human, the shape was so familiar. The head was slightly large, the eyes even more so. It stood around five foot nine and was well muscled. The hand had only four fingers instead of five, but the structure was the same as anyone on *Midway*. Its features were flat, with a small, triangular nose and thin, pale lips. Within that face Hiro could see intelligence and, strangely, fear. There was something else, something incredibly familiar: discipline. This was a soldier.

My god, Hiro thought. *They could have walked off a movie set.*

Two more of the black- and silver-suited creatures emerged, each sporting alien rifles. They looked similar, but at the same time were easily distinguishable. One had dark gray spots running from its brow down the right side of its face. Another had narrow eyes and breathed heavily, its teeth a single ridge-line with valleys and crests. They took position as a fourth creature stepped down from the ship, its multicolored robe extending down to the ground. Standing between the three soldiers, it called out to the interior of the ship. The language sounded like wind rushing through pipes; a melodic, pleasant sound. Finishing the call, the robed alien turned and bowed down toward Hiro. It spoke, but the noises meant nothing to the human. The commander felt his anxiety growing quickly. What exactly was he supposed to do next?

Hiro watched in awe as the last creature approached from the interior of the shimmering craft. Dressed in gold, green, and black robes that dragged in a train behind its feet, the elder alien conjured an image of a wizened monarch. Its emerald eyes locked onto Hiro's, and those watching swore it smiled. Its ashen skin was wrinkled and leathery, but it walked with energy and poise.

"Fa'hnaki Lan, Earthborne," the creature spoke. Its voice came out soft but weathered. "I am honored by your welcome." His words were slightly accented and easy to understand. When no one replied, he asked, "You do speak English, don't you?"

Hiro could barely move as the alien approached, entourage in tow. He stammered a few words out before taking the time to compose himself. "My name is Hiro Osaka, Commodore in the Terran Fleet and Commander of the TFC *Midway*." He paused, unsure if it was enough of an introduction. "It's... I'm honored to have you aboard."

"That we could have met under kinder circumstances, Commodore Hiro Osaka." The pronunciation was impeccable. "I am—we are—forever in your debt for assisting in this battle."

Hiro felt a sea of eyes watching his every move. The gravity of the situation dawned on him slowly, which was a blessing. If he'd had full presence of mind, he probably would have fainted. A thought gnawed at him, that he should call an admiral or a councillor. But there was no time.

The creature turned to face the crowd. "I am called Anduin na'Lanus. I am the leader of my people, the Nangolani." Anduin turned to face Hiro. "You have made a lifelong ally by coming to our aid, but you have also found a ferocious enemy in the Boxti."

"I'm sorry," Hiro said. "The who?"

Anduin's voice lowered. "It would take too long to explain here, but rest assured I will answer your questions. For now, all I ask is your trust, temporarily placed upon my people and me, until we can earn it fully. That and an agreement not to attack my weary flotilla. We have seen your might and know we would not last against you." The alien extended his hand. Hiro was surprised that he thought of the creature as a *he*, but the voice sounded decidedly masculine. "Commodore, I know that a handshake is only a custom and not a contract, but I hope you will accept my plea for help."

Here it is, Hiro thought. *It almost doesn't feel real, being here at this moment.* He had made life-or-death decisions without thought, relying on gut instinct alone. He had charged into battle with faith that his crew's skill would carry them through. But this was wholly different, and the fear he felt gnawed at him. Seconds passed, feeling like hours, before Hiro took the offered hand.

Anduin's grip was strong, far stronger than expected. Hiro smiled and the alien returned the expression. The dam burst and every Terran in the room cried out, cheering and hollering. Crewmen jumped up and down, hugging and crying. Hiro shook hands with each of the aliens, acting as a diplomat more than a commander. Then the lithe soldiers took turns greeting the throng of pilots and crew eager to be a part of history. What had moments before been a tense standoff became an ad hoc victory party.

Across the room, Cameron watched with sober appreciation. Next to him, George bounced around, trading high-fives and clapping soldiers on the back. He stopped when he noticed Cameron's posture.

"Jesus, buddy. What's wrong?"

Cameron tried to shake it off. "Sorry. I just don't know. I mean, this is great, but—"

"No," George said. "No 'buts.' This is huge. This is the biggest thing we've ever been a part of." George stared at the alien craft, an enormous grin on his face. "This is just the beginning."

George pushed through the crowd, leaving Cameron standing in the middle of the celebration.

That's what I'm scared of, Cameron thought.

PART
TWO

TALLUS

"And on that day, for the sins of their fathers and the pride of their leader, the Lord rained fire from the sky onto the fields and homes of the Egyptian people. And so it was then, so it is now."

–Alexander Blightman
Founder of the Red Hammer Union
March 14, 2220

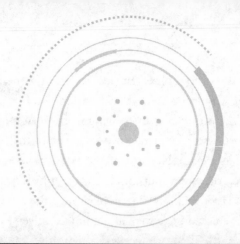

October 14, 2236
Presidential Tower
Vienna, Incorporated States of Europe

"L ADIES AND GENTLEMEN OF the press, High Chancellor
Alexander Burton."

With a sudden explosion of flashes from the thirty
cameras in the room, the high chancellor walked in. Standing
six-foot-three with the build of a linebacker, the chief galactic
executive posed an intimidating figure. It was easy to see why
the common joke in the Council was that Alexander's security
used *him* for protection. Wearing a charcoal gray Kalsin suit,
he took the podium, gripping the cherry oak with his hands
as he gazed over the crowd. His head of security—a gray-haired
agent—stood to the side, his eyes on the line of reporters.

"Please," he said in a deep and slightly British baritone.
"Have a seat." The assembled crowd took their assigned chairs
and waited for the speech to begin. "Hello, citizens of the
Colonial Federate. Earthlings, Martians, Plutonians, and
all who call Sol their home. Good morning to our friends
and loved ones on Tallus, as well as the scientists watching

from the various observatories. To our loyal men and women of the Colorum Belt, good hunting. And of course, good evening to the lucky ones living in Eros. As all of you know by now, yesterday marked a sea change in the history of our humble species. Not just of the Federate or for the people of the Sol system—but for all of humanity. For thousands of years, since mankind first looked into the sky with wonder, we have asked if we were alone in the universe. On October thirteenth, 2236, we received a definitive answer. As Earth rose in the Lunar sky, two alien races met over our home planet to wage war. Though the motivation of each race is unknown to us at this time, their actions spoke to their true intentions.

"As Solus and Terra carrier groups converged on the impromptu battlefield, the alien race known as the Boxti began an unprovoked attack on our fighters that led to an all-out skirmish. With our two largest armadas positioned around Earth, the enemy was outnumbered and outmatched. Heavy fighting continued through the morning, but in the end our mighty fleet emerged victorious."

The high chancellor looked down at his notes, pain showing in his face. "The battle was not without casualties. Two thousand injured, one quarter of that fatally. Nearly one hundred seamen died aboard the TMF *Savanna*, but her sacrifice destroyed the remaining enemy craft and prevented this hostile race from posing any immediate threat to our Homeworld." He paused, letting out a sigh. He pinched the palm of his left hand, feeling a comforting lump of shrapnel underneath the muscle. "All told, some four hundred thirty-six soldiers, airmen, and seamen lost their lives defending our space, remarkable given the extreme technological superiority of these beings. And that sacrifice was not made alone. In this fight, another alien race shed blood alongside our ships, dying to protect their own existence. When the dust settled, they made the first move to offer a peaceful parlay that has since shed significant light on the extent of their dire situation."

He continued: "The silver craft belong to a civilization called the Nangolani. They are, in many ways, similar to us. Their home of Nangol, or 'mother rock,' is built much like Earth. They have different cultures and languages depending on where they grew up. They have arts and science and fashion and, of course, a strong military. For us, the conflict with the Boxti is only hours old. For them, the war has raged for a hundred years. Millions of their people have died, and countless other alien races have fallen to the alien menace. While fleeing their pursuers, the Nangolani found a way to our system, and the rest we'll leave to the historians."

Alexander took a breath. "I have spent the last day in deep counsel with Emperor Anduin of the Nangolani and, with the advice of the Council and the guidance of the generals and admiralty, I have decided that the Terran Colonial Federate will enter into an alliance of faith with the Nangolani fleet. Though there is a long path before us, together we can share a burden that has taken so much from the galaxy."

The high chancellor took a moment to drink from his glass of water. The next portion of his speech wasn't written on the script. He hadn't dared let a leak from a loose-lipped intern start a shitstorm in the press before he'd had a chance to get ahead of it. Taking a deep breath, he dove in.

"It is with this task in mind that I will reinstitute the policy of a draft, compelling all men and women of appropriate age to join into a branch of service, to be started on Reformation Day next week. I understand this will be wholly unpopular, and I don't like the idea of conscription any more than you. But we are now a civilization at war, and everyone must contribute to see this through. I make a promise to you, the united Terran people, that I will repeal the draft when the war is finished. I have much to discuss with our new allies, so I cannot take questions at this time. Thank you."

The high chancellor turned from the podium, dodging the shouts and screams as his aide, Arthur, took the stand. The small Martian native held up his hands and yelled over the din.

"The high chancellor will not be answering questions at this time. Please direct all queries to the press liaison desk."

Cries of "Arthur" and "Alexander" and "Mister Chancellor" followed the politician down the long corridor, all the way to the landing pad on the outside of the building. Secret Service agents ushered the high chancellor to his waiting limo and guided him inside.

The last man standing on the platform, a gruff-looking agent with steel blue eyes, spoke into his cuff.

"Paladin is moving."

New York City
United America

JONAH BLIGHTMAN WATCHED THE broadcast on his tablet. He nodded along to the beats, anticipating the chancellor's every word. This was a calculated political move, and it reeked of panic. An alliance with an unknown alien species? The draft? Alexander was on his heels. Jonah would have started dancing, but his men were wound a little tight. His change to the plan had caused some problems, but there was time to work through them.

ADAM KORENMAN

In one month, the world was in for a big surprise. And no one but the Red Hammer knew it was coming.

November 5, 2236
Seraph Three
Kronos

SERGEANT JOSH RANTZ AND Corporal Dax Shepard's faces stared back from their official photographs, along with other men and women from the 185th.

Dr. Markov Ivanovich looked up from the photos and pressed his face against the glass. His traveling partner, Sasha Otravlyatovich, watched him from a nearby couch. Markov stared down at the fortress, his eyes lighting up like a child's. Every few minutes he would pull back, jot down notes, and whisper something into his personal recorder. Then it was back to the window, hands cupped around his eyes to block out the glare.

Sasha found it hard to believe Dr. Markov had slept at all the last few weeks. Now on Kronos for the wargames, Markov had insisted they move from the comfort of their quarters— where they watched the exercises on monitors—to one of the far more cramped observation platforms on board a Seraph. The move had happened as soon as Markov found his muse, Sergeant Josh Rantz.

"I simply *can't* do my research anywhere else," Markov had said at the time. "We *must* watch from here."

For his part, Sasha had played the grateful guest and kept his mouth shut. The Seraphs were open spaces; there wasn't a designated or reserved area for any of the VIPs. Markov had snagged a small table and sectional sofa early on, and he had a knack for keeping it secure. Sasha was sure money had

WHEN THE STARS FADE

exchanged hands once or twice to keep some undesirable from stealing their spot. Dozens of personnel files littered the area, each one a jacket on one of the soldiers from the games, including the illustrious Rantz and Shepard.

Sasha admitted the last hour had been interesting. With only a handful of soldiers, Sergeant Rantz managed to lure a pair of Alpha's trucks out of the fort and capture them. Everyone aboard the twenty Seraphs wondered what insane plan the young soldier had devised, and why Joshua had waited nearly a month before he took action. The old veteran had a few theories, but figured the simplest would be true.

Nothing was more dangerous than a complacent defense.

The 185th were a part of the Army's Rangers, considered some of the toughest trained soldiers in the general military. They were the first to hit the ground during a fight, and often never left. Sasha had been surprised to learn that the Rangers weren't considered special-forces. That honor went to the Black Adders, though they recruited exclusively from Ranger battalions. Of course, the greatest force in the land had to be Team Hercules. Those clandestine warriors came from all branches, and selection was far more difficult than just winning a Crucible.

It was confusing for the recently released prisoner, so Sasha had spent most of his time glaring across the small shuttle toward a group of civilians. Most were just business men, administrators from weapons manufacturers, or private military contractors looking for new talent. One, however, stood out from the rest. He wore an incredibly expensive and tasteless purple suit, and slicked his hair back. Sasha fumed.

Brent Kerrigan.

Brent hadn't spoken to them for the last few days, preferring to spend his time schmoozing with the politicians and bourgeoisie. It was a well-known and oft-lamented fact that the wealthiest citizens of the galaxy used training exercises like these to poach future security personnel for their estates. The situation with the Boxti only exacerbated that fact. Sasha wondered if there would be any soldiers left after the vultures had their fill.

More than that, however, he wondered what an operative of the Red Hammer was doing in a room of businessmen and politicians.

The brass had made a bold and unpopular decision to keep the Kronos training area in the dark about the brewing war with an alien race. Those in leadership felt the information would only distract the soldiers during a crucial phase of the games. Others found it completely irresponsible to keep such information from men and women in uniform. Granted, only those still active on the field were oblivious; those "killed in action" had come back to the base to find a dramatically changed universe awaiting them. Major General Casey, Kronos' post commander, had considered shutting down the entire operation in lieu of mustering the troops for an eventual deployment. Admiral Walker, now acting as the unofficial galactic commander, had all but ordered a swift end to this "pointless training." Only the urging of the staff kept the Crucible running.

Sasha had been loath to offer his opinion. War would find them all eventually, but better those few soldiers enjoy another day in a peaceful universe. Right now, those on the sidelines were playing a different sort of game. The politicians were looking for a way to appear tough in front of the press. The rich dogs were looking for protection. Brent was looking for new toys to steal and new tactics to learn. With the Red Hammer, it was hard to tell where the line between cowardice and cleverness began. Even the military men seemed out of place. Half were champing at the bit to get out and find the alien menace, while the others were trying to draw out their time behind a desk as long as possible.

And then there was Markov. He was the strangest of them all.

"Any minute now," Markov said, his breath fogging the glass. "I never thought a game could be so exciting."

Sasha stood and stretched. "They play for keeps." He put a hand on his chin and pushed his head to the side until he heard a satisfying crack. His body seemed to make more and more noises the older he got. *Never expected to make it this far,* he thought.

A television hung from the ceiling, playing a news report from Terra Node. Word of the attack over Luna spread fast on the FTL network. A cloud of dread hung over the populace. For some, it was fear of this new and unknown threat. For others, it was plain xenophobia for these new "allies." A month without any sightings of the Boxti had quieted the tension only so much, and the Nangolani were regarded with more and more suspicion.

On Earth, activist groups marched daily outside the offices of the Council, calling for the removal of all alien vessels from human space. Out on the rim, Tallus was yet unaffected by such events, but the uncertainty pervaded the system like a plague.

The images of the cleanup around Luna sent chills down Sasha's spine.

"Does that change your plans any?" he asked.

Markov turned from the window, annoyed at the disruption. His eyes darted from the screen and back to his companion. "If anything, this makes our job easier. The military is always willing to dump money into a project when war looms on the horizon."

"Aren't you worried this will expose us?"

The doctor flashed a grin that was equally charming and disturbing. "Only seven people know enough about this project to be a bother, and one is the chief of staff."

Sasha raised his eyebrows. "Why does the chief of staff know about this project?"

"It was his idea. Granted, I'm affecting the scope just a little bit. But it means that we have the support of the High Chancellor." He coughed into his hand. "In a manner of speaking, anyway."

The Martian scowled. "Doctor, how do you expect to keep a project like this secret when the head of the government is behind it?"

Markov patted Sasha on the cheek. "Have a little faith, Sasha."

But now he didn't recognize himself. How had he become this scarred old man? And why was he with the irascible *synok*?

The young Dr. Markov returned to the window, a glass of some hideous concoction in his hand. Every few minutes he would speak into his data recorder at a whisper. Sasha didn't dare interrupt again. He had no intention of being sucked into another intellectual debate. Those turned into one-sided battles with speed.

Sasha watched Markov's myriad spastic tics and listened to the scientist talk to himself. *Those years on Europa were not kind to him,* Sasha thought.

In his private corner of the platform, Markov doodled on a tablet while mumbling whatever thought popped into his head. Overwhelmed by curiosity, Sasha moved over and sat down. He looked over the doctor's shoulder and saw the monitor was still directed at the fledgling guerrilla squad.

The entire platform, it seemed, rooted for the underdogs of Charlie Company. They had cheered when the ambush on the two trucks went down, and many had fallen silent to watch what would be the final battle of the games. Of course, no one thought the small group of soldiers, determined though they may be, would succeed against Alpha.

"Dr. Ivanovich, have you looked at my suggestions?"

"I told you already. I know my seven."

Sasha ran his fingers over his mustache again and again, an old habit. "And none of them are on my list? I'm telling you, Sergeant Perez is our man, and the rest can come from his company."

Markov put down his notebook and sighed. The chief of staff's words echoed in his mind: *You're better off taking runts.* "Zev is good, I'll give you that, but he's too much the soldier. He doesn't have a single mark in his file after ten years of service."

"And that is not good?" Sasha looked down at the Doctor's files and picked up one marked *Rantz.* "Three marks of insubordination, but all were argued down to minor charges." He dropped the tablet on the table. "This is what you want? Soldiers who *can't* follow orders?"

"I want soldiers who think for themselves. Once we choose our candidates and bring them to the CROWN training facility, it will be pure hell. They'll look back on their time on Kronos with longing. I need to make sure they have the mental strength to handle it. Joshua Rantz single-handedly concocted a brilliant plan to infiltrate Alpha Company's fort. He's creative and cunning and crafty—an ideal candidate for CROWN."

Kronos

THE TRUCKS RACED TOWARD the Alpha fort. Shots came from behind, snapping past the windows, kicking up dirt around the road. The lead Jackal driver weaved back and forth, trying to make his vehicle as small a target as possible. He grabbed the radio from the console and keyed the mic.

"Any station this net, we are coming in hot. Hostiles in pursuit. Need that gate open ASAP!" No answer came, just the crackle of static. "Any Alpha unit, we need support *now!*"

Once the trucks swung into view, the gates opened immediately. Soldiers came into the courtyard to see what the commotion was about.

Zev stood in the doorway to his barracks, watching the vehicles come in. Something caught his attention. The soldiers in the trucks—their uniforms seemed oddly colored. Almost tan. His skin prickled. Maybe it was a trick of the dying light, but just to be sure, he flipped down his helmet's IR monocle. The driver and the truck both sported a glowing "A" glyph, for Alpha company.

But we haven't had a mounted patrol out in weeks.

At the last moment, as the trucks passed through the gate, the drivers jerked the wheels to the left and slid to a stop. The men inside spilled out of the vehicles and disappeared behind cover.

Zev saw the drivers clearer now. They wore tan uniforms with the standard issue hexagonal print.

Who wore tan? Bravo was brown. Delta had blue. Charlie wore...
Lights. Lights. Lights.

The sight of blinking red lights interrupted Zev's thoughts. He saw them on the side of one of the Alpha trucks. Jackals were soft-skinned vehicles, meaning there shouldn't be any armor plates on the side, yet both trucks that had just arrived had small boxes covering their doors.

The boxes were blinking red.

"MINES!"

The trucks exploded. Smoke and simunition pellets fired out in every direction. The soldiers in the open fell like playing cards. Those in the towers tried to hide, but were picked off by sniper fire from the ridge. One of the platoon leaders called for his men to grab the wounded. As they emerged from the tents, mortars screamed down and dropped them. The ground shook as grenades and explosive rounds fell inside the base and filled the air with smoke and shrapnel. Enemy soldiers, taking cover behind the trucks, fired wild bursts into the crowded troops.

"Stay inside," Zev shouted over the clamor. "Hold your positions." A chunk of dirt splattered the wall near his face, coating his cheek in red sand. He spat, choking on the thick cloud. Zev's arm felt numb and he saw his left bicep had taken a grazing shot. The suit produced a mild current to simulate an injury.

"Sarge," one of the privates said. "What should we do?"

He thought for a moment, listening to the barrage outside. "We're going to hold here, fortify the barracks. If they want to take us, we're going to make them pay for every inch. Barricade the windows and doors, and find anything we can use for cover. We need to turn this building into a castle." He pulled a first aid pouch from his vest. It wasn't a real bandage, though he carried several of those as well, but simply an electric pad that ended the suit's "injured" status. He pressed the pad to his arm, and the numbness faded.

The mortars ceased. Zev observed the damage. Another fifteen soldiers lay on the ground, and more were down inside the tents on the far side. The far side of the fort was worse. The mess hall had taken a direct hit. Two platoons had gone in just moments before, and most of the officers as well.

We've lost half the company.

Voices shouted outside the gate. The enemy approached. Zev closed the door to the barracks and strode down the hall. His soldiers had moved cots in front of the doors and prepared defendable positions at key choke points. The cobwebs were shaken off, and the unit stood ready to make this assault too costly for whatever unit had chosen to attack. Zev figured it had to be Delta or maybe Charlie, which meant a platoon of shooters. It didn't matter. It could be a battalion out there, the tactics wouldn't change.

"I need sharpshooters at every window, but watch for their snipers. If you hear mortars, take cover. They won't penetrate this building, so we only have to worry about splash from nearby impacts. We don't have a great view of the main gate, so they're definitely making it into the compound. That means this is it. Today is the last day of this mission. Live or die, this ends now. Ready yourselves," he called out. "No one breaks us. *We are Alpha, and we own this house!*"

New York City
United America

NEW YORK AWOKE WITH A roar, spewing traffic into its already congested arteries. The tiered lanes of cars and trucks stacked almost eighty million people in the tight spaces between the looming skyscrapers. Like all moments preceding a storm, the air seemed charged with electricity.

Since its founding, the city had changed flags only a few times. The Union Jack gave way to the Star-Spangled Banner. Under the United Earth Council, the Big Apple served as capital to an entire planet, though that distinction eventually moved to Vienna after political protest from the Korean Kingdom. Not to be deterred, the great city continued to grow in size and prominence, consuming the surrounding lands under one immense urban sprawl.

With the ground left so far below, travel between buildings required the construction of the Sky Rail, a tram system that led from tower to tower.

Spanning the vertigo-inducing distances between the hundreds of high rises in the downtown area, the Sky Rail carried thousands upon thousands of travelers to and from their places of work and play. On a given day, more than twelve million people used the mile-high trains.

At the station hanging over the Fifth and Broadway intersection, a young man sat on a bench and ate a sandwich from a paper bag. He was barely worth a passing glance. A small backpack bearing the NYU slogan lay on the ground by his feet. Everyday passengers paid no attention to the kid. No one noticed the colorful wires that poked out from between the zipper of his bag, or the way he glanced around fitfully as he ate his food.

Two transit officers walked onto the platform, looking around for anything out of the ordinary. One spoke into his walkie-talkie, his eyes alert as he scanned each face. The other walked around the area, hands resting on his gun belt.

They looked bored. But they weren't. They were working.

On his bench, the young man's phone rang. He dropped his sandwich and answered the call, pressing the device against his face hard enough to leave marks. The nearest officer turned his head slowly, not wanting to seem too interested in the exchange. Without speaking, the policeman glanced over at his partner and tapped the brim of his hat. On the signal, the other officer nodded and moved into a flanking position.

"No," the young man said into the phone. "Everything's fine here. I don't need you to babysit me."

The two cops closed the distance. Surrounding pedestrians sensed trouble and cleared the area. One of the officers stood directly in front of the kid. He didn't draw his weapon, as there was no reason to cause alarm just yet. The cop waited for his presence to be noticed.

The boy looked up. When he saw the cop's uniform, his eyes popped wide. Slowly, he lowered the phone to his lap.

"Officer?"

A train approached the station, shaking the entire platform. Businessmen and students and blue-collar workers moved closer to the boarding area, leaving just enough space for arriving passengers to disembark. A circle formed around the two police officers and the suspicious kid.

"Son," the policeman said. "Would you mind stepping to the side with me?"

The young man looked at his watch. "Is there some kind of problem?"

The officer leaned in. "Is there going to be?"

The young man looked over the policeman's shoulder at the large digital clock on the platform wall. He lowered his head, resigned to his fate, and started to stand. It wasn't supposed to go this way. A few more minutes and the platform would have been almost empty. He held up his phone apologetically, miming a request to end the call. The officer relented, taking a step backward.

"Dad," the boy said. "It looks like I'm not coming home for lunch after all." He snapped the phone shut and dropped it into his pocket. As the police closed in on the young man, he looked up at the sky and closed his eyes.

"The Red Fist Rises!"

Twelve pounds of high explosive, surrounded by nine packets of nitric acid, exploded in an immense fireball. The boy and the policemen were immediately vaporized, as were dozens of the surrounding onlookers. Each packet of acid turned into a fiery cloud. The shockwave shattered three support columns, weakening the structure of the platform. Unable to support its own weight, the station snapped off from the side of the tower, beginning the long descent to the city streets below. The rail line began to crumble under the excess weight. People scrambled toward the tower, trying desperately to reach the safety of the building before the entire area fell.

Fire swept across the side of the tower, preventing any escape as the platform continued to break apart. Glass shattered under the intense heat, raining dull cubes down on the panicked mass. With a horrific groan, the metal supports on the rail itself gave way. With the train still attached and thousands aboard, the entire line plummeted down the side of the building. People screamed as the floor beneath their feet simply vanished and they fell into the fog below. Safeties activated along the rail, separating the broken line from the rest of the track and letting it drop free. Emergency rockets activated on the train, sending the screaming passengers toward a rough but survivable landing.

Then the clock struck ten.

As those inside the tower watched on, every single Sky Rail platform connected to their building exploded.

Bombs destroyed the platforms and connecting supports, tearing the rails down and sending fiery debris tumbling to the ground. Smaller explosions rocked the Galactic Media Tower as the access points on the lower floor were hit. Though they didn't know it yet, everyone inside the building had just been trapped.

In his office on the top floor, CEO of Galactic Media Arnold Rothsburg tried in vain to reach the police. At the moment the explosions took out the Sky Rail, all the lines had been cut to the building. From his vantage point on the two hundredth story, he could see the six armored shuttles approaching. Even with smoke obscuring the view, it was impossible not to notice the blood-red fists painted on the side of the ships.

One of the transports touched down on Arnold's personal landing pad, shoving his own aircraft off the platform. Soldiers poured out and rushed his office, firing through the glass. One of Arnold's security guards shoved him to the floor and shot back, trying to halt the attack. A round pierced the guard's forehead, and he collapsed to the ground. The assault lasted only a few seconds. The CEO's detail was dead and the room secured.

The last thing the executive saw before blacking out was a tall man wearing a long black coat walking into the office, his boots grinding the broken glass into the carpet.

New Freeman
Tallus

NEW FREEMAN, THE CAPITAL of Tallus, covered almost an entire continent. The arid planet stored most of its water underground, only supporting one meager ocean and a few dozen rivers. This kept the temperature aboveground warm and dry, perfect for the scientific communities that called the rock their home. Natives often found it hard to take other atmospheres if they ever vacationed, so accustomed had they become to the vapor-free air. Tourism was nonexistent.

Most Terrans forgot that Tallus, not New Eden, had been the first colonized planet. Though farther out in the galaxy, the orange planet had been the savior of the International Space Commission's catastrophic *Odyssey* voyage. Launched over 150 years before, *Odyssey* used Stride technology to race for new horizons. Only five days in, the massive ship inadvertently entered Blue Space while passing by the asteroid Vesta. Dragged lightyears off course, *Odyssey* found itself floating in the center of a strange and otherworldly formation of gas giants.

Concerned with repairing the extensive damage the ship had taken in the Blue tunnel, the captain of the voyage brought them down on a new, golden planet. Landing near the only source of water, the scientists aboard were baffled to discover how similar the atmosphere was to Earth's own. Days later, the crew emerged from their battered boat and stepped foot on alien soil. Not knowing how far from home they truly were, the crew began their mission in earnest, building a small settlement and starting experiments on the myriad local wildlife.

Nearly eight years passed before contact was regained with Earth. The spinning FTL receiver caught wind of a transmission several lightyears away. Hours later, the captain was able to have a slow, laggy conversation with a controller back on Titan. Days later, the crew was able to talk to families long lost to the distant stars. It was a momentous occasion, not only for the success of the mission, but for the possibility of return.

It took the effort of every person in the *Odyssey* crew to build a suitable relay node and place it into orbit. The ship was too damaged to return to Earth, and the only way to ensure a rescue mission would be to rely on home for help. A plan was hatched and put into motion. Luckily, the years of research on the planet had led to a small but thriving community outside *Odyssey*. Shelters turned into homes, and the center of Freeman—named after the captain—was founded.

The hell of it was, when Earth finally reached Tallus, *Odyssey*'s crew didn't want to leave. They were already home. And with the advent of Blue Drive technology, more and more Terrans flocked to the dry landscape to carve out their own slice of freedom. Platinum mining became an extremely profitable business, and the population grew rapidly. Now united under new government, and still playing home to Fleet's training field in the Valley, Tallus sparkled as a gem amidst the galaxy.

Days on the small planet were only eighteen hours. Schools were letting out as the twin blue suns began to tango their way below the horizon. It was the magic hour, when the city lights hadn't yet drowned out the faint yet visible valley overhead. Third-grader Natalie Barkovski stopped to wave up at the sky toward the slow-moving speck of light that orbited her world. She smiled a toothy grin and shouted.

"Have a good night, mom!"

She skipped her way home, completely oblivious that, in just hours, there would be nothing left alive on the surface of the planet.

ADMIRAL LAWRENCE GILROY AWOKE with a groan, his mouth sour from stale bourbon. Fumbling in the dark, he slapped his meaty palm down on his phone, silencing the alarm. For a minute he thought about falling back asleep, maybe waiting for a steward to come and drag him off his couch. Then as his brain came online, he remembered where he was. With a yawn, Lawrence sat upright and stretched.

Even in the dim light he could see the name of the vessel embroidered on the couch: *Imperion One*, the capital frigate of the high chancellor. Opulent to the point of excess, *Imperion* had been designed during the first years of the United Earth Council, after the Empirical War. Platinum and titanium composites covered every inch of the hull, gilded with a gold-carbon fitting. The sleek and futuristic curves of the frigate made it the source of envy and admiration for every politician in the council.

Lawrence's uniform lay over a nearby chair, more wrinkled than he preferred, but no one would care. Admiral Walker, the Fleet commander, allowed for less-than-perfect appearances as long as work was getting done. Lawrence rubbed his jaw, finding more stubble than he'd expected.

They let me sleep in? He left his top on the chair and shuffled over to his bag, pulling an electric razor from the side pouch. A mirror hung on the far side of the room, lit by a small lamp. Staring at his reflection, Lawrence took stock of his appearance. He'd put on a few pounds since earning his stars, but at six-foot-three it hardly mattered. He ran a hand over his smooth head, his fingers coming away greasy. A minute later he put down the razor and pulled on his clothes, whispering a silent prayer that he be left alone today.

The light in the hallway blinded him for a second. Lawrence stopped short of a small aide, nearly knocking her flat.

"Sorry," he muttered under his breath. It took a full minute before he could see clearly, but he still had to be mindful not to tread on the staffers. Not a one came close to his towering frame. His mind wandered as he walked toward the main conference room. With the exception of one of the Secret Service agents, who might legitimately be a giant, Lawrence was the tallest person aboard the ship. It was a minor point of pride, but one he could enjoy for the moment.

Soldiers stood guard at every door, rifles in their hands. Lawrence scowled at their posture. *Not a one at the low ready. Everyone just counting down the minutes until their shift ends.* He made a mental note to speak with the sergeant-at-arms when his meeting was through. At the end of the corridor he climbed a flight of stairs, following color-coded signs until he found the one pointing toward his destination. When he finally arrived, the double doors to the room were wide open.

"Admiral Gilroy," the chief of staff called out. "Glad you remembered."

Lawrence smiled icily and took his seat. A glass of water had already been set out, along with a steaming mug of coffee. He looked at the coffee.

And then he was somewhere else.

Imperion One was gone. He was sipping piping hot and bitter grounds from a rusty metal can. His senses were overwhelmed by the stench of smoke and blood and shit, and the literally thousands of voices crying out for help or death or mama.

As quickly as it began, the episode ended. Lawrence placed his hands in his lap so no one would notice them shaking.

On his right and left sat the military brass: four- and five-star generals and admirals, all decked out in their finest uniforms. Lawrence felt downright frumpish in his field gear, the rank on his shoulders a subdued black instead of shiny silver. Across the cherry-oak table were the civilians. Lawrence recognized the high chancellor's aide, Arthur, and Jerry Ahmad, the chief of staff. An attractive but very young staffer sat next to Jerry, scratching out notes on a pad of paper. That made Lawrence smile. Every television in the media room showed the same image. Broadcast from helicopters bearing every news logo, the ring of fire around the Galactic Media Tower continued to burn hours after the initial attack. Generals and cabinet members stood silent and watched the reports, each lost in a world of their own. Three thousand people were dead or missing, and that didn't include the countless others trapped inside with Red Hammer soldiers.

The high chancellor sat at the table, a half-emptied cup of coffee within arm's reach. Lawrence knew from his time on the frigate that there were at least two shots of bourbon in that cup as well. Arthur and Jerry paced the room with the other staffers, each yelling at someone on the other end of the phone. Special-forces units had been mobilized and the American ground units were loading up for immediate deployment. But the news in New York wasn't the worst of it.

All over the planet, explosions had shocked the most powerful nations of Earth. In Europe, the United Federal Bank headquarters had been completely destroyed by a truck bomb left in the basement. Another device had taken down six satellite receiver towers across Asia. Brazil was reeling from a series of raids on military bases and prison transports.

The coordination alone was staggering, as each attack had happened at almost the same precise moment, separated by thousands of miles. Groups—no, *armies* of soldiers fought brushfire skirmishes across the globe with local military. Most attacks targeted at infrastructure: fuel and natural gas lines, communication, defense services.

Jerry slammed his phone on the table, fuming. "This is going to get worse before it gets better. We've lost forty percent of our network on the planet."

"What do you mean?" Alexander asked. He was weary from bad news.

"Jonah has his soldiers taking down transmission towers. He wants to control the media on Earth, to put his own personal spin on all this. They're blocking news networks, only allowing one signal through. They're also shutting out receiver satellites. Terra Node is going to lose contact with the planet soon." Jerry shook his head, running a spotted hand over his stubbly chin. Ever the businessman, he couldn't help but look for the angles. "Damn smart moves, if he can keep control long enough to capitalize. This is Mars day one all over again."

Lawrence rubbed his temples and groaned. "How was he able to pull this off? I mean, we're talking about a planet of over fifteen billion people. How big has Hammer become, and how could we not see this coming?"

Arthur was about to start an argument when Jerry stepped in. "Jonah isn't the first head of a Martian splinter group. After the Coalition fell and the war ended, there were millions of rebels still itching to fight. Only their leaders stood down, and that didn't sit right with those on the front lines." He walked over to the monitor, pointing at a report. Jonah's face stared back from an old photograph. The terrorist leader

ADAM KORENMAN

wore his usual expression of mild distaste, and his thin beard was still jet black. His name was blank; only the alias *Jonah Blightman* was printed. "This is what came out. Not just one fanatic, but millions. All Jonah had to do was convince those with his point of view that he was the biggest dog in the yard. After that, they'd follow him anywhere."

"And with a million-man army," Arthur said, "how were we supposed to keep track of every possible citizen who might be associated with Red Hammer? The intelligence agencies had over forty different groups to watch at any given time, and that's just between Earth and Mars. Titan has had operational cells since the war ended. The Sol System has a lot of places to hide."

Lawrence wasn't satisfied. "But this level of coordination, you must have heard something. Somewhere, there has to be an analyst who didn't have their head up their ass."

"If Jonah is good at anything," Chancellor Burton said softly, "it's being anywhere but where you think he is." He took a sip of bourbon and looked up with bloodshot eyes. "He must have been moving people in small groups for years, slowly transferring the entire army to Earth."

Lawrence's leg bounced up and down under the table. He bit his tongue. *You're about to do something stupid, Larry. Think this through.* "Earth's forces are occupied with skirmishes all over the globe. General Burnside is missing." *Please don't get us into trouble.* "Let me have operational command of Earth's defense. I can have bombers in the sky in under an hour. We know he's inside the GMT. Why not just destroy it? The chance to take down Jonah Blightman comes maybe once in a lifetime." *Jesus, Larry!*

"No," the high chancellor said. "I won't condone an attack on our citizens. No matter who stands behind them. I'm sorry, Admiral, but you're not exactly the right man for this."

Lawrence steamed. "The last I checked, sir, there were fifty thousand members of the special-forces units in Sol and about a million men wearing the Red Hammer. The military is still rebuilding, and you need boots on the ground. The draft was a good idea, you just didn't implement it soon enough. It'll be a year or more before we're fielding a true ground force. With Burnside gone, and most general officers fucking away on Kronos, you're down to two options: either you let a few mid-level commanders run the most important defensive operation in Earth's history, or you sack up and let me do my fucking job."

"Lawrence!" Admiral Walker rose from his seat, beet red. "That is the goddamn high chancellor."

"Balls." Lawrence had worked up too much of a lather to stop. "The high chancellor can't seem to forget that whatever I did to piss him off happened when he was wearing the wrong fucking uniform." There were a few gasps at that remark. *Well, Larry. I hope you enjoy prison. You fucking moron.* "I don't want to do the ground and pound any more than you, but the last time I went up against Jonah Blightman, I won. That's what you need right now."

No one spoke for several minutes. Admiral Walker looked ready to choke his officer right there in the boardroom. On the televisions, news anchors reported sudden and mysterious blackouts from their Earth associates. Finally, Jerry spoke.

"He's right."

"Like hell he is," Arthur shouted. "He's a freaking psycho."

"Arthur, shut your mouth." Jerry placed his hands on the table and took a calming breath. "Admiral Gilroy is not the most *eloquent* debater, but he's right. This is a rebellion, and we have a subject matter expert on those in our midst. We would be foolish to waste his experience."

Alexander groaned. "Jesus Christ, we're in the middle of an intergalactic war and we have a rebellion to deal with? Why did Jonah have to pick now?"

"It's the perfect moment," a voice said softly. All eyes turned to Quinn. She handed the chancellor a note and a fresh cup of coffee; *fresh* in that it hadn't been spiked with bourbon. "We honestly can't spare the men to fight at home when such a powerful enemy as the Boxti is on our doorstep."

Jerry read the note. "Alexander, it's from the Nangolani."

"And?"

"They've been tracking a group of Boxti scouts in the Orleani Cloud. That's just outside the Valley of Giants."

Alexander blanched. "Tallus?"

Jerry nodded. "Admiral Walker, we need every fighting ship we can spare headed that way now. How long is the Blue jump from Sol to Tallus?"

"About two hours," Adeline answered.

"Then they had better leave now."

Kronos

THE FORT FELL SILENT after the last mortar landed. Josh and Dax, hugging a wall just outside the perimeter, listened for any signs of life. More than likely the enemy had holed up inside to weather the attack and would remain holed up now that they knew a rush was imminent. It wasn't what he wanted, but it was exactly as he'd planned. Now he had to wait for reinforcements from Alexa. She would remain in her perch with two other sharpshooters and make sure anyone who poked their head out lost it.

"That went well," Dax said with a heaving chest. He looked at the "D" attached to his arm and gave it an appreciative pat. Sweat ran down his face in thick lines. He squeezed Josh's shoulder. "How many do you think're inside?"

"Have to figure at least another platoon, and all of them are gonna be revved up." He checked his rifle, making sure nothing had been damaged in the jump from the truck. "We'll lead with grenades, roll in two by two. Should make it easier to clear the fatal funnel," he said. The entrance to any confined space quickly became a "fatal funnel," a choke point that was a magnet for bullets. "We need to breach and clear as fast as we can. If they fall back, we're screwed. This isn't a siege; this is a full-on, balls-out assault. Either we do this now and win it all, or we don't."

"You really think we can pull this off?" Dax asked.

Josh nodded. "Nope."

Valley of Giants
Venetian System
TFC Gettysburg

KILO SQUADRON WAS PREPARING to turn back in before the signal appeared. They had reached hour three of their patrol without incident, and fuel was too precious to waste. The twenty Phoenix III fighters, combat veterans from the TFC *Gettysburg*, had received an anomalous contact during a routine sweep of their carrier's sector and been sent to investigate. Battle Group Tallus occupied the massive corridor known as the Valley of Giants. Made up of six enormous gas planets, the Valley led straight to the heart of the Venetian system. On one end of the path, the twin stars Romulus and Remus battled for position in a beautiful dance that took almost a full two years to complete. On the other end was the amber planet known as Tallus, the only habitable rock in the entire sector.

With only one colony and a few mining outposts to guard, Tallus group was understandably small. TFC *Gettysburg*, a second-class carrier, only housed two squadrons of fighters and a flight of Seed bombers. Escorted by the destroyers *Cambridge* and *Cape Cod*, the three-ship strike-force existed as a deterrent to the odd rebel group or pirate raiding party, nothing more. On most tours, the twin missile frigates *Tigris* and *Euphrates* would be on the flanks, but both were down for annual services. The crew all agreed that this was the worst time to run short-staffed.

In the silver-striped Squadron Commander ship, Captain Frank Dunham took point on a sweep of the Valley. He shifted his large frame in the chair, trying to work out a kink in his back. At forty-three, he was long past his prime for piloting, but Tallus was short on pilots. He stifled a yawn and began a slow banking turn to port. Over his shoulder he could just make out a winking light. *A little longer*, he thought, *and we'll be back aboard the bus.*

Gettysburg had detected radiological disturbances coming from Venetian Four, the mammoth green orb in the middle of the planet-lined pathway. Given Chief Officer Rodriguez's warnings about a possible reprisal from the Boxti, every anomaly had to be investigated fully. At the end of their fuel capacity, and far beyond the limit of their patience, Kilo wing was almost finished.

"Kilo, this is one," Dunham said. "Send me your sit-reps." He pulled at the straps on his flight suit. The armor was sitting tighter on the chest than it used to. There wasn't much to do aboard the aging carrier, so Dunham spent most of his time at the gym. He smiled. *Could be worse. Could be tight around the middle.* He leaned over and bit down on his water line, taking a large mouthful. Chimes sounded on his console and situation reports from his wingmen filtered in.

Still nothing. Somehow that was worse.

"Overwatch," Frank said over the net. "You picking up anything?"

Aboard *Gettysburg*, Lieutenant Junior Grade Kaileen Nuvarian drummed her fingers on her console. Her uniform was crisp and hugged her athletic frame, bulging out under her left knee to make room for a thick plaster cast. The dark orange jumpsuit made her pale skin even lighter. She refreshed her display. Still nothing.

Behind her was the ship's CO, Captain Gregorovich. The aging war vet sat placidly in his chair, smoking a fat cigar. He hadn't said a word in almost an hour, and most of the crew thought he had fallen asleep again.

"Negative, Kilo. Skies are clear."

Inside the tactical center for *Gettysburg*, the young officer aided her fellow pilots in the snipe hunt. She'd rather have been out in her bomber, flying alongside her friends, but she was the only officer aboard with any training time on the new projectors. That and a broken tibia put her out of action for the time being. It meant a comfortable room near the bridge, but also excessive boredom.

"Roger, overwatch." Frank sighed audibly. "We're ten mikes to bingo out here. Show us RTB."

"I copy, return to base," Kaileen said.

For the other pilots in the wing, the tedium was palpable. "This is some fucking borex, sir." Kilo three, a rat-faced Tallus native, griped into the net. "Pucker factor is zero."

Another voice said, "Who sent us on this snipe hunt?"

"Would you believe this came from our new gray buddies?"

"Fuck that," Kilo seven added. "I don't need some bug-eyed freak telling me what to do."

Dunham barked, "Cut the chatter." The radio went silent. "Keep some discipline until we land." He didn't actually care. It was a local net; *Gettysburg* could only see that they were talking to each other, not listen in on the conversation. But like the chore itself, their griping had become painfully routine.

Back aboard the carrier, Kaileen's terminal chirped as an unknown signature winked into existence. She tapped the screen, resolving the contact until it stuck. Long-range radar had something but couldn't identify the object at this distance. *Couldn't be them,* she thought. *Intel says we can barely track the aliens with our systems.* Her pulse quickened all the same.

"Kilo, this is overwatch. Come in."

"Overwatch, Kilo. Go ahead." Dunham let his mind drift to the bottle of Belgian ale he had stashed in his quarters. He'd never needed a beer more.

Kaileen reset the radar and gave it a moment to refresh. The same unidentified objects appeared. Kaileen pulled at her hair, concerned but certain of what needed to happen. She opened the channel to Kilo and waited for the tone. "Kilo, this is overwatch. You have neighbors in your yard, quadrant nine-two-one, sector one-thirteen. Identify and report. How copy?" She waited while the pilot confirmed with his own radar before responding.

Frank looked down at his screen, finding it clear. "Overwatch, are you sure that's a good read?" Suddenly a small green dot popped into existence, just on the far side of the planet. "Check that, overwatch, I have contact on approach. We're low on fuel, so this is going to be a quick peek."

"Roger, good hunting. Overwatch out."

Kronos

JOSH AND DAX HUGGED the side of the building, weapons ready. Two soldiers from Dax's fire team moved in close, practically stepping in each other's footprints as they approached the entrance. With only two flashbangs remaining, the room clearing would have to be quick and violent. Specialists Valenzuela and Burko were the fastest shots in the squad. Standing there, an entire platoon of rifles waiting, Josh felt as though his stomach would leap through this throat.

"Breach and clear," he said.

Burko stood in front of the door while Dax prepped the flashbang. Dax nodded and Burko stepped forward, planting all his weight into a thunderous kick aimed at the door. The wood splintered and exploded inward. Burko stepped out of the arcing path of Dax's grenade.

A massive bang shook the ground. Shouts could be heard from inside as the effect of the grenade took hold. Josh and Dax charged in, flowing through the doorway in opposite directions. They dropped three enemy soldiers in seconds. Burko and Valenzuela were through the door moments later, covering every inch of the room in fire. A round snapped past Josh's ear, and he jerked his sights over, sending a salvo into the chest of a tall enemy fighter. Simunitions skipped off the floor, peppering the wall and door frame.

Burko pushed in past the upturned cots, firing at anything that moved. Suddenly a soldier leapt up, planting his knife into Burko's stomach. The suit activated, and Dax's support gunner fell to the ground. Valenzuela shouted, firing round after round into the Alpha troop. As quickly as it began, all was silent. Ten soldiers lay on the ground, faces as peaceful as sleeping children.

Dax ran over to his downed soldier and checked him, but Burko was already "dead."

"Shoot," Dax said. "We got a little less than a squad. They must be holed up in the rest of the building."

"Then let's keep moving." *Down to eleven. And they've got at least thirty.* Josh stepped over to the next doorway and paused. He touched the handle and looked over his shoulder to see everyone behind him. With his team ready to move, he pushed the door open and stepped inside, rifle already up and firing.

Valley of Giants
Venetian Space

"Contact, vector Nine-Zero."

Dunham looked at the distant curve of the approaching gas giant and saw light reflect off a glossy black hull. He brought his fighter to bear and saw the convoy: a black vessel, almost as long as a Terran frigate, orbited Venetian Four. The pilot could hardly understand what he was seeing. A large funnel dangled by a long tether into the swirling gasses, sucking up the emerald cloud. Five fighters—four Y-shaped ships and a larger command variant—circled the vessel.

"Overwatch," Dunham said. "This is Kilo. We have visual on enemy targets. Eyes on five fighters and one...looks to be frigate-class, if not bigger."

Kaileen tried to adjust her radar controls to pick up the enemy signal, but the planet's gravity played havoc with the system.

"Sir, Kilo has enemy contact. We're within striding distance."

Gregorovich glared at Kaileen. "And waste fuel? Kilo has twenty fighters. What are they looking at that they can't handle?"

Kaileen confirmed with Dunham over the comm before answering. "Captain Dunham says he has five fighters and a frigate-class vessel."

The commander laughed. "Tell him to stop begging mommy for help and to face the big bully on his own. Weapons free. A few Harpies and the whole show will be over. We'd arrive about thirty minutes too late, lieutenant. No reason to even spin the engines." He tapped the ash off his cigar into a waiting cup. "Comms, send a notice to Fleet that enemy ships have been spotted. Hell, we'll probably get medals out of this."

She didn't like the captain, but there was no reason to argue. He was, on all accounts, making a sound judgment call. After reviewing the tapes from Luna, the odds were clearly stacked in Kilo's favor. She passed along the order to Dunham to engage. Seconds ticked by while the dots on her holographic display danced. Suddenly, every single friendly light winked out. Kaileen's heart jumped.

"Kilo, report!"

Silence.

"Kilo, this is overwatch. Report your status." She looked at Gregorovich, frowning. "Sir, I've got nothing. We need to head over there and make sure they're alive."

The elderly commander sighed, easing himself into a more professional sitting position. He paused, gathering his thoughts for an interminable few seconds before responding. "Are you giving orders now, Lieutenant?" He smiled, but his eyes were cold.

Kaileen let out a short breath. "No, sir. I'm recommending that we investigate and make sure our fighter squadron is alive."

Gregorovich yawned, stretching. "But they're so far away. At stride speed we're a half an hour from Venetian Four, and I had every intention of heading back to Tallus after Kilo returned."

"But sir!" She threw her arms in the air and turned toward the communications officer. "Can we get a visual on that sector of space? A satellite or something?"

Gregorovich's face reddened. "Lieutenant, belay that order."

"Goddammit," Kaileen said. She hobbled over to the communication terminal, shoved the scrawny soldier aside, and scrolled through the various contacts on the screen. She found one she liked and flicked it toward the main terminal. An image of the gas giant appeared, though nothing else could be seen. "Move us up a few hundred kilometers and we should have an angle over the top. We'll be able to see where they reported the contacts."

"Lieutenant Nuvarian," the captain said. "Your shift is over. Go back to medical."

Kaileen wheeled around, her eyes full of fire. "Sir," she began.

"Not another word. Lieutenant Marcos can run the projector. Now get back to your physical therapy before I make it an order. There is nothing going on here."

"We've lost contact."

"They're on the far side of a gas giant. Gravity plays all manner of hell out here. They'll come back on in five minutes, bored out of their minds."

Her mouth was open before her brain could register the danger. "We've lost contact with twenty fighters, and this is the first interaction with the enemy since Luna. What if this was an ambush? What if they're all dead already?" She was breathing hard now. "How can you be so fucking stupid?"

A second passed before her words struck him.

Gregorovich rose from his chair, his face red. "Get her the *fuck* off my bridge!" He shook with rage, his cigar tumbling to the ground. "I want her remanded to the brig. A *week* at half rations!" Two MPs appeared, hands on their holsters. They didn't appear worried that the 110-pound pilot with one good leg would be a threat.

But Kaileen wasn't going quietly. When the first MP grabbed her arm she brought her elbow back hard. The poor sergeant collapsed against the wall, gasping. The other soldier grabbed her wrist and bent it behind her back until she cried out. Together the two men cuffed the lieutenant and dragged her from the room. She looked at her feet as they dragged her briskly down the halls to the brig.

After an oxygen tank had proven faulty a week earlier, the brig had been temporarily moved to an adjacent escape pod. The small space was actually less hospitable than the brig cell, and the controls were all hardwired to a panel outside the airlock. One of the soldiers opened the door to the pod and guided Kaileen inside. Before shutting the door, he handed her a combat ration with a grin.

"I'll be here if you want to go another round." He sealed the hatch and disappeared from view.

Taking a seat inside the escape pod, Kaileen rested her head against the cool wall. The vibrations from the ship calmed her nerves and carried up inside her cast to soothe her sore leg. Before long the adrenaline wore off, and she fell into a fitful rest.

She woke when the first explosion threw her to the deck.

The automated alarm sounded at full blast, mixed in with warbling klaxons and flashing red strobes.

"Alert! Battle stations. All crew are to report immediately. Alert!" From inside the modified escape pod, Kaileen could only watch the throngs of soldiers and crew run past her small window, their voices a cacophony of confusion. Another hit knocked her to the ground again.

Finding the intercom, Kaileen contacted the MP outside. "What the hell is going on?"

"We're under attack," the response came. The MP's voice was pained. He'd been injured.

"How many of them?" She longed for a way to see what was going on outside.

A cough. "I dunno. Maybe five."

Five? She couldn't believe it. Fleet engaged hundreds of fighters at Luna, and it was a turkey shoot. "Let me out," she said. "I can help. I can fight."

His response was cut off by another explosion. Something smacked into the bulkhead, a sound like a ripe watermelon exploding. The pod shook and began sounding its own alarm. Kaileen looked over at the controls, watching them light up like a Christmas tree. A countdown appeared on the monitor, running backward from sixty seconds.

"Shit."

ON THE BRIDGE, GREGOROVICH gripped his chair as the ship lurched to starboard. Fires raged in five compartments, effectively cutting the carrier in half. All of the ship's fighters and bombers had been launched, and all floated dead in the slag-filled space around *Gettysburg*. The battle had lasted minutes, the Terrans' weapons all but useless against the alien onslaught.

It made no sense. The captain had watched the Luna tapes again and again. He'd listened to the debrief from Commodore Osaka and Commander DeHart. The enemy could be beaten. And a Phoenix III fighter was said to be a match for seven Y-fighters.

So how had only *five* managed to annihilate one destroyer, incapacitate another, and cripple a carrier and her escort?

Another missile drove into the engine room before exploding, taking out the gravity generator with it. Crewmembers floated about the bridge, trying desperately to attach their tethers. Gregorovich made his decision. He activated his handheld mic, ready to order the evacuation of all personnel.

But before he could speak, a barbed black missile drove straight through the top hull, embedding itself in the tiled floor on the bridge. The commander had a moment to register the impact before the warhead exploded, vaporizing everyone inside.

IN THE POD, KAILEEN strapped into the control seat, bracing herself for launch. As the timer hit zero, the docking clamps released, and the engines engaged. The *Gettysburg* broke apart around the ExoPod, debris and shrapnel pinging off the hull. Kaileen saw something hit the windshield and roll past. She caught a blur of clothing, arms, and legs, and a face frozen in fear. Squeezing her eyes shut, Kaileen rode the shockwaves and prayed.

As the tiny pod raced away from the fray, the Boxti fighters cleaned up. The two destroyers were pounded with fire until all that remained was melted slag. Finally it was just *Gettysburg*, limping along with one remaining engine and an exposed core. The Boxti frigate closed in, warming up its weapon systems. As Kaileen's cell tumbled away into the distance, the massive ship fired into the heart of the Terran carrier, obliterating everything. A glowing blue shockwave spread out from the explosion, the heat dissolving everything it touched until all that remained of the battle were specks of melted glass and pieces of hull.

Their enemy destroyed, the Boxti fighters returned to dock on the outside of the frigate. When all the smaller ships had returned, the large vessel tore off in search of bigger game.

Behind them, barely conscious inside her spinning prison, Kaileen drifted along with the rest of the dead.

Tallus Orbit

THE PLANET WAS UNDER siege, though no one on the ground would know it. Floating high above the only civilized landmass, watching with cruel intent, the Boxti frigate beamed FTL coordinates from a spiky transmitter on its dorsal tower. Seconds later it received a coded response.

They dare attack the King's army?

Dozens of small probes shot from the warship, setting up a node for the incoming war party. The beacons broadcasted a navigation lock, coded to the alien's frequency. On the surface, radio and television programs broke into static, overpowered by the intense transmission.

Khuum...khuum...khuum...

Within minutes, blue motes of light began to appear in the sky over Tallus. The nearest Boxti group was hours away, but the frigate would use the time wisely, gathering intel. Already, the creatures aboard the vessel had plotted the various population centers of New Freeman and begun preparing firing solutions for all of them. Covering an area the size of Australia, the metropolis made a difficult target, but a coordinated assault was well within the Boxti's skill set.

With incredible patience and inhuman banality, the Boxti planned the destruction of the planet.

TFC Berlin
Valley of Giants
Tallus

THE SCOUT CARRIER *BERLIN* entered evasive maneuvers only seconds from exiting Blue Space. Followed by three destroyers and a dozen frigates, the strike group entered a battlefield littered with the dead. *Gettysburg* floated in pieces, none bigger than the smoldering hangar wing from the flagship. The two destroyer escorts were nowhere to be seen, having been blown out of existence only minutes before.

The Terran vessels navigated the sea of debris, hulls resounding with every impact. Inside *Berlin*, crewmembers clung to bulkheads as each strike reverberated throughout the carrier. A smaller fuel frigate, TFF *Atlantic*, struck a floating munitions room and blew off its starboard reserve tank. The explosion caused a fury of action until the commander of the fueler reported all clear.

Captain Newman, standing on the bridge of *Berlin*, watched the scene with horror. What could do this much destruction? He turned to Captain Shandras, *Berlin*'s commanding officer. It was strange to bear the same title but sit significantly lower on the rank ladder. By Sector Patrol's standards he was an O-3, while the ship's commander was an O-7. Newman could never figure out naval rank.

Why couldn't they just keep it simple, like the Army?

Merging Sector Patrol with Fleet had been a matter of convenience more than tactical thinking. Under the orders of the Federate's draft, any soldier within the reserves, or having been discharged in the past five years, was called into service with the active component. It had pissed off a huge number of people, but war was never meant to be fair. Newman took his new post as a battle captain in stride. He was still managing the same squadron, just aboard a carrier instead of the safety of Yonkers.

Captain Shandras wiped a tear from his eye. Standing near the center of the room, he whispered a prayer for his dead brothers in uniform. A full head shorter than Newman, Shandras was revered as a man of faith by his loyal crew.

"Flight, report," Shandras said in his usual soft voice. His eyes never moved from the screens in the front of the room.

Lieutenant J.G. Vega worked the helm, guiding the wide ship through the field. "We're clear of the larger fragments, sir. I've got us on a path to double back around for a better view."

"Engineering?"

"Hull is ninety-nine percent and holding. We didn't take too much, sir." Lieutenant Gordon leaned back in his seat at the engineering position and rubbed his face. "Shields moved to full front until we clear the debris."

"Good work," Shandras said. "Let's set up position in Q-seventeen, let our search-and-rescue craft have a chance at combing through the derelicts. Comms, send the report to Fleet at once. CBG Tallus has been completely destroyed."

"Aye, sir," came the response from all stations.

Newman quickly moved to his commander, speaking low. "I'll have Wolfpack in the air to provide escort, Captain."

Shandras nodded to his subordinate. "Good. Have them run the same frequency as the Valkyries."

Newman picked up the handset by the communication officer and connected to the Quick Reaction Force. "This is Captain Newman. Wolfpack is clear to launch. Flight line Hotel, channel two-five-two." After his order was confirmed, he hung up the line. He turned his attention to the monitor and watched as fighters launched from the hangar out toward the battlefield. Fat-stomached Valkyries, the all-purpose military transport, rocketed out on four engines, their bubble-domed cockpits reflecting light from the distant stars.

The rescue ships charged headlong into the wreckage, scanning for any signs of life. Every now and then a Valkyrie would launch a tow cable and pull a piece of metal away from a portion of the carrier, but no living crew were found. The fighter escort weaved in and out of the debris as they patrolled the ominous landscape. Nimble Sparrows dropped sensor pods into the smoldering husks of *Cambridge* and *Cape Cod*. The latter barely existed anymore, save a steadily disintegrating section of hull.

IN HIS FIGHTER, CIRCLING the remains of one of the fallen destroyers, Cameron gaped. From all reports, this attack had come at the hands of five Boxti craft and a frigate. It just didn't add up. He vividly remembered the fighting from only a few weeks before. What had been so different here?

"Wolfpack, this is *Berlin*."

Cameron pulled his thoughts back to the moment. "Go for Wolfpack." It didn't feel right to still use the call sign. Only four of the original squadron remained since the draft, with the rest still in recovery back in Sol.

"We're showing residual energy from a Stride outside of the debris field. Investigate and report, out."

George pulled up alongside, rolling his eyes. "And here we were, hoping for a leisurely flight through a graveyard."

"Hey," Cameron snapped. "Have a little respect."

George blushed. "Did you know anyone here?"

"Does it matter? We're all in the same uniform."

The younger pilot closed distance so he could look the other in the eye. "What's going on, Cam?"

"What do you mean?"

"You've been like this since Luna. Every time we fly." He paused while he dodged a frozen body. "McLane was green, but he was a grown-ass man. We risk it every day out here."

Cameron stared straight ahead. "I should have seen it coming."

"I'm sick of the moping. We're all hurting. Hell, I'm beating myself up about him, too. But this is war. Get your shit on straight. There was nothing you could do."

"Sure," Cameron said dismissively. "Whatever."

For a moment all George could do was fume inside his cockpit. Then he angled his wing down and rammed his friend's ship, sending sparks flying out where metal met metal. The diamond-glass cracked from the impact.

Cameron shouted, "Christ, what the hell are you doing?"

"Normally I'd slap you, but these damn fighters were in the way. You've lost people in a fight before. What makes this different?"

"He was my responsibility." Cameron's eyes were red. "Any other battle there was someone else in charge. Another officer making all the calls. Not now. I'm the flight leader, this is all my fault. Any lives lost are on me."

"There was nothing you could've done."

Cameron was about to respond when his radio squawked. "Wolfpack, this is *Berlin*. We saw a collision alert on the tracker. Is everything all right?"

George shook his head, turning his attention back to the sky around them. Cameron tapped his headset. "Just passed a little close to a debris field. We're fine." He looked over at his wingman. "I'm fine, George. But thank you." He cut the line, whispering to himself. "Until the stars fade." His left hand found the tiny cross hanging off his flight suit. He squeezed it tight.

A signal lock shook him from his thoughts. Passive radar systems chimed to life, identifying a small blip on the screen only a few kilometers away. Cameron used his left hand to tap commands into the console, pulling the yoke with his right to guide the ship toward the unknown contact.

"*Berlin*, this is Wolf One. Traffic in the sky."

The radio squelched. "Wolf One, *Berlin*. You are cleared to investigate. Report coordinates on approach. Out."

"What do you see?" George asked from Cameron's four o'clock.

Cameron squinted, trying to catch a glimpse of the object. Venetian Four hung in the background, an immense green canvas. "Got a hit on passive. Shadow me." He put his foot to the floor, sending the Phoenix rocketing forward. The ship rumbled and bucked, hitting a sudden wake of particles. "George, how's your ride?"

"Choppy. I need to get new shocks." He checked his computer. "Shit, we're in a Blue box."

Cameron activated his net again. "*Berlin*, Wolf one. We have located a recently closed entrance into Blue Space. Sending coordinates now." The small size of the box suggested it was only a transmission line. Larger ships left wakes that could be followed to the source, in theory. At the very least, they could shoot a probe into the mess of particles and hope it found its way to the other side. Cameron saw a flash of light from the carrier, followed by a small blue puff as the sensor pod chased after the transmission signal.

Something danced in the faint light ahead, a tumbling silver craft. Cameron and George closed distance, their weapons armed and trained on the unknown object. Vapor leaked from various cracks in the surface, and the hull showed signs of plasma burns.

"Jesus," George said. "It's an ExoPod." He slowed down, allowing Cameron to take point. "*Berlin*, Wolf Two. We have an escape pod on our location. Should we wait for rescue?" The tow line on the Phoenix wasn't designed to drag the larger pod, though it could do in a pinch. Valkyries had the right equipment to bring the ExoPod home safely.

"Wolf Two, *Berlin*," the operator said. "Rescue teams are working on the main wreckage. Do you have confirmation of survived crew aboard?"

George activated his thermal imaging scanner, but the venting gasses from the pod scrambled the signal. White noise flooded the monitor. "I've got nothing, Cam."

On the other side of the ExoPod, Cameron used his control jets to invert the Phoenix over the escape craft's door. He moved in close, the glass canopy nearly touching the warped metal hull. Inside the pod, lights flickered as power drained. Vapor left droplets of condensation on the glass; a good sign, all things considered.

Suddenly, a small hand smacked against the window, smearing the moisture. Cameron leapt back in his seat. "George," he said. "We've got people inside. I just saw a hand."

"Okay, keep your panties on, son." George angled his fighter closer to the pod. "I'm gonna drop my line nice and easy. Watch the wash on your jets. I just had this baby detailed." He eased his fighter closer. The silence built as the two pilots worked to secure connections to the pod. A blast of static on the radio made them jump.

"All stations this net, this is *Berlin* actual." Shandras' voice came over the net. "Return to the boat and prepare for immediate action. Tallus is under attack from a large hostile force. The *Arlington* will stay behind to alert Fleet via FTL before joining the fight. *Berlin* out."

Cameron's hands felt slick with sweat inside his gloves. *A whole planet under siege? How do you even do that?* It wouldn't be the first time intelligence severely screwed the pooch, but this task force wasn't up for a prolonged engagement. Hopefully Tallus had managed to get the rest of its forces into the air.

"George, drop your line." He didn't wait for a response. Placing safeties on all weapons systems, he armed the tow cable and fired. A magnetic bolt shot out from underneath his belly, catching just behind the blast shields on the escape craft. When the line drew tight, Cameron flipped his ship around and started a slow acceleration. "Snap a brake line on the back."

"Already on it," George said. He attached his own cable from behind. If Cameron stopped short, the pod would no longer ram into his engines. "Ready for hard burn. Pod is clear of blast area."

"Punch it."

The two craft raced back to the carrier, the crippled pod in tow. Rescue craft left their positions and hurried along to *Berlin*, flaring their engines as they approached. One by one, the squadrons landed inside the hangar until all were safely aboard. Cameron and George waited for the last Valkyrie to grab the pod before attempting their own landings. *Berlin* extended two long tubes from her flanks: the Strider sleds. They began to glow as the last fighter arrived.

The hangar door closed, sealing the area off from the rest of space. With air came sound, and the entire area vibrated with the thrum of the sleds prepping for launch. Cameron and George leapt from their fighters, the engines still revving down. They threw their helmets aside and attacked the door to the ExoPod. The panel released with a groan and slammed to the deck. Cameron leapt inside, emerging moments later with a frail form. The thin woman was unconscious, and blood ran from a gash on her forehead. Her left leg was set in a dirty blue cast. She wore the coveralls of a bomber pilot. She was pale, enough so that Cameron thought he must have arrived too late. He laid the injured pilot on the deck.

"She's not breathing."

He started compressions, locking his arms and driving hard with each beat. The woman's ribs nearly cracked with each push. Meanwhile, George reached into her pockets and pulled out her tags. He read the name and tossed the disks aside.

"Lieutenant Nuvarian, can you hear me?" His partner continued CPR. "Kaileen, come back to us."

Two medics scrambled over and shoved Cameron aside. One prepped a syringe with glowing blue liquid and jammed it into Kaileen's arm. Cameron looked around to see a large crowd had formed. Everyone held their breath.

Kaileen sat up suddenly, coughing hard. The crowd cheered, clapping and hollering, while a medic placed a mask over her face and hand pumped oxygen. Slowly, she regained color. Her golden eyes darted around as she raced to process her new situation. Panic quickly settled into relief, and she allowed the medics to help her to her feet. With unsteady legs she hobbled to a waiting gurney and laid down again. Immediately, the medical team strapped her in place and placed an IV line in her arm. They wheeled her from the hangar, escorted out by the crowd of pilots and mechanics.

Cameron caught up with the gurney as it neared the door, and for a moment locked eyes with Kaileen. He laid her tags on her stomach and squeezed her hand. Her face was ashen and slick with sweat, but she managed half a grin. One of the medics pushed her glossy black hair away from her face and set the mask back down. They whisked her away toward the medical ward.

George joined Cameron at the door, breathless. "Jesus, ain't we just the big damn heroes." He noticed his friend staring off at the injured pilot. "Is she gonna be okay?"

"We'll see," Cameron said just as a sudden burst of acceleration shook the hangar. He and George grabbed onto bulkheads and looked out the porthole. The dark void exploded into streaks of white light as *Berlin* tore off toward Tallus. An alarm sounded throughout the ship.

"Alert," a mechanical voice announced. "All crew to battle stations. Refit fighters for air-to-air combat. Alert. Tallus planetary defenses report attack from multiple hostile ships. Emergency assistance requested. Alert. Strike Force Tallus no longer reporting."

The hangar exploded into frenetic activity. NCOs barked orders over the roar, preventing a chaotic mosh pit from forming. Crew immediately took to the fighters, checking ammunition attachments and applying lubrication to all moving parts. Fighters ran to their craft, hopping inside and beginning function checks. Even though they'd just landed, the redundancy helped prevent an unexpected failure. One by one, the vessels were refueled and walked to the rails. In thirty minutes, the entire fighter and bomber wing rested on the magnetic launcher, standing by for deployment.

Cameron saw George a row ahead and to the right of his position on the line. Small mechanical brakes held his Phoenix on the charged rail, preventing him from a catastrophic merging of his fighter with the Seed bomber in front. The entire carrier shook as they increased speed even more, racing toward an unknown force. With each passing minute, Cameron's heart beat faster. He'd reread the briefing from the Fade, but none of it added up. He figured that in ten minutes, he'd have his answers.

One way or another.

Tallus Orbit

A BEAM OF ORANGE light shot through space and tore into a fleeing Tallus ship. The lance bisected the craft in seconds. Oxygen tanks erupted, fueling an explosion that killed all aboard. Its target destroyed, the Boxti ion frigate continued to hunt. Spreading its mechanical arms wide, like a spider descending on prey, the craft surged forward.

The attack was well in hand. Only minutes after arrival, all twenty frigates, coordinating a continent-wide attack, launched a blistering volley of ionized plasma down onto the planet's surface. Concentrating on New Freeman, the rain of fire set buildings ablaze and destroyed key launch pads and hangars. When the carrier arrived, most of the Terran resistance had been put down. Now, aided by Y-fighters, the alien armada began the systematic destruction of the colony.

Boxti bombers, fat craft with stubby wings, charged down into the atmosphere to carpet-bomb the city. Whole blocks disappeared in fire and smoke; the screams of the dying drowned out by the deafening explosions. Across the continent, military and civilian shuttles launched toward the sky in a desperate attempt at escape. They were caught in the blockade, torn apart by an impenetrable wall of frigates and fighters.

Another lance of plasma shot down into the city, destroying a launch pad and killing hundreds of pilots and ground crew. Planetary defenses were gone, the cannons on the ground silent and broken. Save the soft crump that punctuated every explosion, Tallus was dying with barely a whimper.

Imperion One
Earth Orbit

"WHAT IS IT?" THE High Chancellor asked.

Admiral Walker stood with his phone in his hand. The Fleet Commander did not speak, but his face told volumes. He had earned his position crushing a planetary rebellion. He had won a Colonial Medallion for single-handedly blocking the invasion of Titan Academy. There was video evidence that he had killed a man with his bare hands.

Now here he was, shocked silent.

Walker had disappeared for ten minutes after receiving an urgent line from Terra Node. He returned with a peculiar look on his face. Admiral Gilroy grew anxious; he had seen that expression before, when he'd been an ensign under Walker during the Breach of Bellgrove. It made Lawrence's skin crawl.

Walker finally spoke. No one breathed.

"I've just received an FTL signal from the TFF *Arlington*. Tallus strike group engaged a small scouting party of Boxti craft."

"How many ships?" Gilroy asked.

Walker paused to catch his breath. "We had them twenty-five to five, and we had the element of surprise. Dead to a man, with not a single enemy casualty to show." The assembled staff murmured, confused.

Gilroy's chest ached from rising acid. "Those were veteran flyboys. We had green-eyed Sector pilots taking names over Luna. What the hell happened?" *Hey, Lawrence, don't forget he's your boss.* "Sir."

"*Arlington* sent along the black boxes from several craft left over in the Valley of Giants," Walker said. "The news is... troubling. The Boxti were protected by some sort of shielding system, similar to our own kinetic barriers. It made them significantly harder to hurt. They didn't have as hard a time with us."

Walker took a moment. "Honestly, High Chancellor, I'm without words. It's almost like we're facing an entirely different force than we did at Luna. They move differently, work differently, and certainly *fight* differently. Our pilots didn't stand a chance, and they outnumbered the enemy five to one.

"The last word *Arlington* sent was a distress call from Tallus. Enemy frigates had appeared in orbit and started an aerial bombardment of the colony. That was an hour ago. Until we can reestablish communications with *Berlin* and her group, I'm recommending we seal Tallus off from the relay network."

Alexander stood. "And leave the survivors to die?"

"Sir, we need to think about the bigger picture. The Boxti were able to disrupt communications, which means they understand our relays. If they figure out how to reverse the transmission coordinates, they'll follow a buoy back here."

"Weren't they already outside?" Arthur piped up. "If they already have our coordinates, what's the harm?"

"According to the grays, no." All eyes turned toward a holographic display of Vice Admiral Winger. The New Eden Fleet commander appeared larger than life, her dress uniform weighed down by a simply absurd number of medals.

"What do they say?" Arthur asked.

"It's in the report. One small carrier group chased them here, piggybacking on their jump. We've seen the same thing happen at Titan and Rios, so it's not impossible."

"Piggybacked?" Arthur made a face.

The chief of staff glared. "Arthur, we don't have the time to go into the science of hyperspace jumps. Just assume it's magic, and let's move on."

Admiral Winger didn't miss a beat. "If the Boxti followed a jump, then they won't have our coordinates. And we didn't detect any long-range communication during the battle, so they never broadcast our location. There's no way to be sure, but I'm pretty confident we dodged a bullet here. At least, according to our new allies."

"And we're to take their word as gospel?" Arthur asked. "We hardly know anything about these creatures, and we're affording them a lot of weight in our decision making."

The high chancellor pounded the table. "Quiet, everyone! We're done discussing the possibility of abandoning our citizens." The high chancellor stared in stony silence at a nearby monitor. Footage of the attack on New York City played in a constant loop.

The feed on one set played a far different scene. Outside the makeshift Nangolani embassies, protests became riots. Buildings were raided and burned to the ground, and diplomats were dragged into the streets and beaten. Police in Melbourne had to use fire hoses to disperse a crowd that nearly lynched a group of visiting naval officers. It was knee-jerk xenophobia, and it showed little sign of stopping.

Aboard the high chancellor's ship, the mood was dark. Staffers busied themselves with various tasks to avoid getting in the way. Military officers shouted into telephones and slammed their fists on desks. Politicians talked with aides planetside, trying to get ahead of the story. The less scrupulous men and women thought of ways this tragedy could work in their favor.

The high chancellor gave a weary smile. He was only forty, but the past few weeks had taken their toll. "It's terrible, but all I can think about is my election." He leaned back in his chair. "My first one, I mean. I never thought about going into politics before that."

Walker nodded. "I remember. It was about a week after Titan fell, right? All those interviews with you and the surviving members of the Earth Council."

"The Treaty of Tseang, they called it. Take a former rebel and make him into the savior of humanity." He crossed his arms and frowned. "I wish they'd picked someone else."

The Fleet commander shrugged. "You'd have ended up on Phobos, stuck in prison. All things considered, you're not doing too bad."

Jerry approached from across the room. The chief of staff seemed to be holding up better than the rest of the cabinet. His shirt was wrinkled, but his eyes were bright. "Sir, Admiral Gilroy has the rescue going in shifts, twenty-four-seven." He handed over reports, detailing the reconsolidating effort on the homeworld. "He's prepared to move to the surface to lead the counteroffensive. Walker can take the fight to Tallus."

The high chancellor stared out the nearby porthole. "How did this happen? How could someone do this?"

"We can't think about them as people, Alexander. This is an alien race, something we've never dealt with before. Who knows how they justify this genocide?"

"We do," a voice said from behind.

Admiral Walker looked over his shoulder. There in the hall stood Anduin and his entourage. Two soldiers guarded their leader, rifles slung. Behind them walked a shorter Nangolani wearing a simple green blouse and black pants. Though he had only spoken with the aliens a few times, Walker had started to notice the differences in the sexes. Men of the species seemed taller and more muscled, and their faces were often long and thin. Females tended toward the smaller side, with round faces and large expressive eyes. Their features were much closer to what humanity perceived as normal, a trait xenobiologists found mind-boggling. They also were the only members of the species that grew hair, straight and shiny black. If you squinted, they could easily be human.

This one's skin had a blue tinge that seemed iridescent. That had been another startling discovery. Television and films tended to paint alien life as monochromatic. Nature, it seemed, just didn't work that way. Like humans, the Nangolani came in all colors and combinations. Some bore intricate birthmarks or a pattern of lines and dots. They ranged from pale blue to dark charcoal, and everything in between. The admiral wondered if their species had the same trouble with racism as his own. He could recall with painful ease the ignorant and hateful letters read on the news after Burton had been named high chancellor. Six hundred years had done little to calm that fight, apparently.

Anduin stepped forward, his eyes moist. "I am so sorry, but I fear your world is lost. If the Boxti have begun siege of a planet, they will not rest until it is either in their hands or destroyed."

"How could you hold this information from us?" Arthur demanded. "Millions are at risk. *Millions!* Can you even understand that?"

Anduin held up his hands. "We had no idea the Boxti had a force of that magnitude this close to one of your planets."

"Bullshit," Arthur shouted. "It was your intel that led our group to attack their scouting party." He glared at the alien emperor. "What did you think would happen?"

"We thought you would win." This came from the new, shorter alien. The voice was clearly feminine, with a strange accent that placed the emphasis slightly off. Her glossy hair fell to her shoulders and her eyes shined like amber. "The Boxti posses powerful technology, greater than even our own, but they are not invulnerable. Your ships are weaker, but your pilots of much greater skill. That they would fail to eliminate a small scouting party had been thought of as a remote outcome. Unfortunately, the retaliation on a nearby planet was the expected result of that contingency. They are prone to acts of vengeance."

"Who the hell are you?" Arthur asked.

Jerry elbowed him hard in the ribs. "Watch your tone, Arthur."

Anduin held up a hand to calm the group. "We take no offense. Your people have only just learned the cruelty of this alien menace. Anger is to be expected, and we are aware of the tendency to 'shoot the messenger,' as your kind puts it." The emperor gestured to the younger Nangolani. "This is Mara Nox Booren, a historian and senior scientist of our civilian fleet."

"Fa'hnaki lan," she said. "It is an honor, High Chancellor Burton." Mara held out her hand and smiled. She seemed much more at ease in replicating human expressions, and the feeling seemed genuine. The high chancellor took her hand, noting it was far more delicate than the soldiers and politicians he'd met so far. He bowed slightly, a custom observed of the alien race, and this seemed to please the assembled group.

"Civilian fleet," the high chancellor said, curiously. "Emperor Anduin, you never mentioned that there were civilians in your armada."

"It was necessity. What began as a simple convoy for myself and several prominent politicians became a desperate run as the Boxti closed in on our homeworld. We gathered into an endless procession that included several scientific vessels and transports. As we rescued our outer colonies from attack, our military strength grew in numbers, but so did our stock of women and children."

Mara stepped in. "I apologize, Mr. High Chancellor. Our race is known for caution, a lesson proven wise through generations of peace with our neighbors. We weren't eager to reveal every detail of our fleet without learning more about your people."

"I'd say you know more about our people than you let on," Arthur said. "You know our customs, our rank structure. You

WHEN THE STARS FADE

can speak our languages and your pronunciation is exquisite. How long have you been watching us?"

Mara smiled. "We have had scouts watching Earth for almost three hundred of your years. Not piloted vessels, just drones. We wanted to make contact, but the distances were astronomical. Our understanding of—how do you call it—Blue Space is only now growing into something useful. All of our travel was once restricted to a single, all-encompassing system.

"JohGal, our star, absorbed a white dwarf many millions of years ago. The two solar systems combined, merging perpendicular to one another before settling into one solar plane. The combination of planets allowed several habitable bodies to form. When we gained access to the stars, we had a bountiful realm to populate. Only recently have we begun venturing deeper into space, and that came with the help of other species."

"Why watch us then?" Arthur pushed off Jerry as the older man tried to quiet him. "To take our drive technology?"

Mara closed her eyes. When she opened them, her lids were moist with tears. "We are desperate, and there is no shame in that. The Boxti have cornered us time and again, always at grave cost. We reached out to so many species, only to be turned away for fear of reprisals from the Horde.

"But then we found you. Without a means to reach you, we could only watch from afar. We learned new art forms, heard new music, and fell in love with your devotion to each other. The human race is unique in the galaxy for their compassion. No other alien civilization we've encountered would give so much to help out those in need."

Arthur scoffed. "So that's it? We're some shining beacon of light in a cold, dark universe? It sounds more like you're trying to placate us."

"Christ, Arthur." Jerry blushed.

"You're not perfect," Mara said. "But you are strong. And stubborn. The Boxti admire the first but abhor the other. They would be drawn to you eventually, but your hubris would lead to your destruction. We believed then, and I still do now, that our mutual survival depends on cooperation."

Now it was the high chancellor's turn to be incredulous. "You came here without knowing how we'd react? What about the rest of your planet? The rest of your people? What do they think about all this?"

Mara turned to face the emperor, her face contorted.

Anduin frowned. "I don't think now is the most appropriate time." He looked at the humans, emotion rippling across his withered face, before nodding to Mara. "Tell them," he said.

"We lost contact with Nangol less than a year after our evacuation. We had fled across the galaxy, and by this time the armada was larger than what you have seen. Emperor Anduin and the other elders decided that our mission was to continue forward and seek out help. It was my suggestion that we reach out to you, and I was humbled when the request was approved."

"The Boxti caught up with us a few jumps from your home planet," Anduin said. "Not their invasion force, by Darna Wo, but a raiding party. That was what chased us across the galaxy to your front door."

Admiral Walker looked skeptical, but gave the aliens some space nonetheless. "You've said their armada is massive. How is it that they're in so many different systems? How did they find Tallus?"

"The Boxti are not a single race," Mara began, "but rather a civilization built on the backs of slaves. We believe the native Boxti have all but died out, but their goals of conquest remain the same. By the time Nangol fell, over a hundred species had surrendered to the Horde. Their fleet may number in the trillions, spread across the galaxy. Tallus is located near several gas giants, each rich in valuable chemicals. The Boxti most likely stumbled upon it by accident, and they would not have thought to look for any natives."

"Why not?" Jerry asked.

Mara crossed her arms and looked at the chief of staff. "The Boxti are segregated, and only the higher castes are allowed to make contact with alien races."

The high chancellor and his staff stared at the delegation, unsure what to think. There was no way to confirm the aliens' story, but turning on humanity's newfound ally wouldn't solve anything. The high chancellor sighed.

"I understand that you must be cautious, but this kind of secrecy will poison our future." Alexander let out a calming breath. "We need you to be honest with us if we hope to survive."

Anduin nodded. "I agree, High Chancellor. From now on, my people will share intelligence that is vital to the war effort, no matter how small. And furthermore, Mara shall be attached to you, for use in whatever manner you deem fit. She will share our culture and knowledge, and assist you in research and development."

"Thank you," the high chancellor said.

Mara bowed her head. "I will teach you everything I know about our people."

"First," the high chancellor said, "I need everything you know about the Boxti."

Tallus Orbit

CAMERON KNEW SOMETHING WAS wrong. Terribly wrong. Balls-out, what-the-fuck-is-going-on-with-this-universe *wrong*. Within minutes of closing with the enemy, the Y-fighters demonstrated air superiority with a vengeance. They bobbed and weaved with incredible precision, their return volleys tearing through the Phoenix's triple-plated armor. Two of his wingmen fell in the first few seconds, while others lost stabilizers and weapon systems. An escort destroyer, the TFD *Tripoli*, ate a barrage of missiles and split amidships, the giant wound vomiting flames.

The alien craft flew tighter than before, more coordinated within their units. They absorbed the bullets from the gauss rifles with a reflective shield that shimmered with each hit. After double-teaming a fleeing fighter, Cameron and George managed to wear down its protection enough to land a shot into the engine. It knocked the craft out of commission. Another Harpy came along to finally destroy it.

"Jesus," George said, kicking down his afterburner. "When did they find their teeth?"

A glowing red bolt flew past Cameron's canopy, scraping along his starboard wing. "I don't know," he said. "Shit. They're everywhere." He rolled hard to the right, barely avoiding a frontal collision with an incoming fighter. Pulling a stomach-churning 180, he joined his friend in pursuit. They alternated fire, sending hundreds of rounds into the Boxti's shield before the bullets struck home. As the enemy exploded into chunks, Cameron looked at the battlefield with wide eyes. The fight was only minutes old, and already a quarter of the Terran fighters were lost.

The plan had been to distract the enemy while the civilian evacuation continued. With the number of Terrans falling faster each minute, the ruse wouldn't last long. A Seed bomber, attempting to down an enemy frigate, flew into a field of flak, and shattered into pieces. The TFD *Florence* fired a main gun volley into the center of one of the smaller ships. Truck-sized tungsten slugs tore through the enemy's shields, plowing through the hull. Still, the frigate managed to stay aloft, firing a return volley that knocked out *Florence's* engines.

"All fighters," Shandras' voice came over the net. "Focus on their squadrons. We've begun civilian evacuation. Buy as much time as you can."

George and Cameron flew in tight spirals, narrowly avoiding enemy fire. Their kinetic shields flared and sputtered with each near miss. One alien fighter dove toward the pair, guns spitting bright red bolts.

"Break!"

Cameron went left while George went right. The Boxti craft zipped in between, hitting nothing. George pulled his yoke back hard, veering into a collision course. Before Cameron had a chance to warn him, George slammed into the back of the Y-fighter. For a split second, the two ships seemed to be locked together. Then the alien began to break away. George squeezed the trigger, sending dozens of metal slugs into the belly of the enemy craft. It broke apart around him, fiery chunks of metal slapping the sides of his canopy.

"Holy shit," George said. "That's one way to get them."

"Are you okay?" Cameron asked.

George looked over. "Never better. Now don't you ever let me do that again."

"No problem. I think I have a better idea."

Cameron launched a cluster missile, a large munition that exploded into a dozen guided warheads upon launch. The smaller projectiles hunted down three Y-fighters. Traveling at a lower rate of speed, the cluster bombs bypassed the shielding and embedded in the alien hull before exploding. In an instant, three enemy vessels left the fight for good.

"Fuck yes!" Cameron activated his radio. "Wolfpack, this is Wolf One. Switch to cluster missiles, their shields miss them." He launched another munition, watching as it chased down another two Boxti fighters. Going off a hunch, Cameron pulled up his gauss cannons' firing system controller and lowered the velocity to targeting speed. "George, give me some cover. I'm gonna try something stupid."

"Sounds good to me. I'm shadowing."

Cameron found a lone Boxti bomber looping around for another run at *Berlin*. He squeezed the triggers, watching the tracers chase the enemy ship until the system finally zeroed in. The rounds bounced off the shield at first, but the next volley slipped inside and chewed up the magazine compartment. Spiraling out, the bomber blew up from the inside in a dazzling display of gold and crimson.

"Holy shit, Cam." George pulled up into a support position. "What did you do?"

"Switch cannons to target speed," Cameron said. "These are kinetic barriers; they respond to speed, not impact. Spread the word. These bastards are ours."

New Freeman
Tallus

ON TALLUS, THE EVACUATION was finally showing some success. Three shuttles had managed to escape the atmosphere and reach the node. Another fifteen had begun their launch sequence, and two Arks were preparing to make a run for the relay.

In the smoky sky, the Terran fighters fought to buy every second for the fleeing civilians. The fires below raged onward, threatening to consume the entire continent.

This wasn't evacuation. It was the full-scale abandonment of an entire world, all in the space of a few hours. But the planetary immolation continued, and there simply wasn't time for everyone to make it offworld.

In the skies overhead, human ships erupted into pieces, tumbling down into the atmosphere. The mighty carrier *Berlin*, placing itself between the evacuating ships and the enemy, became the prime target for the Boxti war party.

It couldn't take another hit.

Tallus Orbit

THE ENGINES TOOK A critical hit, and *Berlin* listed hard to port. Without the thrusters maintaining a planetary orbit, Tallus' gravity started to pull the carrier into a death spiral. Across a wide gap of space, an enemy hive moved closer to the wounded Terran ship. The word was out, and soon a half dozen ion frigates joined their companion in targeting *Berlin*. The enemy closed in like predators around prey.

"All hands, brace." Captain Shandras held his tether with one hand while the other gripped his midsection. He had at least two broken ribs, care of his own navigation officer. The young man hadn't been tied down when a missile ripped open the after oxygen generator. Shandras came away lucky in that impact. The other officer was dead.

Shandras watched as the enemy carrier arrived at standoff range and prepared to fire. The frigates lined up, charging their weapons for a finishing blow. The captain kept his eyes open, wanting to face death with honor. Around the bridge, to his immense pride, his officers joined in taking in their final moments with dignity and defiance.

Suddenly the enemy carrier pitched to the side, a blinding blossom of fire growing from its midsection. From overhead, the supercruiser *Valley Forge* bore into the battlefield, all stations firing. Missile tubes launched school bus-sized warheads into the frigates, saving the mammoth ten-meter rounds for the hive. Each volley collapsed shields and gouged gaping wounds in the enemy fleet. *Midway* appeared moments later, Phoenix and Seed ships spilling from the hangars and taking the fight to the Boxti. A dozen destroyers and frigates followed behind, picking off fighters and bombers. As soon as they cleared Blue Space, the cavalry let loose a torrent of screaming missiles and lead.

"*Berlin*, this is *Midway* actual." The bridge erupted in cheers at the sound of Commodore Osaka's voice. "Fall back to the rear of our formation and prepare for exfil."

Aboard *Midway*, Commodore Hiro Osaka gazed at the battlefield with furious determination. "I want every bird in the air in the next twenty seconds. Alpha wing, focus on the frigates. Bravo on the fighters and destroyers. And send a message to *Valley Forge*—I want that hive ripped apart." Officers and enlisted snapped to, racing around the bridge to carry out the commander's orders. On the flight line, the hangar chiefs released *Midway*'s complement of fighters and bombers, each armed to the teeth. "Battle Group, weapons free. Fire at will."

VALLEY FORGE UNLEASHED ANOTHER salvo, obliterating one of the Boxti heavy cruisers. Captain DeHart gripped his armrests, his stomach still churning from the trip through Blue Space. "You heard the commodore. All systems lock on that fucking hive. Burn it down!"

Wave after wave of fighters smashed into the enemy fleet. Within minutes, the tide had turned for the Terrans. With renewed energy, *Berlin* and the remaining escort rejoined the fight.

The hive carrier took another hit, losing a chunk of its engine. Drifting and venting from every angle, the ship turned its weapons back toward Tallus. It fired indiscriminately, missing the landmass by a large margin. Seconds later, a round from *Valley Forge* ripped into the center of the Boxti craft, obliterating the engine and the carrier. Explosions racked the hive, splitting it in pieces.

As the Terrans watched, celebrating their victory, they saw a massive blue vortex appear on the far side of the fray. Space bubbled and frothed, the glow casting shadows across the battlefield. A giant dreadnought, easily five times the size of *Valley Forge*, emerged from the ether. Every inch of hull was double-plated and spiked, with turrets in every direction. Four scythe-shaped arms protruded from the front like thorns dipped in blood. Cannons jutted from every surface, all turning to face the human battle group. But it didn't bother engaging them. As every human in the system gazed on, a single black missile launched from underneath the starboard plane. The obelisk-shaped projectile dropped down through the atmosphere, arcing into the center of New Freeman.

Blinding white light blossomed in the center of the city and expanded until it swallowed the entire continent. As the light faded, a mushroom cloud the size of a mountain emerged through the thick ceiling of smoke. From the center of impact, a wall of fire streaked outward, a tsunami of hellfire, destroying everything in its path. Buildings crumbled. The seas boiled. The sky fell. In a stroke, the Boxti had turned Tallus into hell.

Captain Shandras watched in horror from his post. Death had been a simple chore to stare down in the face of such darkness. He swooned, catching himself on his chair. Though he didn't realize it, he was crying. Newman walked over, short of breath. He gripped the commander's shoulder.

"Jesus, sir."

Tallus Orbit

BERLIN FIRED ITS TWO-METER cannon, perforating a frigate on the far side of the fray. Three missiles came back in answer, tearing a hole in the storage compartments. Frozen food and clothing supplies vented into the upper atmosphere of Tallus, lost forever. The crew raced to seal the exposed section of carrier.

TMF *Haifa*, a missile frigate, unleashed a stream of high explosives toward the enemy carrier. Thirty bombs, each carrying a half-ton of explosives, raced toward the hive-shaped craft. A passing Boxti bomber caught one in the belly, detonating its entire payload. The explosion sent another fighter pinwheeling into a frigate's shield, which failed under the impact. Bits of hull and glass floated in dense clouds around the battlefield.

Fireballs bloomed upon the missiles' impact with the alien carrier. Large chunks of hull flew in every direction. Flames raced through the interior, engulfing ships still parked in the hangar. Still the hive drove forward, returning fire with glowing red slugs and barbed projectiles. The enemy frigates, seeing the bigger ship under attack, ceased their assault on Tallus and turned all attention on *Berlin*. Engines flared white hot as the alien craft rushed toward the Terrans.

On the far side of the battlefield, *Berlin* pushed forward to form a physical barrier between the Boxti and the escaping civilian craft once more. Enemy fire peppered her port flank, gouging holes in the thick armor plating. The escort squadron broke off, leaving four fighters to act as a last line of defense while the rest charged in. The *Florence* continued to fire, despite floating dead in the water. On the bridge, the elderly commander barked orders with the energy of an academy cadet while his crew raced to comply. As they began to target a new frigate, a spiny yellow bomb sent by one of the Boxti bombers pierced the stern and obliterated the destroyer.

SINGED AND SCARRED BY narrowly avoided fire, Cameron flew into the sortie. The twin gauss rifles under his wings sang constantly, barrels rocking hard enough to shake the canopy. The ammo counter on his HUD raced toward zero. He figured he only had a few minutes before he was spent. Granted, he also figured he'd be dead in less than that.

An explosion to his five o'clock rocked his ship up and to the left. As Cameron steadied his flight path, he saw George appear. The young pilot burst through a field of fiery debris, whooping and cheering in his cockpit.

"That's six," George said.

"Six what?" Cameron performed a quick system check. He had two hundred rounds of tungsten ammo and a single Harpy left.

George pulled in closer, firing a quick burst to deter a Boxti fighter. "Six beers you owe me." The enemy ship turned away, smoke pouring from holes in its tail.

Red bolts shot up between their cockpits and the two Terrans broke formation. Cameron barrel rolled and dodged a blistering volley of fire until he found himself staring at the crimson glow of an alien engine. He let loose his last missile. It flew into the enemy craft and exploded with a clap. The Y-fighter burst into a red and yellow star. Cameron kicked his afterburner and pushed through the flames.

George's Phoenix shook from the impact of another bolt, which tore through his hull. Already the outside of his fighter looked like swiss cheese. It was amazingly lucky that a shot hadn't punctured his fuel line. He checked his six and found a Boxti fighter sniffing his exhaust. "Fuck," he said. "Cam, I need a little help here."

Cameron pulled up behind his friend's pursuer. This Boxti ship looked different. Though shaped like a Y-fighter, the wings were tipped in red metal, like a thorn dipped in blood. *Must be a squadron marking*, Cameron thought. He squeezed his trigger, firing a short burst into the enemy. Rear shields flared and failed, allowing a few rounds to punch into the hull. Immediately the craft broke pursuit, leaving a smoking trail in its wake.

"Drop it to five beers, George."

George chuckled. "I'm not counting that one. He was falling into my genius trap." He moved his fighter to port, but the engines flared out. The Phoenix shook violently. "Okay, I need to land. Stabilizers are fried." He pressed the pitch down, but nothing happened. "Starboard jets are out. Electronics are shorted. Shit, Cam. I may have legitimately broken it this time. Do you think I can take it back for a refund?"

"Did you keep the receipt?" Cameron asked, steering his ship up and over George's. He released the tow cable. It thunked into place.

"I never keep the receipt," George said.

"You probably should've kept the receipt. I'd put it up for auction." He accelerated until the tow line drew taut and turned toward *Berlin*. "*Berlin*, this is Wolf One."

"Wolf One, *Berlin*. Send it."

Cameron scanned his radar. Most of the fighting had moved off toward the far side of the planet. The Terrans weren't winning. Far from it. Most of the strike group was being chased by the Boxti toward the enemy carrier, which refused to die despite enormous holes punched straight through its body. "I'm towing a downed fighter. Requesting emergency crews on standby in hangar, and refit."

They flew past a dozen wrecks, mostly Phoenix fighters and Sparrows. A Seed bomber limped up beside them, half of its hull simply gone. Cameron marveled that it was moving under its own power at all. He waved to the pilot, a cheery-looking blonde who smiled back. A broken piece of TFD *Florence* spiraled down toward Tallus, caught in the gravity well.

"Wolf One, you are cleared on approach. Be advised, hangar deck is not clear. Watch for crew guidance. *Berlin* out."

"Are we in trouble?" George asked.

Cameron started to answer, then realized his entire body was shaking from the cocktail of fear and adrenaline he'd just downed. He took a few quick breaths to steady his voice. "Nah. This is just like we drilled, you know? Self-recovery in the middle of an alien invasion. You should have learned this shit in basic." His teeth were chattering, but he wasn't cold.

"Just go faster." George slumped down in his seat, smacking the now useless controls with a growl. "Much faster if possible."

Pain crept up Cameron's throat. It felt like acid reflux, but he knew better—his heart rate was in the 150s, easy. Suddenly, waiting in line to land felt insane. An urge to break into a dead sprint made his legs ache. He laughed, sudden and loud.

"Take it easy," Cam said. "They're getting out the good vodka for us."

"You're dead to me," George said, a smile in his voice. "How can you still drink that crap when I've taught you scotch is superior?"

Cameron switched from little, quick breaths to long, slow ones. He tried to think of a comeback, but all of his brain's resources had been rerouted into a full search of the area for threats. He scanned the skies, found nothing—but he felt heat from aft.

"Anyone in our rear-view?"

George tapped on his monitor, but the screen remained black. "Electronics are still out. I must have lost a cell back there. Ask our friend if hers are still reading." He gestured to the pilot in the bomber.

Turning on the jump frequency, Cameron called out. "Wounded bomber, this is Wolf One. Do you read me?"

The blonde turned and winked. "Lima Charlie, Wolf."

"How do our skies look?"

A pause while the bomber checked for radar signatures. "I've got gremlins in my radar. These ghost images keep appearing and disappearing."

The Phoenix bucked hard, and Cameron swore. It felt like they were flying through a thunderstorm. "George, are my engines firing?"

"Can't see from here."

Cameron looked over at the bomber. "Hey, are you feeling this chop?"

The female pilot glanced over. Before she could say a word, two red bolts shot down from directly overhead, shattering her cockpit and destroying the canopy. The craft pinwheeled to the side before the flames reached the fuel reserves. The tanks erupted, taking the rest of the vessel with them.

Cameron looked up, spotting the same strange Y-fighter above his position. It was larger than the rest, with more bulk and armor. The ship dove into them, its blood-tipped wings flashing orange with light from the nearby suns. Its wings spewed spiny missiles that trailed coiling black smokewakes.

Looking back on this moment, Cameron would reflect that it all happened in less than three seconds.

"Cam, look out!" George activated his jets and rammed Cameron out of the way of the missile. The projectile impaled George's broken wing. The tow line snapped. Cameron spiraled away, wrestling with his controls, but by the time he righted himself, fire and shrapnel were already drilling through every part of George's ship. His friend looked him in the eye, face calm and resigned. Flames engulfed him.

Cameron tried to breathe, but his throat was full of cotton.

"Punch out!" he wheezed.

It felt like he was listening to a different person, an older man who'd smoked three packs a day for the last decade. He'd meant to scream the order the instant the Boxti missile struck George's wing, but the explosion happened in the few fleeting instants it took his brain to deliver the command to his mouth.

He spotted the Y-fighter turning for another pass. Cameron looked down at his HUD. Seventeen rounds remaining. His heart rate had dropped to a comfortable sixty beats per minute.

With a sneer, he stomped on the afterburner and charged.

Kronos

ALPHA DID NOT WANT to go quietly. Josh hadn't expected an easy run, but these soldiers fought like they were possessed. He could sympathize. These were, after all, fellow brothers-in-arms defending their home turf. When it was over, they'd be comrades again, but for now, he forced himself to think of them as the enemy.

The last three rooms had been costly. He'd called in Alexa's reinforcements after a stray round clipped Valenzuela. Gordon and Naren had fallen to a tripmine shortly thereafter, and Alberts had taken a round to the throat before they'd cleared the final room on the floor. With only five soldiers left to take the complex, the odds of success continued to dwindle. They'd used the last of their grenades flushing out a nest of heavy gunners in a hallway, leaving them with only their rifles to take the loft. Eight Alpha troops stood between them and victory. If they could kill four more and hold until the siren, they would win the game by a hair.

"Throw down your arms," he called out, crouching by the final doorway. "Let's start discussing terms of surrender." It was a bluff, and everyone knew it. Even if Josh had a full squad, they had to know it was Charlie and not Delta in their base.

A voice called out. "We accept your surrender!"

A few exhausted laughs sounded around the compound. Josh smiled.

"Zev? You still alive?"

"So far. Is that you, Rantz?" Zev said. "Coulda sworn I killed you a month ago. Didn't I shoot you by the resupply post?"

Josh shared a glance with Dax but addressed Zev: "That was you? At our camp?" He signaled for Dax to pull his DaVinci out. The big man grumbled, slinging his rifle over his back and lugging out the heavy weapon. Josh continued: "That was some mean shit. I was taking a nap a few klicks away."

"Sorry about your company. Why don't you come in here and I'll make it up to you?"

Nicholai and Malcolm, Alexa's support gunners, hunkered behind a table and reloaded their magazines. Each tapped their ammo pouch and held up a finger, signaling that they had a single magazine remaining. At the far end of the hall, aiming a machine gun at the door, Felix waved to indicate he was ready. Josh and Dax rose up and prepared to breach.

"Last chance, Zev."

The Alpha sergeant responded with a burst of rifle fire. Nicholai ducked just in time. Josh pulled a small pouch from his thigh pocket. It was a heater from his combat rations. He sucked in a mouthful of water and spit into the sack, sealing it tight. The heater began to boil, gasses building up inside the enclosed bag. When he felt the bubbles reach a breaking point, he tossed the heater inside the room.

"Frag out!"

The decoy worked, exploding with a sudden bang and causing the Alpha soldiers to flinch. Josh and Dax charged the room, firing on full auto. They killed two soldiers with their initial burst and drove in, taking cover behind upturned cots. Nicholai and Malcolm rushed in behind them, shooting from the hip. They took down another two before being cut apart by heavy machine gun fire. Dax growled and lunged at the gunner, leaping over the cot and firing at the same time. He hit the man in the sternum, but took a round to the shoulder from Zev. Felix came into the room but was hit in the face before he could get off a shot. Dax hit the wall, bowling over a young private who had been cowering in the corner. Josh struggled hand-to-hand with a gangly corporal, trying to reach his pistol while fending off a knife.

Zev continued to fire, putting two more rounds in Dax's chest before his rifle suddenly locked up. He slapped the magazine, trying to fix the jam. Josh seized the moment. He brought a knee up into the corporal's stomach, opening a space to draw his pistol and fire two rounds at point blank. The soldier fell back into a cot and slumped to the ground. Josh pivoted and rushed forward, tackling Zev into the corner. The bigger man ripped his rifle away and tossed it aside, drawing a knife. Josh rolled out from under and aimed his sidearm, but Zev was faster. He lashed out with the blade, just barely missing Josh's throat.

Josh fired a round but missed wide, hitting the wall. Zev charged in screaming, driving them both through the window. Boards exploded outward as they fell ten feet to the ground outside, hitting the dirt with a thud that knocked out their wind. Josh scrambled to his feet, fighting to catch his breath as the enemy searched for his knife. The pistol lay in the sand a few feet to the side, just behind the last Alpha soldier. Zev beckoned Josh forward, grinning.

"Just you and me now, Josh."

Josh pulled his own knife and twirled it in his hand, holding it blade down. His heart pounded in his ears as the hulking sergeant rushed him again. Josh sidestepped and brought his knee up, connecting with Zev's solar plexus. The impact spun them both around.

Zev rubbed his stomach, wincing. Sweat ran freely down both their faces, landing in sopping drops on their armor.

The larger sergeant hissed. "Are you done yet?"

Josh readied his weapon. "Nope." He kicked off with his back foot, lunging hard with his knife. They struck at the same time, catching each other's arms at the last moment, blades inches from each other's faces. Josh knew he was overpowered and allowed the momentum to slip his arm inside his opponent. He countered the spin, using his hips to launch Zev up and over his head. The big man flew in the air and slammed down on the ground. Josh leapt on top, using his knees to pin the soldier's arms to the dirt. Zev bucked hard, knocking Josh to the side. He barely was able to keep hold of the knife as they grappled on the ground. Zev grabbed the weapon and threw it to the side. He snatched Josh by the vest and dragged him to his feet. With incredible strength, he threw the smaller soldier into the door of one of the trucks. Zev walked over to the downed man, breathing heavily.

"You really thought you could take me? I've got you by fifty pounds."

Josh lay on his back, sore as hell. He looked at up. "Didn't have to beat you," he said. "Just keep you occupied long enough."

Zev realized he was standing alone on the battlefield.

Josh touched a finger to his headset. "Take the shot."

On the ridge, Alexa squeezed the trigger. The bullet nailed Zev in the chest. He dropped.

She jumped and let out a shout that echoed in the canyon.

Josh crawled to his feet as Alexa ran down the ridge toward the base. He pulled his radio from his belt and twisted the knob to the command channel. He leaned against the J10 for support, his right arm tingling. He felt like he'd been hit by a truck. Considering the size of his enemy on the ground, it made sense. Lights snapped on overhead, and Josh saw nine separate Seraphs floating low over the complex, the glowing windows filled with onlookers. He waved.

"Eagle One-Two, this is Caveman White One. Enemy company has been destroyed, vicinity Foxtrot November eight-three-four-two-one-three. Requesting immediate evac and class six support." Alexa and Felix jogged in, sweating from the run. They grinned as Josh waited for the response from the command net.

"Caveman, this is Eagle. Endex declared. All suits powering down. Stand by for immediate pickup and debrief. Outstanding job. Eagle out."

Seraph Three
Kronos

APPLAUSE SOUNDED FROM ALL aboard the floating platform. Even Sasha stood as the triumphant Charlie Company collected their brethren and marched out into the open. In the history of the Crucible, no company had ever scored this kind of a come-from-behind victory. Ever.

The observer shuttle was emptier than just a few hours before. Word of a Boxti attack at Tallus had spread over the Net, and several politicians remembered that they had constituents on that planet. Markov and Sasha didn't mind. It meant a quieter environment to observe and decide.

"You have to admit," Markov said. "Rantz ended that with spectacular flair."

Sasha shrugged. "Flair is showy—not something you want with special forces." He pointed to the enormous staff sergeant on the ground. "Zev is the man you want. Maybe Dax, but his sports career will cause us problems."

Markov scoffed. "No one follows the Grudge anymore, at least not in fifty years. If anything, they'll be happy to have the dozer spot open up." He tapped Josh's file. "I'm telling you, this is the candidate."

"He scored lower in all events than his squad," Sasha reminded. "He's not that great a shot, and he lost that fight handily. Why would you ever want him for the program?"

The scientist stared out the window with binoculars, watching the young sergeant scramble around the fort. Josh checked on each of his soldiers, making sure they were unharmed. He made them drink water, or strip down if they were too hot. Markov nodded knowingly. "He's got heart." He smiled at his traveling companion. "And more than that, he's got balls."

CAMERON CHARGED, ENGINES SPEWING white-hot fire. He could just make out the Boxti ace attacking a small group of bombers. He slalomed through a few other Y-fighters, sights trained on George's murderer. As he neared the ace, a Boxti destroyer appeared from nowhere. One moment Cameron was looking at clear skies, the next he was staring at the belly of an enemy ship. The pilot banked hard, firing off his forward rockets, but his momentum was too great. With a sickening crunch, the Phoenix plowed into the destroyer.

Alarms sounded as smoke filled the canopy. Cameron fumbled for his emergency ejection handle. As he tumbled, he was faintly aware of a sudden bright blue glow that flooded his cockpit. The Boxti ship turned, giving Cameron a view of the planet's surface. His stomach dropped. *When did another ship join the fight?*

Cameron stared in mute horror. Through the smoke and chaos in his fighter, he saw the sun rise on Tallus and erase the human presence from the system. His fighter shook uncontrollably, clearly in its death throes. The ejection system had malfunctioned, sealing him inside the spiraling Phoenix. He didn't know if there was anyone out there to rescue him. In a way it didn't matter. Even if they had won the field, how many had died in that bombing? Who could hope to win against such a foe? Cameron closed his eyes, tears streaming down his smoke-charred face.

"Cam?"

The voice came from nowhere. It was faint, distant, and almost imperceptible. Cameron ignored the sound and focused on the sounds of his fighter's demise. The air filter wheezed as it tried to push oxygen through ash-clogged screens. The engine stumbled, turned, and finally stopped altogether, leaving only the hum of the energy cells. Silence began to rule inside the cockpit when the voice came again.

"Cameron?"

Each breath came painfully, often punctuated with a choke or cough. Cameron tapped his radio, trying to clear the signal. "I'm here," he said, his own words barely whispered. "I'm here," he tried again with more conviction.

"Don't move, buddy. I'm coming for you."

Something moved in the darkness, a sudden burst of speed. "George?" Cameron barely had time to register the glossy black metal before blue light surrounded him. His fighter slammed violently to the side. His head connected with the canopy.

Black.

TFC Midway
Tallus Orbit

THE MUSHROOM CLOUD ROSE higher, consuming the entire sky over New Freeman. From the bridge of *Midway*, Commodore Osaka watched the horrific display with the calmest disposition. That serenity lasted until the Boxti opened Blue exits and started to flee.

"What?" Hiro glared at his comms officer.

"They're breaking contact, sir. All Boxti ships are exiting the system."

Hiro grabbed his radio. "All ships, this is *Midway*. Target the enemy's engines. Don't let them escape." It was hopeless. By the time the other ships radioed in their affirmatives, the aliens had already slipped into the ether and beyond their reach. Hiro watched helplessly as the genocidal vessels simply disappeared. He seethed, storming over to his navigation officer's console. "Fire every buoy we have into the Blue box."

"Already on the way, sir. Salvo two is firing now."

Hiro crossed his arms and watched the small pods disappear in puffs of blue. Moments later, readings appeared on the navigation computer.

"Well?"

"Sir, it takes a few minutes."

Hiro pinched the bridge of his nose. "Why?"

The officer shook his head. "Are you asking me to explain the science of plotting Blue jumps? Do we really have time?"

"I'm asking you to remember the rank on my shoulder."

The young man squirmed. "I'm sorry, sir. It should be coming up now."

The computer spat out information rapidly, slowing to a crawl after a minute. Coordinates appeared, with the last two numbers of each set snapping up and down.

"It'll get more accurate in a minute, but that's the best estimate for where they're headed." The navigation officer looked up at his commander. Hiro's face was focused off in the distance, his eyes wide with fear.

"I know those coordinates. Every commander does." He walked back to his chair and pulled the radio from its cradle. He typed a quick command into the armrest computer and waited for the line to connect. "This is Commodore Osaka to Fleet Command. Send an alert to Primus right away. The Boxti are headed to Eros." He ended the transmission and brought up a map of the Eros star system, which included the New Eden colony, as well as the training moon Kronos.

The war is coming to the Crucible sooner than we hoped, Hiro thought with grim humor.

New Eden Node
Eros

THE RELAY SYSTEM AROUND New Eden was far more complex than any other node array in the Terran galaxy. Surrounded by seven moons, each one populated, the blue and green planet represented the pinnacle of colonization. Though Tallus had been the first, and Colorum remained the most profitable, New Eden was the gem of the Colonial Federate. Almost exactly the size of Earth, and with an atmosphere rich in oxygen and nitrogen, the heavenly body had been the discovery of the century. Now, almost one hundred years since its founding, the "diamond of Eros" was close to paradise.

Located a perfect distance from the blue star Eros, the planet earned its nickname. Founded by an Israeli Ark ship, the planet had originally been called Gan Yarok, or the Green Garden, due to endless expanses of land. When more and more settlers arrived, the lush landscapes and crystalline waters invoked an image of paradise, and the moniker had stuck. New Eden's tropical climates attracted tourists by the millions. The more temperate areas to the north and south were populated by some of the largest corporations in the galaxy. Scientific research labs on the poles provided incredible opportunities for some of the best minds the Terran academies had to offer. Despite all these amenities, the cost of living was still surprisingly manageable, and New Eden hosted the largest extra-Earth population at almost seven billion inhabitants.

HIGH IN THE SKY over New Eden, resting in a gentle swell of gravitational pulls, the massive space station began its morning. Aboard the node, the team of civilian technicians monitored a constant flow of traffic. Scientific vessels routinely used Stride drives to travel to the mineral and gas mining operations on the other planets in the system. Civilians, politicians, and of course the Federal Fleet jumped in an out of system on varied trips and missions. All of this had to be carefully controlled, lest a miscalculation cause a cruiser to exit Blue Space in the path of a striding chemical hauler. It was not unlike an air traffic control network planetside, if airplanes traveled at seventy thousand miles per hour. The circular command deck was divided into three separate sections, spread like slices of a pie from the central control desk. Standard drive coordination only required five technicians, while Stride drive took up the largest footprint.

At his console near the center of Blue Traffic Control, Charley Bruins watched a small detachment from the Meir Academy disappear into the ether. It was fascinating to see the radio signature simply vanish as the ten-ton scientific research vessel entered Blue Space. He'd only had a chance to watch the event live twice, and each time the sight of that eternal maw opening and swallowing a ship whole had left him breathless. He often wondered how a scientist endured it, jumping into the unknown. The statistics attached to hyperspace made it seem so safe, but Charley couldn't bring himself to enter the void as often as the brainiacs from Meir.

He noted the movement on his log sheet—why they still used digital books was beyond him—and opened his travel sheet for the day. Blue Jumps were still controlled events, and it was unlikely he would have more than twenty in a given day. He was halfway down the list when his computer

WHEN THE STARS FADE

chirped. Charley looked up, surprised to see a new contact reading at the edge of the controlled zone. The computer chirped again, and then there were two contacts. Then three. Then seven. Then thirty.

Charley tapped on his screen. *What is happening here?* he thought. The red mass of enemy vessels continued to grow. He felt a pinch in his chest. In seconds, he had his phone in his hand.

"Sector Patrol Eros, how may I direct your call?"

Charley watched the screen, waiting for the red dots to start moving. "This is New Eden Node. I've got some strange contacts at the edge of the turnout line. It's a pretty large scattering, so I'm thinking an asteroid cluster. Still, wouldn't mind a set of eyes on."

"Understood, Eden Node. Send the coordinates and we'll have a patrol conduct a flyby."

"Much appreciated."

The operator spoke calmly. "Havoc squadron is en route, but I have been asked to check on your contingency nine plan."

Charley's throat tightened. "Ronin Protocol?"

"Are you prepared to execute, should the chancellor make the call?"

He almost didn't hear her over the drumming of his heart. "We will."

"Roger that, Eden Node. Sector out."

Charley hung up the line, his mouth filling with saliva. His stomach gurgled. His gag reflex kicked in, but he suppressed it. A full minute passed before he started to feel normal. Charley reconnected the line to the operator at Boden Pass near his home. "Operator? Can you connect me to thirteen-eleven Norfolk Avenue? I need to speak to my wife."

The Void

CAMERON AWOKE IN BLUE Space. Blood covered his right eye, casting the world in shades of purple. Around him, the cockpit vibrated with a steady hum. He looked around, trying to establish some semblance of bearing, but there was nothing; only blazing sapphire skies everywhere. The Boxti frigate that had towed him into the void was long gone, having found its exit. He was all alone, somehow still traveling through hyperspace.

Trapped.

PART
THREE

KRONOS

"I am Death, the Destroyer of Worlds. Even without
you, all the armies arrayed in opposition shall cease to be.
Therefore get up and attain glory. All of these warriors
have already been destroyed by me.
You are just an instrument."

–Bhagavad-Gita
Chapter 11, Verse 31-33
New Arjun Translation

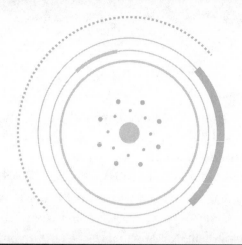

Presidential Tower
Vienna
Incorporated States of Europe

"OUR PEOPLE ARE NOT willing to divulge secrets of that nature, Magistrate."

Adeline Quinn, standing in front of the Nangolani delegation, glanced over at her boss. Jerry Ahmad hadn't said more than two words the entire negotiation. He preferred to see how his well-practiced students handled the heavy lifting. By the smile on his face, she could tell he was impressed.

You ain't seen nothing yet, she thought.

Adeline stared into the magistrate's dark eyes. "Tallus cost you a lot of clout with the administration. If you want to keep this alliance on track, you're going to have make a few concessions. Access to our mining operations are off the table."

The alien began to chant under his breath, his musical language coming out in short bursts. Finally he looked up at Adeline and nodded. "Colorum can then remain an undisclosed location. The Nangolani shall establish our own personal safe haven away from human systems, and in return you will identify areas where we may set up triage and local housing."

Adeline smiled. It had taken the better part of the evening, but the negotiations were finally drawing to a close. Far from just serving as an attaché, Adeline took center stage for the talks, owning the room and controlling the tempo with the alien delegation. She was grateful to have had Jerry in the room, just in case, but knew she did this on her own. *Diplomatic Liaison has a nice ring to it.*

Jerry beamed at his goddaughter, prouder than ever that she'd allowed herself to be dragged into this world. Even with his help, she'd faced an uphill battle to attain her position.

Emperor Anduin had been absent, leaving in place his own version of a chief of staff: the magistrate intercessor. The surprisingly tall alien wore a scarlet uniform gilded with golden lining. Bronze and silver crescents adorned the fabric, creating a flowing pattern that cascaded from his shoulders to his belt. Crimson fringes hung from his shoulder boards. He spoke with a deep baritone, another oddity after hearing the mostly soft voices of the species, and enunciated each syllable. After the pleasantries were over, Jerry had laid down the Terran requests while Adeline handled the back-and-forth. With Mara helping to translate some of the nuances of the language, the treaty was pitched.

Jerry was having fun. Talking with the Nangolani diplomats afforded him invaluable insight into their government, which differed radically from the human's.

The Colonial Federate was based around the Three Pillars, divvying power of legislation and execution amongst the high chancellor and his cabinet, the Centurial Council, and the colonial delegation. *And the military, though no one would admit how much power the admiralty wielded.* Each position was elected by a majority vote of its subordinates. Countries elected their own representatives, who voted for presidents, who elected governors and ambassadors. Those then invited the best and brightest to fill any vacant seats in the Chamber of the Hundred, as Council members ruled for life. The high chancellor was elected after a thorough vetting process and served up to three six-year terms. At least, that was how it was all intended to function. Jerry often reminded himself this was barely their tenth year as a government.

The Nangol magistrate was a different game altogether. Emperor Anduin ruled with near-absolute authority. The members of the magistrate, known as the elders, advised the head of state and executed his orders. Under them were the Domin, commanders of ships.

Jerry called it a militant monarchy. In any case, the two species at least could agree that power and responsibility had to be shared.

For obvious reasons, Nangolani ships were only allowed in Terran systems with an escort group. Fleet had enough on hand to release a small contingent of cruisers and destroyers for the duty, and the intercessor accepted the condition. As he put it, if the situations were reversed, the same would be expected.

"One must guard their home, even from supposed friends," the intercessor had said.

The aliens possessed technology that the humans did not understand, namely their proficiency with plasma and laser technology. In the hundreds of years since mankind dropped the shackles of fossil fuels in favor of fusion and fission, they still relied on archaic methods of combat. The gauss cannons, though modernized and effective, required significant stores of ammunition and limited the effective range of fighters.

The Nangolani resisted the idea of sharing their military secrets, but found a compromise. Their own knowledge of hyperspace was limited compared to the Terrans. In exchange for a look at the humans' drive systems, they would release several weapons for study.

A more tender point of the discussion focused on the recent anti-Nangolani violence that had plagued every inhabited system. What had started as a few isolated attacks was now a weekly event. The intercessor insisted that the humans deploy better security measures around the embassies. More than that, the Centurial Council needed to raise awareness among the human populace that the Boxti, not the Nangolani, were responsible for the tragic events at Tallus.

Adeline had no objections to that. In fact, steps were already in place to help calm the animosity.

Mara Nox Booren enjoyed her time in the room. It felt a treat to both take an active part in the intense negotiations and observe human interactions up close. Years of study from afar and through recorded video could not hope to capture every detail or nuance. She spoke sparingly, more content to just listen and learn.

As the talks came to an end for the day, Adeline rose from her chair and offered a hand to the magistrate intercessor. He accepted, though his face showed no emotion. Unlike some of the other aliens, he had no concept of human expression and did not try to fake it. His grip was strong and confident.

"Naku am do, Marmakan," Adeline said, her tongue tripping somewhat with the alien language. This produced a reaction, and the aliens clicked aggressively to each other.

For a moment Adeline feared she had inadvertently spoken an insult.

"Naku mai sholo." The delegation bowed their heads. "The honor is mine, Chieftain Quinn." The intercessor and his entourage collected their data pods and left the room. Before he walked through the door, the intercessor turned to face Adeline. "Your pronunciation was adequate, but try to soften the consonants next time." He left the human standing dumbfounded.

Mara and Adeline remained with the staffers and tidied up, while Jerry made small talk with some of the alien aides. Adeline ended up doing most of the work while her two cohorts simply stood and gawked.

"Why don't you boys make sure the car is ready?" Adeline asked sweetly. "Or do you want to take some photos for your personal collections?" She snapped her fingers and pointed out the door. The two aides, embarrassed, grabbed their things and fled the room.

"They can be big, dumb animals sometimes." Adeline shook her head.

Mara's head cocked to the side. "Your colleagues?"

Adeline smiled. "Those two," she pointed to the fleeing staffers. "Related to members of the Council. Do you know what we call that?"

The alien paused, her body completely still. "I believe the word is 'nepotism.'"

"Bravo," Adeline said, giving Mara a brief applause. "Someone's been studying her thesaurus." She walked around the table, collecting used cups. "Actually, though, I was looking for 'the status quo.' Sadly, hiring qualified, intelligent people like me is more the exception than the rule." She snapped her briefcase shut. "I'm sure you knew that about us. Hey, I have a question. Why English?"

Mara didn't even need to look up. "We found that seventy percent of your population spoke it fluently."

"How many languages do you speak?"

"Nangol or human?"

Now it was Adeline's turn to stare. "Let's start with mine, but now I'm curious. How many languages are there on Nangol?"

Mara stopped and stretched. "I've spent years learning English, Mandarin, and Russian. They were fairly simple compared to the ten thousand dialects once spoken by my people. Not that we still use them all."

"Fascinating."

"What's that?" Jerry asked, entering the room.

"Not that it's any of your business, but Mara here is a master linguist." Adeline handed her boss the signed treaty in a sealed folder. "How'd I do?"

"Very impressive," he said. "No, that's not accurate. You were on fire." Jerry grabbed his briefcase, slipping his phone into his pocket and throwing his bottle of water into the recycling bin. "Mara, I can't tell you how much I appreciate the assistance with translating." He winked at his goddaughter. "Though I'm sure Adeline would've loved the challenge."

Mara nodded, still focused on the task of cleaning the table. "This was different than I expected. You are a skilled negotiator. I don't think a single concession was made without equal compensation from our side."

Adeline nodded. "The art of building a treaty isn't about leaving the table happy. You have to be willing to make sacrifices; otherwise, you're not going anywhere. Give and take." She handed Jerry a stack of folders. "Today just had less of the former."

Jerry pulled his phone out and activated a note from Alexander. He showed Mara. "The high chancellor provided us with guidelines about where and when to draw the line. All we had to do was start the conversation way above expectations and walk them down into our comfort zone." He didn't admit that the entire ordeal had been significantly easier than predicted. In fact, in his fifteen years working for the government, no single table talk had ever ended so amicably. And those were between members of the same species. "I hadn't expected your people to be able to eat human food. That opened up a few possibilities we hadn't thought of."

Mara patted Jerry's shoulder. She seemed more comfortable with physical contact than the rest of her kind. Some of the Nangolani were downright skittish about being touched. "In any case, you displayed remarkable poise. I find that every minute spent with your race delivers mountains of observations. It is no wonder you have become such a dominant force in your systems."

"That and a lack of anyone else on the food chain," Adeline said.

Mara looked up, suddenly worried. "You have to eat those below your station?"

For a second she didn't respond. Then she and Jerry laughed so hard tears streamed from their eyes.

The Void

CAMERON WAITED TO DIE. The hours dragged on, and his focus blurred. Carbon dioxide was slowly building up, overwhelming the small filter in his ship. More than once, he looked outside the canopy and saw George's escape pod on his wing. In those brief moments, he believed his friend was still alive. But the mirage only lasted a moment before reality came crashing back in. He would check the filters, make a quick call out on the radio, and then relax back into his stupor.

The collision alarm sounded. Soft at first, as the object in question was far enough away not to warrant immediate action. It was just the computer saying, *Hey, you might want to turn at some point in the near future, if you don't mind me pointing it out.* Cameron checked his radar, forgetting it was powered down. That meant the alarm was from the auxiliary. He couldn't see behind him, and didn't want to risk using any more fuel. His air filter read six hours remaining, but he couldn't use it as an accurate gauge. It fluctuated every few minutes as the system prepared a new guess at Cameron's time of death.

A tear broke free from his face, danced around in the absurd gravity for a moment, then slammed into his headrest.

He decided to turn on the radar. He knew he was biding time against the inevitable, but having some active control over the end of the line was keeping him moderately sane, for the time being. He flicked the master power back on and waited while the computer rebooted. It took several seconds longer than normal, and Cameron wistfully imagined he would yell at the chief on the *Berlin* when he got back and make him replace the damned thing once and for all.

When the radar screen winked to life, the collision alarm sounded in full. Cameron watched as a large red dot appeared on the screen, racing toward his ship. Before he could make any decisions, something slammed into his fighter from behind and pushed him forward. He looked up and lost his breath.

He was back underneath the Boxti frigate. He could tell from the marks on the underside of the sensor array that this was the very same vessel that had dragged him into Blue Space. It was a medium-sized craft, about five times as big as his Phoenix. From his position, he could see the impact his fighter had made to the alien hull. *That's impossible.* The best he could guess was that their ships must be able to travel through the same wormholes at will. *Like those space whales near Eros.*

"Knock off the chatter," Cameron mumbled. "It's a miracle. Now, don't blow it."

He drained the last few drops from his water line and strapped back into his seat. No matter where it went, he was riding this fare all the way home. He looked at the filter readout and grinned at the flickering numbers. Two hours and dropping. A moment later, they redlined completely.

Cameron groaned. "Come the fuck *on!*" He punched the panel and the dial jumped back up, showing a half hour of oxygen remaining. "Just don't let me die as a bug on some alien's windshield."

The ride was not easy. The frigate dragged Cameron's ship through hyperspace at unfathomable velocity. His canopy bucked and popped and crackled. He could see the exit opening in the distance, a small point of darkness that rapidly expanded. It was an amazing sensation, riding the turbulence in a small fighter. Aboard even the largest carrier, Blue Space could be a rough journey. Cameron couldn't help but feel some excitement at being the only human to ever survive this. If, he reminded himself, he did end up surviving. It felt like riding huge swells on a surfboard, each break dropping his stomach to his feet. The world lurched, turned upside down, and they were out. Cameron took one look around and shouted in triumph.

What was it George said? 'Stars all look the same, seeing as they're giant balls of burning space magic. But Eros, that guy is something else.' Cameron would have recognized the system anyway, but his onboard computer told him so as well. Eros meant New Eden. New Eden meant humanity.

From his cockpit, Cameron saw the winking lights of different stations and satellites, all within range of his radio. If he sent a message, the alien ship would detect him and destroy him. Same if he ejected, same if he ran. Every choice would lead to him getting shot. He drummed his fingers on the console.

Without warning, the frigate fired up its engines and raced forward, closing distance with a lone red moon. *Tritan? No, Calypso? Shit, why can't I remember the goddamn—KRONOS!* The dark side loomed ahead, with only a few glowing spots marking the various bases. The pulsating engines of the thorny ship cast a red glow throughout Cameron's cockpit. Each burst rattled the pilot's teeth.

Almost an hour passed before the frigate slowed to a stop in low orbit. Cameron noticed a tingling in his fingers, another sign that his CO_2 filters were failing. He bit down on his gloved hands, savoring the pain. At least he still had feeling. But for how much longer?

The catch-22 lasted until the blinking red warning light became a solid glow on the console. If he waited much longer, he'd die anyway. The slowly overheating fuel rods meant the Phoenix was fast becoming a death trap. Cameron sat in his canopy, sweat dripping down his face, and planned.

A shudder brought his attention to the Boxti frigate. From the far side, something flailed in the dim light of distant Eros. As Cameron watched, jaw dropped in amazement, a strange creature emerged onto the hull. It crawled in zero gravity on five prehensile limbs that doubled as both foot and arm. It wore a jumpsuit and mask to protect it from the harsh environment. For a moment, Cameron sat and stared. He'd only seen some of the aliens on TV, but they were at least *humanoid.*

This was...unreal.

It dawned on him that the creature must be a Boxti crewman conducting a routine inspection of the ship. It wouldn't be long before the Boxti saw Cameron.

His timeline, it seemed, had just been accelerated. Cameron closed his eyes and thought back to a mechanical lesson regarding the Phoenix drive core.

While larger Terran ships ran on cold fusion systems, fighters operated with compressed hydrogen slush and powered fuel rods. Given the warnings that persisted even in auxiliary power, Cameron figured he didn't have much time before the entire ship became less hospitable. And less not-on-fire.

He worked quickly, flipping switches that deactivated key safety features in the fighter. His fingers hit buttons that he had been expressly told never to touch, causing alarms to activate even in low power. The entire ship seemed to be asking what exactly he thought he was doing. Cameron paused to wipe sweat from his eyes, knowing how precious each breath was as the air turned warm and sour in his mouth. Finally, figuring he'd done as much damage as possible, Cameron prepared to leave his perch.

A fighter pilot comes to see his ship as his home, and Cameron had come to love his battered, old Phoenix. She wasn't his first, but this model had kept him safe for the last few years. It seemed a shame to leave, but the only thing left inside was death. He strapped into his seat, tugging each strap of the five-point harness. As he looked up and pulled his helmet on tight, the Boxti crewman turned to face him. Its black eyes widened in a comical expression, and it pointed with a three-fingered hand-foot. He waved back and floored the afterburner.

Flames shot out the back of the Phoenix, scorching the alien hull. The journey had fused the two ships together, and instead of shooting away, the human fighter began to rotate the jumbled vessels. Slowly but surely, the larger frigate began to turn. Holding on for dear life, the Boxti crewman screamed and shook its head.

Another alarm sounded, this one even more dire than before. The engine compartment had reached a critical temperature. Cam's neck burned from the intense heat generated behind him, but he kept the afterburners rocking. He gritted his teeth, counting the rotations in his head and watching the moon spin past every fifteen seconds. His timing had to be perfect. He released the afterburner and tapped his foot against the canopy, finding the rhythm in the spin. At the last moment, as the moon began to rise into view, he gripped the yellow handle by his seat and pulled as hard as he could. The canopy exploded outward, rocketing past the frigate and out into space. Centrifugal force shot the pod at breakneck speed, pressing Cameron deep into his seat.

Cameron used small bursts of his control jets to spin around just in time to see the Phoenix's engines go critical.

Heat from the fuel rods burnt into the hydrogen chamber, igniting what remained of the accelerant. The chemicals mixed and blossomed into a bright white fireball. The explosion tore the frigate to shreds, sending chunks of the alien ship spiraling in all directions. He braced himself for the shockwave, which hit like a jackhammer moments later. Shoved by the force of the fireball, Cameron's escape pod shot toward Kronos, trailing smoke.

Seraph Three
Kronos

"I SAY AGAIN: ALL guests, please strap in for an emergency evacuation to the base. Remain calm."

Markov hadn't heard a word from the overhead speaker, so Sasha had to lash him into a chair. The scientist still had to narrow down his list to seven people, and nothing else in the world mattered at the moment. Not even an imminent attack.

No one aboard the platform had actually seen the Boxti enter the system, but they knew what the sirens meant. Red Hammer certainly had no interest in New Eden, mostly because they would lose that fight handily. If an invasion was actually happening, it meant something far worse had found them.

"Liane is a talented sniper, but we already have Alexa." Markov tapped his lip with his stylus. "Maybe we could merge them somehow, using a surgical grafter." He looked up and grinned, but Sasha was in no mood for jokes. "Maybe I need to put you in an MRI, see what happened to your sense of humor."

The old vet closed his eyes and counted to ten. The long scar on his face grew red. "If we survive the next few hours, I'm going to hit you very hard in the face."

Fort Peterson
Kronos

A STEWARD BURST THROUGH the doorway of the command room, her face red and dripping sweat. She weaved around the other soldiers on her way to the general. General Casey had taken up residence on a platform in the rear of the space, away from the glowing blue monitors and war tables. Two captains, the general's aides-de-camp, gathered and sorted information in growing piles on a nearby desk.

Fort Peterson was more an outpost than a traditional military base. The inhospitable summers on Kronos tended to chew through most large buildings, so the entire complex ended up as a series of one- and two-story metal containers welded together. The fort had been built as a temporary rest home for the training soldiers, so amenities were sparse. Now Peterson had a new purpose: preparing for the defense of the moon.

General Casey had been up already, watching the conclusion of the games, when the alarm sounded. He'd barely had time to don his jacket before his aides ran into his makeshift office and told him the bad news: Boxti warships had arrived in the system. The timing worked somewhat in his favor; he was already on Kronos for the conclusion of the Crucible. A few phone calls later and the entire moon was on alert for the incoming alien invasion.

"General Casey," the steward called out. She leaned against a war table, a large computer projection showing a massive section of Kronos. "General, the Seraphs are just now reporting in."

Casey adjusted his body armor and crossed over to the steward. Kinetic shields on the fort would protect him against bombardment, but if the invasion got this far, he wasn't about to die without a fight. He snatched a phone from one of his aides and connected the line to the games warden.

"This is Major Ashford," a female voice said.

"Ashford, this is General Casey. Why are the Seraphs just now coming back?"

The major gulped audibly. "The civilian, the doctor. He said he wouldn't leave until the fight was over. He needed all available data."

"Are you fucking kidding? I gave you a direct order to suspend the games and bring the civilians back here. For Christ, we have members of the fucking Council on those skiffs. Get them docked and load that imbecile onto the first boat to New Eden."

She stammered. "R-roger, sir. I'll get it done."

"You fucking better." He hung up and immediately sent out a new call. The line rang several times before a husky voice answered, that of Cora Winger.

"This is Vice Admiral Winger."

"Admiral," Casey said. "Where is the battle group?"

Winger shouted something over her shoulder. The sound of engines reverberating through metal echoed in the receiver. "*London* is under way, and I've brought every serviceable ship to bear. We're about thirty strong and growing."

"Make up?"

"Mostly destroyers," Winger said. She mumbled the names of ships as she read off a roster. "Counting me, we have two supercruisers. Most of our carriers are getting refit for those new sleds, so I'm short on fighters. Six of my frigates will be air denial."

Casey closed his good eye and processed the information, playing out a mock battle in his head. "We need some support. What's DeHart's ETA?"

"Another two hours?"

"Jesus," Casey swore. "How about the lift from New Eden?"

Winger tutted. "Best estimate is twelve hours to mobilize and deploy the locals. Most of Fort Metts is already emptied out supporting your training event."

Casey almost argued more, but he knew it was useless. He had fifteen thousand soldiers and only enough ammunition for a fraction. Most of the riflemen were carrying modified weapons that could only fire simunitions. He'd rarely felt so terrified.

"Cora," he said softly. "If the fight is lost up there..."

Winger cut him off. "You shut your mouth, Booker. You're too old to be playing the martyr."

"New Eden cannot fall."

"Then don't let Kronos go." She screamed at her weapons officer to bring all systems online. "When they get close, I'll get their attention. They won't have time to look your way." She paused, her voice coming back strong. "This we'll defend."

"Until the stars fade," Casey replied. He set down the phone and looked at the glowing map of Kronos. Blue symbols indicated the location of his troops in training. He waved over one of his captains. "Get ahold of the units in the field. If they're not armed, they need to be brought back here. Admiral Winger is going to have one her frigates dump a few crates of munitions at the LZ. It won't be enough, but it's a start."

The captain nodded. He took off toward the center of the room, leaping over a railing to talk to one of the communication sergeants. Casey pulled the other aide in close.

"If we can't hold this position, we'll need to fire off all of our GReMs."

"Sir?" the young captain said.

"Ground Reduction Mines. This moon is full of them, all around key locations. Coordinate with the command sergeant major and get the codes. I want a remote programmed in the next hour."

After the aide disappeared, the steward approached. "Sir, what do you want me to do?"

Casey leaned on his desk, his eye running over the details of his field reports. "Stay on the line until Captain DeHart arrives. I need him here as soon as possible." The steward turned to leave. "One more thing." Casey stared into the young girl's face. "Find a rifle."

Kronos

ALEXA GRABBED JOSH IN a bearhug, squeezing him so hard his ribs hurt. He laughed out loud, putting his helmet against hers. When Alexa finally let go, Josh walked over to where Zev lay on the ground and waited for his eyes to open.

"You dead?"

Zev's eyes remained closed. "Feels like." He blinked, grimacing. "Damn electrodes hurt like a sonofabitch."

Josh held out a hand and helped the big man to his feet. "You know I could have taken you. I just let you think you were winning."

Zev smirked. "I'd love to have seen that. I threw you into a car. That's basically a superhero move."

The Alpha sergeant hobbled to the vehicle and sat down in the passenger seat, rubbing his legs. He took off his helmet, taking a long drink from his CamelBak. "They coming to pick us up?"

Josh looked up at the sky, surprised that no Seraphs hovered overhead. "I hope so. I don't really know the way back from here." He leaned against the door near Zev. "That was a good fight. Thanks for not breaking anything important."

"Superheroes are nothing if not merciful."

They shared a laugh as the rest of the soldiers began filing out of the tents and buildings. Dax helped an Alpha gunner who'd twisted her ankle during the attack, easing her down against a wall. A few people pulled out cards and sat to play while they waited for the shuttles to arrive for pickup.

If he hadn't been waiting for the shuttle, he might have missed it. Overhead, clear in the night sky, a brilliant star briefly flashed into view. Josh and Dax looked up and shouted, pointing to the other soldiers around them. Zev, who had been resting in the truck, peeked his head out and glared. But his face softened when he saw the brilliant display.

"What was that?" Dax asked.

Josh shrugged. "Maybe a satellite?"

Zev shook his head, pulling himself from the vehicle. He still favored one leg as he hopped over to the two men. "Couldn't be. They don't carry enough fuel to make that big a boom." He pulled out his night-vision goggles and turned them on, staring up into the dark. "There's a lot of debris. Jesus, must have been a collision or something."

Josh frowned. Something had suddenly caught his eye that was significantly closer to home. A burning light, growing brighter every second. At first he thought he was imagining it, but there was definitely a sound as well—a roar that grew louder and louder. By the time he realized what it was, he was already shouting, "Incoming!"

The burning ball of light roared just overhead before crashing down in the canyon nearby with a momentous *boom*. The earth shook from the impact. Josh was moving before anyone even registered the sound, racing toward the smoking crater. Dax and Zev were right behind him, with Alexa sprinting to catch up.

"Where are you going?" Dax called out.

Josh led the way, wind whistling in his ears.

"It was a ship," he yelled back.

They arrived at the impact area a moment later, out of breath and panting hard. Josh was the only one standing tall, his heart racing but his face bright with excitement. He leapt into the crater, moving quickly but cautiously toward the smoldering wreckage. From this close, it was obviously Terran, and most likely a smaller craft. The glass canopy had held up remarkably well, and the impact-absorbing polymaterial had deployed as designed, completely engulfing the pilot inside. Josh stepped in closer, donning his gloves and pulling at the canopy to break it apart.

"Come on," he said. "The pilot can't last forever in this stuff." He waved for his friends to join him. "Put on protection. This shit will get under your skin and stay there."

"It sounded like a bomb going off," Dax said. "You think anything will be left?"

Josh looked up at his friend. "Deceleration rockets. Look at the crater." He pointed at the three large black circles around the impact zone. "These pods touch down gentler than a Valkyrie."

Dax jumped in, lending his strength to the task. He ripped the hull apart, chucking huge pieces over his shoulder. Zev took the other side, and together the three pried the escape pod loose, leaving just the white, spongy foam. Josh reached into the substance, rooting around for something to grab. He grunted with effort, found what felt like an arm, and pulled hard. Slowly, a hand emerged. Zev grabbed the arm under the elbow and they removed the pilot, carefully laying him on the ground next to the wreckage.

"Careful with his neck." Alexa shouted from the edge of the crater. "He might be injured. I called for a medic already."

Josh unstrapped the pilot's helmet but left it on. He loosened the man's suit and unlaced his boots. Dax popped the snaps on the pressure cuffs that looped around the pilot's arms and legs. The man's uniform identified him as an SP pilot from Luna wing. Underneath the crescent patch was another patch, a small broken wall over a raised fist. Josh shared a look of confusion between the other soldiers. They threw sand on the flames to douse them, allowing the cool night air back into the pit. Josh wrinkled his nose at the acrid stink that permeated the crash site. Dax slumped down against the ramped earth, grunting with the effort. He took off his vest, sweat shining on his bulging arms.

The pilot moaned and reached for his helmet. Josh grabbed him by the arms and firmly held them in place.

"Don't move," Josh said. "You may be injured."

The pilot's hands fell like stones. Josh thought he'd lost consciousness, but his voice soon warbled out: "Where am I?"

"Kronos."

"Did they follow me?"

A rustle of unease passed through the contingent. Josh asked, "Did *who* follow you?"

He didn't answer. Josh eased the ballistic visor back on the man's helmet, revealing a pair of bloodshot blue eyes. The pilot lifted his hand weakly, which Josh took in his own.

"Hi," the pilot whispered.

"Hey there. Where did you come from? What ship?"

"Did they..."

Josh was getting worried. This guy needed medical, soon. He raised his voice a little: "Still with me, flyboy? How about you tell us your name and rank?"

"Cameron Davis. Lieutenant."

"Nice to meet you, Lieutenant Davis. Can you tell me where your carrier is?"

Cameron's eyelids fluttered. "Blue Space."

Josh frowned. "You're saying they jumped away, left you here?"

"I came from Blue Space. With them. Did they follow me?"

His eyes rolled back in his head. He was out. Josh stood up. Dax stood and helped Zev to his feet. They both walked over to Josh and the injured pilot.

"The hell's going on out there, Sarge?" Dax asked.

"I don't know." He spotted a medical shuttle a few klicks to the north. He looked at Alexa and nodded. In response, she popped a flare and waved down the shuttle. Behind the craft, several transports appeared, headed toward a clearing near the fort.

"Picked a pretty good place to land," Zev said.

Dax nodded. "Lucky. Must have a whole squadron of angels on his shoulders."

He looked up as two combat medics slid down the ramp into the crater, dragging a litter between them. They pushed Josh aside and gently moved Cameron onto the stretcher and strapped him in place with nylon belts. With a silent countdown, they lifted the pilot up and onto their shoulders. Zev and Dax moved alongside as they marched out of the crater, spotting them. Josh followed behind, but glanced over his shoulder at the last remnants of flames.

What is going on up there, he wondered, *and how the hell did a pilot from Sol make it all the way out here?*

He had just turned around when a sound drew his attention skyward. More objects streaked through the moon's atmosphere, dragging fiery trails across the sky. Josh almost dismissed them as pieces of the pilot's ship when he noticed that they were slowing down. He pulled his radio out and switched to the administrative channel.

"Eagle One Two, this is Caveman White One. Are we expecting any landings in our area?" The line hissed for a minute without response. "Eagle One Two, this is Caveman. Come back, over?" He was about to try again when the radio squelched.

"All stations, this is Eagle. Hostile forces in close orbit."

Josh shot a look toward Dax. His heart pounded faster and louder. The handset shook in his hand.

"I say again. All stations. *Prepare to repel!*"

November 6, 2236
Galactic Media Tower
New York City

JONAH BLIGHTMAN SMILED FOR the camera. His normal coat was replaced with a fresh suit, and his face was trimmed and clean. He wore his long brown hair in a ponytail down to the small of his back. The lights in the studio blinded him, but he forced his face to remain stoic.

Across the way sat Gregory Kent, looking more disheveled than his normal handsome self. Around the room, Jonah's men trained rifles on the crew of the news program.

"Good evening, viewers. This is Gregory Kent with an exclusive update to our breaking story. With me is Jonah Blightman, the leader of the militant group known as the Red Hammer. Jonah, you had something you wanted to say to the audience?"

Jonah nodded. "Thank you, Greg. People of Earth, I want to begin by condemning the violence seen yesterday. What began as a strictly military operation ended up taking the lives of hundreds of civilians. The original plan would have minimized the damage to the rail lines, injuring no one but shutting down the transportation system. It was the sudden and violent response by local law enforcement that caused the damage you've seen here.

"As for the target strikes around the globe, the collateral damage has been mostly contained. With the exception of Africa and Brazil, where I'm told secret weapons reserves were ignited, non-military casualties have been under ten. Now you might think that any violent action is unwarranted, and I don't begrudge you your opinion. Truth be told, I would love for nothing more than a peaceful settlement to the affairs of my organization. Sadly, the Terran Colonial Federate is not interested in negotiation."

Jonah took a sip of water and assumed a pained expression. "I want you all to know that with the Red Hammer, the buck always stops with me. I take full responsibility for the attack on the New York Sky Rail. When the situation here in New York finally ends, I promise that I will present myself to the proper authorities to face charges for my crimes. But I came here with a mission, and I aim to see that mission through."

Behind the two men, a green screen flashed. Images of Mars played in silence, depicting the various battles fought only a decade before.

Jonah watched the carnage onscreen. He wiped a tear from his eye. "I'll bet the majority of you don't know the numbers from the war. It just so happens I have them memorized. The Earth forces—your so-called Alliance of the Free—lost just under three hundred thousand soldiers, sailors, and marines. Martian revolutionaries died in the *millions*, mostly from orbital bombardments and targeted strikes on our oxygen generators. Add to that the nearly thirty million civilians killed and you have a tragically one-sided fight.

"We would launch an attack against a military convoy, and the UEC would destroy three blocks of apartments. Why? We had no such means to retaliate, and the disproportionate response by Fleet cemented the relationship between Mars and Earth. We were second-class citizens, just bugs waiting to be stomped. I ask you, what would you have done different? If that was your reality, day in and out, what would it make you become? What would you be willing to do?"

Greg maintained a calm and respectful mask of concern and interest, but the corner of his eye twitched at the mention of the civilian deaths.

Jonah had him.

TFC Sidney
Earth Orbit

ADMIRAL GILROY WATCHED THE live feed from the bridge. He didn't care if his crew saw the anger on his face. He wanted them to know he was angry. He wanted them to share the emotion. He wanted them pissed and ready to kill.

"Admiral, are you ready for your in-brief?" The man speaking wore an impeccable black suit and dark shades, despite the relatively dim light on the bridge. The crew gave him a wide berth wherever he went aboard *Sidney*.

Even Lawrence felt uneasy around the spook. It was unnerving to know that this nondescript man held clearance well above most admirals in Fleet. There was a menacing quality about him, a feline grace that didn't sit well.

There was a reason Lawrence had avoided dealing with Ghosts of the Fade in the past.

"Whenever you're able, Agent."

"Please," the man said. He smiled, showing all of his teeth. "Call me Mr. Blake."

"You don't like your title?"

The agent frowned. "It's not that. I just don't want you to get the impression that you outrank me. When people call me 'agent,' I assume it's so they can imagine 'admiral' or 'general' or 'chancellor' somehow stands above. I am not in your chain of command, but I assure you I would not stand in your shadow. Now, let's begin."

Mr. Blake pulled a tablet from his briefcase and handed it to Lawrence. As soon as the admiral touched the clear plastic, the screen came to life. It verified his identity by his fingerprints before starting a slide show he'd prepared. Mr. Blake, standing close by, narrated.

"Red Hammer currently controls twenty-three percent of the land mass of Earth. That in and of itself presents little concern. They do, however, manage to control roughly seventy percent of the infrastructure, and nearly one hundred percent of the media. This has allowed them unfettered access to the population. While most of our sources on the ground report a general sense of unease and distrust, a good majority don't even know what's happened. They know about the attacks, of course, but not the situation in which they now live."

Mr. Blake continued: "Militarily, Red Hammer owns the planet. We have just over a million soldiers in uniform spread across the globe, including many types of special-forces. Red Hammer commands four times that."

"How?" Lawrence asked. "When did they get there?"

Mr. Blake cocked his head to the side. "They've always been there. When Buenos Aires went off, the entire police force revealed themselves to be Red Hammer operatives. They've been planning this for over ten years, the so-called 'Operation Family Reunion.' We're just surprised they were able to pull it off with the war long lost."

"So what does the Fade recommend?"

The agent took the tablet away, clearing the screen with a swipe of his hand. "Observe and report. Any military action right now would lead to a media nightmare for the Federate."

"Bullshit. If we sit here and do nothing, it only gives Jonah time to consolidate his forces and strengthen his hold on the planet."

"I'm not saying you sit here with your thumb up your ass, Admiral. I'm saying you let the remaining forces on the ground do their job. Specifically, the job of maintaining the peace. You want the people of Earth to see Federate uniforms cleaning streets, keeping the buses running, and generally making their lives easier. If you fail at that, rest assured that Red Hammer will be right behind you. If you give them the chance, they'll win the people over. If they win the people, they can call for an election and win the planet. If they win the planet, then we are going to be in quite a tight spot. You think watching a planet *burn* is terrible? Try watching it *elect* itself into oblivion."

Lawrence wiped a meaty palm over his face. He was sweating alcohol from every pore on his deteriorating body. He scowled at the intelligence agent. "You know, you people make for shit-awful houseguests."

Mr. Blake shrugged. "There's not much of a social life for ghosts. You asked my opinion, and there it is. If I were you, I would fight fire with foam. Broadcast your own messages. Terra Node can still override broadcasts, at least until they manage to break the tether."

"You think I should be on TV?"

"Not really, but it's our best option." He snapped his briefcase shut and stood. "You've got a really shitty post here, Admiral. I hope you've punished whoever's responsible for you getting it." He left through the side entrance, disappearing into the ship.

Lawrence rolled his eyes, unable to look at his crew.

He's not wrong, Larry. How the hell are we getting out of this mess?

Invasion Drop Zone
Kronos

THE FIRST SHUTTLE TOUCHED down at one in the morning. Engines fired up clouds of orange and red dust, obscuring the landing zone. Alien craft flew through the thin air, engines wheezing and popping. When the first pod hit the dirt, the doors stayed closed for almost two minutes. The Boxti were in no apparent hurry.

Josh watched from his hastily dug foxhole. Moments later, dozens of crab-shaped shuttles joined the first. Each ship's collision lights dimmed in unison to a dull purple. The smoke and dust cast wandering shadows on the surrounding canyons. The hiss of hydraulics and the groan of metal echoed in the still night. Josh hoped it would mask the noise made by his hastily assembled squad.

The exhausted and terrified soldiers of the 185th lay prone behind clusters of rocks and natural barricades, their training rifles rattling against the orange stone. Other companies were slowly filtering into the front. The call to arms had come only moments after the official end to the gauntlet, and the truth hadn't yet sunk into the collective psyche of the troops. All they had been given, before being ordered into a hasty defense, were two sentences from General Casey.

We're at war. They just came here.

"They" began to emerge from the shuttles, bathed in dim blue light. Immediately the landing strobes cut off. The landing zone went from bright to pitch black in a half second, and the silence seemed to grow deeper. Josh reached up slowly and activated his low-light enhanced vision. His visor lit up and a black-and-white view of the clearing appeared clear as day. He nearly screamed.

Holy shit. Monsters.

That was all he could think. Monsters had arrived and they were invading his little slice of hell. The first soldiers out of the shuttle stood a little over six feet tall. Dull metal plates covered them from top to bottom. They didn't seem to have heads; just a rocky line stretched between two enormous shoulders. They communicated with hand and arm signals, made more complicated since they had four arms apiece. Behind them emerged slender, wispy creatures with faces like geckos. They wore long coats over form-fitting armor and carried absurdly long rifles.

"Are you seeing this, man?" Dax craned his neck to see over his cover. He had spent almost an hour scratching at the unforgiving terrain, trying to dig out a space to hide his bulk. Josh had proofed the defense before settling in, but he was still surprised the enemy hadn't spotted them yet. The heavy gunner's elbows and knees kept slipping outside the boulder's shadow.

Josh swallowed hard, wincing at the noise. "What the fuck are those things?"

"Aliens, dude. Little green monsters. Our Father who art in Heaven hallowed be—" Dax slipped into a spitfire rendition of the Lord's Prayer. "—forever and ever, amen. I've got your back, man. No matter what, you're going home in one piece."

"Stop it," Josh said. His teeth chattered, so he pinched his jaw to still it. "You're freaking out, and that's making *me* freak out. I need you calm, Dax."

"I'm holding a squirt gun, man. They didn't have any live ammo." Dax ran a beefy hand underneath his belted ammunition, stretching out the line until Josh could clearly see the blue simulator tips. "This is just gonna piss them off."

Something warm and wet ran down Josh's leg, and he fought down a sudden urge to whimper. His breathing grew faster, until he thought his lungs were going to froth and burst from his mouth. He closed his eyes and focused on his combat breath. *Four in, hold. Four out, hold. Four in, hold. Four out.* The sound of scraping rock broke Josh's concentration.

Two of the geckos had closed on the front line. This close, Josh could make out their faces in detail. Their features were identical with the lizards of Earth, down to the oddly independent eyes. The aliens wore no breathing gear of any kind; apparently oxygen worked just fine for them. The long coats shimmered as they blew in the wind and seemed to blend into the ground perfectly. Josh gawked at the six-foot rifles each creature held. They had to be at least .50 calibers, if not bigger.

Suddenly Zev's voice sounded over the radio: "All stations, this is Ravage. Hold your fire. Let them draw in. The ambient heat on the rocks is blocking your signature. They won't know you're there."

This is stupid, this is stupid, this is stupid. The screaming voice in his head spoke faster and faster: *Are you fucking crazy? There are aliens out there. Real life, fuck-you-and-your-mother aliens. Sweet holy fuck, look at those monsters. Where the fuck did they come from? What the fuck are they doing here?* He didn't realize he was shaking until a hand came down on his shoulder to steady him. Josh opened his eyes and looked at his battle buddy. Dax nodded comfortingly.

"We're getting through today, man."

Josh shook his head. "I don't think I am." His eyes burned hot and sweaty. He wiped at them with dirty gloves, which only made them tear up more. "I pissed my fucking pants, Dax."

The heavy gunner shifted carefully, spreading his knees until Josh could see the darker area in between. "So did I. How's that for some shit." He adjusted back to a good firing position. "Now let's spread that fear around."

The LZ went quiet, save the soft footfalls of the aliens. Josh felt a hand squeeze his shoulder. His stomach twisted, knowing full well what the touch meant. Holding his breath, Josh flipped the selector switch on his rifle from SAFE to SEMI and sighted his first target. Every drop of moisture in his mouth evaporated.

Through the low-light scope, Josh could see like it was daylight. The bipedal gecko-things had set up in an observation post a hundred meters from their shuttle. Two of the ungainly creatures lay prone on an outcropping of rock, chattering aimlessly to one another. Or at least Josh thought it was aimless. It looked to him like they were trying to pass the time until their shift ended. Like any other soldier in the history of warfare.

It was a strange realization, and Josh wasn't alone. In their half-moon ambush around the alien LZ, every human took a moment to appreciate that they were up against another uniformed army. The being underneath might look foreign, but the actions were all the same.

The moment was shattered, seconds later, when the first shot rang out.

Josh didn't fire at first. He'd been given only two magazines of live ammunition, each heavier and colder than his own. Once he'd burned through that, all that was left was simunitions. The heavy chalk round would sting, and could possibly blind the aliens, but they wouldn't kill.

One of the geckos popped its head up at the first round, unsure if it actually heard a shot or not. Josh bit his lip, held his breath, and squeezed the trigger. The gecko dropped down so fast that Josh thought he missed. Then he noticed that the alien's arm remained draped over its cover, not moving.

Rifles barked and machine guns sang as the humans let loose a swift barrage. Boxti soldiers, caught in the open, fell in a spray of ichor and gore. Screams joined the roar of gunfire, shouted in a dozen new tongues, adding to the fear and chaos. Grenades landed in between the shuttles, exploding in flashes of light and clouds of shrapnel. In seconds, the stink of blood and death covered the LZ.

Josh and Dax worked in silence, picking off targets with extreme care. Every few seconds his rifle bucked against his shoulder. He would breathe in and out slowly, his senses thrilled by the smell of a live battlefield. Each squeeze of the trigger came easier and easier. Soon the humans were on their knees, firing and screaming as they mowed down the monsters from the sky. Slowly, the roar of their weapons quieted down.

Seconds later, the roar of something else started up.

TFC London
Kronos Orbit

ADMIRAL CORA WINGER'S BODY tingled with adrenaline. With every passing second, her battle group drew closer to the enemy line. Already her long-range destroyers had loosed dozens of seeker missiles. The fire-and-forget warheads slid past the alien shields, burying themselves in metal before exploding.

The first return was unimpressive. Two Boxti frigates fired thick blobs of green energy that sailed harmlessly overhead. Cora ordered her own ship to hold fire until they were within all weapon ranges. Her sights were set on the alpha warship, a mean-looking dreadnought.

Unlike the battle over Luna, this enemy armada flew in a controlled and tactical formation. Gone were the wild swarms of fighters and near collisions from frigates. Every vessel maintained speed and heading, and they seemed rehearsed in the battle plan. It was intimidating as hell.

The Boxti brought all manner of ships to the fight: thorny destroyers, hive-like carriers, acorn-shaped cruisers, and the mammoth dreadnought. From the reports Cora had read, that was the bastard who had killed New Freeman. She marked him on her board. There wasn't a chance he'd flee this battlefield.

Images of the battle over Tallus played in her head: Snapshots of Terran vessels drifting lifeless in orbit over a burning planet, a KIA list filled with the names of friends— no, family.

She returned to the present. Typing into the keypad on her armrest, Cora brought up the command line for the ship.

"This is the admiral," she said. "I want all weapon systems locked. Arm air-denial and missile defenses. Ready the one-two and tether down." She took a quick look around the bridge, making eye contact with each member of her team. Her final glance lingered on her XO. "Godspeed and good hunting."

The XO moved quickly, but with discipline, snapping down the crew's personal lines and checking on the people to her left and right. Computers chirped and tweeted, bringing every weapon aboard the massive carrier to bear. Everything fell into place like the tumblers of a massive, ultra-complex lock. The final sound came as the *London* crossed over an invisible line, entering into firing range for all the cannons, missiles, and lasers aboard the ship.

Cora's stomach lurched forward. The carrier's engines were in full reverse, with forward rockets firing blinding streams of light. Enemy rounds plinked off the kinetic barrier. A lucky shot from one of the spherical destroyers punched a hole through the TFF *Kennedale*, but the rest of the group entered the battlefield unharmed. Cora stood, leaning into the deceleration, and shouted.

"All ships, this is *London*. Alpha strike!"

THE BOXTI DREADNOUGHT TOOK the first few shots in stride. They were pathetic, wasteful efforts, like insects nipping the heels of a giant. The armada, known as the King's Golden Spear, marched on toward the red moon. Drop pods had already delivered a small scouting force, but the larger shuttles required a safer approach. No matter. These creatures had yet to put up a decent fight.

The Warlord Eruk djun Tolan had been a part of the vanguard since his graduation from training. He was one of the privileged few to have been joined with the Parasite and allowed to retain most of his essence. Though his mind often went over to the Druuma, he was trusted to carry out commands without oversight. It was truly an honor to be on the frontline of the great conquest, seeking out the unknowing and converting them to the cause.

Unlike some of the indoctrinated, he was a true believer in the journey. He read the Grol 'Nahja every day, touching his face to the cold, glassy floor of his quarters before dressing and leaving the room. If he were ever to allow a moment of pride, it would be to think himself worthy of becoming one of the Clerics when his usefulness on the battlefield ended. The Parasite would laugh whenever that thought entered the warlord's head. Only the purebred Boxti were allowed such an office. The lower species, even Eruk's own Cthanul, were never chosen.

Eruk watched the approaching Terrans with interest. In the weeks since the war with the humans began, he had taken time to study the species, as he did with all the ones before. Sitting in his chair on the bridge, he took a moment to admire their bravery.

Human ships, as he had quickly learned, were fairly well-made. They could take a beating before succumbing to fire. More than that, the fleshy creatures inside were bred for war. Of that the Cthanul had no doubt. He could sense the fighting spirit of the creatures and respected it. They were, however, an underwhelming threat to the Warlord.

So he ordered his ships to hold their position and wait, allowing the Terran armada to close distance and enter the kill zone. What looked like aimless drifting put the Boxti frigates and destroyers in perfect flanking positions, all while allowing the carriers to nestle safely to the rear.

Eruk was about to bark a command when the leading human carrier exploded. Or rather, the sky exploded around it.

Missiles streaked from every pore, lasers flashed and shells erupted, blossoming around the massive ship in glowing petals of death and destruction. Eruk watched in awe as every single human vessel followed suit, unleashing a surging wave of incoming fire that shook the very space around it.

Smaller destroyers and frigates never stood a chance. Three scouts, out to collect intel, dissolved. One cruiser took a powerful hit to its engines, sending it careening into its sister ship. Both vessels went up in a short but brilliant blaze.

Warheads smashed into Eruk's dreadnought, rocking the ship from side to side. Alarms sounded as different areas decompressed, venting hapless crew into the upper atmosphere of the besieged moon. The Warlord weathered the storm, watching as the rolling fire washed over the line and faded into the shadows beyond.

"Impressive," Eruk said, almost bored. He turned to his weapons chief, a fellow Cthanul, and clicked an order. "Destroy that carrier."

Guns dropped from the dreadnought's belly. As one, the cannons fired.

TFC London

CORA FELT THE FIRST impact. *London* shifted off axis as the penetrating laser cannon bit into her hull. The second volley sheared the port hangar completely clean and sent the carrier into a spin. Cora's weight leapt from her seat to her throat and back down again. Klaxons sounded and strobes flashed and the world turned upside-down.

"Evasive!" Cora cried out. Something heavy slammed into her face. She saw a flash of white. Blood filled her mouth. Deafening explosions rattled the bridge, sending shrapnel through the corridors. A flaming scythe of pain slashed her leg. She looked. A chunk of metal had torn an inch-thick gash in her thigh.

Wind rushed and roared, and the smell of smoke gave way to the foul odor of burnt ozone. The temperature dropped thirty degrees in an instant. Cora's sweat frosted over. She blinked again and again, but her vision remained blurry. She shivered.

Hands grabbed at the admiral, disconnecting her tether and dragging her from the command center. They were halfway down the hall before her vision returned. Lena, her XO, had her by one arm. Doc Roe, Lena's brother, led the way to the infirmary. Minutes later, Cora stared at the ceiling. Something pricked her arm. A needle.

"Lena?" Cora murmured. She tried to focus, but it was harder to breathe than normal. Looking around the room she saw dozens of bodies covered in stained bedding. The air was thick with smoke. Alarms rang incessantly. Cora sat up and immediately regretted it. She placed a hand gingerly on her stomach. It came away red.

"Don't move, Admiral." Doctor Roe appeared, snapping a fresh pair of gloves onto his hands. He was a spitting image of his sister, with just the slightest change toward the masculine. With a mask over his face, only his dark brown eyes showed. Doc had thick eyelashes, so he always looked like he was wearing eyeliner.

The doctor probed her stomach and chest. She winced at every palpation.

"Why did you take me off the bridge?" Blood splashed from her mouth. She took a corner of the bedding and spat into it, wiping her mouth clean.

Doc Roe gave a pained look. "Admiral, the bridge was hit. The XO managed to pull you out, along with a few others. *London's* in pretty bad shape."

"Where is Lena?" Cora asked, her voice cracking. Her heartbeat quickened. Suddenly a warm hand landed on hers. Cora smelled the familiar scent of lilacs and engine oil.

Lena wrapped her arms around Cora, bringing her close. "I'm here. I'm here, and I'm fine." She kissed Cora on the cheek.

"What happened?"

Lena brushed aside strands of greasy hair and blood from her forehead. "They punched right through the shield. Melted the hull. We had no idea they could do that." She leaned against the bed. "*London* was split amidships. We've lost the hangars, the barracks, and most of the engine."

Cora put a hand on the captain to steady herself. "How long until the core breaks down?"

Lena shrugged. "That part of the ship is blocked off. Could be hours. Could be less. I've already given the general order for evacuation." She stared at her injured crew. "The Boxti seem content to let us drift. We aren't much of a threat anymore."

"And the rest of the group?" Cora didn't like the looks from her staff. "Can we even see them?"

Lena shook her head. "Unless they fly by and wave, we can't see or talk to anyone. I'm readying the command pod for evac. You and I will head out so we can get a better picture of the field. We can call for a pickup and get aboard one of the remaining ships."

Cora pushed Doc Roe aside and slid off the bed. Her right leg screamed in agony when she tried to put weight on it. A loose-fitting bandage barely covered the six-inch gash where a piece of hull had nearly nicked her femoral. A small sliver of glass still protruded from her stomach. Cora pulled the shard out with a hiss and dropped it on the bed.

"Just get me a new boat, Lena." She wiped blood and dirt from her face and stared defiantly. "I've got a battle to win."

Invasion Drop Zone
Kronos

THEY'D GONE FROM KICKING ass to turning tail in a head-spinning instant. Josh couldn't believe it. One second the enemy seemed completely routed, and the next they were surging toward the line, charging through the humans without fear. Dax grabbed Josh by the elbow and dragged him back toward the rally point, unloading his training rounds at the oncoming aliens.

Bolts of purple, red, and yellow flashed overhead, splashing into the surrounding rock with a hiss and sizzle. Superheated sand sprayed against Josh's neck as he ran, crunching underfoot as glass. Someone nearby took a hit to the chest and dropped. Their screams died a moment later when the second volley hit. The crisp commands from the higher ranks dissolved under the decimating counterattack.

"Return fire," Zev shouted. He stood tall amidst the flying rounds, grabbing soldiers and spinning them back in the correct direction. "Goddammit, hold the line!"

Josh and Dax slid to a stop behind a large boulder. A bolt from an alien rifle hit the rock, blasting a large chunk into fine powder. Josh spat out bits of the dust, choking to catch his breath. "Zev," he called out. "We need ammo."

A sniper bolt tore through the air, whistling toward Zev. He ducked the shot. "I know. We're all out."

"So shouldn't we retreat?"

"To what?" Zev asked. "There's no ammo in the rear. Just more of this."

Dax pointed toward the alien advance. "But fewer of them."

A shrill barking drew their attention. At the center of the enemy front, a barrel-shaped alien approached on four legs, carrying a huge gun. Each burst sent hundreds of red bolts streaming at the humans. The alien cut a swath through the Terran line and fired. A heavyset human officer shoved an enlisted man out of danger and absorbed the blast. The officer collapsed to the ground, nearly torn in two. It took Josh a minute to recognize who it was.

Jesus. Captain Thornton.

Thornton was dead, but he still had grenades. Josh dropped to the ground and snatched one.

A new voice said: "*Row kass.*"

Josh looked up slowly, trying to make as little sound as possible. The massive alien gunner stood over him, staring off into the distance. Up close, Josh saw that the creature wore heavy scale-armor over a loose cloth covering. Its face was small compared to the rest of its body, perched on a stalk-like neck that twitched back and forth. Three eyes looked out from its lower jaw.

Behind the heavy gunner, a gecko appeared. It chittered in a strange language, gesturing with its hands. The heavy gunner swung its head around. "*Bora kros ka-changa. Dakka na.*" Its voice was like a bubbling pool of melted rock. The gecko nodded and disappeared.

Josh remained frozen, willing his heart to shut the fuck up. His limbs were lead. Goosebumps tingled hot and cold across his body. Josh tried to take a breath—but he coughed.

"*Jo?*" The alien looked down. Its three eyes grew wide. "*Sna-doo.*" Reaching down with a thick arm, the alien lifted Josh into the air by his neck.

The creature's hand tightened. *Like a vise,* Josh thought. *Of course it's like a vise.* Josh struggled to breathe, vaguely aware of yelling behind him. Something zipped past his ears. Dark shadows began to cloud his vision. *Huh. This is the moment I die. I'm about to experience that moment.*

The world returned with a whoosh of air. The alien's grip was loosening. His feet found ground.

"Josh! Are you okay?"

"Put him down! Put him the fuck down!"

Zev and Dax stood on a low ridge, rifles pointed at the four-legged alien. Josh shifted his weight as best he could, gripping the creature's bony forearm for leverage. His peripheral vision registered that his comrades had no magazines, a fact he hoped was lost on the invaders.

Three geckos took up position opposite the humans, brandishing green and blue weapons. They squawked, clothes flapping in a sudden gust of wind. Every few seconds one would hop forward, bray, then dance back. Frills on the sides of their heads flapped in a colorful posturing maneuver.

"Josh," Dax shouted. "We're not gonna leave you."

"Thanks!" he choked.

Zev stepped forward, sneering. The four-legged alien growled and lifted Josh higher. Its mandible ground together. It lunged toward Zev, throwing its massive arms back and roaring.

"*Jo-graw!*"

Josh saw his moment. He kicked the creature in the jaw. Its claw released, and he hit the ground with a thud, coughing hard. His chest burned. The air was hot embers, his vision nothing but dancing red dots.

Heavy hands fell on his shoulders.

Dax hoisted Josh into a fireman's carry and took off running. The aliens cried out, firing their rifles and giving chase. Zev appeared a moment later, sprinting hard. Josh bounced along on his friend's shoulder, taking in short gulps of air.

"Zev," Josh croaked. "Where's your gun?"

A flash of red singed Josh's face. Behind them, the geckos were giving chase...and gaining, their long legs covering the rocky terrain in great, loping strides. Josh was about to shout an order in Dax's ear when he felt a familiar weight in his hand.

Oh, cool. Thought I dropped you, buddy.

He twisted the top of the grenade and armed it. Winking lights appeared on the side.

Josh didn't get a chance to throw the grenade. Dax took a running leap over a gap and landed hard on the other side. The device clunked to the ground and bounced until it settled by a small crater.

"Frag out," Josh muttered.

Dax turned his head. "You say something, Sar–?"

The grenade exploded with a dull *crump*, spraying rock and shrapnel in every direction. The three geckos disappeared in a cloud of smoke and blood. Dax cried out and fell to the ground, throwing Josh to the side. Zev landed nearby, hurled by the concussion wave.

Dax groaned. "What the hell, Josh?" His hands went to his leg, gingerly touching a hunk of shrapnel embedded in his calf. He pinched the metal between his fingers and pulled, gritting his teeth. It didn't move. "Damn." He fell back onto his arms, hissing through clenched teeth.

Josh crawled over. His left arm tingled painfully from the elbow down. Each breath came with a price. He could feel pieces of rib shifting under his armor, scraping at his lungs. Josh rolled over onto his back, staring at the starry sky above. "Sorry, buddy."

"It's all right," Dax said. He grabbed Josh's shoulder. "We have to move."

"Nah." Josh massaged his elbow, swallowing a cry of pain. The arm was broken, no doubt. "I think we scared them off."

The crunch of rocks got their attention. The four-legged demon stomped toward them. With each step it grunted, its nostrils venting steam. In one hand it dragged the lifeless corpse of a shredded gecko. The alien glared, lower jaw quivering.

"*Mar daka. Rach drok-graw.*" It dropped the body and started toward the two soldiers.

Josh sucked in a deep breath.

SHIT!

Kronos Orbit

ADMIRAL WINGER WINCED AS the command escape pod smacked into another object. Kinetic shields flared, bathing the cramped quarters in purple light. She closed her eyes to block the sight of frozen blood splattered across the diamond window. Another jolt sent searing fire through her gut. Her bandages were soaked through with blood.

"ETA, six minutes," the pilot said. Unlike regular escape pods, the command module had dedicated engines for maneuvering in space. With rank came privileges, and Cora's pod had been manned and ready when the order to evac came down.

Lena held Cora's hand and kissed her forehead. "It's going to be all right, love. We're almost there." Red and black smears covered her face and neck. They'd made it off *London* just in time.

On the rear-mounted camera, they could see the remains of the carrier falling to a decaying orbit. There had to be crew onboard, as engines and weapons still fired valiantly trying to save the ship. The hangars were long gone, peppered by enemy attacks until nothing remained but slag and tumbling steel. A lone Boxti frigate launched missiles aimlessly into *London's* belly. They weren't content to merely cripple the Terran ship. They wanted it gone.

Doc Roe tapped a syringe and injected a syrupy orange cocktail into Cora's IV. A strange numbness crept through her body. It started at her fingertips and spread, inch by inch, until she was floating in air.

"Where is the Seventh?" Lena demanded to know. "They should have been here by now. They should have helped us."

The doc shook his head. "I don't know. I wish they'd been here too, but that's not important right now. We need to get aboard a ship. Preferably something well armored."

Lena absently cracked her knuckles. "Who's even left?"

"They'll come," Cora said softly. She kissed Lena's knuckles. "They'll come. Sam DeHart doesn't know how to lose a fight."

Kronos

THE ALIEN WAS ABOUT to stomp on Josh's head.

He rolled onto his broken arm and screamed in pain. The alien's boot landed on empty ground. It howled, then took a swipe with its claws, barely missing the solider. Josh lurched to his feet and hobbled away, only to get knocked back to the ground. His head connected with the dirt, protected only by his helmet. Bells rang in his ears. He spat out a wad of blood.

With a yell, Dax jumped onto the creature's back and grabbed its scrawny neck. The alien shrugged its shoulders and tossed Dax end over end. He jumped up in an instant and struck a stance. It was like he was back in the Grid, squaring off during a game of Grudgeball. His muscles stacked on top of each other, tensing for another attack. He ran at the alien, catching it under the arms and peppering it with powerful blows to its chest. The creature grunted, spitting up dark blood. Finally it ducked a swing and countered with a devastating kick, using two of its legs. Dax tumbled back and landed hard.

Zev charged in next, body-slamming the four-legged monster to the ground. He stood over it, kicking and shouting and spitting. It finally got a limb free and clipped Zev's ankle. The big sergeant dropped with a high-pitched cry.

Josh pulled Dax to his feet with his good arm, backing away from the alien. Zev scooted on his elbows, joining them. They made a poor front against the creature: two broken giants and a one-armed shorty. The alien rumbled and chittered.

Something else was making noise now too. Josh noticed that a crowd had grown while they'd been fighting. Some human, but also many aliens. The fight seemed to have stopped around them. No more rounds flew overhead. No more explosions rocked the canyons. Just three humans and an alien beating the crap out of each other.

Not exactly a heart-warming first contact, Josh thought.

Zev climbed onto one foot, hopping to maintain his balance. Blood ran from a savage cut over his eye. He sneered with a mouth that was a red mess. "Come on, you fucker. Let's do this." He drew his knife.

"Zev," Josh rasped. "You can't take him with that. It's a safety knife." The dull blade had a foam cover. Josh was about to say more when he heard a roaring in the distance.

"It's not so safe." Zev placed the edge of the knife against a large rock by his boot. He stomped down, breaking the metal in half and leaving a ragged edge. Now properly armed, he took up a fighting stance. "Come on!"

Josh turned toward the sound. It came from the sky. The sun had just started to curve around the horizon, and the reds and oranges of the dawn were barely making their appearance. Far above, streaks of fire rained down. Everyone present gaped at the sight.

They were ships, or at least bits of them. Debris from the battle in orbit. Frames and wings and massive engines disintegrated in the upper atmosphere and pinwheeled down. Josh swallowed a mouthful of bile.

They'd lost the fight.

Zev beat his chest with his fist. Each movement was calculated, intended to impress—and to hide. Josh could see it, just as he saw it a day before during their own fight. Zev was beat.

"Don't wimp out on me now," Zev said. "You afraid of an audience? Afraid you'll lose to me? Fight me. Come on, you piece of shit. *Fight me!*"

A deep voice bellowed: "*No.*"

Something massive pushed its way through the crowd of aliens surrounding the fight. It wore layer after layer of silvery plated armor. Each of its four arms bore a spiked gauntlet. Heavy boots stomped the ground. It settled in the center of the ring, staring down the humans.

"Fight over."

A spindly creature skittered over, like a cross between a sea urchin and a spider. Its voice was a mixture of hisses and hums, but somehow they could understand it.

"Warlord Eruk djun Tolan grants you one day to gather your forces." Its eyes popped up from its body on a long stalk and stared directly at Josh. "War shall resume in one cycle."

Zev's entire body shook. "What the hell is this?"

"Do not waste your time. Let your leaders know. You have one cycle."

Dax found his tongue. "What do we do until then?"

The large alien leaned over, butchering the words but still managing to get the point across.

"Bury your dead."

Eros System

SAM DEHART'S ANGER HAD turned his bridge into an oven. His rage radiated at the sight being delivered to him from every viewscreen: New Eden's armada of warships rendered into scrap, while the Boxti horde began to invade Kronos.

Valley Forge had arrived with the vanguard, securing the exit space around the ultragiant star Eros. Roughly the size of twelve Jupiters, Eros marked the center of the system. Its incredible gravitational pull sucked in every dangerous object that would otherwise threaten the livable planets and moons. Its girth also blocked radar signals, providing a perfect staging ground for the Terran fleet.

Seventh Section floated in a stable orbit high above the hydrogen clouds, scouting out the enemy fleet. *Valley Forge* had only brought six other ships for the advance unit, and after seeing the carnage from the orbital fight, they knew they were outgunned.

Aboard the supercruiser, Sam's XO stood a safe distance away from the captain.

"All ships have arrived, sir." Captain Fuller handed over a tablet with the full report. The names of the various frigates, destroyers, cruisers, and other ships of the line seemed endless. "When should we begin the attack?"

Before Sam could answer, space near the massive planet swelled and bubbled. Blue light poked through the starry sky until a gate formed. A large, gray vessel emerged headfirst into the formation. Sam's face lit up.

"We were just waiting on him."

In the radar shadow of Eros, surrounded by almost two hundred other ships, *Midway* came online. As soon as the mighty supercarrier took its position, the entire fleet powered their engines and began to march toward Kronos at Stride speed. Commanders barked orders and seamen ran to battle stations. Part of Sam longed for the good, old days, when a midshipman would play a drum to send everyone to quarters.

The ships were all different classes and sizes, with varying armaments. But they did have one item in common. In the command room of every single Terran warship, a banner hung at the front. Simple orange fabric bore only two words, but it was a rallying cry that would be heard around the galaxy.

On his own bridge, now leading the charge, Commodore Osaka smiled and nodded. He wondered if the enemy even contemplated what was coming.

"For Tallus."

Imperion One
Colorum Belt

HIGH CHANCELLOR ALEXANDER BURTON stood at the great window in the observatory, staring out into the brilliant backdrop of the Colorum Belt. Light from the system's star reflected off hundreds of thousands of floating rocks, some as large as Earth. Lights from the distant mining facilities glittered and pulsed, marking the very small human presence.

Alexander watched this and realized, with a sinking feeling, that his species was doomed.

"Alec?" Jerry walked into the room, dressed in a light brown suit. Behind him, peeking in from the doorway, stood the alien historian Mara Nox Booren. "I know this is a bad time."

"Twenty-four hours," Alexander said. "They arrived in the system, destroyed over thirty ships, and invaded a military installation. All this in just twenty-four hours."

Jerry walked over to his boss. He wanted to reach out, to express some modicum of comfort, but he couldn't find the words. "The Boxti are far more powerful than we ever considered. The *London* was one of our newer carriers, designed with a stronger hull than *Midway*. Somehow that dreadnought bit right through it. After that, the rest of the group broke."

"If you're trying to make me feel better, you're failing."

The chief of staff shrugged. "I won't bullshit you, Alec. We're in the fight of our lives, and a lot of good men and women are dying in it. Estimates are putting our losses at just under ten thousand."

Alexander swallowed hard. "How many were down there?"

"On Kronos? We had a fighting force of fifty, but most were in the wrong place, and few had live ammunition. That moon is a training base. They only carry live ammo for the firing range."

The high chancellor sighed and walked over to his desk, taking a seat in the leather high-back chair. "And now they're giving us a respite before finishing the job."

"Not quite, sir." Mara entered the room, her dress flowing behind her. The sapphire material glittered with each step. "This is a Cthanul method of fighting. They call it a *dereth nu'a*. New enemies are given a chance to prepare for the next round after receiving a taste of battle."

"Why?" Alexander stared with tired, red eyes.

"Cthanul are a warrior race. Every part of their culture revolves around battle. It brings them no honor to crush an ill-prepared enemy. They were a perfect thrall for the Boxti during the opening centuries of its conquest." She crossed to the window and pointed out. The bright center of the galaxy dominated the center of the view. "Somewhere out there is Boxt, the homeworld of the true Boxti. Not far away, near the center, is the Cthanul planet."

Mara continued: "The Boxti followed the arms of the Milky Way, conquering civilization after civilization. Every culture they absorbed shaped them as a whole. It's one of the ways they've managed to survive all these years."

"But each generation feels the same?" Alexander asked. "There's never been a new group of Boxti who don't want to destroy the galaxy?"

Mara stared blankly. "You do not understand. The Boxti who began the conquest are still alive. They've been commanding this army since the beginning, serving the same King."

Jerry shook his head in wonder. "I honestly didn't believe it the first time she said it. A species that could live for hundreds of thousands of years? It sounds nuts, I know. But we checked it out."

"How?" Alex asked.

"Simple science, actually." Jerry pointed at the stars. "Light travels a finite speed, and everything we see is just a reflection. The center of the galaxy, as we see it from here, is what it looked like about thirty thousand years ago. You put a telescope in the right place, you can see anything from the past."

"And you saw their planet?" Alexander asked incredulously.

Jerry shook his head. "Not exactly. We'd need a telescope the size of a damn moon to do that. But we saw some of the planets they'd conquered." He leaned in. "Alec, there are signs of life. Other civilizations from thousands and thousands of years ago. Incredible."

Alexander placed his hand against the quadruple-paned glass. "Since when are you an expert in all this?"

Jerry shrugged. "Since aliens arrived. I've been absorbing every book I can find, trying to understand the science. Maybe that way I can understand how this is happening."

The high chancellor nodded, then looked at Mara and said, "Where is your military in all this? After Tallus, your Emperor promised to support us against this threat."

Mara shifted uncomfortably from one foot to the other. "The Domin are not united in this decision."

"What the fuck does that mean?" Alexander snapped.

Mara stared up at the High Chancellor, fretting. "It means that, while Emperor Anduin has the best intentions, he is not the sole steward of our species. The Domin are sworn to protect the Children of JohGal against all threats, including from within. We are so few now that risking even one ship must be done only in the most dire of circumstances."

Alexander bore down on the alien. "We signed an accord, and now your people want out because the going is tough? Over three hundred million of my people are *dead*. I don't care if it takes every ship you have. You owe us."

Jerry stepped in. "Alec, please listen." He set a hand on his shoulder. "The Domin—the military commanders of the Nangolani—they want to have a sit down with the Fleet Commander. We need to get the Council's support for what comes next."

"And what is that?" Alexander asked.

Mara stepped up. "We want to share resources. And talent. Have some of your pilots come aboard our ships, and the same with ours. Begin to build a closer military relationship."

"Walker's gonna love that."

"He won't have a choice if the Council makes the call," Jerry said.

Alec didn't say anything for a minute. Jerry started to speak, but the high chancellor held up a hand. "Don't. I know." He let out a long breath. "Council doesn't jump unless *they* say so."

"So we need to get them on board," Jerry said. "There hasn't been so much as a peep since Luna." Jerry rolled his eyes. "If we make a show about getting the Pillars to unite, they'll take notice. Maybe we can get off the leash a little bit."

Alexander nodded. "Then let's go put on some theater." They walked toward the door when Alexander stopped. "What about Gilroy?"

Jerry shrugged. "That one, we should have on a shorter leash."

Vienna
Incorporated States of Europe

ADMIRAL GILROY HAD NEVER felt more uncomfortable in his life. His uniform had been taped down and coated with hair spray, his face was buried under makeup, and a young woman continually dabbed at his head with a soft cloth. He didn't understand the fuss. Once he was old enough to learn about genetics, he took a look at his father and mother, did some math, and figured he'd be an ogre for the rest of his life.

The news anchor opposite him seemed to have a similar thought, but managed to keep a straight face as they set up the interview. Lawrence had asked the man his name a dozen times, heard it, and summarily thrown that knowledge away.

News of Kronos had come in only moments before he sat down to be interviewed. Admiral Winger was gravely injured, and most of CBG Eros had been destroyed. Lawrence knew Cora, considered her a personal friend, and he had no doubt that she was the perfect choice for the post at New Eden. There were only a handful of officers in the universe he would trust with his life more than her. How in the hell had some alien group managed to rout her forces?

"We're on in two, Lek."

Lawrence turned his whole body to search for the source of the words. He had tissues coming out of his collar to prevent makeup from staining his uniform. *I'm a fucking clown right now.* There were too many people in the room, too many civilians. He'd brought a fair share of soldiers down as well, just to secure the room. He wasn't about to hand himself over to Jonah on a silver platter. That wasn't the point of this circus.

Just think about it like a recon by fire. You're not sure if this is going to work, so take a shot and see what jumps. If nothing changes, you only wasted a little ammo.

"And we're on in five...four...three..."

Lawrence felt the tissues disappear and the light came on, blinding him completely. He could just make out the well-dressed man to his left. *Here we go.*

"Good evening, ladies and gentlemen of Earth. I am Osaf Lekshman and this is *Orbit with Osaf.* My guest tonight is a highly decorated veteran, and claims he is the savior of the planet. Please welcome Admiral Lawrence Gilroy."

There was no applause. This wasn't a studio with an audience. Lawrence squirmed in his seat for a moment before he realized he was supposed to speak.

"Um, yes. Hello. I am Admiral Gilroy with the Federate Fleet. Currently I'm assigned to Sol Group Three, more specifically the carrier *Sidney*."

"And we are so grateful to have you here with us tonight," Osaf said. "Please, tell us about why you've come to Earth."

Lawrence swallowed. He'd practiced this speech in his mirror only once before, but it felt right. Not the cameras or the makeup or anything else, but the words felt right. He just hoped they were enough.

"Citizens of the Federate, I come before you with a wish. I wish that the sins of the past hadn't returned to Earth to visit such pain upon you. I wish that the ghosts of Mars had stayed where they belonged, buried deep in the mines of the red planet. I wish that scar on our species' history could ever heal. But this is the world we live in now."

Gilroy continued: "Terrorists, under the guise of some fabled mission, have taken over key parts of our homeworld. They claim to be revolutionaries, shining a light in the shadows, revealing the dark secrets of the government. These are lies. Red Hammer, under the command of Jonah Blightman, is a group of madmen, driven by greed and bloodlust. They will destroy all that we have built and salt the ground so nothing can ever grow again. Please, people of Earth. We outnumber them a thousand to one. They may be well-armed and well-organized, but we are united by a common cause: the continued existence of our species. In case you've forgotten, we are at war. In the past month, we've seen alien ships in the skies over Earth, watched a planet burn, and now they even attack out military outposts in Eros. If we divide ourselves, we are asking to be destroyed. We are begging for the killing blow."

The admiral took a breath and concluded: "I'm not a politician. I'm a soldier. All I know is how to fight. All I know is how to win. I can tell you, with perfect certainty, that we will lose everything unless we can agree on just one thing: Red Hammer must be stopped."

Osaf's face remained passive for a beat, then he put on his news anchor smile and turned to the camera. "Wow. A passionate plea from a powerful patriot. Let's go to commercial and we will take your calls when we're back."

Lawrence pretended he felt smug by his words, but something was off. This wasn't how he fought wars. Still, he had tried to reach the people without violence. No one could deny him that.

Your move, Blightman.

The Tomb
Kronos

"Ow! FUCKING CHRIST, YOU asshole! Watch out." Josh gripped his arm. Hot knives cut into his bones and muscle, spiraling around to his fingertips. Even in the cast, the slightest nudge set off fireworks. Josh waved off the nurse, sweat beading on his forehead.

Dax appeared in an instant, creating a space around his friend. His skin was shades darker from his time in the sun. Both arms were wrapped in sticky gauze, and a blue, metal splint encased his right leg. He used his crutches like batons, holding back the doctors and nurses.

The infirmary swelled with injured soldiers. They suffered every possible injury, from severed limbs to exposure. Boxti weapons were tough. Most fired projectiles packed with plasma that burst on impact—like balloons filled with radioactive napalm. They passed straight through ceramic plates and into the soft flesh beneath. Medics, both military and civilian, fought to save every life brought in. It was a losing battle. Almost three hundred bodies filled the black bags in the morgue.

Josh allowed Dax to lead him through the scrum, holding onto the big man's shirt. His broken arm hurt something awful. The doctor said the bone was fractured in a half dozen places, courtesy of the four-legged alien freak. Had it not been for the gargantuan cockroach commander, he'd most likely be dead.

"This is fucked," Josh said.

Dax turned his head but kept walking. "That's a nickel for the swear jar. You're making Jesus cry."

Josh's face turned bright red. "Oh, is my foul mouth tainting my soul? Will God not let me into his magical white sandbox if my lips are stained with naughty words?" A young private collided with him and Josh hissed. "Son of a fuck bomb!"

"Josh, I'm serious. Stop it." His voice lowered almost an octave. That was usually the sign that he had taken about as much as he was willing. Dax spread out his arms and pushed aside the sea of injured soldiers.

They waded through the bleeding crowd in silence. The wounded alternated between screaming in pain or begging for painkillers. The dying whimpered softly, crying for their mothers or fathers. The dead said nothing, but their eyes spoke volumes.

The sweet smell of burnt flesh mixed with the acrid stink of biofoam and antibiotic sprays. Josh's mouth tasted sour, and he smacked his lips as a familiar gag reflex kicked in.

A mess of red hair and freckles appeared in front of him, flashing white teeth. "Josh!" Alexa grabbed Josh in a surprisingly tight hug, kissing his cheek. Her tears left his face wet. "I thought you were dead. Oh, my god, it was terrible."

Dax wrapped them both in a huge bear hug, weeping openly. His broad shoulders lifted and dropped like pistons with each sob. Josh bit his lips, his tears coming from the burning sensation in his arm more than relief.

Josh gently pushed out of the embrace, pinching just above his cast. "Where's the rest of the squad?"

Alexa started crying again. "Burko is dead. Felix, too. We were on the north side, protecting the command team. These...things overran our position. Josh, we were firing dummy rounds at them. They walked right through us."

He wanted to reach out, to comfort her. Something pulled at his stomach, twisting and churning until he couldn't bear it anymore. Before he could move, Dax had his arm over her shoulder. Josh kept his face stoic.

Dax brought Alexa's head to his chest. She stood on tiptoes to reach. He brushed her hand, rocking her steadily. "We're okay. We made it through the night."

"But our friends..." She squeezed Dax's arms, her hands like a child's against the large man's biceps.

Josh turned away and walked across the infirmary. He thought he heard his name called, but he ignored it. Every few steps someone would jostle him, causing another explosion of sparks from his crippled arm. After a few minutes, he found himself standing by the ICU.

Most of the soldiers on the dozen beds were already dying. Their wounds ranged from broken spines and shattered ribs to plasma burns. Josh couldn't differentiate the smells in all the chaos. One of the men shifted under the covers, groaning. Josh stepped closer.

"George," the wounded man murmured.

Josh leaned forward. "Lieutenant Davis?" He found a fold-out chair and pulled it over.

The pilot opened his eyes and pushed his blanket aside. His face was puffy and red. Half of his head was shaved to the skin, and dozens of sensor pads covered his scalp. Still, he managed to smile when he saw the soldier.

"I hope I don't look as bad as you."

Josh shrugged. "I'd say it's a toss up."

Cameron struggled to sit up, but his body wasn't having it. He finally settled on a casual lean. "What's going on?"

"The aliens are giving us a day to recover, then they're going to attack again." Josh rested his head on his good hand. "This is fucking unbelievable. We're being invaded by another species."

Cameron nodded. "Several, actually. And there are good aliens."

"No shit?"

"Would I lie to you?" Cameron coughed, interrupting his grin. The fit lasted almost a minute. In the end, Cameron spat out a mouthful of phlegm and blood and settled back into his pillow. His face seemed shades paler.

Concern crossed Josh's face. "Do you need a nurse?"

"No," Cameron said, shaking his head. "They said this was normal. I was exposed to a lot of radiation." He pulled his left arm from under the cover. A small white patch covered his hand. The center glowed yellow.

"What does the color mean?"

"Yellow means I got about ten gray."

Josh laughed. "What the hell does *that* mean?"

"Gray...it's how much radiation I absorbed. I mean, I think. I'm on a lot of stuff right now, and the doctors don't speak the same English we do."

"But yellow is good?"

"Better than red." Cameron fought a wave of nausea, barely keeping his meal down. "You know, I don't even think red is on the chart. Is there a chart on that wall?" He pointed to the curtain separating his bed from the main area.

Josh put a hand on Cameron's arm. "Sure is, buddy. A real nice one too."

"Cool." He closed his eyes, drifting. "I hope I make it through this."

Josh was about to speak when he heard a deeply accented voice call his name.

"Sergeant Rantz?"

He turned to see a barrel-chested old man in civilian clothes holding a clipboard.

"That's me," Josh said.

The older man smiled, but there was nothing comforting in his face. A scar ran from an eyebrow to his lips, giving him a permanent scowl. "The doctor would like to see you."

Josh held up his cast. "I've already been seen, sir."

"He just needs to administer some antibiotics." The old man gestured with the clipboard toward a cordoned area of the infirmary.

They slowly wove their way through the injured and arrived at a small bed surrounded by a blue curtain. A young man with jet-black hair worked at a small table, his back to them. Josh entered warily.

"I'm Sergeant Rantz," he said. "Well, actually it's 'specialist.' My promotion in the field doesn't actually count."

The doctor turned, flashing his teeth. His eyes lit up when he saw the soldier. "Of course. Joshua. Welcome. I'm so happy you made it." He sounded like the host at a restaurant, as though Josh had made a reservation. He pulled out a chair and motioned for Josh to take it. "With everything going on, we just wanted to make sure you were taken care of."

"I already saw another doc. They said my arm'll be fine." He pointed at the cast again. "Almost a pound of biofoam and a bone bath."

The doctor clicked his tongue, as though scolding a child. "Army medics are hardworking and truly wonderful people, but they are not doctors." He took a syringe from his table, along with a glass vial. Josh couldn't make out what was inside. "This won't hurt a bit, and you'll feel right as rain in a few hours."

The doctor mixed the serum around before drawing it into the needle. Something about the scene made Josh's instincts prickle, but he dismissed the feeling. The doctor pulled up one sleeve and wiped off dirt and blood with an alcohol swab. He jabbed Josh's arm, and a warm tingling sensation flooded the soldier's body.

"There," the doctor said. "All better." He placed the syringe aside in a small leather holder.

"Thanks, Doc." Josh stood, using his good hand to push off the chair. "Am I going to need any more of that?"

The doctor turned, licking his teeth. "Let's see if this takes first." He collected the vials and his syringe in a leather bag and clicked it shut. "And please, call me Markov. Now, I know you're going to be heading out soon. Can't stop the grains from falling. What I would like to offer is a chance to do more on the battlefield."

"I don't follow."

The doctor scowled, searching for the right words. "I have access to...certain hardware. It may give you a competitive edge in the fight."

The word *hardware* made Josh's stomach do a slight, sickly turn. "What kind of hardware are we talking about."

"Simply an armor upgrade. Should help against the more advanced alien weaponry. Can't guarantee anything, of course, but I do have enough ammo to keep you in the fight."

"And what do you want in return?"

Markov laughed. "This isn't a quid pro quo thing. Just bring back the armor, or at the very least the data recorder." He shuffled through his pockets, searching for something. "You don't have a history of seizures, do you?"

"Um, no?"

"Any allergies to latex, penicillin, or boron?"

"What?"

"Are you, or are any of the past five generations of your family, a natural redhead?"

"I'm not...no."

"No to the allergies or no to the redheads?"

"No to all of it."

"Perfect. Follow me and my associate and we'll get you all set up." He pulled aside the curtain and the large old man was waiting. "Tell me, Mr. Rantz. Have you ever heard of CROWN?"

Kronos

ERUK KNELT AND PICKED up a clump of dirt. The red and orange sand felt rough and sharp and foreign. Everything about this place felt wrong. Alien. The word popped into his head and in a moment he knew it was right. It was the same feeling he'd felt on countless other worlds while staring down the endless mutations of the cosmos.

He wore his formal attire rather than his body armor. His long chata robe dragged the ground, each of its forty braids representing a war won. Today was a holy day, the dereth nu'a. After walking the grounds, feeling the blood-soaked earth between his fingers, Eruk would bathe and dress for battle in the armor of his clan. It infuriated him that the glory on the ground would go to a Battle Chief. Warlords were forbidden from leaving their ships during combat. There was no reason to feel ashamed; his position aboard the Hand of the King was critical. Yet he was Cthanul, and none of the changes brought by the Druuma would take that from him.

"You are a prideful creature, Eruk." The Druuma purred. It shared some of the emotions with the Warlord and enjoyed the thrill of anticipation for the coming fight. "The Great King cautions against such arrogance."

Eruk stretched out his jaws and shoulders. Each of his four arms popped in sequence. "Leave me alone, worm."

The Druuma feigned hurt. "I only live to serve you, Warlord. Part of our symbiotic relationship is constructive criticism. Surely you can understand that. How else can you hope to rise to the ranks of the Clerics if you don't better yourself?"

The Cthanul growled. "I don't have time for another lecture." He hissed, grabbing his chest. The Druuma wriggled and bit inside him. "I could cut you out, worm. Throw your carcass into the dirt and let you bake."

"And you would die as well, and much more painfully than I. My consciousness is connected to the Great King eternally. Death is simply an inconvenient delay in my lifespan."

"How is that possible?" Eruk asked. "You are flesh and blood."

"The Boun are rock and little more, and they live. And for much longer than you. I once met a Boun that claimed to be almost three epochs."

Eruk grunted. He stepped over the bodies of several Poliadon, taking care not to move their scaly forms. The dead should not be disturbed. They served in life and have earned their peace. As their commander, he ought to at least be able to say a few words of encouragement in their native tongues. At least, for those with tongues.

"You mourn for them," the Druuma said. "Your kind killed more of the Poliadon than any other species during the sacking of Holas."

That surprised Eruk. He normally had a strong memory for such things, but couldn't recall that planet or that battle for the life of him. "When was this?"

"Before you and I joined. That is why you struggle to remember. A Ruall often loses a part of themselves during the burrowing. It is an intensely painful process, after all." The Druuma gurgled at its own joke. "But you will dream of this battle for years to come. Until your carapace hardens and cracks, you will be known as Eruk the Conquerer."

The Warlord beamed. He'd never heard the Druuma speak this way, and it filled him with energy. He set out deeper into the battlefield, searching for a place to say his prayers. Eruk planned to commune with his ancestors today, to draw in their power and strength for the coming battle. He would go back to base camp renewed, ready for anything.

Tomorrow, he thought, *I will eradicate this planet.*

GENERAL CASEY WOKE UP and realized a day had passed. His skin felt hot and grimy with sweat, and his feet ached from wearing boots all night. Even with the air conditioner running constantly, the temperature in the command center had soared into the high 80s. He had sweat stains in his pits and around his neck.

The Tomb had become his home only hours after the failed ambush on the surface. Fort Peterson had been hit with a series of crippling orbital strikes, rendering the base uninhabitable. During the painfully short respite, members of Casey's staff had labored to move the entire operation to the underground bunker. Now, with only an hour before the fight, the small hideaway had become crowded.

Politicians and arms dealers shoved and cursed alongside soldiers and technicians. Tempers flared and fistfights broke out regularly. Casey had to deploy the MPs to keep the peace. No one would say what everyone was thinking: this could be their last night alive.

"General?"

Casey looked up and saw the steward standing at attention. The general let out a long breath and sat up straight.

"Is it time?" Casey asked.

The steward shook her head. "The Boxti are preparing their next attack at a location known as the Lion's Mouth. There's still an hour before the deadline."

He yawned, stretching until his body hurt. "Any updates on the ammunition run?"

"Major Garcia went to the depot, but we haven't heard anything yet. They should've been back by now, even with cargo."

Casey mulled that over. "It's going to take more than one trip. Most of our resupply burned up in the sky last night." He pulled out his canteen and poured water over his face. "Christ, I need one thing to go right. Just one."

The steward shifted from one foot to the other. "I can see where we are with the Gremlins."

The general sighed and nodded. "That's fine."

A sudden commotion on the far side of the room drew Casey's attention. Guards at the door shouted and brandished their weapons in response to a tall man who barged in. He was dressed in a black and blue plated uniform and wore a pistol on his thigh. The Black Adder captain's rank was sewn onto his chest. His eyes were hidden behind small, round glasses, but widened when he saw the general.

Casey stood and marched toward the interloper. "Captain Hendryx, what exactly do you think you're doing?"

"I'm sure as hell not waiting for the next act of this goat show." He was filthy, covered in dirt and grease and layers of sweat. "Adders don't wait in the wings, General. We're front line. Find, fix, fuck up. You're wasting us in reserves."

Casey crossed his arms. He wasn't fond of pulling rank, but this captain failed to see the stars before him. "We don't have the fuel or the ammunition to field you. Besides that, you're one company against *how many* battalions of enemy soldiers? It's a suicide mission."

"It's not...that's just stupid, sir." Captain Hendryx set down his helmet on a nearby table. Its smell pushed a few of the technicians away. Hendryx stepped closer to the general. He was a few inches taller and used his height. "Your infantry got it handed to them the other night. We need to bring the big guns to bear, and I'm all you've got on this moon."

"And all you've got," Casey said, "is training ammo."

Hendryx groaned. "It's still a fucking bullet. And I've got plenty of live grenades from the range. Let me take the company into the shit, and we'll block their advance. The only reason my troops are even here was to support your infantry brigades. Now they need some real support."

Casey wanted to argue, but his energy was gone. He slumped into a nearby chair and closed his eyes. Finally he looked up at the insolent captain. "Load up everything you've got, but only what you brought out here. Not a single round from one of the other lines. And tell your battalion commander that I'll be speaking to him when this is all done."

Hendryx grabbed his helmet and started toward the door. "Roger, sir. Just make sure you spell my name right."

"On what?"

The captain turned and walked backward, grinning mischievously as he donned his helmet. "The award you're gonna give me for saving your ass."

Kronos Orbit

TWO BOXTI HIVES ROTATED at the center of the alien formation, positioning themselves directly over the planet. Each massive carrier used engines mounted all over its hull. The design wasn't aesthetically pleasing, but served its purpose. With infinite patience and ponderous speed, the vessels readied for deployment.

Inside the alien ships, grotesque creatures climbed limb over limb into the open cockpits of a thousand Y-fighters. They didn't look like a cohesive species; just limbs and eyes and fingers, all custom designed to be a pilot. They moved in jagged, spastic bursts, like they were having a never-ending series of seizures.

One larger creature stopped short of its ship, admiring the view from the open hangar. Far below, the orange and red planet awaited, ready to be cleansed of its infestation. Unlike the rest of the pilots, this alien wore a darker uniform with glittering red dots around the neck. It also wore another unique object: a Parasite. This Druuma was smaller than the Warlord's, and younger, but just as passionate about its task.

"Own the air," the Parasite spoke. "Own the air, and the ground will follow. That is the way of war."

The pilot climbed into the belly of its ship: a large Y-fighter with blood-rep tips on each wing. The fighter was larger than the rest, with blood-red tips to the wings. Black lines had been scorched on the hull, representing confirmed kills. The newest were shaped like human ships.

With a grunt, the Boxti ace settled into its fighter and began start-up procedures. "For the glory of the Horde."

Kronos

JOSH SAT ON A crate inside the impromptu barracks above the Tomb. Along with a few hundred soldiers, he prepared for the fight ahead. The doctors had protested against him leaving the infirmary, but he wanted back in the fight.

His arm hurt, but somehow less than before. The cast itched terribly, like it was full of ants. His shoulder hurt too, from Markov's injection. Josh pushed it all to the back of his mind. He chortled.

"What's so funny?" Alexa asked. She had strapped on the last set of scout armor and was busy adjusting the plates.

Josh shrugged. "Something my dad used to say. Any time things were bad enough, he'd go, 'If we're lucky, we'll be dead before dawn.'"

Alexa made a face. "That's awful."

"Helped him cope." Josh went back to cinching up his boots and leg guards. "It's not as bleak as it sounds. You don't actually *hope* to be dead; it's just a way of prioritizing."

She shook her head and went back to fixing her uniform. "A little dark for me."

"The dead don't have to worry about paying bills, or keeping up with schoolwork, or fighting off an alien invasion. The dead are the lucky ones." Josh clipped another plate on his forearm. Satisfied, he stood and let the armor fall into place. He felt a hundred pounds heavier. The mechanical suit looked cobbled from scraps, and felt like wearing shrapnel. "Do I have this on right?" The powered suit made him a half foot taller and added an inch of metal all around his body.

"No." The old man—Sasha—pulled at the plates and rearranged them into neater stacks. "You had your ass under your chin."

Josh bit his tongue. "So you could say I had a shit-eating grin waiting to happen?"

"No."

"Oh, come on," Josh complained. "That was gold." He looked at Alexa and Dax, who watched nervously. "My audience isn't feeling too cooperative today."

Alexa ran her fingers over the strange suit. "Are you sure this thing is safe? I've never heard of power armor of this size."

Sasha growled. "It's a new design."

"Really?" Alexa raised an eyebrow. "It looks old as shit."

"Make fun all you want," Josh said. "I feel pretty."

Alexa smiled warmly. She grabbed her rifle and started inserting magazines into the pouches around her midsection. "I don't think the dead are lucky."

"Why not?"

She leaned over and gave his good arm a squeeze. Her eyes lingered on his for a moment. "Because only the living get lucky." She winked and walked across the room, leaving Josh speechless.

Sasha finished with the armor and set the helmet down over Josh's head. All was pitch black, and then the system activated. Immediately, the armor felt lighter.

"Sweet."

"This only adds about forty kilo to your total weight, so don't act like a wrecking ball. You can still break inside there."

Josh nodded, then realized his mechanical head didn't bob with him. "Gotcha." His voice was projected by speakers in the jaw. He sounded awesome.

Above the barracks, the hangar-sized warehouse over the Tomb roared with activity. Jackals were outfitted with heavy cannons, Sparrows had their guns adjusted and armed, and mortar tubes were prepped for support. Anyone not mindfully tasked stared out the open doorway, waiting for the sun to rise. Any moment now, the enemy would begin their assault.

CAMERON SAT IN A wheelchair, watching the scores of injured soldiers load onto shuttles to New Eden. The distant planet could barely be seen through the early morning haze. Blue oceans turned purple when seen through the thick atmosphere.

"All full here," the loading sergeant called out, halting the influx of infirm with an upturned palm. A few minutes and a few whistles later, the shuttle pushed away from the ground and roared into the sky. Stubby wings folded in to streamline the craft's shape. It broke the sound barrier and cut into the upper atmosphere, sending shockwaves down below.

Soon after, another shuttle screamed down from above. Landing gear scraped at the ground until it found purchase, kicking up swirling clouds of red dust. The pilot immediately began prepping a course for a swift exit. Cameron smirked, noting that the pilot failed to engage the ERG rockets.

He's gonna burn half his fuel before he makes it out of atmo, Cameron thought.

Nearby, a Sparrow pilot sat fiddling with his DaVinci. The three-barreled gun was broken into pieces and scattered in a semicircle around the young man. Cameron wheeled himself over, stopping just short of the pile.

"Need a hand?" Cameron asked.

The pilot looked up with a start. "Shit, you scared me." He grinned sheepishly. "I'm fine. I mean, I'm not fine, but I can do this."

Cameron raised an eyebrow. "Are you sure?"

"Yeah. I mean, no. I mean...could you?" The pilot seemed overwhelmed with gratitude. He slid over to make room for Cameron. "Name's Parker."

Cameron held out a hand. "Cameron Davis. Lunar SP."

Parker shook the offered hand incredulously. "Lunar? How did you get out here?"

"Wish I knew." Cameron picked up the DaVinci's feeder assembly and pressed down on the graspers. "Well, here's your problem. Your graspers are bent. Are you using the guns as a stepping stool when you climb in?"

The pilot blushed. "How'd you know?"

Cameron laughed. "Don't sweat it, man. I used to do that all the time. But it bends these little fingers right here, and then they won't grab your rounds correctly. Makes it awful hard to shoot without bullets."

Another shuttle came and went. Parker turned toward Cameron. "Shouldn't you be getting out of here? The aliens will be back soon."

"You're not wrong. We should be getting out of here." Cameron scanned the mess of weapon parts, searching for any further defects. He was surprised to see a figure dancing in the middle of the pile. Leaning closer, Cameron saw a tiny, naked version of himself performing some sort of salsa. That...can't be a good sign.

He blinked. The nude man vanished.

"Are you all right?"

Cameron looked up, wide-eyed. His sudden grin did nothing to calm Parker's nerves. "Totally fine. Nothing to worry about. Doc gave me a few shots, told me to take it easy. I need your Sparrow."

"You should probably go lie down...wait, what?" Parker scooted back.

"Look, Parker." Cameron maintained eye contact, but his hands moved in a blur, assembling the machine gun. "I know you and I just met, but I feel a real connection. We're two peas in a pod, two fish in a barrel."

Parker squirmed.

"You want to help save some people today, so do I. My plan is just a little better. A little more fresh. More tactical. For god's sake, Parker, will you answer your fucking phone?" Cameron shoved the assembled DaVinci forward. He noticed, suddenly, that there was no ringing. "I'm sorry.

Didn't mean to yell. But I am taking your Sparrow. Now, are you going to give me the engine code or do I need to beat you to death with my chair?"

Kronos Orbit

THE BOXTI DIDN'T SEE the attack coming. One moment they were orbiting peacefully above the besieged planet, the next they were fighting for their lives. Terran cruisers, carriers, destroyers, and frigates leapt into the gravity well at Stride speed, hulls bristling with weaponry. Missiles arced and shells rained onto the alien fleet, breaching shields and shattering frames. In seconds, five ships were destroyed.

Aboard *Valley Forge*, Sam DeHart held tight to his tether as a return volley left potholes in his port wing. "Hit them again." Every bolt and screw aboard the supercruiser shuddered as the twin cannons Thunder and Lightning sounded, launching heavy slugs toward the dreadnought. Each round plowed through sections of hull, erupting in brilliant blossoms of red and yellow. The alien ship replied with a barrage of laser blasts that melted straight through *Valley Forge's* armor.

Midway dropped down behind the cruiser, unleashing an endless stream of fire-and-forgets into the side of a thorny battleship. The Boxti ship shivered before cracking into pieces, each fiery husk drifting down toward the planet below. Fighters and bombers shot out of the hangars like bullets, seeking out targets and knocking them down.

"Captain DeHart," the navigation officer shouted. "Emergency rescue has picked up Admiral Winger."

Sam registered the news with a small nod, eyes never straying from the screens arrayed before him. "Bump three loopers toward their rear flank. I want them following targets of opportunity. Get our escort to cover down on the starboard side."

Another blast from a laser cannon shook the supercruiser, but *Valley Forge* surged on unhindered. Flak burst in a golden wall around the ship, intercepting enemy fighters and shredding them to pieces. Friendly birds pushed through the debris and continued the assault.

John, his XO, appeared at his side and said, "Captain, Commodore Osaka is on a secure channel for you."

Sam squeezed John's arm, smiling appreciatively. "You've got the ship."

"Aye, sir." He swapped seats with Sam, tethering down and activating an open channel. "This is John Fuller, XO, taking control of the bridge. All call signs acknowledge."

Sam headed toward his quarters. Officers and enlisted soldiers sped past, not bothering to salute. A part of Sam's brain registered that the ship was actively fighting, and that such pleasantries had no place on a battlefield. Still, it was hard to shake the feeling of being slighted.

He arrived in his room seconds later, sweating despite the cool temperature. Sam secured the door and activated the communication line on a nearby screen. "Authenticate, Captain Samuel DeHart."

The screen came to life, and Commodore Osaka's face appeared.

"Sam," Hiro said. "We're moving our group around to the outer quadrant. Keep them focused a few minutes more and we can enclose them."

"Roger." Sam paused. "Sir, did this need to be on a secure line?"

Commodore Osaka pursed his lips. "I heard you found Admiral Winger."

"We caught her pod about ten minutes ago. Everyone on board is alive, but shaken. They were pretty low on air when we caught up to them. Nearly twenty-four hours in one of those flying tombs...Jesus."

Hiro remained stoic. "Please have them transferred to *Midway* as soon as possible. We need to get the Admiral on a secure transport to New Eden for debrief."

"With respect, Commodore, we're right in the middle of something here. She'll be safer when surrounded by a few hundred tons of cruiser than in a shuttle." Something crashed into the ship. Sam braced himself. Lights flickered overhead. "Better than that, we should be giving her another ship. I'd rather have her in the fight."

The commodore seemed genuinely worried. "Sam, Cora is a dear friend. I'm entrusting you with her care."

Sam pursed his lips. "She's also an admiral of the Federate Fleet and a grown-ass woman. And, she may be the best commander on the field right now, us included."

Hiro clenched his jaw, but softened a moment later. "Then get her whatever she needs."

Kronos

THE SURVIVING SOLDIERS FROM the 185th joined their brethren from the Black Adders and began a slow and tense advance toward the Lion's Mouth. They wore a mixture of combat and training armor of every color—not exactly tactical, but necessary. Each carried as much live ammunition as could be spread over so many men and women. Every step brought them closer to the enemy, closer to the monsters that already haunted their dreams. Over the jagged horizon, the blue star Eros began to warm up the day.

They marched slowly in a wide formation that covered almost a kilometer. The Black Adders, in their shades-of-gray camouflage, led the way. Josh was about halfway down the line, still struggling to make his mechanized suit work. Every few minutes the group paused and took cover, collapsing to the ground and waiting. Josh would halt and use the suit's enhanced optics to scan. Inside the dense helmet, dozens of readouts fed him a firehose of information.

Sills, Josh thought, recalling an old pneumonic. *Stop, Look, Listen, Smell. Well, I'm stopped…standing tall like a fucking moron, but I'm stopped. I can see everything, which is nice. Can't hear or smell for shit, though. What else am I supposed to be doing?* His neurons fired at a blinding speed, and suddenly he remembered every page of his training manual. Closing his eyes, he could see the crude drawings on the tablet as though they were right there in front of him. He came back to reality with a start. His stomach churned. *What the hell was that?*

He brought his left arm near his face, rotating the wrist and bending the elbow. There had been hardly any pain before they'd left the Tomb. Now there was none. The doctors had told him that, at best, he'd be facing a two-month recovery. Josh fought against a sudden and overwhelming feeling of fear.

"Hey," a voice hissed. "Are you okay? We're moving."

Josh jumped, waving off the friendly soldier and moving out. His right arm was a little heavier than the left; a machinegun was mounted across his forearm. When he pointed his hand, a reticule appeared on the HUD. A flash of light blinded him, and Josh was suddenly seated at a lecture hall at Fort Metts, listening to a wrinkled war veteran discuss the finer points of mechanized infantry theory. Then he was back on Kronos, stuck inside a rusted bucket, with a magically healed arm.

The fuck?

A voice sounded in his commlink: "Josh." It was Alexa. "I'm in an OP about a klick ahead of you. I can see them. The aliens."

"Be careful." Josh quickly made his way to his squad leader. He didn't recognize the name of the captain, but the patch on his arm was unmistakable. The coiled snake and skull of the Black Adders was as infamous as the unit itself. Josh took a moment to find his voice. "Sir?"

The larger man turned and grabbed Josh by the chest plate. He pushed Josh hard against a nearby rock wall. The officer wore a full face mask painted to look like a screaming demon. His ceramic plates were chipped and scraped from repeated use. When he spoke, each word came out crisp and quiet.

"Maintain. Noise. Discipline."

Josh gripped the captain's wrist, pulling it down from his throat. "Sorry."

"What is it?" They started walking again, with the Black Adder leading the way. His every movement came out smooth as silk.

Josh tried to avoid stepping on every loose rock and pebble, with little success. Anything louder than a cotton swab hitting a blanket drew a harsh glance from the squad leader. It certainly didn't help that he sounded like a dump truck falling into a rock tumbler. "Our OP has the enemy moving toward us about a klick out."

"Fine." The sergeant quickened his pace. He raised his gauntlet to his mask and spoke rapidly. "This is Shogun.

Hostiles moving toward engagement area Roadkill. Need fire support on standby." A tiny voice replied, too faint for Josh to hear. "Roger. Show me on the move. ETA, five mikes." The sergeant turned to Josh. "Keep up." And he was off.

Josh couldn't catch the faster soldier, no matter how hard he ran. The added weight of the combat armor dampened his speed, and the suit refused to respond to his body. The Black Adders vaulted over cover into a narrow canyon pass and disappeared. Josh hit the low rock at a run, jumping as high as he could. His knee plate caught on a small jutting stone and stopped him cold. He rolled over the stone, landing in a heap on the other side.

It took a few seconds before he could breathe right, and by then the Black Adders was long gone.

"Alexa," Josh croaked. "Are you still there?"

Silence passed for a moment, and then her voice came through. "Josh. They're right below me. There's so many of them."

His blood turned to ice. "Don't move. Don't make a sound."

"There's a whole army here. They're going to see me." Her voice cracked. "Josh. Help."

He was already off and running. His legs and arms pumped together, propelling him through the narrow passages. Every movement synced together, and soon he was bouncing off walls with his toes. The heavy combat armor felt like terry cloth on his shoulders. He cleared the canyons and found himself in a small covered ledge overlooking a plateau. Down below, the massive Lion's Mouth stretched for miles.

Standing in the shadows, masked face unreadable, was the Black Adder's squad leader.

"Sergeant," Josh whispered. "We have to extract Corporal Haines."

The squad leader barely turned. "No. We'll lose surprise."

Josh balled his fists. "She's all alone out there."

The sergeant wheeled around. "Specialist, do you understand what's happening here?"

"It's an alien invasion."

The squad leader shook his head. "This is a *war*. We've been fighting these guys for a month now."

"What're you talking about? They just showed up the other day."

"First contact happened in October, Specialist. Less than a hundred killed in a huge battle over Luna. A few weeks later, they came back and burnt Tallus to a cinder."

Tallus? Josh didn't realize he was backing up until his shoulders hit the rock wall. "Why wouldn't anyone tell us? Why weren't we warned?"

"That's above my pay grade." He took a menacing step forward. "The point is, we have an opportunity here. You see, in every fight so far, humans have lost. We aren't as good at making war as we thought. This here is a chance to take back a little momentum." He turned around slowly, placing a hand on the low ceiling. "It's about fucking time they felt pain."

Josh crept forward, heart pounding. "But what does that have to do with Alexa? Why won't you help her?"

The Black Adder's squad leader glanced back. "Corporal Haines is in an optimal position to observe indirect fire. She may even survive the barrage."

"What?" Josh said. "You can't be serious. She'll be *killed*."

"Then she'll take a few thousand of those monsters with her." He brought his gauntlet to his mask again. "Red Leg, this is Shogun. Immediate suppression, codename Vesuvius." He gave Josh a sympathetic nod. "Danger close."

THE INCOMING REPORTS FROM the warzone drew chorus after chorus of cheers.

The collection of politicians, aides, officers, and reporters breathed a sigh of relief as *Midway* confirmed the destruction of yet another Boxti ship. Video feed from Eros lagged heavily, but Commodore Osaka's voice rang loud and clear.

The tides had turned.

They'd been waiting for hours, sitting in the cramped room drinking stale coffee and making small talk. The staff had prepared a sizable meal, but no one was in the mood to eat. Admiral Walker paced in a wide circle around the table, intermittently chewing on his fingernails and texting messages to his staff. Jerry sat by the high chancellor, whispering information as it was passed to him. Several of the Council Secretaries snored quietly in their chairs, exhausted from several days of overstimulation.

"Admiral Winger is secured," a voice said over the loudspeaker. A dozen people let out their breath, and a few people applauded. Admiral Walker paused mid-step and stared at the group before resuming his march.

Alexander picked up his cold cup of coffee and drank deep, ignoring the bitter taste. His hands shook slightly, but he moved quickly to avoid notice. Not that he needed to hide much. Everyone was watching the fight unfold on one of the dozen screens around the room. Already the sky over Kronos was littered with shattered frigates and destroyers and cruisers. Molten slag bobbed and stretched in zero gravity, freezing into metal asteroids that cluttered an already chaotic battlefield.

"Alec," Jerry said. "I heard back from the colonial delegation. They're not thrilled with the idea of an alliance, but almost everyone is willing to sit down and negotiate."

The high chancellor tapped his chin. "I bet I can guess who our holdout is."

Jerry nodded. "Mars will never go along with anything we propose. They rejected bills specifically designed to provide aid. They just want to oppose you. We should be grateful that it's been nonviolent these past few years."

"Grateful," Alexander said. He didn't like the taste of the word. "You know who didn't have this trouble? Norton."

Jerry shrugged. "He also ended his career publicly and bloodily. Do you *want* a rope around your neck?"

"I don't want to start a new empire. I just wish people would look at the facts before passing judgment on every single thing that I do or say."

"The public is fickle," Jerry said. "And easily bored. They like scandal because it's interesting, not because it is in any way good for them or the Federate. Hating you isn't a personal thing. They hate the rank, the position. They hate that you have power, or that anyone has power. And they're about as literate as a tree stump when it comes to politics. So they'll write their angry messages on the Net, or protest outside the embassies. As long as it doesn't get rough, they can enjoy the circus a little longer."

Alexander sighed. "But they're wrong. They're wrong and loud and infuriating." He pointed to a smaller television, the only one not showing the battle over Kronos. On the screen, the Galactic News anchor reported on anti-Federate protests happening all over Earth. "They're supporting him. Jonah. They're buying his bullshit and calling us baby killers and racists. Christ, it was a different administration that ran that awful campaign in the first place. I'm supposed to represent the new humanity, one unified and progressive. How can I do that if half the population thinks I'm the devil incarnate?"

"Listen," Jerry said. "John Q. Public doesn't give two shits about the truth. He's an emotional wreck and his opinion is dictated by crappy television. He's a sheep who follows the crowd. Now that's not necessarily a bad thing. Sheep are law-abiding, at least for the most part. They'll come back to your side if you take care of the wolves."

The high chancellor gestured at the battle. "Am I not?"

"No." Jerry eyed the other guests in the room with suspicion. "Jonah Blightman is the wolf. As long as he's taking control of Earth, the sheep are going to play his game. Take out Jonah, and the public will swing back to your side, even if it's for the wrong reasons."

Alexander downed his coffee, grimacing at the hideous flavor. "Politics suck."

Kronos

JOSH WAS ALREADY RUNNING when the mortars fell. He heard the ordnance drop over the radio and took off, dismissing the warnings from the Black Adder captain. He leapt from cover and sprinted straight at the enemy formation. A few tall stone ridge lines kept him concealed from the alien scouts, but not for much longer. The terrain carried him toward a peak that overlooked the entire pass. Once he crested it, he'd be in the enemies' sights. He didn't care. His friend was in danger.

Time to see what this tin bucket can do.

The sound of battle rose up on either side as the forward elements made contact. Rifle fire and laser blasts made a strangely musical sonic cocktail. Over the rises, smoke and dust exploded upward as the enemy hit trip mines placed the day before. Alien screams echoed against the canyon walls.

"Specialist Rantz," a voice said over the radio. "You are off grid. Return to formation immediately."

Josh kept on his path. "I'm almost to her."

"Jesus. Rounds are incoming in two mikes. You're not going to make it."

"Then I don't have time to talk to you." His lungs burned and his limbs ached, but he refused to stop. *Come on, come on, come on!* By the time he reached the top of the ridge, he could barely catch his breath. He collapsed to his knees, his face red and dripping sweat. Each gasp pulled in too little air, and the heat was unbearable. The suit was an oven. With his strength waning, he managed to pull himself to the lip of the landing and look over.

Josh looked out at the Boxti horde and saw conquest displayed in full view.

There were thousands of them. They wore heavy armor and marched in a line formation. There was no concern about losing a few hundred soldiers. This was an army meant to overwhelm. Their uniforms were varied and multicolored. Josh sensed an army assembled from dozens of assimilated civilizations.

"Josh," Alexa spoke softly, without emotion. "You need to leave me."

His eyes burnt. He told himself it was sweat. "I'm almost there."

"You'll be killed."

"I can do this." He searched the field until he found her. She'd climbed a spire above the enemy soldiers and set up her camouflage netting. From the ground, she would look like just another scraggly plant. But there was no way she'd be able to move without alerting the entire force. Josh scanned every nook and cranny within sight, willing his brain to come up with some sort of solution.

He was about to look for higher ground when he got thrown to the dirt. Josh rolled twice and came up with his gun pointed at his attacker. Three soldiers stood opposite him, their rifles slung behind their backs. In the center, standing tall, was the Black Adder squadron leader.

"You just don't give up, Rantz." The squadron leader clenched his right hand into a fist, but relaxed a moment later. "Looks like I'm going to have to help you so you don't waste that sweet armor."

Josh's amazement turned to anger. "You're the one who called in the fucking strike."

"And I'll keep calling them in until the tubes break. We're outnumbered, outgunned, and outmatched, soldier. Wake the fuck up. We lose *here*, where do you think the next battle is going to be?"

Josh knew the sergeant was right, even if he *was* a total asshole. "Then what are we gonna do?"

The captain pointed toward the edge of the landing. "Those first rounds are to disrupt, and they'll be low yield. Unless your friend is very unlucky, she'll survive. The Boxti are marching too close together for a clean break to cover, and we can use that confusion to get in close." He put a heavy hand on Josh's shoulder. "But understand, if the opportunity comes to level these fuckers, I'm going to take it. Not one of our lives is more important than this mission."

Josh had just started to nod when he heard the whistle from above. All four soldiers looked down on the enemy as the first shell streaked toward the ground.

"Incoming," Josh whispered to no one.

The first round hit with a sudden crunch, burying the force of its explosion under the weight of a dozen alien soldiers. Body parts scattered in a grisly fifty-foot radius.

Josh and the soldiers started moving. The Adders dropped over waist-high boulders, landing softly on their rubber-soled boots. Josh's armored legs sounded like a truck barreling through gravel.

Leading the pack, the Black Adder squadron leader paused at every intersection, sweeping around the corner with his rifle at the ready. They moved forward cautiously. By the time they reached the last bit of cover, Josh was dripping with a cold sweat. And a hot sweat. Basically all the sweat.

"All right," the captain said. "From here on out, we're fighting. Keep your bursts low and centered, and don't stop moving. A stationary target is too easy to pass up." He glanced around their cover. "Rantz, are you wearing a cold pack?"

Josh's face was unreadable inside the metal suit. "I...I have no idea what that is."

The captain growled. "They're dropping HE and Willie Pete. You catch that too close and you're going to bake inside that armor."

"Then I won't try to catch them. Are we going?"

"Two teams," the captain said. "Ray, you're with me." He didn't wait for any more questions. In three steps he was in the middle of the warzone, sprinting and knocking aliens aside.

Josh turned to the remaining soldier. Below the tan helmet, his skin was black as slate. "Who are you?"

"Pierre Roman," he said, giving a two-fingered salute. His accent softened the consonants and rounded out the words. "After you, Mr. Robot."

With a deep breath, Josh barreled around the corner and into the fray. He immediately regretted it. There were too many enemy soldiers to count. They flooded his vision with a sea of alien faces. There were lizards, rock monsters, giant insects, humanoids, and so many combinations of eyes and mouths it made Josh's head spin. He forced his way through, ignoring the arms and claws and limbs scraping against his armor. When a gecko got too close, Josh squeezed the trigger inside his gauntlet. The machine gun bucked and split the alien in half.

The first mortar hit a few hundred meters away and sent up a huge plume of dust and fire and bodies. Josh felt the impact in his gut like a hammer, but he kept moving. More and more rounds shook the earth. Boulders tumbled from the walls, crushing alien soldiers into paste. Sprays of orange, green, and black blood painted the dusty ground until it ran like a river.

Josh nearly slipped in a pile of entrails, but Pierre caught him. They ran side by side, huffing and puffing with exertion. Josh's heartbeat had turned into a drumroll. The burning smell of cordite and metal mixed with the stench of meat and blood. He dry heaved even as he fought for breath.

The first white phosphorous round struck a moment later, sparking into a massive explosion. Steaming clouds of white smoke billowed from the impact, consuming the alien soldiers. Screams of panic and pain grew louder than the mortar fire as skin and carapace melted into slush.

Josh blocked it out as best he could. He ran until his thighs burned. Pierre broke into the lead and guided them toward a cave in the canyon walls. The ceiling curved thirty feet overhead. Josh hit the far wall and collapsed to his knees, sucking in deep breaths and hacking up smoke. The temperature dropped a few dozen degrees in the shade, and both soldiers shivered. Outside, the shells continued to drop.

After a minute, Josh had enough air to speak. "This is awful." He tried to wipe drool and bile from his lips, but only succeeded in scraping his gauntlet against his helmet. "Listen to their screams."

Pierre stood behind a cut in the blue stone wall, peering out at the enemy. "It's war, Rantz. It isn't meant to be pleasant."

Josh lifted himself off the ground with shaking limbs. He leaned against the wall and pulled his helmet off. *Oh sweet Jesus, glorious air, air, air.* He searched for his water line and bit down, sucking in greedy mouthfuls of liquid. Satisfied, he keyed his radio with his chin.

"Alexa," Josh said. "Are you still there? Can you hear me?" Nothing. "Alexa, we made it to one of the Lion's Eyes. I think it's the North cave, but I can't be sure."

Pierre turned his head slightly. "It is. We went right after the ridgeline."

Josh nodded appreciatively. "Alexa. Please answer me."

"I'm here," she said. "The pillar is holding for now."

Something drew Josh's attention. Small rocks cascaded down from the ceiling further into the cave. Josh squinted but couldn't see more than twenty feet in front of his face. He slid his helmet back on and activated the low-light enhancement. The tunnel took a hard dogleg left and disappeared, trending downward. Strange noises echoed from deep below.

"Hold on, Alexa. We're coming." He started toward the decline, his feet lifting and dropping slowly. His brain protested each step. *Nothing good will come from this, you know.* Josh ignored the feeling, creeping closer to the turn. "Pierre, have you made contact with the captain?"

Pierre stayed at his post, watching the aliens burn and die outside the cave. "Nothing yet, *fre*." He swore. "We're going to need a miracle to get out of here."

Josh reached the edge of the tunnel and stopped. A cold breeze carried a foul odor. He increased the sensitivity of his visor and looked around the corner. His entire body froze immediately. "I don't know about a miracle," he said. "But how about a nightmare?"

Kronos Orbit

ADMIRAL CORA WINGER GRITTED her teeth as another explosion sent shockwaves through *Valley Forge*. Metal popped and groaned under the stress, and pipes burst overhead. Streams of water ran down the walls and flooded the corridors outside the ship's infirmary. The admiral, along with Lena and Doc Roe, braced until the world settled back down.

"How much more of this can we take?" Doc Roe asked.

"Enough," Cora said. "She's the best built cruiser in the fleet." She sat up on an open bed, gripping the railing. Most of the infirmary was full already, though the injuries were mostly minor. The supercruiser's durable frame meant that, aside from a few broken bones and burns, the crew had held up remarkably well.

Lena paced nearby. "Where's the commander? He should've come down here to meet us."

"Why would he do that?" Cora asked. "He has a battle to win, Lena. He's right where he needs to be."

"And what about us? We just have to sit here and wait for something to happen?" Lena balled her fists. "You're a fucking two-star, Cora. You shouldn't be put aside like some used napkin. I don't know why you trust that arrogant ass.

You're more important in this fight than Sam DeHart or anyone else."

"I agree."

Cora and Lena turned to see Sam enter the infirmary. Guards snapped to attention, only to relax with a wave of the commander's hand. "Admiral, Captain. It's good to see you both alive."

"Captain DeHart," Cora said. "We appreciate the lift. How goes the battle?"

"We're making do, ma'am." He stopped, suddenly shaking his head. "No, that's not right. We're getting our asses handed to us."

Cora's chest tightened. She'd seen Sam DeHart stare down three-to-one odds before, against a full Martian armada no less. He always took her at poker, and he could hold his own with even the youngest officers in the boxing ring. Now she saw something new in the veteran commander:

Fear.

"I don't understand how they got your boat," Sam said. "Kinetic shields were up. Your armor had just been replated."

"And it wasn't enough," Cora answered. "We–I underestimated the enemy. It won't happen again."

"But how can we hope to win against this?"

Cora took a step closer to Sam. "They may have better ships, but we have better officers." She looked at Lena. "My XO and I are all patched up, Captain. We need to be back in this fight if we're going to make any kind of difference."

Sam nodded. "*St. Nichols* is headed our way right now. They're crewed up and ready for your orders once you're aboard."

Lena scowled. "I thought she was mothballed a year ago."

Sam shrugged. "Returned to duty, apparently. Until then, Admiral, *Valley Forge* is yours."

Cora's eyebrows shot up. "Sam, this is your ship. I couldn't take her in the middle of a battle."

Captain DeHart reached over and grabbed a handset off a nearby intercom. "Cora, I'm good. Really good. I mean, I've been featured in fucking textbooks." He held the microphone out toward the admiral. "You're better."

She didn't know how to react. Cora felt Lena's hand take her own and squeeze. The admiral reached out and accepted the handset, bringing it close to her lips. She keyed the radio and heard the squelch as the line reach out to the entire fleet.

"This is Admiral Cora Winger. I'm taking command of this fleet. Rally at *Valley Forge* and stand by all fighters. We're going to show these invaders how humanity makes war."

The Lion's Mouth
Kronos

JOSH'S SKIN CRAWLED AT the sight. He peered through his scope at a seething, breathing nest filled with...he didn't know what. Behind him, Pierre shook his head.

"Please, *fre*," he said. "I mean, if I'm being serious. Please? Please don't do this?"

"You scared of them?" Josh asked.

Pierre nodded. "My whole life, man. Give me the heebies and all that."

"Me too," Josh said—and pulled the trigger. The round struck the nest with a sickening *splat*. Immediately, hundreds of *things* crawled from the broken nest. Roughly the size of dogs, they were covered with bristly fur and skittered on eight spindly legs that hit the ground with a *click-clack*. Blood-red streaks ran through their brown and black carapaces. With an ungodly screech, the spiders ran out to defend their home.

Josh and Pierre broke from their positions, and scrambled up some nearby stalagmites. The giant bugs crawled underneath and swiped at them, venom dripping from their six-inch fangs. A few of the smaller spiders tried to climb up after the soldiers. Josh and Pierre lashed out with their boots and knocked the shrieking creatures back into the mob.

Great idea, Josh. Fight monsters with monsters? Are you a fucking nutcase?

But they caught a break: the spiders followed the scent of battle out of the cave, where a group of fleeing Boxti met the crawling horde head on. Five geckos stopped in their tracks, shouting and hissing and firing their weapons. They'd barely begun to fight when dozens of the giant bugs overwhelmed them. Fangs came down like daggers, stabbing the geckos to death.

Josh turned his head away from the grisly show, only to see a group of adult spiders on the march. There were three pairs, each the size of a truck. Heavy whiskers concealed a powerful set of mandibles as big as Josh's forearm. The large creatures paid the two soldiers little attention, focusing on the louder and more aggressive aliens outside. As they passed, a putrid and acrid stench flooded the cave. Josh's eyes watered. Pierre jabbed him with an elbow. His armor clanged from the impact.

"Let's get out of here."

"Roger that," Josh said.

They took off at a sprint, leaping over the smaller spiders and weaving around the larger ones. More than once, Josh felt a claw swipe at his back, but he focused on his stride and let speed be his defense. In seconds they were outside the cave, breathing in the hot stink of the battlefield. Only then did Josh realize the extent of what he'd started.

Spiders owned the ground. Swarms chased after fleeing aliens, leaping onto their shoulders and injecting venom into their necks. Larger creatures stayed near the fresh kills, feeding. Mortars fell on the far side of the clearing, but the enemy was too spread out for the strikes to be effective. With the exception of a few platoons of Boxti soldiers, the front had been cleared.

Josh quickly located Alexa's hiding place and ran toward it. He saw the rough netting of her ghillie suit and called out. Pierre drew his rifle and fired at any spiders bold enough to give chase.

"Alexa!" Josh stared hard at her post, praying to see movement. "We're here!"

Her head popped out from the hammock. Her eyes were red and puffy, and her face was covered in black soot. "Josh? Oh my god, I thought you'd left me."

"That's because you're dumb," he shouted with a grin. "I always knew there was a reason you went infantry."

She disappeared, and seconds later a rope descended from the netting. Alexa slid down as fast as she could, landing on two feet with a soft thud. She quickly pulled up her carbine and checked the chamber. "The mortars ceased fire."

"Why?" Josh asked.

"They've got this whole area wired up with Gremlins. The mortars were just meant to break their formation and force them into the canyon passes."

Josh scanned the area. Most of the Boxti were already gone, and the few that remained had their hands full with the spiders. "Then we can't go back the way we came. That road is probably set to go. Can we get a lift?"

"Not likely," a deep voice said. The Black Adder captain walked up to the trio, his rifle held over his shoulder. New cuts and holes in his armor told the story of an ugly fight. "Didn't make you for a strategist, Rantz. Or an entomologist."

Pierre stood a little straighter. "Captain Hendryx, where is Doherty?"

"Dead." The Black Adder rolled his shoulders. "Hit with some sort of plasma rifle. Melted right through his armor." He knelt down, touching a dead gecko. "They're not invincible. That's a plus." He looked up at Josh. "Vesuvius goes hot in ten minutes, Corporal. What's your exit strategy?"

Josh balked. "What do you mean? Don't you have a plan?"

"My plan was to watch the sky fall on these fuckers from the safety of the Lion's Brow. You're the genius who wanted to go into the Mouth."

"I don't know," Josh said. "I just had to get to Alexa before they did."

The captain shook his head. "And good for you. She's safe. And in another nine minutes we're all going to be dead." He poked Josh's armored chest with a gloved finger. "Figure something out."

A loud roar cut off the conversation. All four soldiers turned toward the canyon passages. Rock and dust shot into the sky as a ground reduction mine lit off. Some of the spiders fled for cover, braying. The ground bucked.

"Shit," Alexa said. "They're starting early."

The Front
Kronos

CAMERON BANKED HARD TO dodge an incoming missile. The sky over the battlefield was alive with ships. Terran Sparrows danced with Boxti Y-fighters mere meters over the ground. Laser fire and missiles crisscrossed in the air, leaving smoky trails in their wake. Cameron flew low and fast, slaloming in between the canyons to avoid the enemy. A few brave Boxti pilots gave chase, only to lose ground to the more maneuverable Sparrow.

A missile curved wildly past Cameron's port side and exploded into a wall. The Sparrow rocked from the shockwave, but righted itself quickly.

"Hey, Six," Cameron said to one of his fellow pilots. "How about you provide some cover for once? Might be a nice change of pace."

"Who the fuck is this? Where's Parker?"

"Never mind, just fucking fight."

Cameron searched the sky for a familiar shape. Every Y-fighter that flew by got a cursory scan before being ignored. If they were dumb enough to linger in his sights, he sent a quick burst from his DaVincis to get them away. He turned down the radio so the constant shouts and curses from the other pilots wouldn't bother him.

Only one thing mattered: finding the Boxti fighter who killed George. It was insane. There was no way to be sure that a single pilot would be in this same battle group, but Cameron could feel it in his bones.

"Where are you?"

Far overhead, the Boxti hive dumped out more and more fighters. The lithe craft dropped through the atmosphere with a screaming howl, only engaging their engines when they reached the fray. Cameron watched with awe, admiring the skill of the alien pilots. One ship came to a stop only a few feet away. Its engines chugged to life and blasted it toward the Boxti front line.

More Sparrows arrived, releasing another flurry of cluster warheads. The charges broke apart into a dozen smaller bombs, each one hunting for a target. Y-fighters took the hits and fell like wounded birds, spiraling to the ground.

Then, in an instant, it arrived. The ship fell into place at ten thousand feet. Cameron recognized it immediately with its extended wings and red markings. It was the Boxti ace. *The* Boxti ace. It immediately started spewing dozens of rockets in every direction. Sparrows erupted like firecrackers.

Cameron pushed his throttle forward and squeezed the yoke tight. His body ached from the effort. He glanced at the gauze wrapped around his arm. Yellow pus oozed from underneath. No matter—he gave chase. His feet controlled the ailerons and kept the bird between the rocks. The ace flew a few hundred feet over the deck, shooting at targets as they popped up. Terran ships fell in pieces on either side of the canyon. Cameron remained on target, despite the adrenaline surging through him.

"Gotcha, you sonofabitch." He was about to fire when his radio squawked.

"Any station this net, this is...well, this is Shogun. I need immediate evac."

No one responded.

Cameron sighted the ace in his crosshairs and spun his DaVincis up to full RPM.

"Any station, this is Shogun. We're in the Lion's Mouth and cut off. Charges are lit. We need help now!"

Cameron's eyes burned. *Dammit, you're on a mission, Cameron. Keep your head in the game.* He gritted his teeth and pressed forward, but couldn't shake the nagging voice in his head.

Leaving those guys would be a real dick move, Cam.

"Shut the fuck up, George." His tears ran sideways to his ears. The engines roared, and Cameron sank deeper into his seat. He was still wearing his hospital gown instead of a flight suit, and the rushing blood swelled uncomfortably in his body. Dark shadows flooded his vision.

There was no way you could have saved me, Cam. Not even one in a million. I was lunch since launch, and you know it. Don't let someone die on my account.

"I won't let you down again."

The benefit of being dead is not caring about that sort of thing.

Cameron felt the weight of the words in his chest, and he started to slow down. The Boxti ace continued on its path, oblivious to its pursuer. Slowly, the Sparrow began a wide turn outside the canyon. Cameron locked in his destination and opened up the throttle.

"Shogun, this is Wolf. I'm coming for you."

Kronos Orbit

ERUK COULDN'T HAVE ASKED for a better show.

Aboard his ship, he had the perfect seat to watch the battle unfold. Below, on the rocky canyons of the human world, thousands of thralls gave their lives for a feint. The distraction bought his ships time to prepare for the next phase of the journey.

A few frigates and destroyers had fallen in the surprise attack. It mattered little to the warlord. Other ships could fill the ranks, and each life lost only brought greater glory to the overall campaign. Like every other species the Horde had come across, humanity would fall.

One way or another, they all did.

"Warlord," the navigator called out. "A message from the *Shatadon*."

Eruk made a small involuntary sound in the back of his throat. *The Clerics?* He rubbed his lower hands with his upper ones, taking a moment to ready himself for the briefing. When he was prepared, he gave the subordinate a subtle nod.

A shimmering orb rose from the floor and exploded into a massive sphere that cast brilliant shadows around the command room. On the facing side, glaring down at the warlord, the elder Cleric appeared. Its genderless face was angular and immense, with six eyes arranged in sets between its elongated forehead and pointed jaw. A thick gray carapace had grown over its flesh, a byproduct of evolving under intense radiation. *The true Boxti.* Its mood was easy to infer.

"What is the meaning of this, Warlord?" It spat its words as though they were poison. "You were sent to investigate an attack, not start a war."

Eruk remained motionless and tried to keep his thoughts clean lest the Druuma punish him. "These creatures attacked members of the Horde."

"And you decided to act without orders? To play King?"

Eruk shook his head. "I would never presume—"

"Hold your tongues before I take them from you." The elder Cleric blinked its eyes in sequence. "You will cease these hostilities at once and return to Drova for disciplinary hearings."

Eruk rose from his seat, muscles rippling under his armor. "All I have done has been in the name of the King. I have sacrificed my ships—my men—all for His glory. I will not be treated like some insolent thrall."

The Cleric made a sound like a nest of hornets. Its eyes narrowed. "You have done these tasks to further yourself, and you have brought nothing but trouble for our conquest.

The Presagin did not identify this species for your personal gain. Leave that system now."

"I see no reason to leave." Eruk puffed out his chest and clicked his mandibles. "There is no threat to me here."

The Cleric's small mouth curled upward, almost like a smile. "Is there not?"

Eruk was about to answer when the alarms sounded across his ship. He looked over at his crew, suddenly aware of their panicked voices. They shouted to each other in tongues he never bothered to learn.

This can't be happening, the warlord thought.

The Lion's Mouth
Kronos

EXPLOSIONS RATTLED OFF ONE after another, ripping the rocky ground apart. Josh could barely keep his balance. Stones tumbled down from the canyon walls around them, cracking into rubble upon impact. Spiders climbed over everything. They screeched and clawed at the soldiers. Alexa shot three smaller arachnids before they could get too close. Pierre had already exhausted his ammunition and switched to his pistol.

The Black Adder squadron leader took charge, moving them in a tight diamond formation. They walked briskly, taking care to only shoot at direct threats. Bodies of the dead Boxti carpeted the clearing, and puddles of blood pooled in the low ground. Each step had to be taken carefully across the blood-slick ground. The spiders seemed drawn to Josh's armor, though they couldn't break through it. He shot, punched, and stomped his way past them.

Josh ran up a boulder near the center of the clearing. Canyon walls rose to all sides; they were blocked in. "This is

Shogun, we're at the center of the Lion's Mouth. The charges are going off." He shielded his eyes from the sun and spun in a circle. "Where the hell are these guys?"

Pierre kicked away an aggressive spider, putting a round in its abdomen. His pistol's slide locked to the rear. "Fuck. I'm out, *fre*." He pointed off toward the north pass. "Josh, we've got a problem. Look!"

Josh followed Pierre's finger to a large opening in the rock wall. A platoon of Boxti soldiers streamed out like angry hornets. They sighted the humans immediately and charged, hollering in their alien tongues. The Black Adder squadron leader used the laser sight on his rifle to determine range.

"Six hundred meters." He slung his rifle and started piling up bodies. Soon he had a grisly barricade established with the large boulder in the center. Pierre and Josh helped stack it up higher, until all four soldiers could lay down and have some semblance of cover.

Josh stared down his sights. "Make every shot count," he said. His machine gun was rock steady as he tracked his first target. One tall and lanky alien had limbs that stretched and shrank like taffy. Josh aimed for center mass and waited for the order to shoot. The ground continued to shake as the Gremlins drew closer and closer.

"Now!"

Alexa, Josh, and the Black Adder opened fire. They loosed single shots, striking down the Boxti soldiers mid-run. Some hit the ground and tried to rise again, only to be trampled by the hundreds of others behind them. Josh saw a flash of purple overhead and shifted his rifle. A lone gecko had climbed up a pillar to try to flank them. Josh put a bullet through its throat.

The Boxti returned fire, but it was chaotic and unfocused. A few rounds hit their meat barricade, filling the air with the stink of burnt flesh, cordite, and smoke. Alexa gagged but never stopped shooting. The Black Adder ran through his magazines in seconds and tossed his rifle aside. Before long, all three were down to their pistols.

"Heads up," Alexa shouted, pulling a grenade. She yanked the pin with her teeth and sent it sailing at the enemy. "Frag out!" The explosion sent blood and bone spraying everywhere.

But the Boxti kept coming.

Josh fired at a mean-looking rock creature, but the rounds bounced off its face. He squeezed the trigger again and nothing happened. *Shit.* He swung the weapon hard, cracking the alien in the head. That didn't stop it either. The Boxti slowed short of the humans, weapons raised. One by one, the soldiers stood up and raised their hands. The Black Adder was the last.

A gecko stepped out front, brandishing a strange gun. It pressed the weapon against the Black Adder's chest and spat out a curse. As one, the Boxti raised their rifles and hand cannons.

Alexa reached out and squeezed Josh's arm. She smiled weakly. "Thanks for the rescue."

Josh felt oddly calm. "Don't mention it." Something gnawed at the back of his head. There was a ringing in his ears, like a motor spinning too fast. He stared down the barrels of the firing squad and gritted his teeth.

The aliens barked some order again, this time more urgently. Their next words dissolved under the sudden and violent sound of flesh popping. Down the center line of the

Boxti formation, bullets tore the menagerie of creatures apart. Sound caught up a moment later and the group scattered.

Rising over the canyon was a single Sparrow. Its DaVincis sang a long note, sending a tight stream of bullets into the alien soldiers. Josh and the soldiers attacked the Boxti line. They drew their knives and lunged in, stabbing and hacking and kicking and punching. Blood sprayed and screams rang out. Hands and claws tore at Josh's armor, but nothing else mattered. He closed his eyes and suddenly recalled his hand-to-hand training in vivid detail.

He was like a computer calling up a familiar subroutine.

Josh took a kick to the chest and flew backwards. He rolled to a knee, grabbed a nearby rock, and charged back in. The Boxti line broke and started to run back toward the passages. Explosions drew closer as the mines reached the edge of the canyon, but the aliens were too crazed with fear to rally. The Sparrow made a final pass and showered the battlefield with bullets.The pilot brought it in for a quick landing, skids scraping the dirt.

Alexa went in first, climbing into the tight space behind the pilot. Pierre sat in the door and strapped a tether to his body. Josh tried to fit on board, but his armor was too bulky.

"Shit."

"Lose it fast," the pilot shouted.

Josh ripped at the panels, pulling his armor apart. Pierre hopped out and helped, breathing hard as he lifted each heavy panel. Finally Josh was free, save a shoulder guard that seemed glued on. He climbed aboard the Sparrow, only to jump right back off.

"What are you doing?" Alexa cried.

Josh picked up his discarded helmet, reached inside, and pulled out the data recorder. He leapt back onto the jump-seat and strapped in. "Good to go!"

The Black Adder squadron leader came on last, limping and cradling his gut. He sat next to Josh and motioned for the pilot to take off.

"I thought you were evacuated."

Smiling back, Cameron pulled the Sparrow off the ground and out toward the horizon. Below, the Gremlins erupted with a powerful blast, burying the last open ground in the Lion's Mouth. The ship bucked from the concussion wave, nearly tipping sideways.

"Please buckle up," Cameron said.

"Jesus," Alexa gasped. "That was...thanks for the pick up."

The pilot nodded. "You're welcome. You're all welcome. Now please buckle up."

Josh reached over and squeezed the pilot's shoulder. "You were out solid, Lieutenant. Are you good to fly?"

Cameron wiped sweat from his eyes. "Okay, full disclosure. I'm on a cocktail of about sixty pain killers and antibiotics, not to mention I'm wearing eight radiation-blocker patches. It feels like I have bees in my mouth, and I'm pretty sure I've hallucinated a few times since I took off. Also, my left eye won't focus." Cameron glanced over his shoulder. "So like, really, could you buckle up?"

New York City

"THIS IS SOME LUCK," Victor said. He looked over at Jonah Blightman, nodding and smiling. "Fucking pigs. Deserve whatever those freaks give them."

Jonah sat splayed in a large leather recliner, his head resting on his hand. Along with a whole platoon of soldiers, they'd been watching the newsfeeds coming out of Eros. He rolled his eyes. "They're just soldiers, Vic. They aren't the enemy."

"Bullshit," Vic said. "They're the same breed we've been fighting since Mars."

The rebel leader sat up, brushing his hair back behind his neck. "No, the breed *I* fought on Mars wore green and blue. This is the Terran Army, and there may be more Martians in that casualty list than here in this city." He stood and paced around the room, grumbling to himself.

Victor walked over and stopped Jonah mid-step. "Boss, I don't know why you're so upset. This is the best thing that could have happened. Gilroy's speech didn't do shit to move the polls. We can call for an election, put Kerrigan into place, and have this planet locked down within six months."

Jonah pushed his lieutenant aside. "A world isn't as fun to have when it can so easily be taken away."

Victor frowned. "What's that supposed to mean?"

"It means open your fucking eyes," Jonah snapped. "Kronos is a military stronghold. Thousands of soldiers training for just this sort of event. And now it is partially owned by aliens. Fucking aliens. How does that put us in a better place? Best-case scenario is that the aliens stop at Kronos. Burton surrenders and New Eden is under some manner of garrison for the foreseeable future. Worst case? They trace back one of the relays to here and wipe out our whole goddamn civilization."

Victor shook his head. "Burton may be a bastard, but I'd never think him a coward. He'd let the entire species die before waving the white flag."

"If you think that, then you really know nothing about Alexander Burton." Jonah looked back into the recreation room. They'd taken over the upper floors and found the amenities more than satisfied the troops. "We need to find a way to lock this system down."

Victor laughed. "That's great, Jonah. Next you'll ask me to catch a celestial whale for you. It can't be done. We don't have access to any ships strong enough to break the blockade. Mars is still playing dumb to this whole thing, so no luck there. Not to mention it would cut off millions of Martian sympathizers in Colorum."

Jonah pulled Victor aside and down the hallway. They didn't stop until they'd entered a long meeting room. Dark wood furniture filled every bit of space. "Have you heard of the Ronin protocol?"

Victor lost his whimsy. "Jonah, you can't seriously be considering this."

The rebel leader stared back. "If this is the only way to ensure the survival of the human race, you can be assured I am. If it means rebuilding the colonies from the ground up, so be it."

"Ronin Protocol has to be approved by one of the Pillars. You're sure as shit not getting the Council, and the colonies will be just as bad."

Jonah smiled. "I know. That's why we have to go to the source." He reached into his pocket and pulled out a small remote. When he pressed the button, the door to the meeting room locked and the windows drew shut. Panels rotated in the walls, revealing maps and drawings and photographs. Schematics for various high-profile ships and installations covered the walls, and screens showed video surveillance of various politicians. "I think it's time I brought you in on one of my pet projects."

Victor spun around, marveling at the sight. "What is all this?"

"We need to secure the planet, and there's only one man who can help us do that." He pressed the remote again, and the screens displayed the same image. A middle-aged black man in a fine suit, smiling before the flag of the Terran Federate.

A chyron underneath him read, HIGH CHANCELLOR ALEXANDER BURTON.

Jonah smiled. "We'll just need to ask the right way."

Kronos Orbit

COMMODORE HIRO OSAKA SAT on a silent bridge. Moments before, his crew was one chaotic scramble. Now all eyes in orbit over the red moon of Kronos turned toward the blue star, Eros.

There, streaking in with engines glowing, were six pearl-white ships.

The forward screen flickered and an alien face appeared. Its gray skin had specks of white and blue along the right side. Hiro had never met the Nangolani commanders, but he recognized the uniforms. He straightened and gave a curt nod.

"This is Commodore Osaka. To whom am I speaking?"

"This is Hanweh Shodow, Domin of the *Barrenon*." He spoke in a soft tenor. "We are at your disposal. Where should we focus our attack?"

Hiro stood at once, giving a quick glance to the holographic battlefield display. "I want everything you've got on their dreadnought. We'll handle the rest."

Hanweh relayed the orders in the sing-song language of the Nangolani. "Commodore, stay clear of our main cannon. It will not discriminate."

He'd no sooner spoken than the first shot rang out. Leading the pack, the *Barrenon* charged along the axis of the cruiser. The cigar-shaped vessel flashed bright green before unleashing a stream of energy directly at the Boxti flagship. Metal boiled. The intense beam peeled open the dreadnought like an onion. Powerful decompressions warped the hull of the ship.

The other Nangolani cruisers picked up targets at will, releasing streams of energy that bit into the frigates and destroyers. Boxti ships burst at the seams. Smaller fighters crashed together in the mad dash to escape the sudden assault.

Red missiles shot out from the Boxti line, slamming into the Nangolani ships. Each warhead punctured the smooth white hulls and detonated inside, sending out sprays of debris and bodies. Y-fighters joined the battle and peppered the enemy with blasts from their cannons. It was too little an effort to regain the momentum, and the Boxti knew it. Their ships began to break orbit and beat a hasty retreat.

Hiro called out orders as fast as he could plan them. "All fighters to Q-two-oh-two. I want that hive disabled immediately. Third and fourth groups, hit their escort. All missile frigates need to unload on their supply trains." He knew that aboard *Valley Forge*, Captain DeHart had the same notion. The supercruiser's escort was already launching a swift counterattack.

Make them pay dearly for this attack, he thought.

"Hiro," the XO shouted. "They're out of range for our guns. Missiles at fifteen percent."

Hiro stood tall. "Don't give them an inch. I want to make them bleed all the way into Blue Space."

Valley Forge's twin cannons, Thunder and Lightning, pounded the fleeing enemy, destroying another frigate in the process. The aliens answered with a wild shot that missed by a mile. The TFC *St. Nichols*, under the command of Admiral Winger, pulled ahead of the pack and emptied its store of missiles. Her voice echoed over the radio.

"Next time you'd better make sure I'm dead!"

Under withering fire, the Boxti fleet pulled ahead of their pursuers. Led by the disabled dreadnought, the alien fleet charged their engines and tore off toward the edge of the system. Blue light flashed as the black ships fled into the void. The Terrans fired a final salvo, but the projectiles sailed into nothing as the gates closed. Letting out a collective breath, the humans and Nangolani cooled their engines and powered down weapons.

Aboard the supercarrier, Hiro sat back down. He was suddenly more tired that he had ever been in his life. He felt like he'd just stepped out of a warm shower, he was so sweaty. "Get a line to Admiral Walker," he said. "Let him know that Eros is safe."

There were no cheers from the room. A few seamen shook hands or hugged, but all remained at their posts. Word was relayed to all sectors of the human galaxy as quickly as it could be typed. The battle was over, but the next would be right around the corner.

RIDING HIGH OVER THE battlefield, Josh finally took stock. As the Nangolani arrived overhead, the battle below began to wind down. Supported by a company of tanks, the line outside the Tomb held fast. Boxti soldiers fell against the barricades a dozen times, only to be repelled, minus hundreds of their dead. General Casey organized the remaining infantry into an impenetrable wall.

The Gremlins served their purpose and then some. Of the twenty thousand Boxti troops that landed on Kronos, only a few hundred survived long enough to be captured. The rest lay buried underneath tons of rock along the many canyons of the moon.

Alexa slept peacefully behind Cameron. Pierre muttered a prayer over and over again, holding onto the frame of the Sparrow for dear life. *He's right to be scared. The only thing between him and gravity is a thin cable connected to the frame.* Only the Black Adder squadron leader remained awake. He had a jagged blade protruding from his stomach, but didn't seem too upset by it. Josh stared.

"It's mortal," Captain Hendryx said. "I can feel the other end of it in my back." He pulled off his helmet. A black balaclava covered his face underneath the mask. The helmet slipped from his fingers. "Are you ready for what happens next?"

Josh shook his head. "I don't know what's coming. I just know it's bad."

"Handle yourself like you did today, and you'll be fine." The captain tugged at his balaclava, but couldn't get a grip. He gestured for help.

Josh pulled off the mask. Underneath, the man was average looking. His hair was completely shaved off, but his eyebrows were dark and thick. His skin was intensely pale, as though he hadn't seen the sun in years. He smiled gratefully.

"Keep the call sign," he said. With some effort he dipped a thumb under his collar and pulled out his dog tags. He broke the chain and handed it to Josh. "Let General Casey know."

Josh nodded. He bit his lip, debating what to say. "Why did you help me? Why didn't you just stick to your mission?"

The Black Adder grinned with bloody teeth. "Any soldier willing to leave a man behind is no soldier in my book. You definitely earned your place on the team."

"Team?"

The sergeant tapped his nose. He groaned, gripping his stomach. "Okay," he said. Reaching back, he gripped his tether and drew it taught. Before Josh could move, the Black Adder snapped his line free and tipped forward. He slid off the skids, dropping down the three thousand feet to the rocks below.

Josh held the dog tag and watched him disappear.

November 9, 2236
Fort Metts
New Eden

JOSH STOOD AT THE entrance to the banquet hall and fussed with his dress grays. The uniform looked great; no doubt about that. Scarlet piping ran down his arms from shoulder to cuff. The buttons were polished silver with the arrows and stars of the Federate Military. He adjusted the golden chevrons on his lapel, wiping off fingerprints.

"Josh?" Dax hobbled over, taking care not to smash his foot into anyone. The leg of his uniform had been cut off at the knee to make space for the massive cast. He'd spray-painted the gauze black to make it fit in.

The two soldiers stood in the doorway and watched the wait staff finish their setup. Josh looked up at Dax. "Does this feel right? It doesn't *seem* right."

"They're calling it a 'memorial dinner.'"

Josh nodded. "Yeah, but...isn't this a bit much?"

The banquet hall looked like it was ready for a state dinner. Round tables filled the floor space, surrounded by comfortable chairs. Each setting had a full assortment of silverware, giving the whole affair a more elegant air than just a military ball. Josh found it gaudy. He'd grown up in a working-class family and had never seen a truly fancy dinner before. In his class-A uniform, Josh made an impressive figure. Dax, on the other hand, couldn't have looked more out of place. The man was a mountain, even without eighty pounds of gear.

They walked inside and looked for their table. Alexa waved at them from across the room, holding out two chairs. Josh had to pause when he saw her. She looked stunning in her service uniform, and her hair was neatly tied in a Martian braid. Make-up hid the bruises on her face well enough, but her glowing smile made them hardly noticeable. The two men crossed the floor briskly, not wanting to get sucked into conversation with any of the brass. Josh knew it shouldn't bother him, but talking with officers always felt forced. Most of the lieutenants were his age or younger, and the field grades just seemed out of touch with the soldiers.

"Can you guys believe this?" Alexa asked. She squeezed Dax's arm, but hesitated at Josh. They settled on a brief hug. "This is something, isn't it?"

"Definitely not what I expected," Josh said. His voice was distant.

Dax leaned over. "Are you okay?"

"There's a lot of empty settings here."

There had been a mini-riot when they'd first come home. Mailboxes were full of letters from mothers and fathers, husbands and wives all wanting to know if their loved one was still alive. Some of the senior NCOs had gone to the command board demanding answers for the media blackout. Why had so much been kept from the soldiers? Even the officers were up in arms, defending their company's right to know. Almost a third of the battalion had lost someone in the last few months, and to find out this way had been heartbreaking. Every soldier wore an orange ribbon on their lapel, in memory of those lost on Tallus. Many sported fresh injuries from the fight only a day before.

Alexa sipped white wine. "It's surreal," she said. "Luna. Tallus. But then there's this whole other side we haven't even talked about yet. I mean, we're actually becoming friends with aliens. Real, live aliens." Alexa had been lucky. Her family lived on Earth in a small town in the Americas. Aside from a terrified message from her father, she was untouched by the chaos.

"They look so strange," Dax said. "I mean, they look human. Well, not *human*, but they have arms and legs and everything."

"Humanoid," Josh said, detached. "I wonder what they're like. Whether we can actually trust them."

Pierre sat down at the table, setting down an armful of beers. His face was drawn and glossy. Deep circles ran under his eyes. "At least the brass kept the open bar." He twisted off a cap and drained half the bottle in one long gulp. "I hope you don't mind. My company isn't making much of a showing at the dinner, and I'd prefer not to drink alone."

Josh leaned over and grabbed a beer. He flicked the cap off with his thumb and knocked the neck against Pierre's drink. "We'd be honored to have you join. You can show me which fork to use."

Pierre smiled. "Just because I look like royalty doesn't mean I am one." He took a long swig. "Thank you, *fre*."

"This is awful fancy," Alexa said. "You think they're going to cancel the leave passes? I bet they do. Wouldn't make sense to let everyone go off and play when we've got an intergalactic war to fight."

Josh didn't answer. He was watching the main table at the front of the room. General Casey had taken his seat, along with a few other senior staff. The post commander stared out at the sea of gray uniforms with one clear blue eye. His cybernetic patch covered one end of a scar that ran from temple to jaw across his face. The old man seemed weighed down by the sheer volume of medals and ribbons and cords lashed to his uniform. At fifty-five, he was a veteran of more battles than anyone had a right to survive. Down the table, a wiry young man with slick hair and glasses sat near the end. Brigadier General Hennesy, the post XO, took to the podium and tapped on the microphone, silencing the room.

"Good evening, soldiers," Hennesy said. The crowd applauded politely. Hennesy leafed through his notes, shaking his head. "I wrote a speech a few months back. It was a very good one. Would have left you all feeling powerful and accomplished. Now, reading over it, I can't find a single line that fits anymore. 'Congratulations on surviving'? After what you've been through...calling this a baptism by fire doesn't cover it. You were all great soldiers before you arrived on Kronos. Now you're goddamn heroes. I won't tell you that you served the cause or some other bullshit. I won't say that you rose up against insurmountable odds. I'll just say that we are all alive now because of your efforts. That survival was purchased with the lives of thousands of soldiers and seamen. We're still burying our brothers and sisters, and that ache is very fresh. Look around the room and you'll see the empty seats where they should have been. Without warriors, our great civilization would be but another footnote in the history of the universe. We must accept upon ourselves the responsibility such a position demands, and give our all for the safety of our families, our loved ones, and our citizens."

Hennesy took a sip of water and continued: "The last few days have featured a few small, but significant victories. In New York, the terrorists inside the Galactic Media Tower have begun releasing hostages. Admiral Gilroy has assured the Council, as well as the rest of the galaxy, that a swift resolution is imminent. The rescue operation on Tallus has recovered some five thousand survivors of the horrific attacks. And here in New Eden, our resident fallen angel Lieutenant Davis is expected to make a full recovery. For his bravery at the battle on Kronos, and for his efforts to return to us with such pertinent intelligence, Lieutenant Davis has been awarded the Distinguished Service Cross."

More applause, this time as much from the main table as the floor.

The XO continued, his face pained. "I know that many of you wonder why we even held this ball, after everything that's happened. I don't know if you still care about the results of a game when the blood is still drying on Kronos. But the

Crucible began with a solemn purpose: to select the best and bravest for special operations training. That need is now greater than ever before." A murmur of agreement rose from the crowd. "With that, allow me to introduce our honored guest. He is one of the brightest minds of our time, and the most brilliant scientist in all of the Federate. Ladies and gentlemen, please welcome our speaker tonight, Dr. Markov Ivanovich."

As one, the soldiers stood and clapped, welcoming the thin Martian to the podium. Markov waved and smiled, clearly enjoying his return to celebrity status. The noise died out quickly and the audience took its seat, continuing to eat their first courses as Markov began his speech.

"Thank you, General Hennesy, for that introduction. I am truly humbled. Officers and soldiers of the Terran military, I am privileged to speak before you. I, too, prepared a different speech. Now those words seem self-serving. I want to be honest with you. You deserve nothing less. Many of you are probably familiar with the name CROWN, either through anecdote or perhaps in study during your military training. The half trillion-dollar project lives in infamy as a painful waste of resources during the height of the Martian conflict. There were many scientists and generals attached to that failure, but I personally take responsibility." The crowd whispered in wonder. "I was young, I was cocky, and I made a terrible error in judgment."

Markov continued: "I wanted to create the greatest weapon on the battlefield. CROWN failed because I wanted to *improve* the soldier. I thought, incorrectly, that you needed my help. A belief, I must admit, that stemmed from a lack of interaction with you all. But I learned my lesson. Over the last few years, I have been creating a new and exciting training program for the special forces of the Federate. Through these simple exercises, soldiers found their combat efficiency increased dramatically. With the permission of the Kronos training staff, the last few months have been a part of a grand selection, one that concluded only nights ago.

Josh listened intently. He absent-mindedly squeezed the skin around his arm, checking for any spots of pain. Only days before, the doctors had said he was lucky to keep the limb at all. Now it seemed completely healed.

What was in that shot?

The doctor, maybe sensing the eyes upon him, locked his gaze with Josh. "Seven names have come from the midst of thousands." Markov's voice rose, his excitement growing and spreading within the crowd. "For those of you selected for this new training program, you will travel immediately with me to a secure location on New Eden. From there, at a remote facility, you will train with the most elite of the elite and become a new breed of special forces. For those of you who remain here, you will also receive new and powerful training tools for use within your units."

Markov smiled, looking over at General Casey. The elder officer wore a sour expression. Turning back, Markov continued: "For now, please enjoy your meal. We'll announce the candidates after dessert. Thank you all once again." He walked back to his seat, accompanied by a smattering of applause. He sat down in the chair next to Casey, waving a final time to the crowd.

"I want weekly updates on these soldiers," Casey said. "You're taking some promising men and women away from me."

"I'm giving them a chance to make a difference in the war," Markov answered. "They're not just going to be cannon fodder, against the Boxti or Blightman or anyone else. I don't understand why you can't appreciate that."

Casey leaned in close, the sweet smell of pipe smoke ripe on his breath. "I've spent my life in uniform, Doctor. These soldiers are my family, and you want to take them away for your little science project. You're not the first brainiac with a new way to 'make war easier' on the troops." He tipped back his glass, swallowing a mouthful of scotch. "We had a young kid just like you when I was a captain. Wanted to fix whatever causes a man to stress out about fighting. Only took a few dozen grunts losing their minds before they stopped tampering with our brains. We don't need supermen, Doc. We need infantry."

Markov raised his hands in surrender. He lifted his own glass and grinned. "To the infantry, then."

Casey mimicked the toast, but his eyes never left Markov. He drained the tumbler, savoring the burn. "If you'll excuse me, gentlemen. I have to make a call." He walked away from the table and out the side door, his medals jangling with each step.

Irwin Cove
Colorum Belt

BERLIN HADN'T LEFT DRY dock since Tallus. Attached to the repair station Irwin Cove, the carrier underwent a massive overhaul. Floating far on the outskirts of the Colorum Belt, the Cove serviced ships from all over the galaxy. It had been placed in the remote region of space as a mining depot, but grew in function and size over the course of five decades. One of the largest man-made structures in the galaxy, the station had a surprisingly small crew. Only ten thousand engineers worked aboard, servicing hundreds of frigates, cruisers, and carriers over the course of a year. This left more than enough room for the pilots and soldiers of the broken vessels to live.

The infirmary, easily the nicest section of the floating base, was state-of-the-art and fully stocked. Irwin Cove often took ships fresh from battle, when the crew was as in need of attention as the crafts themselves. The chief medical officer, Doctor Patel, made his rounds down the hallway, stopping at each room to check on patients. Near the far end, he stepped inside a curtained-off area, closing the cloth behind him.

"And how are we feeling today?" he asked.

Kaileen put down the book she'd been reading and glared at him. "I'm still stuck here, so not great."

Dr. Patel smiled, though there was little warmth in the expression. He'd been working with the military too long, and his bedside manner had all but vanished. "Still working on that Miss Congeniality award, Lieutenant Nuvarian?" He picked up her chart with a manicured, caramel hand and read. "I'm impressed, you've gone through almost every nurse on staff."

Kaileen scrunched her face and groaned. "Come on, I'm a pilot. There has to be a ship out there that needs flying."

The doctor lifted the sheet covering the woman's feet. He was only half-surprised that she had, again, removed her cast. "You know, broken legs don't heal very well when you continue to aggravate them. I'm going to recommend you get time in the exercise room. Supervised, of course. You need to train yourself back into health, and then we can talk about you flying again." He scribbled on the clipboard before attaching it to the bed. "For now, get some rest. I'll have a nurse escort you to the gym in an hour."

"I don't need a personal trainer."

Patel chewed on the inside of his cheek. "It takes sixty pounds of pressure to hit the afterburner on a Seed. Eighty for a Griffin. I doubt you're up to thirty yet. So let a professional get you there faster. Then you can go annoy someone else." He didn't wait for the inevitable outburst before walking away.

Kaileen sulked in her small quarters. She'd spent the better part of the year in infirmaries. First aboard the *Gettysburg* after the accident. Then *Berlin*. Now here. It was becoming a nasty habit. She had to admit, the food was better on the station, but the boredom the same. With the doc gone, she picked up her book, stuck the placeholder a few chapters back, and continued to read.

Fort Metts
New Eden

"ALEXA HAINES."

The crowd roared, cheering on the spry team leader as she stood and danced in place. Already four soldiers had been called out, three from Alpha Company. Josh remained seated, half hoping to walk away unmentioned. Dax had been the first named announced. The big man walked over to Alexa, picking her up in a big hug. They jumped in a circle, surrounded by Charlie Company comrades.

"We're down to our last two candidates." Hennesy stood at the microphone, his face shiny and red. He'd been enjoying a few drinks with the good doctor at the head table. "This next soldier demonstrated an ability to think on her feet during the early days of the event. Though she was taken out before the end, her personal score rivals entire platoons.

The best shot in all of Kronos. Please congratulate Specialist Liane Lu."

Across the room, a petite Asian woman stood and shouted. Her table rose with her, cheering and stomping on the floor. The Delta soldiers cheered her on, clapping their hands and whistling.

Josh turned to Pierre. "How well did she do?"

"Forty-eight confirmed kills during the exercise." He leaned in closer. "And I heard about sixty during the invasion."

Josh joined in the applause, duly impressed. It took five minutes for everyone to calm enough for the last announcement.

Hennesy beamed at the soldiers as he prepared to speak. "Our final candidate led his unit to the very end, taking the fight to the enemy without fear. He exemplified the warrior ethos, risking his own life to ensure no man was left behind. Our last soldier exemplifies what we look for in a leader."

Josh scanned the room and found Zev staring back at him. The Alpha sergeant sat in a wheelchair, wrapped up like a mummy from all his injuries. Zev still managed to put on his war face. The two soldiers locked gaze, neither one breaking contact.

"In fact, this soldier's ability to read a combat situation was so impressive, that he will not only join his brothers and sisters in arms in this experiment, but will receive a battlefield commission to second lieutenant. Ladies and gentlemen, let us shake the very roof as we welcome our final candidate into this program. From the number-one company in the number-one platoon in the top-ranked squad for the *entire* event, Corporal Joshua Rantz."

The room erupted as the soldiers, officers, and guests shouted and cheered for Josh. They pounded the tables as he stood from his chair and waived, somewhat taken aback by the whole affair. Dax clapped him on the shoulders and nearly knocked him over. The two friends hugged and toasted their beers. Across the room, Zev smiled bitterly and lifted his own glass.

Josh spun around and saw Alexa grinning madly. She wrapped him in a tight hug and rocked him back and forth. Before he could stop himself, Josh leaned forward and pressed his lips against hers. The world seemed to stop, then started back up even louder. He pulled back, his cheeks turning lobster red.

"I'm sorry," he mumbled. "I didn't..."

Alexa recovered quickly. "It's fine. Go, get congratulated." She touched her lips gingerly as Josh was pulled away by the crowd.

Josh kept Alexa in sight as long as he could, but the ground fell away as Pierre and Dax lifted him onto their shoulders. The entire mood of the room had changed in just a few minutes. Instead of a wake, the banquet hall was a celebration. Josh shrugged his shoulders, ready to go along with the feeling as long as it would last.

"Yeah!" he shouted. "Go me!"

Hask Medical Center
Fort Metts

CAMERON WAS STILL AWAKE when Josh entered the room. He looked up, not entirely surprised to see the soldier standing in the hall. Ever since they'd returned from the Lion's Mouth, the pilot often awoke to find Josh sitting in a chair reading. In his brief lucid moments, they'd shared a quick joke or two. It hurt to think about, but Josh was the closest thing Cameron had to a friend.

"Don't you have a girlfriend or something?" Cameron asked.

Josh rolled his eyes. "You clearly haven't seen Army women before." He pulled two beers from behind his back. "I brought some medicine from the doctor. He said you should take it quick, before the nurse comes back."

"You are a king among men." Cameron twisted the top off and took a swig. The bock was a little warm but tasted amazing. "That's right, tonight was your big ceremony. And you left it for me? All that free booze is just going to waste."

Josh laughed, pulling a stool around to take a seat. "Don't worry. Delta company took whatever was left for the after-party." He stopped, his smile fading. "Well, now it'll have to be for the road. They're deploying the entire division tomorrow."

The pilot's face became serious. "Shouldn't you be with your friends?"

"Nah," he said. "I see them every day. Besides, I just found out I'm leaving with you tomorrow, so I figured we should get better acquainted." They clinked glasses. "You didn't finish your story."

"Yes I did."

Josh took a swig of beer, his eyes never breaking contact. "You need to say it out loud."

Cameron looked away. "It doesn't get better from where we left off."

"I know."

"A lot of people died there. Everyone I've ever served with..."

Josh held up a hand. "Cameron, you've been through more circles of hell than anyone should have to endure." He put his drink down and leaned in. "I lost three soldiers this past week. It still hasn't hit me, but I know it's coming. What I'm saying is that I'm here, and I think you need to get it off your chest."

Cameron wiped his face, ashamed of his tears. "He was my best friend for ten years. We'd taken on everything the universe had ever thrown at us. He saved my life a dozen times. And I couldn't even tow him a kilometer to safety."

"Stop it," Josh said sternly. "It wasn't your fault. Some alien with a dozen sticks up its asshole pulled the trigger, and he's living on borrowed time now. This is war, Cameron. This is what happens. And we keep fighting until it's over." He rocked back and retrieved his beer.

"He's right, you know."

They both turned and hid their drinks. Josh stood at attention, his jaw clenched tight. "Sir."

General Casey took a step into the room. He was still in uniform, still the spitting image of a war hero. He walked over to Cameron and placed a wrinkled but strong hand on his shoulder. "War is the worst thing any of us can live through. The honest truth is that we envy the dead for their peace." He turned to Josh. "Are you going to offer me a drink, or do I have to make it an order?"

Josh quickly pulled a beer from his coat and handed it to the general. Casey twisted off the top, taking a long swig. "You want to hear the first time I lost a soldier?" The two men nodded. "Thirty-two years ago. I was here. Well, on New Eden. Some warlord in Foster's Glen started lopping the heads off anyone he didn't deem worthy to live in his neck of the woods. We rolled in hot, firing up the neighboring area and straight murdering anyone who looked at us for too long."

He continued, "My platoon ended up walking the long road in, hiking through jungle so thick you couldn't see more than a few feet in any direction. I had a battle buddy back then, a short, little grunt named Mosley. He couldn't have been more than five-three. He always had the other joes ragging on him. Called him 'short shit.'" He smiled, remembering the tiny man's beady eyes and sharp grin. "Mosley was fearless. He once went off to take a piss, came back with five prisoners. Said they'd tried to jump him, but he'd beaten their leader to death with his dick and wrestled the others down." Cameron and Josh busted out laughing at that. "I'm serious, he was fucking crazy."

"What really happened?" Cameron asked.

Casey shrugged. "We found another insurgent back where he said. But he wasn't beaten to death. Gunshot through the eye. Mosley wasn't the best fighter, but he was scary with his pistol. Must have put away one piece and pulled out another. In any case, no one made fun of him after that." His voice softened. "So there we were, crossing that bush and trying to be as quiet as we could. And then we heard it. A click." His green eyes burned and watered. "They'd set up minefields all over that area. Hell, the ground was fat with explosives. We always joked that if anyone would set off something it would be tiny, little Mosley." Casey wiped his mouth. "He didn't make a scene. Just told us to keep going, that he was gonna work it out. He gave me his pistol, said I'd need it more than him. Then he started whistling. We left him there, walked away while he smiled and waved at us, as though we were just headed out for a smoke and would be back soon. I can still remember hearing the soft whump as he lifted his foot."

Josh didn't speak for a few minutes. He sat there, silently drinking his beer and staring at the wall. Cameron could barely move. It was an entirely different world of fighting, going from the sky to the ground. Cameron never had to look his enemies in the eye as he killed them. Or watch his friends bleed and cry for their mothers. The horror of it all affected him in a way he hadn't expected. His stomach was still in knots, but the general's story had done the trick. He realized he wasn't the first to feel this way.

"I'm sorry," Cameron said softly. "And thank you."

Casey looked up, eyes red. "You're welcome. It's a hard business we're in, Lieutenant. But I've met the best people in the universe while in uniform." He punched the pilot's arm. "And more women than I can remember." He stood up, stretching. "Oh, to be thirty years younger. You boys stay safe. The war may need you now, but the galaxy will need you later." He lumbered out into the hall, yawning wide. His heavy footsteps followed him down the corridor to the elevator.

Cameron looked at Josh quizzically. "Where's your rank?"

Josh looked at his shoulders. "Oh yeah. I was honorably discharged tonight."

"What!"

He laughed. "Part of the bargain. I'm moving to a new unit, and I'm earning a gold bar along the way."

"Lieutenant Josh Rantz," Cameron said. "I think that works."

"And, now I don't have to feel so weird hanging around with an officer all night."

Cameron swung out a fist, but Josh dodged with a laugh. "Do you have any cards, smart ass?"

Josh shook his head. "But, I do have these." He pulled two more beers from his jacket pockets and they drank. It felt good, having something to be happy about. They stayed up late, talking about sports and women and booze. They left politics and the war behind. There'd be plenty of time for that in the morning.

December 1, 2236
New Eden Orbit

TRAFFIC AROUND HUMANITY'S MOST prosperous colony had finally begun a return to normal. Cargo ships from Earth arrived with emergency supplies, docking at the massive New Eden Node before turning around for a quick jump home. Travelers from all over continued their pilgrimages to the gorgeous waterfalls and scenic beaches. The Sky Guard continued to patrol, flying in packs of six in a constant swarm around the planet.

Far away from the civilian traffic, orbiting at four-hundred kilometers, was the military station Primus. Almost twice the size of Irwin Cove, the Fleet stomping ground was a moon unto itself. Each of its sixteen docking bays housed one of the Seventh Section's wounded ships. *Midway* and *Valley Forge* rested next to one another, jutting out from the station like thorns on a rose.

The command room aboard Primus sat at the very top of the spindle-shaped platform. The circular room housed the primary controls for every major function aboard the floating city. Dozens of technicians, both civilian and military, sat at their desks monitoring every inch of the station.

Standing near one of many windows, Hiro had a perfect view of the beautiful planet below. He saw a small speck of dust on the glass and wiped it away. Satisfied, he turned back toward the room. Sam DeHart waited impatiently.

"Are you done reflecting?"

Hiro ignored the jab. "I'm ready to begin. Do we have him on the line?"

"I don't see how this is supposed to help." Sam walked with the older officer toward the communication section. Massive computers connected the station to every point in the known universe via FTL transmitters. News networks from across the galaxy broadcast their reports about Kronos or New York or the Federate. Sam scowled. "The Terran Space Initiative is a civilian force. They can't handle this sort of thing."

"I disagree," Hiro said. "The Initiative is the reason we caught Luna in time. Their observer network records every significant event in each of the controlled systems. If anyone is up for this task, it is them." They stopped next to a pimple-faced technician. Hiro motioned for the young boy to connect the line. "Besides, TSI has unrestricted access to the Nangolani. And that's exactly what we need."

The central screen flickered off, then came back on to display a clean white computer lab. Scientists in the background wore the blue uniforms of the Initiative, with the golden comet on their backs. A young man's face appeared from the side, his eyes wide and nervous. He pulled at his shoulder-length black hair and pushed it behind his ears.

"Hello, sirs." He coughed into his hands. "I'm Ray. Uh, Raymond Lee. Sir. Commodore." He blushed. "Can we start over?"

Hiro held up a hand. "Mr. Lee, there's nothing to worry over. Have you read my report?"

"Yes, sir." Ray held up the thick packet. "It's...well, it's pretty dense. I mean, there's just a lot of theory and speculation thrown around in here. I can go through some of the points with you."

"That's not necessary," Sam said. "We need to know if you can research it."

Ray stared blankly. "Guys, this is way above my pay grade. I can get you Director Chavez on the line."

"We already spoke with him. He said you're the best tech he's got." Sam crossed his arms. "Mr. Lee, can you or can you not investigate the commodore's claim?"

"I mean...I guess I can. But do you really want me to?" He flipped through the packet, shaking his head. "Sir, if this is all correct, then the fallout would be—"

"Catastrophic," Hiro said. "But the truth needs to come out. Humanity survived the first shots of this war, but just barely. I think we deserve to know exactly how this began."

Ray nodded. "And what about the Grays? Sorry, the Nangolani. What happens to them if you're right?"

Sam scowled and turned away. Hiro watched him go. "I pray that I am wrong," the commodore said. "Every night I think of another way this could have been, and every night it is the same conclusion." He looked into Ray's eyes. "If I am right, then this war is about to get much worse. If I am right, then we are betrayed." Hiro let out a long, slow breath, centering himself. "First we must know the truth, and then we can bring our evidence to our new allies."

Ray hesitated before speaking. He glanced around the room at the oblivious staff. His voice trembled. "And then?"

Hiro's visage darkened. "Then we will visit our vengeance upon them."

EPILOGUE

JANUS
AWAKENS

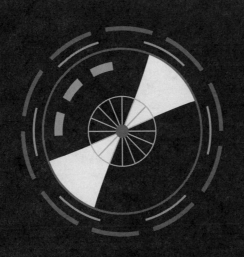

Imperion One
Colorum Belt

THE TRAITOR GLANCED OVER his shoulder at the door, making sure the handle hadn't moved. There was no reason for anyone to come into this room at this time of night, but he had to be sure. Too much was at stake to be taken down by such a foolish error.

"No...no, I'm absolutely *not* ready. That's why we had a timeline. That's why we had all of those meetings. That's why I fucking *told* you I needed more time."

The young man bit his tongue and listened to the voice on the other line. The man went by many names, but they stuck to code even over secured lines.

"Brutus, I'm not going to ask you to calm down again. If you keep raising your voice, I'll be forced to do something very rash. You know how I hate making rash decisions."

The traitor swallowed a lump in his throat. "I'm sorry. But I'm the one risking my neck aboard the fucking imperial limo. If they suspect anything..."

"If they suspected anything, you'd already be dead. Or in jail, which would end worse for you." The man on the other end of the line snickered. "Alexander has no idea."

"Maybe," the traitor said. "So how will this go down now?"

"The same as we discussed before. They're going through with this ridiculous conference, so we'll have to use it to our advantage. With the aliens there, you should be able to find a moment alone with the high chancellor. Once the fire alarm goes off, you guide him to the emergency escape pod and make sure he gets in. We'll have taken care of the rest."

"And what about me?"

"You need to stay behind. The damage to the ship won't be severe. You'll be fine. But when the smoke clears, you'll need to be our eyes and ears during the panic. I have to know what they're planning before it happens. That's the only way we're going to keep Alexander secure."

"Okay." The traitor felt sick to his stomach. "I can do this. I know I can."

"I know, Brutus. You're ready for the big leagues. And you will be greatly rewarded for your work in our campaign."

"Thank you, sir. I won't let you down."

"The red fist rises," the voice said.

"With hammer in hand," the traitor replied. The call ended, and the young man wiped the phone clean. He made sure he hadn't left anything out of order and went to the door. He was reaching for the handle when it swung open. He stared open-mouthed at a Secret Service agent, unable to speak or move.

"Huh." The agent flipped on the light switch. "Oh, it's you. Why are you hanging out in the dark?"

The traitor's mind raced. "I was taking a nap."

"I heard someone talking."

"Yeah, I talk in my sleep." He slipped by the larger man and started down the hallway. "I'd better get back to work. You too."

"Sure." The agent returned to his post, erasing the interaction from his head. It wasn't an important event in the scheme of things. Just another run-in with the high chancellor's chronically weird aide.

Arthur Roden.